T
MEA

BOOK ONE IN THE HUNT

# the Beast

## LINDSAY MEAD

**THE BEAST**

Cover and Interior Artwork by Mooney Designs

Interior Design by QA Productions

*I dedicate this series to Trisha Wolfe.*

*I knew how to write (for the most part), but you taught me how to tell a story. You were the cheerleader in my corner and my toughest coach. Thank you.*

*To everyone else— go read her books.*

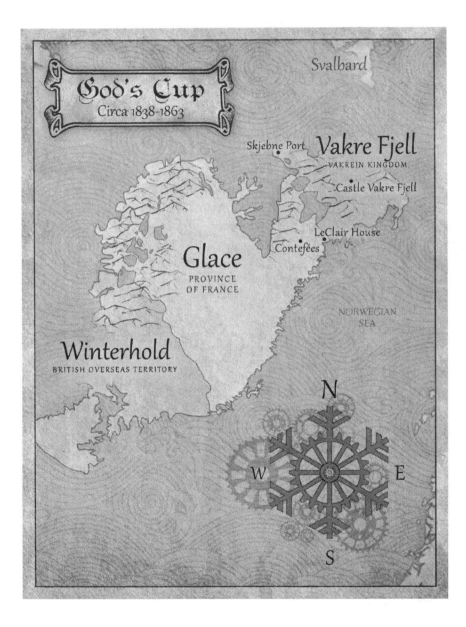

# The Hunter's Creed

Oh Holy Angel, attendant of our wretched souls and afflicted life, forsake us not.

Give no place to the evil demon to subdue us with the oppression of these mortal bodies; but take us by our outstretched hands, and guide our weapons to smite the minions of hell who now walk the earth.

As warring angels of God, we give blood for the blood of the demon possessed, should He so choose it.

Pardon us for the evil we must do in thy name, For we deliver to thee the souls of all the lost departed from the pains of hell and from the bottomless pit.

In nomine Patris, et Filii,
et Spiritus Sancti, Amen.

# Chapter One

It was a good night for a hunt. Delicate snowflakes flurried to the ground, adding to the already thick, white blanket that coated the forest floor of Vakre Fjell. Its hush was the only sound to disrupt the hum of burning gas lamps lining the dangerous paths.

Belle's trusty Friesian horse, Charming, huffed and pawed impatiently. His steamy breath swirled up before being absorbed by the cold. Belle's gaze waded through the darkness that lay beyond the trees. She listened, waiting for the devils to be drawn to her warm flesh.

Then she heard it; the thudding of swift moving, heavy paws. She tapped the reins against Charming's neck. He spun on his heel as Belle drew one of her revolvers.

A hellhound raced toward her.

He was big, feral, and his lips curled back in anticipation. He came within range, a snarl ripping from his chest.

She exhaled, then squeezed the trigger. A silver bullet burst forth in a smoky explosion, destroying the forest's peaceful silence. The hound plunged into the snow and skidded several feet. Blood trickled from its head wound; a stark contrast against the white snow. The twitching body claimed half the path. Belle pressed her boot into Charming's side, cuing him toward it.

They walked casually, unafraid, up to the hellhound. It didn't breathe, its eyes didn't follow her. Snowflakes started to gather on the tips of its thick, brown fur. There was no doubt the devil was dead. She'd given it a far quicker death than it would have given her.

Satisfied, Belle urged Charming away from the carnage. The familiar ringing, like an angel's voice, sang into the air. Lights jetted out before her, dancing over the trees and glittering snow. Without looking back, Belle knew that as the illumination faded, the hellhound's corpse would be gone, replaced with a clothed, human body.

The belief was that, five years ago, the Devil took hold of Vakre Fjell for its sinful ways. He'd claimed the Vakrein people as his own and turned them into hellhounds. The proof of this was found when they transitioned in death—with rays of gold light—from hound to human. Death freed them.

That's why the Hunters existed. To protect the village of Contefées and exterminate the demon spawn, the Catholic Church had formed a small army of defenders. Led by Belle's father, Henri LeClair, the group of civilian men became protectors, and "Hunter" became their title.

Two soft pops drew Belle's gaze from the forest. Over the trees, a scarlet flare soared brightly through the night sky. Tiny red sparks trickled in its wake like an ever-growing tail.

"A pack," Belle whispered. Faint, distant shouts and gunshots followed. "Yah!" Charming sprang like a living bullet. He covered the ground at a gallop, his hooves thundering. She leaned into him, giving him enough rein to run unhindered.

They had to hurry. Hellhounds were hungry, ravenous demons. A single Hunter could handle a few on his own, but when they gathered in groups, they took on a terrifying pack mentality. Though it was rare, it could mean certain death if a Hunter was alone.

A second flare went up. Belle and Charming ran parallel with the ambush. She wanted to cut through the woods and get there quicker, but she couldn't leave the trail. The forest of Vakre Fjell was vast and easily disorienting. Many Hunters died while creating the lit paths, and the first thing every new recruit learned was to never leave them.

Charming sped down the trail, eating up ground and scattering snow with each step. His long, black mane lashed her cheeks like tiny, stinging whips. The battling Hunters and hellhounds weren't far off now.

A hellhound jumped from the woods at Charming's head. The horse jolted to the side, evading its deadly paws. The devil crashed ungracefully into a snowbank. She raised her gun to aim, but an unseen set of claws sank into her shoulder.

There was no chance to cry out from pain as she was wrenched from the saddle, then slammed to the ground. The collision shook through her body, briefly dazing her. Belle forced her eyes open just in time to see sharp teeth descending. She jerked away and fired on instinct. The bullet shot clean through the hellhound's skull. It fell limp to the ground, almost on top of her.

*Two bullets down. Four left*, Belle noted as she pushed herself up from the blood-tinged snow.

Charming was rearing up and slamming his hooves down at the first hellhound. There was no fear in the horse, only the pure animal need to survive. The creature growled and snapped at him while trying to avoid those large hooves. Belle took aim, and when her Friesian reared again, creating an opening, she shot. The hound's head whipped back with a snap and it tumbled over itself.

Belle couldn't help but smile. *Three head shots in a row—not bad. Three bullets left.*

Trotting over to her, Charming nickered from deep within his chest.

"Well done, boy," Belle said, as she hoisted herself into the saddle.

Pain seared hot in her right shoulder. Warm blood seeped down her back. She ignored it; no time to tend the injury now.

The stallion rushed around the last curve. Cold air swept Belle's fur cloak up off her back as they approached the battle. Her Hunters were all alive and fighting. Two were still mounted, but three fought from the ground with their well-trained Friesians helping to defend them. The quiet night was filled with noise; howling, growling, barking, and Hunters shouting to one another between gunshots.

From beside his horse, Gastone slashed his sabre at two attacking hellhounds. As Charming brought Belle into the fray, she aimed, pulled the trigger. Aimed and pulled again. Both hounds dropped. Gastone looked up at her and relaxed his bloody sword.

"Merci, mademoiselle," he said with a breathless smile. His face and clothes were smeared with crimson, but she was certain the blood wasn't his.

"Are you out of bullets already, Gastone?" she teased.

"My body, or should I say *bodies*, of work." He gestured to the surrounding dead hounds, a few of which had already returned to their lost human forms.

"Reload. I'll cover you." Belle removed her second revolver as Gastone pushed back a fallen strand of his black hair, sheathed his sabre, and began reloading. One hellhound leapt over another, eager for the distracted Hunter. Belle put a round in its chest, emptying her first pistol.

Growling rumbled nearby, alerting Belle. She turned in her seat and shot with her left hand, which was nearly as good as her right. *Nearly* as good. The bullet grazed the attacker's ear, not stopping the hound's charge. Belle stayed calm, waiting for it to jump—knowing it would jump. Its muscles gathered as it advanced and, sure enough, it sprang. From two feet away she fired again. The creature flew backward with a yip, dying before it hit the ground. *Four bullets left*.

A cluster of hellhounds pressed in on the men. In quick succession, Belle dispatched three hounds, missing once from her perch atop Charming. Still more demons appeared from all sides. The scent of blood called to them.

No time to reload, Belle tucked away her empty gun and drew her sabre. The sword's weight in her palm felt good, strong. She clenched the hilt, shifting it beneath her gloved fingers. Belle dismounted and took up arms alongside her Hunters. With silver and steel, gunpowder and muscle, they killed each devil that tried for them.

A dead hound reverted to its human body, sending out a blinding light. One hellhound tried to take advantage of this by dashing past Belle, but she was fast. She struck out, slicing open its side. It yelped and lunged for her. With a twist of her body, she ran the sabre through its temple. Before it could drag her down, she yanked her weapon free.

"More on the approach!" bellowed Andre.

Delano responded with a wicked twinkle in his eye, "Holy damn, the devils are out tonight."

Belle was already moving. She grabbed her rifle from the saddle holder. It was loaded and ready to go, but she only had one shot. Belle dropped down behind Gastone and Andre, her skirts billowing on the snow around her. Letting her sabre fall to the ground, she needed both hands to take aim. One of the snarling fiends was in her sights. The following blast was bigger, louder, than that of her revolvers. The hound went down, and the men made quick work of the others. Sabre and shotgun in hand, Belle got to her feet.

The last gunshots echoed into oblivion. The sudden onset

of silence was alarming and so were the number of corpses surrounding them. Dozens by the look of it. It was barely a speck, no bigger than the snowflake that landed on her eyelash, compared to the countless she had killed over the years.

It pained her to see women and men lying dead in the snow, dead by their hands. At the beginning of her hunting career, Belle would have reminded herself that they were fighting the devil— freeing these people. Belle believed it wholeheartedly then. She had to; for her sanity's sake. But then Belle killed a hellhound that turned into child . . . No amount of Holy Scripture could repair the damage done by seeing that dead little girl. Because in the end, how could a *child* be a sinner?

*"I know what we do is difficult to face because we don't really understand what happened to these poor souls. But we know what will happen if we fail in our duty."* Henri had told her that between her broken-hearted sobs. He didn't need to voice that Contefées would be overrun, and then the hellhounds would move throughout all of Glace. Killing and killing. *"We hunt so that we can protect. Above all else, remember that."*

Belle always would.

"So, what is your count, Belle?" Gastone asked. She blinked, allowing the memories to fade and bringing the present into focus. When she didn't answer straight away, he said, "I had thirteen."

The smugness in his voice made Belle smile. He thought he had bested her. She walked over to Charming, replaced her rifle, and remounted before answering, "I had thirteen as well."

Gastone's face fell. "You jest."

She laughed with a shake of her head. To the others she said, "Are you gentlemen ready to call it a night? I think we've reached our quota."

The siblings, Delano and Nicolas, remained on the lookout for loan hellhounds. Jean Legrand, a mountain of a man, reloaded his many guns and Andre, Gastone's closest friend, checked his horse for injuries. They each looked up from their tasks and chorused their enthusiastic approval as one.

Belle reached into her saddlebag to remove a flare gun. She then tapped the Electro-Phonic Chip hugging her right ear.

"Friar, we are ready for you. Bring two carts." She positioned her finger over the communication device. "Standby for the flare."

Each night, while they hunted, Friar Clemens and a Hunter waited outside the forest. Their job was to collect the dead. Belle touched the ear chip again to stop it from sending out her voice. Extending her arm, she fired the flare gun. Green sparks exploded with a pop.

Franck's voice came through the earpiece's receiver. "Location confirmed."

Franck was one of the original Hunters who served under Belle's father. When she took command of her own hunting party, the older Hunters stepped down from full active duty to serve in a smaller, safer, capacity. A Hunter never retired.

Belle's hunting party was on the lookout as they waited. She removed the cover to her gun's bullet chamber, placing the thin piece of metal between her teeth. Reaching into a small pouch at her waist, she grabbed six rounds. Handmade by the Hunters, each silver bullet was etched with a black cross into its side. Belle popped them, one by one, into the tight compartments.

As she worked, Belle admired her gorgeous revolvers. Designed just for her, they were shaped like a lowercase 'L' with no sharp edges and an easy curve for the handle. Silver vines, comprised of leafy accents, wrapped the guns' wooden frames from tip to handle. The depiction of a gold, shooting star stretched across their barrels—As though, instead of bullets, Belle shot cosmic fire. Secured to each barrel's underside were spring-loaded twin bayonets that sprang forth at the press of a button.

She had loaded three shells when movement caught her attention. Belle paused, watching. From the thick tree line two hellhounds dropped onto the snow-tousled path, running straight for them.

Accepting that she would have to do this with only three, Belle stuffed the last of her bullets back into her pouch. She snatched the cover from her teeth and shoved it over the gun's chamber. From the corner of her vision, she saw Gastone watching her. He hadn't yet noticed the coming hellhounds, and this was her chance to steal the lead count. Confidence filled her—but then one growled.

Gastone smiled knowingly.

# Chapter Two

Gastone turned his shameless smirk to Belle. Magnanimous, his stallion, sensed their rising energy and danced in place. Acting faster than Gastone, Belle cued Charming and the horse launched first down the path.

The hellhounds and horses sped through the snow, barreling straight for one another. On this current course, Belle could kill the closest hound, giving Gastone time to kill the other, but that wouldn't break their tie. Belle thought through her vast répertoire of riding tricks. She'd practiced with Charming over the years and had the perfect one to secure her both kills.

"Okay, Charming, the Flying Angel." His ears flicked in her direction, listening to her instructions. Belle released the reins and placed her hands on the saddle's pommel. Shifting her weight onto her arms, she raised her body up off the horse. With stable breaths and complete focus, she dragged her feet beneath her until they rested on the seat. Belle was poised, Charming's stride remaining steady to give her balance. "Get ready."

Beneath her, she could feel Charming's muscles gathering— but not yet. The hellhound had to be in just the right place. They drew closer. She could hear the demon's growl. Closer still. Then, she gave the command. "Down!"

Charming skidded to a halt, throwing his momentum into

his back. Belle uncoiled her legs and, like a tightly wound spring suddenly released, she propelled into the air. Up she went. Body straight. Arms out. Over the hound she sailed. Her free hand smoothly grabbed the throwing knives strapped to her chest. With practiced grace, Belle flung them at the hellhound below. Each blade struck his body in perfect order. His yip wretched the silence.

Altitude waning, Belle arched her body, flipping and twisting to the ground. She landed in a crouch, skirts tumbling around her, and aimed her gun at the other nearing hound. A second to steady her hand—she fired. Snow dusted against Belle's cheeks as the hellhound bashed into the ground a few feet away.

She stood, already smiling at the trick's success, and turned to see the gloriously shocked look on Gastone's face. She curtsied. "Fifteen."

Gastone tensed, then he drew back his shoulders. With a high-hatted expression, he cued his horse by Charming and stopped over the hellhound stuck with knives. He pointed his gun, tugged back the hammer, and sent a bullet into its head. A tendril of smoke swirled over the barrel and up his arm.

Belle tossed up her hands and trudged back toward her horse. "What did you do that for?"

"I was killing the hellhound. *Fourteen.*"

"Oh, I do all the work and you claim the kill?"

"Your knives hit his back muscles. Flesh wounds at best. He wasn't dead yet, so I finished him, making it fourteen to fourteen." Gastone shifted around to watch Belle gather up her knives and remount. Sauntering his horse by, he added, "And *I* did it without all of the fancy."

This made Belle laugh. Fancy was the perfect word for the stunt. It was unnecessary and a silly risk, she could admit, but still she had to do it. Just once. "Sometimes, a little fancy is completely needed."

"Indeed." Gastone guided his Friesian over, making room for Belle to ride alongside.

Dual acts of high-pitched songs and an eruption of yellow light trailed them back to the group. Belle and Gastone approached as Friar Clemens and two other Hunters arrived. Friar Clemens drove one cart while the new recruit steered the second. Franck rode his own horse, eyes on the forest and gun at the ready.

"Hello, messieurs. How goes it?" Belle greeted.

"Very well. Merci, mademoiselle," Clemens replied. He didn't wear the same traditional society clothes as everyone else. His style was little more than basic; brown monk's robes with a plain cloak for added warmth. "Simple clothes for a simple man," he'd once told her.

"Aside from the dead ones." Franck pointed to the carted bodies they'd picked up along the way. "We didn't encounter any hounds. The forest seems pretty well cleared."

Belle nodded. "That's what I wanted to hear."

"Well then . . ." The new recruit, Jack, hooked his reins to the wagon and climbed down. "Let's get these bodies loaded. I'm pert near sick of this cold."

That was typical Jack Lloyd. He was brash, cocksure, charming, hardworking, and the only American Belle had ever met. He'd traveled all the way from the Colorado Territories in search of an adventure. Said he'd worked on his father's cattle ranch till he finally decided to see if the world was as pretty as the prairie. He hopped on a train, then boarded a ship, went from Australia to Europe, and somehow found himself in Glace—broke and looking to make some fast cash. Instead, he became their latest recruit.

"Come on big fella." Jack slapped Jean's thigh. "Why don't you give that horse's back a break and help us."

With a grunt, the ever-massive Jean dismounted. He, along with Franck, Jack, and the friar, set to work loading the bodies. The others kept a lookout. The woods seemed empty, but the forest could be deceiving. Belle knew better than anyone what they were dealing with; her life had been irrevocably shaped by the dangers within Vakre Fjell.

Five years ago, her father was attacked while traveling home from the Inventor's World Fair. Not knowing what exactly he'd shot, he carted it straight to the cathedral. Belle remembered waking up to the call of the church bells, running past the unusual guards at the entrance, and pushing through the swollen crowd of onlookers. Most of all, she recalled seeing the bloodied hellhound on the floor. Henri thought he'd killed the creature, but given it took so long to become human again, it must have clung to life before it finally died.

Questions were shouted. The crowd's fear was palpable. But when the demon suddenly shifted into a human, stunned silence took the room.

It was Bishop Sauvage who broke the quiet. As Archbishop, he often traversed the province, visiting the churches in his care. He'd heard tales of hellhounds in his travels, and explained how some sinners could be claimed by the devil. He then foretold of how these creatures would try to consume the world.

The town hung on his every word, rapt by the power behind his voice. When he proposed forming the Hunters (or holy warriors as he called them) everyone agreed. Being the first to kill a hellhound, Henri LeClair was given the charge.

To accommodate the volunteers coming from all over, the LeClair family uprooted to the local inn, and their home was redesigned. Continually more and more hellhounds were finding their way south, forcing every second to be devoted to the cause. Henri desperately sought to perfect their hunting skills and weapons, and oversaw the building of the gas-lit paths. Many men died in those days, so by thirteen, Belle was in training. Barely a year later, she was hunting alongside her mother.

They were just starting to find a sense of normalcy, then her mother died and again everything changed. Her older sisters were shipped off to live in Paris with their aunt, where they could join society like normal young ladies. Henri put new pressure on training, especially on Belle's. More men were recruited, and in a short time, she was named captain of the next hunting party.

Five years, that's all that had past—yet it felt longer. Even now, as Belle stood guard with her Hunters, it was hard to fathom all that had happened. Many great changes—she watched as Jack and Franck swung a body into a cart—and much of it terrible.

Once the corpses were loaded—which took some time as there were many—the group traveled farther into Vakre Fjell. The lampposts looped the trail around and throughout the woods, then led back to the original entrance. To collect the deceased, the Hunters walked the entire path before they returned home. Absolved in death, these sinners needed their last rites to be laid to rest.

Though, at times, Belle was conflicted over the truth behind these hellhounds, she did not doubt this ritual. These people may have been victims or maybe they were sinners, but they did deserve peace. Likely, more than others.

Nearly an hour later, they reached the blessed Glace border. Belle pulled her fur cloak tighter around her. A sheet of white fluff had settled over her and Charming. She had a high tolerance for the cold, but after several hours on horseback it was starting to get to her. Despite her leather gloves, Belle's fingers were numbing. That is until she flexed them, then they exploded with sharp pain. Her toes weren't faring any better.

"Headed to Le Géant Tranquille?" Franck asked as he rode up next to her, a glint in his eye.

Going to the pub after a hunt was a long standing tradition. No doubt he was remembering his own escapades there with Henri and fellow Hunters. Belle could practically taste the awaiting mug of ale, and feel the warm fire on her skin. They moved onto French land and a gust of cold wind slipped up her sleeve, reminding her that she wasn't there yet.

"Yes, we are." Belle indicated the corpse-filled carts as they rolled out of Vakre Fjell Forest, the rest of her hunting party in tow. "Would you like some help before we leave? That's going to be some work."

Franck looked at the carts. "No, I don't think even that comes close to the weight you and your men took on tonight."

She glanced up at the sky. A small break in cloud cover unveiled a stretch of twinkling stars. "How long does that kind of weight have to be carried?"

"I don't know." Franck sighed. "I'm still carrying mine."

Belle dropped her gaze to the ground, nodding. "You have a good night, Franck."

"You as well," he responded.

Steering Charming onto the main road, Belle started for Contefées. Her hunting party also bid their farewells to accompany her. Franck and Jack would stay behind to tend to the dead. Not a desirable job, but until Jack swore the Hunter's Creed before the church and God, he had to pay his dues.

The stallions' long legs trotted effortlessly through the heavy snow, hastening their journey. Full manes and tails glided behind them. With coats as black as night and necks arched, the Friesians exuded both elegance and power.

For good reason, the majestic breed was the only kind that Hunters rode. They were locally bred, trained for survival, and Hunter and horse often bonded for life. When Belle was astride Charming, she felt his strength empowering her own. He would fend off the wolves at her back and carry her through the most brutal of snowstorms.

Reaching the hilltop, Belle halted Charming with a softly uttered command. The other Hunters did the same, stopping in a line abreast with her. No one spoke as they looked down the hill at their sleeping town. Tonight, it was safe.

# Chapter Three

Montefées sat quiet and settled for the night. The great Catholic cathedral loomed above the snow-topped buildings like a dark Goliath. Two sparkling lanterns hung at its doors; a welcome to any late night worshipers. The Hunters made their way down the hill and onto the cobblestone. As the Friesians walked along, their clopping hooves echoed off the buildings.

Illuminated lampposts lined the streets, showing that most shops and homes were shut tight. Save for Le Géant Tranquille, which spilled light and music out into the town's center. Here were some of Belle's favorite buildings; the church, tavern, bakery, and the bookshop.

In the middle of the circling cobblestones was a fountain, topped with the same style lantern that dotted the streets. It was too cold the majority of the year for the water to run, but instead of the structure being a waste, the town's people started a tradition of placing candles along the fountain's edge. Candle after lit candle, they built up and consumed the stonework. Now, solid waterfalls of wax drooped over the sides. There was nothing more lovely than a still night when old and new candles flickered around the fountain, and the overhead lantern cast a warm glow upon it all.

Outside Le Géant Tranquille were a set of hitching posts.

They were fashioned into tiny horse heads cradling metal circlets in their mouths. Belle dismounted and looped the reins loosely through one of the rings.

From the back of her saddle, she removed and unrolled a large blanket. She spread it over Charming. The other Hunters did the same. Just a little something to keep the snow off the horses while they waited. Delano and Nicolas used the butts of their rifles to break the ice in each trough, allowing the Friesians access to the water beneath.

"Shall we, messieurs?" Belle asked as the men finished up their tasks.

She unbuttoned a clasp at her waist, which released her skirts, and they fell freely to the ground. Belle had sewn the buckles into her dresses years ago. It didn't take her long to realize that running or even mounting a horse was much more complicated when her legs were engulfed by layers of fabric. With a button on the outside of her dress and a strip of cloth stitched underneath, she could lift the skirts over her right hip and pin them up with ease. It revealed entirely too much leg for a proper lady . . . but the rules of higher society didn't have much place on a hunt. However, so as not to offend anyone's sensibilities or to sully her own reputation, Belle covered her legs in the presence of non-Hunters.

"After you, mademoiselle." Gastone pushed open the tavern door and waited for Belle to enter.

She smiled as raucous music, laughter, singing, and slurred speech filled her ears. The Hunters followed close behind, eager for warmth. As cold air swirled into Le Géant Tranquille, the patrons glanced their way, and the crowd broke into a cheer, welcoming the Hunters' safe return.

For Belle it was a tradeoff; being a Hunter hurt any prospects she had for marriage, but in its place came great respect from the town's folk. As was the way of the world, the men did not have this issue. In fact, being a Hunter made them more desirable as suitors.

Belle accepted this reality. Her duty to protect Contefées always came first. The only time this bothered her was when she thought of her parents. They'd loved each other deeply, standing together against many enemies. Her mother's death was a devastating shock. More so for her father, who disappeared into his workshop for weeks afterward.

Even now, Belle would catch a certain look in Henri's eyes. A look that said he wasn't with her at that moment. He was with the memories of his wife. She knew because his eyes somehow shown both love and sorrow. Belle might give up hunting for that sort of love—a love that gripped the soul and didn't let go.

"Gastone!" Medford, a nearing middle-aged miner, stumbled his way over. He was scruffy and unkempt; the sort to only keep his money long enough to gamble it away.

"Medford!" Gastone brushed back the loose, black strands of his ponytail, the side of his mouth upturning in a half grin, and grasped the man's shoulder with strong, wide hands.

Belle eyed the way the gas-light fell on the stark line of his jaw and it was no wonder that eligible women flocked to him. He was the handsome son of a Count, who was also a remarkable Hunter. Any young lady would be lucky to have his attentions.

Upon Belle's seventeenth birthday, Henri intimated that she might be just such a woman. Though he would never push the subject, he did tell her that local gossip expected Belle and Gastone to begin courting. Apparently, despite her not coming from a family of great financial means, she did come from a respected name and her position as Hunter captain afforded her some social standing. Moreover, her beauty remedied any damage done by her having a man's profession. But this was idle talk and nothing more. All that really mattered were the thoughts of Gastone and his family.

Unfortunately, if Gastone gave Belle the same consideration for marriage as the town had, he never verbalized it. The way he looked at her sometimes set her nerves on fire, but no tokens were ever given, and until Gastone made his intentions clear, a courtship between them couldn't happen. Society gave way on some rules for Belle to be a Hunter; such as her living in a house with potential suitors. On other rules, they would not bend. Belle still had to conduct herself as a lady and follow courtship etiquette.

"The guys and I have a bet on who can fit more escargots in his mouth, you or Ivon. I'm betting on you, of course." Medford took hold of Gastone's arm in return and dragged him toward the bar. "Oh yeah, and the Pêcheur sisters have been asking about you."

*Of course the Pêcheur sisters have been asking about Gastone,* Belle rolled her eyes and her gaze fell on the voluptuous two. Odette and Josette were the only other set of identical siblings born in Contefées—the other being Belle's two older sisters. The Pêcheur twins were the daughters of a local fisherman. As such, they had little money and no social standing, which meant their corsets were kept tight and their bosoms high. They often frequented any establishment filled with eligible men. Currently they pressed their chests against the wooden piano, singing along, and gawked after the group of attractive Hunters.

Gastone seemed unsurprised by the twin's attention and didn't bother looking their way. "Who can fit more escargots, huh? With or without shells?"

Medford thought briefly. "Uh . . . With. Definitely with."

Smugly, Gastone raised his chin. "Challenge accepted."

Belle chuckled. One minute he's saving the world, making young ladies swoon, and the next he's stuffing snails in his mouth.

Belle began weaving her way through the maze of tables and

patrons. The other Hunters went about their own business, join-
ing friends, placing bets on Gastone and Ivon, or going straight
for the ale. At Le Géant Tranquille, Hunters drank for free.

The tavern's décor was truly something to behold. Filling every free space, the walls were covered in animal trophies hunted
by the townsfolk. But it even went beyond that. The chandeliers
were enormous, pointy concoctions of candles, gas lamps, and
antlers. Horns were hidden throughout the pub's furnishings,
furs covered the chairs, and a massive bear rug, complete with
roaring head, rested in front of the hearth.

The fireplace in Le Géant Tranquille was an elaborately carved
masterpiece that filled the entire room with its heat. The frame
was designed to be a collage of wildlife. They toppled over one another and blended together. The fire's glorious blaze illuminated
some animals perfectly and cast others into shadow.

Fireplaces may have been essential tools against the bitter
cold, but in this arctic land they were also a fashion statement.
They had to be big, and they had to be works of art. This was so
important that, when invited into someone's home, it was considered impolite not to remark on the size and aesthetics of their
hearth.

Stopping at a table of her usual town companions, Belle removed her cloak and draped it over a chair left empty for her.

"Hey Doc!" she called to a man drinking alone in the corner
and waved him over.

"He's a doctor?" said a stranger from the table next to her.

"Yes, monsieur." Her eyes swept over his group. They were
outsiders to be sure. British, by the look of them. "He's the only
doctor for miles and miles."

The man watched the physician trip into his own table as he
tried to get up. "He's not fit to do any sort of doctoring."

"Doc's the best at what he does," Belle said simply, refusing to defend the doc's soft soul to someone who couldn't understand what it was like here.

"You never said you were injured before." Gastone appeared behind her.

His hand went to her arm, and she felt the other upon her back. Peering at the cuts, he twisted her in the light. Several deep punctures bled down her back, painting her skin and dress. His touch was gentle and warm; she inwardly reveled in their feel.

With a quirk of her lip, she replied, "I thought you were eating snails."

Gastone chuckled. "Snails can wait."

Belle bobbed her head back and forth, pretending to weigh the value of his words. "Hm, they are rather slow."

"So can death be." He turned her to look at his face. "Don't go dying from something as trivial as an untreated wound."

Being so close to him, Belle noticed that his dark eyebrows arched in the most interesting way. She fought the urge to reach up and trace one softly with her thumb. Immediately aware of how indecent her proximity to Gastone was, Belle stepped away.

"For the love of God, get out of my way!" Doc shouted to part a crowd of ambling drinkers.

Doc was young, but it was impossible to determine his age. He kept his hair short and parted down the middle, causing his bangs to create half-moons around his forehead. The bifocals he wore were perfect circles resting on the bridge of a small nose. He could have looked like a man fresh out of medical school, but this life had left its imprints on him. Lines creased his otherwise youthful face and melancholy shaped his features.

He stopped before them and took a calming breath while adjusting his vest. "Let's see it then."

Belle turned, allowing Doc to examine her wounds. She wondered if he was seeing double.

"Mm, not bad. No stitches necessary. Some bandages should do the trick." He reached into his bag and brought out a jar of alcohol and a cloth.

With deft fingers, he worked till the wounds were cleaned and covered. To finish, Doc repaired her lacerated dress with a few swipes of his needle and thread. He didn't need to tell her that the punctures would scar. At this point, Belle had more scars than she could count and was no longer concerned by them.

Unexpectedly, the table of strangers all came to a stand amid a chorus of shouts. They were looking at Andre and Delano. One man was dangerously close to Andre's face and whispering something that was sure to be rude. From across the room, Jean and Nicolas were making their way over. Clearly a bout of fisticuffs was brewing.

Shockingly fast, Andre's fist shot out and crashed into the whisperer's face. He went down hard, hitting the ground unconscious. The outsiders stared in disbelief, as the downed man had been much larger than Andre. To answer their unspoken question, Andre removed his glove and raised his hand. Metal parts gleamed in the tavern light.

"Metal prosthetic, lost my hand to a hellhound." He reached down with the same hand and rapped his knuckles against his leg, creating a *thunk*. "They took my leg as well."

"Well, maybe the French are just too soft." This man was tall and heavy-chested. Judging by his bearing, he was the leader of this little group. "I say there's plenty of Vakrein bounty worth killing a few wolves over."

*Mercenaries.* Belle scoffed. Their ilk had been coming around since the world learned of Vakre Fjell's demise. Every one of them thought they could fight their way in and come out with a king's wealth. None ever returned rich. Most didn't come out at all.

Belle slipped between the doc and Gastone, making like she

intended to get out of the way. Instead she walked through the crowd, seeking to position herself just behind the mercenary leader. No one paid her any attention as she drew her revolver and pointed it at the back of his head. She pulled back the hammer, letting it click loudly.

"Bloody hell!" one mercenary shouted.

The room looked at her; the leader wide-eyed with surprise.

"I don't care how you messieurs want to risk your lives. My only concern is two days from now. My father is traveling through Vakre Fjell to reach his transport to the Inventor's World Fair. It's last minute, so it can't be missed. But mostly I can't have you all riling up the hellhounds." She'd been looking between all the mercenaries, but now her gaze focused solely on the leader. "So I have a proposal. You wait three days. Spend all the money you have at our inn, shops, and good tavern. After three days, you may treasure hunt without any hindrance from us or this town. If you're as good as you say, you'll walk out of Vakre Fjell with more riches than you can imagine, and this town gets a little boon from your short stay."

"She's bluffing," said some spindly fellow to her left. "She couldn't pull that trigger and—"

With speed acquired from years of practice, Belle drew her second revolver. She put a bullet in his foot, cutting off his sentence. Several people flinched and the mercenary fell to the ground, howling like a stuck pig.

Belle looked back at the leader. "Now you have another reason to wait three days."

He chuckled and grinned, then put up his hands in surrender. "Three days of rest and relaxation sounds plenty good to me."

"Wonderful." Belle gave him her sweetest of smiles and stowed away her guns. "I'm glad we could help one another. It being so close to Noël and all."

The man nodded and went to his wounded friend. Just like that, the whole tavern calmed. Conversation and drink started anew like nothing had happened.

"I would like to thank all ye Hunters," A young Irishman named, Davin, said coming over to her. "I know the world hasn't exactly shown its support for yer efforts. Not just cause of these awful mercenaries, but our leaders as well. If they did—support ye that is—armies would have been sent years ago to kill off dis hellish menace. Instead, they're all too worried about invading, and angering Vakre Fjell's old motherland, Norway."

"Politics," Nicolas spat. He and the other Hunters had made their way over.

"Indeed. So the brunt of it all has been placed on you lot. I want to express my gratitude. Not just for me or my hometown, but for all of God's Cup. We know what yer doing here." Davin referred to their island by its nickname; called such for its resemblance of a wine goblet spilling into the Norwegian Sea.

The isle was occupied by their French province at the center, the Vakrein kingdom to the north, and the British territory in the south.

"Looks like I got here just in time for the entertainment," came a voice beside Belle.

She looked over to find Jack. In one hand, he gripped his cowboy hat and his other ran through his light blond hair. The snow on his black duster was starting to melt. He'd been in Glace for over a year now, but Jack still dressed and acted American in every way. Belle actually found that quite endearing, though she'd never tell him. So did many of the women in town, and they *did* tell him.

It was not uncommon for Jack to join them at Le Géant Tranquille after his duties were done. The man drank like . . . well . . . an American, and made friends fast too. Almost seamlessly, he'd integrated himself into their Hunter family and, except for the occasional tavern brawl, got along with everyone else. Belle was happy to have him soon officially join her hunting party.

"Can I get you something to drink, cowboy?" asked a barmaid while she pushed out her chest. Belle snickered.

He rocked on his heels, grinning at her. "Whiskey, please, ma'am."

Was it just Belle or did Jack's accent thicken when a pretty lady was around?

# Chapter Four

Belle started up the church steps carrying a single rose she'd bought from the town greenhouse. The cathedral's two great, looming steeples reached for the heavens as a thousand tiny peaks tried to do the same. Three arched front doors set next to each other; the center standing taller than the ones at its side. A single ornate, circular glass window encompassed the center of the church's front.

The morning sun caused melting snow to drip from above, as she traversed through the cathedral's entrance. Giant chandeliers hung from the ceiling. Rows of pews lined the floor leading to the dais where a gold crucified Christ suspended. Complex stonework brought saints to life in every available space, hand painted murals depicted various biblical scenes, and massive stone pillars were a canvas for both. Sun shined through the great stained-glass windows, casting the cathedral in a rainbow of colors.

The room's stillness made every sound more palpable. An elderly man shifted in his seat, his eyes staring at the savior. A woman whispered to her candle's flame. A friar's mop sloshed sudsy water onto the lovely floor.

The clergyman acknowledged Belle as she crossed the wet marble to reach the catacomb's entrance. Into the stairway she delved, her pace slowing as the light receded and the air grew colder. Voices traveled up from below. Orange-hued light broke the darkness as she neared the bottom, pausing on the steps.

"Hall of the Unknowns . . ." a woman said, reading the placard above one of the three entrances into the catacombs. They were high and arching, their words etched in gold.

"Those are the remains of souls we could not identify," the clergyman attending her said. "The majority are souls redeemed by our Hunters."

Belle noted the pride in his voice. She'd only walked through there once and the many unnamed graves—the forgotten souls—had made the Hunter's burden feel like a deep, jagged cut. Yet she considered herself lucky to have that hardship. At least she will not be lost in death like those poor souls—At least she will have a name, and the living will come to pray for it.

"Oh, I see." The woman's eyes widened and she looked to the next hall. This dainty, but well-proportioned woman was American, judging by her accent. She had dark brown hair pulled back into a tight bun. Her dress was burgundy, with an almost military style. Around her neck was a thin, gold chain that sported a small pair of tinted bifocals. In her hand was an official-looking briefcase. "And the Hall of The Beloved Dead?"

"That's where our own are put to rest," the friar responded, and Belle followed their gaze down the long stretch of tombs.

The woman wiggled her nose from the stale air and turned to the final hall. "Now why is the Hall of the Hunters sealed?"

Unlike the first two halls, the Hall of the Hunters was cut off by giant metal doors which were not open to the general public. Black metal elegantly shaped the double doors and the visible gears that made up the lock. It was a worthy tomb for those who died protecting the town.

"In the beginning, people feared that Hunters who died by a hellhound would soon rise and become one of them. Everyone had heard the tales of werewolves who turned others with a bite," Belle spoke up, making them aware of her presence. "As a precaution these doors were built to keep the dead in. Those who were bitten, but didn't die, were quarantined in the jail. Time revealed that there was no truth behind the stories, but the doors were never removed."

"Fascinating." The woman's eyes danced with excitement. "How does one get in?"

"Hunters have a key," The clergyman said with a tone of finality and gently took the woman's arm, guiding her to the stairs. "Come, Dr. Caskin, I'm sure the Father is free by now."

The ladies curtsied to one another in passing, then Belle watched the doctor and friar disappear up the stairs. A woman doctor? Was it possible that Doc had found a replacement? Walking over to the great metal doors, Belle hoped that he had not.

From her side, Belle untied her rosary. The ebony beads were held together by gold links. Its matching gilded cross was large enough to span her palm and carved with a complicated pattern. Only a few knew it, but the key was this very rosary. It was one of the three gifts every Hunter received upon initiation. At death, the key was given to the Hunter's family in a funeral ceremony so that they may visit the one they lost.

The cross slid easily into the lock. She twisted it. The mechanism clanked loudly, setting off the many gears. Movement started near her key. Small and large cogs clicked and turned, their teeth snapping into place, causing others to do the same. Like a technological ripple, it spread, triggering pieces all over the doors. Bars slid from the center seam. Metal scraped on metal. Each bar halted with a resonating boom, one by one, into the recesses of the doors.

*Click. Click. Snap.* The clockwork went silent. Belle removed her key and the doors cranked open. She stepped inside. The doors glided shut behind her.

The Hall of the Hunters consisted of white marble walls, brass nameplates, and floor-to-ceiling crypts. Like the drawers in a dresser, they stacked on top of one another—each small compartment containing a bed for the eternally resting.

Belle retied the rosary to her hip, drawing it through added loops so that it dangled against her skirts. She walked along the graves. Rolling the rose in her fingers, she gazed at the many scarlet folds. They looked like satin. Her feet moved, but she didn't need to see where they took her. The path was all too familiar. Belle stopped knowingly before the wall and finally peered up at the precious tomb.

The nameplate read, *Liliane Verdandi LeClair—Beloved wife and mother—Died on the hunt.* She set the rose into the holder and traced her gloved fingers over the engraved words. With her hand upon Liliane's name, she silently prayed. Belle lingered for a while after that. She didn't cry. The time for that had come and gone long ago. Belle simply remained there, picturing her mother, remembering the sound of her voice.

When she left, the cogs to the Hall of Hunters were still locking as she made her way back up to the main floor. Instead of exiting the cathedral, as she normally would, Belle made a detour to the priest's office. The door was open and the voices from within wafted out.

"We send them refusals. We then ignore their continued requests. Yet they still send someone all this way." Belle did not need to see the voice's owner to know why her stomach cringed at its sound. "And a woman scientist no less!"

A scientist! So the woman wasn't a medical doctor at all. Just like the mercenaries, scientists have had an immense interest in Vakre Fjell for years. Their pursuit wasn't for wealth of gold, but for that of knowledge. Not believing the theological explanation given by the church, they wanted to study the hellhounds. Unfortunately for them, they would have to go through the Pope to do that and the church wasn't budging.

"I'm not sure we should write them off entirely." Belle entered the office, seamlessly inserting herself into the conversation. "Studying a live hellhound might help us learn how to save their souls without killing them. Even letting them examine the body of a former hound might do just that."

Father Sinclair smiled kindly at her. The office was small, but its ceiling was high. The priest sat behind his desk, which was mounded with papers and books, writing something before the light of a large stained-glass window. Belle had known the Father her entire life. He was much loved by his congregation. "Ah, Belle, so good to see you. Did you know that Bishop Sauvage arrived today?"

The source of Belle's cringing stomach, the Bishop, sat near the window dressed in the traditional archbishop garb of purple velvet robes. A white fur shawl wrapped his shoulders and a square, plum-colored hat sat in his lap.

"No, I didn't know he was visiting. Pleasure to see you again, Bishop," she lied and before the Bishop could respond, she said to Father Sinclair, "I'm here for the Hunter's weekly allowance."

"Oh?" he replied. "I hope Henri is well?"

"Yes, he has some last minute work to do before he departs for the fair, so I have come in his stead."

"You?" interjected Bishop Sauvage. "Surely, there is a man who could do this?"

Belle felt the slight like it were spit at her feet, but she didn't immediately react. She had to be careful. Bishop Sauvage was already a thorn in her side and could easily become a powerful enemy. Still, Belle had to show she was capable. "As Hunter Captain the duty falls only to me."

"What?" The Bishop clenched his hat. "Captain? They made you Captain?"

"Yes—"

He cut her off, asking the Father, "Why was I not told about this?"

"It was Henri's decision." Father Sinclair sighed, keeping his eyes on his papers. "The town has full faith in his choice, and in Belle."

"This is a lapse." Bishop Sauvage stood and planted both hands on the desk, leaning toward the priest. "A woman is not fit to be a Hunter and is not worthy to be leading them."

Belle took a step forward, forcing their attention on her. She was polite, but she was not weak and would not allow someone to act as though she were. "Bishop Sauvage, I can assure you, I am more than capable to lead my men."

"*Your* men? Dear girl, it was one thing for the church to allow you and your mother to serve, but to give you a station above men . . ." His voice was thick with condescension. ". . . is heresy."

Horror tightened Belle's throat. This was the sort of belief that she feared most. With it alone, Bishop Sauvage could strip Belle of her title, ruin her name, and deny her a Hunter's burial. He could do the same to her mother, even after death. This was the power Belle was afraid of. She collected her thoughts, wrangled in her anxiety.

"Bishop Sauvage, if God believes that my position is an act against him, then I ask that he end me. Let me die in the forest." Belle filled her voice and face with as much softness as she could muster. She had to say just the right thing to quail the Bishop's anger for now. "However there is no one that has been groomed for this job as I have. The men trust me and so do the people. If I

can no longer serve in this capacity, then one of them must take
my place. One of their husbands or sons. Who will they blame for
that? Me, God, or *you*?"

His eyes burrowed unblinkingly into her.

"For now, I will not push this subject." Turning away, Bishop
Sauvage walked to the window. "Instead I will leave this wrong in
God's hands to right."

Father Sinclair frowned and held up a brown envelope. "Belle.
Here is the payment."

"Merci, Father. I'll be on my way then." She gave him the
faintest of smiles, attempting to alleviate any guilt he might have,
and accepted the billfold.

"You are welcome." His return smile was sincere. "Good day,
Belle."

"Good day." She turned toward the door, reaching out a hand
to push it open.

The Bishop's voice stopped her.

"You are correct, mademoiselle. God will surely strike you
down as he did your mother." He had turned just enough to see
her face. "Knowing that, if the hellhounds do not kill you, it'll be
a sign that you are not a servant of God—but, in fact, a mistress
of Satan."

Belle inhaled. Shock splayed across her face. It was almost
inconceivable. In one swift statement, he'd implied that Liliane
LeClair's death was an act from God—a punishment for being a
Hunter—and that Belle was possibly the Devil's lover.

Father Sinclair opened his mouth but seemed to choke on
his words. He looked from the Bishop to Belle. She could see the
sympathy in him, but he said nothing. No matter what sorrow
he felt, it wasn't enough to make him stand up to his better. His
mouth closed and his shoulders sagged. Finally, he looked away
from her.

Belle's heart beat grievously against her breastbone. Breathing became harder. Belle drew her shoulders back, pressing her lips into a thin line. The turbulence of emotions raged inside her and thundered for release. Painfully, she held them back, refusing to break in front of these men.

With the ghost of a grin, the Bishop watched her. "Though, I am sure God will come through."

Unable to stand there any longer, unable to speak, Belle pushed through the office door. She rushed through the church, along row after row of pews. Raw emotion tumbled out of her in waves of gasping, shallow, breaths. If there were people around, she didn't see them. She just wanted to get away from there—away from those awful words.

Tears welled in Belle's eyes, blurring her sight. Delicately made murals and sculptures became smears of color. The front entrance was open, washing the floors in natural light. Street noises breached the cathedral's threshold. Belle stopped short of the entryway. She couldn't go out there like this; heart racing, tears brimming over her eyelids and down her cheeks.

Her breath caught and, quick to hide, Belle dashed behind one of the large pillars. She covered her mouth, trying to stifle her sobs, and leaned against the column for support. Her throat was tight with pain; pain from humiliation.

How could the Bishop say something so terrible? To not just call her a whore, but to also insult her mother's memory, was unthinkable. Belle was not unfamiliar with the meanness of others, but no one had ever spoken so cruelly to her. The vulgarity alone was appalling. Worse yet, Father Sinclair had done nothing.

Not wanting anyone to see her so undone, Belle rested her head against the stone column and closed her eyes. One last tear slipped by. She took her hand from her mouth, placing it on her stomach to lend fortitude. With deep breaths, Belle summoned her composure.

It struck her then, the oddness of her emotions. Belle killed for a living. She'd seen things—grotesque things. Belle had buried family and friends, stood alone in a dark woods while creatures stalked her, but little of it ever got to her the way the Bishop's words had. Only words, but they'd cut deeper than claws.

Swiping away the last obstinate teardrops, Belle opened her eyes. She pushed off from the pillar, letting her own feet support her. Needlessly, Belle smoothed her dress. She blinked several times, feeling strangely lighter.

Holding her head high, Belle left the cathedral—vowing that the next time she saw the Bishop, she would be ready for his callousness. She might even dare to strike back.

# Chapter Five

Henri slashed his sabre through the neck of a champagne bottle. Foam erupted forth, spilling onto the wood floor. The Hunters cheered from around the dinner table. Henri held it out until the foam receded, then handed it to Friar Clemens who started filling glasses.

"Oh, I *like* that French tradition!" Jack pounded the table, making the dishware rattle with his enthusiasm.

The Friar's dinner for their early Noël party had been wonderful. Dishes of all sorts had been laid out. A variety of platters— breads, cheeses, and pastries—were now only crumbs. Roasted duck had been reduced to a carcass. Dessert was a cake made by Andre's parents, the local bakers. Everything had been delicious and they all ate their fill, leaving spirits high.

"No. No, my dear boy," Henri said, quieting the room. "Not a French tradition—a Hunter tradition."

"I was there, the night the tradition began." Belle looked at her father, absently fiddling with a curl at her shoulder.

"Were you?" Grabbing his napkin, Henri wiped the foam from his hands. "At your age, you should have been in bed."

Belle chuckled. "The town was at war with Hell and my inventor father was Commander of our army. The LeClairs didn't sleep much in those days."

"So, how did the tradition start?" Jack prompted.

"It's a good story," Gastone said, watching Belle. There was warmth in his eyes that caused her chest to tighten. "She told it to me once."

"Well, I want to hear it!" Jack insisted, flinging out his hands and the other Hunters vocally agreed.

"We were still living at the inn then." She didn't speak loudly as she started her story. The men would quiet for her, just as they did for Henri. "I'd slipped out of my room and hid on the stairwell, peaking through the railings. I could taste the despair coming from the men gathered below. A large pack had crossed the border and far more men than we could spare had died. The doc was there, I remember, he walked around the group, administering treatment."

She paused to thank Friar Clemens as he handed her the first glass. No one spoke, they hung on her words. "Père stood before them, holding his bottle of champagne. He spoke of the battle and of the men that were lost. It was the best thing I'd ever heard. Grown men had tears in their eyes. Père finished his speech with a booming voice like I'd never heard before. He tried to open the bottle so they could drink to their victory—"

"Damn thing refused to open," Henri added with a grin. He held his glass in one hand and rested his other on the hilt of his sabre.

"It made him so angry." Belle went on over the men's chuckles. "He unsheathed his sword with a slur of horrible curses and sliced off the top." She tilted her head to look up at her father. "When the applause died you said that you'd stand by them. No matter the loss, you'd stand by your Hunters. *Till my heart stills*, were your words. And they repeated them back to you. It was the moment I decided to become a Hunter."

"Well." Henri held up his glass. "To that then!"

Everyone joined in with the toast, tipping the champagne into their mouths.

"Who's in the mood for some music?" Andre asked, flicking back one of the spiraled locks he called dreads.

"Splendid idea." Henri swallowed down a mouthful of drink. "Should I crank the piano or would Jean like to do us the honor?"

Without any further urging, Jean moved to the piano bench. He checked the gorgeous gold and green scarf wrapped around his neck, making sure it still covered the ghastly scars beneath. Where once Jean could have been an operatic singer with his voice gifted by angels, he was now mute—his voice taken, instead of his life, by a hellhound. Pushing back the piano cover, he poised his hands above the keys.

Then his fingers were moving, twinkling over the keys with the grace of a dancer. It was beautiful. All of the talent Jean had once contained in his voice must have transferred to his hands. Transfixed, they all watching him, listening as the music filled the room.

A hand appeared in front of Belle. Her eyes traced the arm up to its owner. Gastone stood there, happiness shining in his eyes. She'd been so distracted by Jean's playing, she hadn't even noticed Gastone move.

"Care for a dance?" There was something in his voice. Something new. A softness perhaps.

Belle placed her hand in his. "I would."

He guided her out of her chair and to the small dance floor. Belle caught sight of her father. He was beaming. For just a moment, she wondered what he was thinking. Gastone turned her so that she faced him.

Belle subconsciously touched her hair. Part of it was clipped up in a bundle of curls that dangled around her face. The rest sat loose, cascading in ringlets and waves past her shoulders and nearly to her waist. Her mother's watch necklace, embossed with a rose, rested on her chest. Belle's dress was one of her nicest, one she reserved for special occasions.

Gastone held his arms out, waiting for Belle to step into them. She took a deep breath and moved into position. Belle's red and green dress hugged her frame—and she could feel the heat of his hand through the fabric as they waited for the change in music.

Gastone moved with its cue. Belle followed, letting him guide her about the floor. It was slow and gentle. Gastone had the grace of a lord's son. His eyes trailed along her face, causing a blush to rise into her cheeks.

The way he looked at her—the way they danced together—it was new, but somehow familiar. Like she'd known they would dance together her whole life. Too soon, the song came to an end.

"Gastone, that is not how you dance with a woman," Jack said as they stepped apart.

Raising an eyebrow at him, Gastone smiled boldly. "Does the Yank think he can do better?"

"Absolutely!" Jack pushed to his feet, tossing his napkin aside and walked around the table. He met Gastone's challenging stare as they past one another. "Ladies love to dance. They dance often and with nearly anyone who offers. The key is to give them a dance they'll remember."

He pulled Belle into his arms, not bothering too much with posture. He leaned over to look at Jean. "Give us something fast."

"Oh!" Henri jumped over to the piano, tinkered with some dials and started cranking.

When he finished, a set of dual violins, displayed in a glass compartment at the top of the piano, came to life. Their bows scraped along their strings, fiddling out a tune to get toes tapping. Jean picked up the song, and soon Jack was twirling Belle around the floor.

They laughed and smiled, moving through the fast steps. Delano and Nicolas started clapping to the rhythm, which the whole room picked up. Jack's style was nothing like Gastone's. He didn't hesitate to throw an arm around her waist or to spin her so fast, she'd fall without him. The dance ended with a flourish, leaving her flushed and breathless.

"Wonderful! Just wonderful." Henri came over as Jack and Belle bowed to one another. He grabbed her by the shoulders and planted a kiss on her forehead. "I'd say now was a good time for presents, wouldn't you?"

"I would." Belle put a hand to her stomach, trying to catch her breath, and laughed. "Better now, before Jack does me in!"

They moved into the parlor, which was done up in ribbons and evergreens. A large tree sat in the corner, decorated to the fullest and bundled by presents. Belle sat on the loveseat as the Hunters found spots around the room.

The great clock above the fireplace ticked to the next hour. Many oversized gears ornamenting the hearth danced, their teeth rocking together. Puffs of steam issued forth as the gears movement reached the brass bells above the clock. *Ding. Dang. Dong.* The sound moved through and around her. Belle sighed; that sound was home.

"Wonderful!" Henri entered last, heading straight for the hearth. "Our timing is impeccable."

As the last bell tolled, a hidden compartment above the mantel opened. A thin arm, holding a delicate teacup and saucer perturbed. Likewise, out came a pitcher. The arm tilted, pouring dark coffee into the flowered porcelain. Steam rolled into the air as Henri reached over to accept the hot beverage.

"Wonderful. Wonderful," he mumbled to himself and inhaled the steam. "Would anyone else care for a cup?"

When all declined, Belle's father turned a rather well-concealed knob. The metal arms retracted, taking the pitcher with it. The door then flipped shut to hide the compartment once more.

"Confound it!" Henri nearly shouted, suddenly glaring at the hearth. Belle discreetly covered her mouth, stifling her snicker. Her father slammed his fist against the wall. "Blast this thing, give me my pipe!"

Noisily the hearth clunked and moaned. With a sigh, a different compartment door popped open. Inside, held up by two small pedestals, was Henri's smoking pipe. He reached in and snatched the pipe with vigor, placing it between his lips and softly inhaling.

A smile quirked the corner of his lips. "Now let us open presents!"

In no time, the presents were all opened. The boys had worked together on her gifts. Andre had bought her the design plans for a dress. Jack purchased ribbons for her hair. Jean, Delano, and Nicolas had selected the fabrics. Then with Gastone's present of a lovely burgundy top hat, an outfit was in the works.

Jack was just thanking Jean for his new cowboy hat when the last present beneath the tree started to slide out. Pixie, Belle's childhood mechanical fairy, pushed from behind. Her metal was green, her eyes slanted black opals, and she was small enough to fit in a woman's hand. She huffed with mock effort and left the gift at Henri's feet.

"Well merci, Pixie." He reached down and picked up the small brown parcel.

Pixie parted her lips and a string of musical notes tumbled out—in lieu of a "you're welcome". Her voice box was a tiny version of the cylinder and comb mechanism used in music boxes. When Pixie opened her mouth, the instrument could be seen turning at the back of her throat. Leaping, her metal wings carried her over to the fire where she pretended to warm her tiny hands and posterior.

"The present is from you, Belle." Henri smiled, ruffling his thick white mustache. He tore off the heavy paper. Beneath was a polished wooden box with the words, *Liberty Watch Co.*, engraved on the lid. "Oh, the famous watch company in America?"

"Open it," she prompted.

Needing no further encouragement, Henri drew back the lid. Sitting safely among white satin was a pocket watch. The timepiece's face was brass with a leaf-etching design. Pulling out the watch, its chain dangling around his fingers, Henri pressed the top and it snapped open. The numbers were elegant and dainty. But the thing that made this watch unique was its back. Instead of brass coverings, the inner workings were protected by clear glass. Henri was likely already imagining the little cogs ticking away behind their glass wall.

"My fille, this is wonderful. Merci." He tugged Belle into a hug. "It's your turn now. Come everyone!"

Henri ushered them all out of the parlor and into his workroom. Every inch of the space was taken by tools, gadgets, spare parts, and gizmos. There were a slew of strange, abandoned inventions on one counter. On the wall were blueprints for projects yet to be undertaken. Henri walked over to a large, covered object; his invention for the World Fair. Everyone gathered around, eager to see it for the first time.

"I'd like to present to everyone the Responsibly Fiscal Currency Counter—Or just Currency Counter, as I'm sure they'll call it." With a flourish, Henri then ripped the white sheet off of his invention.

The brass machine was beautiful. The front was made of glass, with tubes inside for each sized coin. The gold tinted sides were decorated with fauna accents. A large man-shaped hand rested at the top.

"Will you demonstrate it for us?" Nicolas asked with eagerness.

Henri held up a finger to stave him off. Pointing to another covered object, this one much smaller, he said, "That is for Belle."

Feeling so proud of her father, Belle took hold of the sheet and whipped it away. There was a miniature version of Henri's invention underneath. He pulled a coin out of his pocket and slid it between the fingers of the much smaller hand.

"I give you, the Responsibly Fiscal Currency Counter—At Home Version." Yanking a lever on the other side, the device started to purr as tiny puffs of steam rose out of a pipe in the back. The fingers tightened around the coin, then moved along the tubes and released it into the correct spot.

They applauded, giving Henri plenty of praise. He took it in stride, agreeing to demonstrate the larger unit several times and answering all their questions. After a bit, Belle pointed out the late hour and reminded them of tonight's hunt. As everyone left to get ready, Henri asked her to wait a moment.

"You have one last gift." He placed a thin, sealed letter in her hand. "I'm going upstairs to finish packing. I'll see you when you return."

With a kiss to the cheek, he left her alone.

Belle turned the letter over in her hands. There was no name on it, but the seal she recognized. It was the Chevallier family crest. This was a letter from Gastone. Sliding a finger along the parchment to break the seal, her mouth went dry.

> *Dearest Belle,*
>   *No doubt you are aware of the rumors that persist in regards to my future. I apologize if they have caused you any form of grievance. I have tried, somewhat in vain, to separate you from the dramas associated with being the next Count Chevallier . . . at least until I knew for certain. However, it has become very clear to me that there is no better woman in all of Glace than you.*

*I would be remiss if I did not act on these thoughts and increasingly undeniable feelings.*

*On the next cloudless afternoon, I would be honored to accompany you on a stroll through town.*

*Yours Truly,*
*Gastone Chevallier,*
*Heir to the Count of Contefées*

Belle reread the letter three times. Her heart raced as though she'd been dancing with Jack. Suddenly she understood the change in Gastone. More than a few times in her life, she'd imagined what it would be like to marry him. What girl hadn't? But never—not once—did she ever think it was a real possibility. All of the pieces seemed to have fallen into place now. Except, as she clutched the parchment to her chest, she wondered . . . did she love him?

# Chapter Six

The moon was gone, hidden behind a canvas of smooth cloud cover. Belle noted the icy wind that sliced her cheeks as she rode toward Vakre Fjell Forest. From beside her, Andre tugged his glove further over the flesh of his still-human hand.

"Snowstorm?" she asked him.

"It just crossed my mind." He looked up at the sky, glaring through the increasing darkness.

They'd all spent enough time outside to recognize coming weather. It was in the way the clouds moved and the feel of the air. Snowstorms had a way of sneaking in, eclipsing the sky without anyone noticing. When they unleashed their power, it filled every space and shrank the world down to mere inches. It could be terrifying—and deadly.

Gastone rode Magnanimous up. "Do we turn back or proceed?"

Nervousness shot through her chest at the sight of him. Belle was suddenly so aware of Gastone. He was a man. An attractive man. A man who was interested in her. Was she interested in him? She honestly didn't know. Searching herself, Belle couldn't see past the fear and uncertainty that had taken up residence in her stomach. If she could get away from him, then maybe she could relax . . . and breathe.

"We proceed," Belle said, pushing the love nonsense aside and focusing on the issue at hand. "My father needs the forest clear for his trip in the morning. If we don't, his men could be overwhelmed. So we hunt."

They rode the rest of the way to the border, stopping just at the tree line. Loud engines came to life with the sound of massive mechanical workings cranking together. Belle looked behind her, toward the noise and the Norwegian Sea. Arm-like beams, which secured their metal-domed house to the cliff side, now moved it away from the land. Systematically, it lowered out of sight and into the crashing seas below. There it was safe from all manner of storm and hellish creature. Only the lighthouse and fortified stable remained above.

Belle turned back to the dark forest. She lowered her head and the men followed suit.

"Oh Holy Angel," she began the prayer, her voice a solo sound in the night. "Attendant of our wretched souls and afflicted life."

"Forsake us not." The men joined her, the rumble of their words mingling smoothly with hers. "Give no place to the evil demon to subdue us with the oppression of these mortal bodies." The gas lamps began to ignite—one pair at time—throughout the woods and winding paths. "But take us by our outstretched hands, and guide our weapons to smite the minions of hell who now walk the earth." The light flickered through her closed eyelids, reminding Belle of church candles. "As warring angels of God, we give blood for the blood of the demon possessed, should He so choose it. Pardon us for the evil we must do in thy name, For we deliver to thee the souls of all the lost departed from the pains of hell and from the bottomless pit." As the Hunter's Creed came to a close, they formed the cross over their heads and torsos. "In nomine Patris, et Filii, et Spiritus Sancti, Amen."

They raised their heads and opened their eyes. Belle looked at each one of them, then set out first into the woods. The Hunters followed, each taking side paths that spread them out along the border. Soon Belle was alone, with only Charming and the beating of her heart for company.

The first snowflakes to fall came down in a rush of speed. Steadily over the next few hours it increased. The snow now fell at a slant, pelting her face. The wind howled through the trees, like the wail of a sea monster. Belle and Charming huddled into themselves, their backs to the wind.

Her Electro-Phonic Chip crackled.

"I need help. *Christ.* I need it now." Delano's voice was weak, broken up by interference from the storm, but she heard his panic clear enough.

Belle's head shot up, her body straightening. She tapped her communication device. "Flare, Delano. Give us a flare."

A second later, the faintest of reds appeared through the snowy sky. Belle hadn't even heard the pops over the crying wind. She encouraged Charming into a gallop. They sped down the path and slowed only for turns.

Belle was just getting concerned that she'd overshot him when Delano appeared on the path. Charming skidded to a halt, barely stopping in time to avoid a collision. Pushing back her fur hood, Belle gaped at the sight before her.

Delano's horse, Honor, lay on the ground. He wasn't dead, but his shoulder was ripped open. Delano leaned over him, stroking Honor's neck and talking into his ear.

Belle followed the splatters of blood to the dead hellhound. Lights sprang from his body, causing her to quickly close her eyes. When they dissipated, the body of a well-dressed man remained.

Belle tapped her earpiece. "Sending out another flare. Expect the wind to carry it northward."

As she reached into her saddlebag to retrieve her red flare, Nicolas arrived. His face fell at the sight of his older brother. Belle fired the flare gun, then immediately called for Friar Clemens to bring his cart.

Soon the remaining Hunters approached. Leaving Delano to his horse and Nicolas to his brother, Belle drew the others aside to discuss the situation. No one else had killed or seen a hellhound; clearly the demon spawn had chosen shelter from the storm over food.

"All right then," Belle said with a nod. "Let's get Delano and Honor home swiftly."

Coaxing the stallion to his feet was horrible and took time, but Honor struggled through the pain. By then, Friar Clemens and Jack had arrived. They loaded the human corpse as the Hunters took up positions around Honor and the cart. Delano stayed at Honor's side, refusing to ride double with another. He encouraged the Friesian through every limp.

When they finally made it to the barn, the Hunters were desperate for its heat and a break from the wind. But still they waited, letting Delano lead his horse in first. Nicolas and Jean assisted in getting Honor back on the ground. Belle and the others picked up the slack, tending to the rest of the horses.

Depositing the last saddle and bridle in the tack room, Belle then went to where the others had gathered. Most of them were on the ground, prepared to hold down the stallion should he try to rise. Jack stood in front of the iron fireplace and withdrew from the fiery belly a long, red blade. Carefully, he handed it to Delano, who was crouched next to Honor's head.

Delano looked at the sword with red-rimmed eyes. He gulped and squeezed the hilt as he nodded to himself. Honor's eyes were wide from either fear, pain, or both. Delano whispered reassurances to him.

Finally, Delano sat back and let the hot steel hover over the wound. He took a few steadying breaths. "Be strong, Honor."

He nodded to the men. They carefully leaned on the stallion, putting pressure on his body and legs. Then Delano pressed the sword onto the wound.

Flesh and blood sizzled from the intense heat, blackening instantly. Honor tensed and thrashed. Delano cooed to him as he continued to cauterize the injury. Honor listened, squealing from the pain, but not fighting their restraint.

Belle had pushed herself against the wall, tears brimming in her eyes. She turned away from it, heading down the line of stalls. She opened Charming's door and stepped in. Putting a hand to her chest, she blinked back the tears.

Charming left his water bucket, water dripping from his chin, and came over to her. He nickered softly and shoved his muzzle in her hand. She stepped into him, wrapping her arms around his neck and breathing in his comforting scent. "I hope I never have to do that to you."

"Hey now, don't bite, Magnas."

Belle dropped her arms slightly and turned toward the voice. Gastone was in the adjacent stall, petting Magnanimous. She watched him seeking comfort in his horse, just as she was. His shoulders were slouched just a little and his movements soft. Melted snow dampened his hair and skin.

Gastone met her gaze and she saw his sadness. Keeping one hand on Charming, she reached over and grasped the railing separating their stalls. Gastone cupped her hand, running his thumb over hers. It was as good as being hugged.

There was no reason for her to be afraid of a future with Gastone, she realized. He was her friend, and already family. He understood her in ways that no one else would. He understood the challenges they faced—and he faced them by her side. A comforting warmth spread through her hand, reaching straight to her heart.

*This will be good,* she thought.

When there was nothing more to be done for Honor, they headed for bed. Except for Delano, who insisted on sleeping next to Honor. LeClair House was now fully out of sight and hidden beneath the sea. Only when the sun rises will the gears carry the metal structure back up the cliff side, where it will reside above ground until the following night. The Hunters walked single file to the lighthouse, each using the one in front to shield from the wind.

Belle followed Gastone into the large stone building and stomped her boots to rid them of snow. Jean took the rosary from his hip and slid it into the lock. With a twist, the metal doors unclasped to reveal the lift within. It was small, but the only way to get down to the house at night.

Nicolas volunteered to take the lighthouse watch from Andre, claiming his own distress for his brother would prevent sleep. No one argued, seeing it written in the red of his eyes and the pale of his skin. He left them to follow the long winding stairs up into the Watch Room.

With the Hunters cramped somewhat tightly into the elevator, the doors cranked shut. There was a moment's pause as gears and mechanical bits shifted noisily around, then gradually the chains holding them aloft began to descend. Small portholes in the walls showed the passing of rock and the water that filled the elevator shaft—water that helped control and protect the lift's movements.

The speed of descent slowed; the rock disappeared as they passed into the underwater house. The elevator came to a rest and the frames around the door sealed with a sucking sound. The lift opened to a domed, metal room.

Belle stepped out onto a grated walkway. She followed the path down a few stairs and out into the hallway. Here the floor was suspended, giving a flatness to a circular hall. She turned right into the armory where she removed her cloak, weapons, and Electro-Phonic Chip.

Henri met her on the way to her bedroom. She assured him that she was well and informed him of the situation with Delano and Honor. After a kiss on the cheek, she bid him goodnight and entered her room.

Belle stripped off her clothes with the aid of the Governess; a wall-mounted device that worked both corsets and hair. Then she pulled out her pins and turned the dials on the machine's display. Deft, metal hands reached out and gently tied her locks into a nighttime braid.

But it wasn't straight to bed, Belle desperately needed a bath. The large porcelain tub filled quickly with clean steaming water, pulled and filtered from the ocean. She settled in for a long soak.

Three extra spouts hung over the tub. Belle pulled the first, letting rose oil drop into the water. The second was holy water, ordered by the church to cleanse their souls. The final spout was the wonderful invention of liquid soap. Belle went through all three of these, then rested her head on the bathtub's rim.

A large half-moon shaped window took up most of her wall. Outside there was no sky or stars; only the black abyss of the Norwegian Sea surrounding the house. Belle stared into it till her water grew cold, thinking of what tomorrow would bring.

Her father was going to travel into Vakre Fjell, hoping to evade all hellhounds to reach a far off port. For much of that journey, his Electro-Phonic Chip would be out of signal range. She'll have no way of knowing if he made it safely until his hunting party returns.

This was a trip Belle had been worrying about for weeks. But he just had to reach Skjebne Port, and his hunting party was far more experienced than hers. Not one of them was worried about this journey. So why couldn't Belle shake this strong feeling of dread?

# Chapter Seven

Henri pulled Belle in for a hug, squeezing like she didn't have a shoulder wound. She clenched her teeth and squeezed back. They stood, along with a small crowd, outside the border of Vakre Fjell. Henri's hunting party was assembled and ready for the dangerous trip. The Responsibly Fiscal Currency Counter had been moved to a cart, which was harnessed to Magnificent and draped in a protective cloth.

"Please be safe, Père." Belle pleaded into his ear.

Henri patted her shoulder and pulled back to rest his forehead against hers. "Do not worry. My Hunters are the best—even better than yours."

"I've never known you to be a liar, monsieur," Gastone said, coming over to shake Henri's hand.

"Watch it, boy!" Henri pointed a menacing finger at him, then gave Belle's forehead one last kiss. "Love you, my fille."

"Love you too, Père."

Before Henri could mount, he accepted the well wishes of local officials and a blessing from the Father. To Belle's relief, Bishop Sauvage hadn't come. The crowd of excited townsfolk would have kept Henri there all day, but he eventually shooed them off. Henri waved to Belle from atop Magnificent and signaled to his men.

The crowd moved out of the way as the Hunters positioned

themselves around Henri and his invention. Vakre Fjell looked like a winter wonderland straight out of a fairytale. Several feet of fresh snow coated the trees and weighed down the branches. It was beautiful and almost made her feel better about the dangers Henri was facing.

After Henri's hunting party was well out of sight, Belle said au revoir to those who'd come out. She thanked them for their support and many assured her that Henri would reach Skjebne Port unharmed. Belle smiled at each one but rushed for the house the moment she was free.

"Belle." Gastone blocked her path, stopping her just outside Henri's workroom. "Have you thought on my proposal? Do you have an answer?"

Belle scrunched her eyebrows at him, affronted that he would bother her with this now when she was so worried about her father. "No, Gastone, I've been a bit preoccupied."

She made to move around him, but he stepped once more in her way. "Wait, you actually have to think on it? You can't be serious?"

"I most certainly am," she said, bristling at his arrogance. "I will give you my answer when I am ready, but right now I want to make sure my père is safe."

She gathered up her skirts and stepped around the stunned Hunter, but only made it a few paces.

"Belle, wait," he said, holding the bridge of his nose. She paused to hear him out. "I apologize for my behavior just now. Thinking of the dangerous journey ahead of Henri prompted me to pay my own père a visit this morning."

Belle's arms relaxed as her anger quickly faded. Gastone's father hated him. It was common knowledge, as the man did little to hide it. No matter what Gastone did, he would always be a failure in his father's eyes.

"I told him that I'd made my regard for you known." Gastone sighed. "He said I was a fool. A woman of your good character could never love the likes of me. That's why I pushed you now. I didn't want him to be right. But when you didn't have an answer for me, I was afraid that he was."

"Gastone. Your père is the fool, not you." Belle came over and grabbed his arms, forcing him to look at her. "In your letter, you said that you wanted to be certain of your feelings for me before you made any declarations. I've only just learned that it was safe for me to see you in such a way. Like you, I need to take the time to know how I feel. Can you understand that?"

He looked down at her, a glimmer of hope twinkling in his brown eyes. "How long will I have to be patient?"

Belle turned toward the workroom. "It'll be easier to think tonight when I know my père is closer to safety."

"So tomorrow morning, then?"

She laughed. "Yes, tomorrow."

But as Belle crossed the threshold into Henri's workroom, she noticed the unsettled feeling in the pit of her stomach. Surely, that was not how the beginnings of love felt.

"There's nothing to report, Belle," Andre said as she appeared.

Henri's workroom doubled as his workspace and the core of Hunter communications. Andre sat at a table, manning what they called the vox. Essentially, it was an over-sized Electro-Phonic Chip. While working his inventions, Henri could listen to their communications and speak to them if he needed to.

Andre had two large head-speakers attached to his ears that allowed him to listen privately. He twisted a dial on the vox, adjusting the signal. Andre had a knack for technology. One born out of necessity since he can't always rely on Henri's expertise to repair malfunctions in his prosthetics.

Jean wrapped his knuckles on one of the workbenches, grabbing Belle's attention.

"Want to help us make bullets?" Jack asked for him.

She did need to pass the time somehow. "Okay."

Belle took a spot along the table, choosing to paint the black crosses on the side of each bullet. Gastone and Jack filled the cylinders with gunpowder. Using his brute strength, Jean sealed them. She tried to let the men distract her with their political talk, but every now and then she still looked at Andre, watching for any sign of concern. Mostly, he just looked bored.

By the time Nicolas came in from being out in the stable with Delano, they had a small army of finished bullets lined up. He sighed, looking around the room. Belle dipped her thin brush into the inky paint. "How is Delano?"

Nicolas shrugged. "Haggard."

"I'm sure." She paused before painting the first stroke. "And Honor?"

"Holding up well." Sitting next to Jean, Nicolas rubbed his hands over his face, scrunching up the skin. "No sign of infection."

"Well good. That is truly a relief—"

"Belle," Andre cut in, turning rapidly in his chair.

He flipped a switch on the vox. The transmissions left Andre's head speakers and was broadcast to the room.

"LeClair House. LeClair House," Henri was hurriedly saying. Belle leapt from her seat at the sound of gunfire and growls. "A pack . . . Too many." His breathing was labored. Franck shouted in the background. Henri fired his guns between words. "LeClair House, are you there?"

The transmission stopped and Belle dashed across the room, smacking a button on the vox. "Père? Père?!"

"Belle? This is . . ." The signal wavered, only transmitting fragments.

Belle pressed the button again. "Say again?"

She let the button go. Static.

Andre frantically twisted the knobs and dials. "They must be right at the edge of this thing's reaching capabilities."

Belle's heart raced. She could hardly stand it as she listened intently to the white noise. When the signal came back, they managed to catch one word.

"Hurry—" A loud scream, the sound of a violent death, and the transmission went out again.

There was the slightest of pauses, a moment to let the horror of it sink in, then Belle was headed for the armory with her men just steps behind. They grabbed their shooting irons and swords, strapping them on quickly and snatching communication chips from the cabinet. She unpinned the nice, cobalt top hat she'd picked to see Henri off with and tossed it on one of the wall hooks. Tying her cloak at the base of her neck, Belle was the first to reach the front door. Thankfully, the house was above ground now and she didn't have to waste time with the elevator.

Lifting her skirts, Belle raced across the snow-covered lawn and into the barn. With the Hunters close behind, she converged on her stall and began saddling her horse. Delano came out of Honor's stall at the sound of their commotion. "What's going on?"

"Another pack," Belle said, hefting the saddle onto Charming's back. "Père's in trouble."

Delano stumbled over his shock and looked back at his horse, as though to confirm he was in no shape to be ridden. "What can I do?"

"You're staying behind to guard the border." Belle led the saddled Charming out of his stall, just as Friar Clemens reached the barn. "Friar, ride into town and fetch the doc. We'll need him."

Delano closed up Honor's stall and ran from the barn, likely to grab weapons. Friar Clemens started saddling one of the cart horses. The other Hunters emerged from their stalls as Belle was heading out the door. It was the fastest they'd ever readied. In the sunlight, they each mounted.

Belle cued Charming into a jog, gradually speeding him up as they neared the border. There was no time to stand on formality—no time to stop and pray. So Belle did it on the fly. "Oh Holy Angel, attendant of our wretched souls and afflicted life . . ."

". . . forsake us not." The Hunters joined in, riding at a close gallop. They passed into the woods, finishing the creed as they followed the path of Henri's hunting party.

Belle shouted over her shoulder, "Watch for hounds coming from the sides. Let your horses follow me."

There were plenty of tracks to guide her from both hoof and cart. But it wasn't necessary. Henri's party was to stick to the main gas-lit path until they reached its farthermost point and headed into the unknown.

After awhile, Belle slowed Charming to a trot. The group seamlessly matched her pace. They'd been riding for awhile; they had to be getting close.

Belle tapped her ear chip. "Henri? Franck? Adam? Anyone there?"

She pressed it again and waited, but there was no response. Belle looked back at Gastone. He met her gaze and she could see he expected the worst.

His eyes pulled from hers, drawn up the trail. "There's something up there."

Belle turned around. He was right, there was something ahead. It was big and obscuring the path. As they came closer, she started to see the bloody snow—the figures of corpses. She grabbed her revolver and held it up, signaling her men to ready themselves.

The large object revealed itself to be Henri's invention. They rode past a dozen or more bodies. Many Belle didn't recognize, but more than a few she did. Jean dismounted to check them but shook his head when she inquired if they were alive.

"My God." Belle gawked at the surroundings. Her heart pounded heavily in her chest, feeling like it was about to fall out. Never before had she seen so many dead hellhounds in one place. "How many are there?"

Andre rode up. "Counted three dozen so far."

Belle heard growling and followed the sound around the cart. Her gun was ready, waiting for the creature to leap. Just beyond the trees the hellhound stood over the remains of a Hunter named Adam.

It snarled and lashed out as Gastone and Jack came over. It reached down and grabbed Adam's body, dragging him a few feet away. Was it guarding its food? Revulsion rolled through her stomach. Gastone raised his gun to end it.

"Belle!" Andre leaned over someone just down the path.

There was blood all around the area, along with more corpses. A shot rang out as Gastone put down Adam's killer. Belle dismounted and ran, fearing what she would see. Holding her breath, Belle pulled Andre back. But it wasn't Henri.

Franck lay there. His shirt was shredded, as was his body. His eyes saw through them. Blood trickled from the corner of his mouth.

"Friar Clemens, we need the doc now," Andre said into his chip and his voice echoed into her own.

It was too late though. Franck was already on his way toward the light. She'd seen it before. When her mother died, she'd looked right through her—right into the light.

Belle walked away, leaving Andre to him. Her chest ached. She pressed her palm into it, trying to ease the strain. The other Hunters were checking every body, attempting to account for the rest of Henri's hunting party. There were so many bodies. He could be anywhere. Belle palmed her chest again and rested against the cart.

She looked over at it, wondering what had happened to Magnificent. An idea struck her. Belle swiveled around, counting the dead horses. Six. There was one missing. One had gotten away.

Belle walked to the end of the cart, lifting up the harness straps. Hope flared in her chest. They'd been cut—not torn. There was a chance, even a small one, that Henri had cut them and attempted to escape with his life. Surely he would have tried to save his men, but failing that—when there was no doubt they'd been lost—he would have tried to save himself.

Walking away from the group, she searched the disturbed snow, looking for a set of tracks to separate from the others. Escaping toward LeClair House would have been the smartest plan, but Henri may not have had a choice. He may have been forced farther into Vakre Fjell.

Something glinted in the snow, causing her to stop. Belle crouched down and carefully brushed the white fluff away. A timepiece stared back at her. At its center were the words, *Liberty Watch Co*. Hand trembling, she grasped the watch and turned it over. The back was glass. The clockwork inside no longer ticked.

# Chapter Eight

My legs are buried deep in the snow, but I'm not bothered. I can feel the crisp air on my cheeks and cold snow against my skin, but it can't hurt me. Nothing can. Within this earthly plain, I am untouchable. I am as old as time.

Unlike the humans I watched now. They walked among the carnage of their dead and that of my wolves. I sent the creatures that slaughtered the older Hunters and forced Henri to retreat farther into Vakre Fjell. With my power's reach bound by another, I need Henri's talent for killing. He'll remove the threat to my task.

The young woman, Belle, held the watch she found. She stared down at it thoughtfully, then looked out into the forest— in the direction Henri had taken. So she intended to go after him. The girl, normally such a stickler for Hunter rules, surprises me.

She could help my cause, I suddenly realized. Where her father might fail, Belle will succeed. Either way, the threat will be gone, my bindings will be lifted, and I'll be free to do what I came here for.

I could not drive Belle to the castle as I had done Henri. Too many of my wolves had died today and only a handful were near. But I had other ways.

I reached with my mind, calling the wolves. They will be

*there soon. But before they can drive Belle, I must cut her off from her own group. Lifting my hand, I held it palm up. Softly, I blew as if I were sending a kiss. White fog descended from my lips, pouring over my fingers. Frost crystallized upon the sur-rounding snow and crept up the trees. I held it back, waiting for just the right moment . . .*

Gripping her present to Henri, Belle examined the scattering of prints. A set of horse tracks veered off on their own, and wolves appeared to have followed. If her father had been forced to flee, as she suspected, the hellhounds had been intent on running him down. The idea sent waves of nausea into her stomach.

"I found my père's watch and a set of tracks," she said, walking back to Charming and remounting. "I'm going to see where they lead."

Gastone finished closing Adam's vacant eyes. "Wait till we're finished here and we'll ride out with you."

"I'm not going far." She cued Charming forward, shouting over her shoulder, "I won't sit by when my père might be just beyond those trees. Keep watch with the others and I'll come back if I don't find him."

Without looking, Belle knew Gastone frowned at her back as she passed the final lamppost. There was no reason for him to worry; she really had no intention of putting herself in danger. Belle trained her eyes onto the ground, focusing on keeping the trail.

Eventually, she came upon two human corpses, and this was where the hellhound tracks ended. But Magnificent's prints continued onward. Why hadn't her father turned back?

Then Belle noticed a trickle of blood spattered on the snow.

It was too far from the hellhounds . . . it couldn't be theirs. She pressed on. The trail of blood started to grow larger, coloring the snow every few meters. If Henri had been wounded enough, he may have lost consciousness and allowed Magnificent to carry him unguided.

Looking up, Belle saw that Magnificent's tracks led to an area clear of trees; a path that was a straight shot to the north. It must have been an old road, likely the main road right into Vakre Fjell. It would eventually lead to a house or a town. There was a chance that Henri might have taken shelter there. Timid hope fluttered in Belle's chest.

Static simmered in her ear and Gastone's voice broke though. "Belle, did you . . . Clemens . . . here . . ."

Belle tugged Charming to a stop, thinking that she wasn't yet far enough away to be out of signal range. Peering around, Belle realized she was wrong. She couldn't see or hear her Hunters.

The singing started then. The Electro-Phonic Chip began to pitch and whine as though it were serenading her. Belle quickly tapped the earpiece. "Incoming ice fog—"

The ethereal song increased, drowning out her own voice. They no longer heard her, if they even did in the first place. Ice fog was rare but potentially dangerous. It only happened in special weather conditions and generally brought with it a cold so strong it touched her bones. It also somehow made their earpieces sing and cut off all communications.

Tiny ice crystals began to form over the nearby trees. There was a soft crackling as frost flowers spread over her reins, reaching toward her fingers. As the ear chip sang to her, Belle held up her hand and watched as the rime blossomed on her leather glove. The intricate design was beautiful.

White fog rolled around her like a cloud of ice dust. Within seconds, she was engulfed and her visibility was reduced to mere feet. Turning Charming, she had to retrace her steps and join her men.

Panting sounds alerted Belle. Among the trees, a blur of brown appeared and disappeared as a hellhound raced past. It was circling her. Making things worse, it had the advantage with its predatory sense of smell and hearing.

A growl came from in front of her. Belle's breath caught as her eyes just made out the faint silhouette of a stalking hellhound. More growls followed. It wasn't alone and they stood between her and her men. Belle held up her revolver, prepared to shoot if one pounced.

A frosted vine curled around her barrel, covering the engraved shooting star. Charming's steamy breath vanished into the thick fog. Belle shook her head. It was folly to try and fight with this kind of visibility. She patted her pocket, as she turned Charming northward, making sure Henri's watch was secure. They were going to make a blind dash and she didn't want to lose it.

"Yah!" Charming leapt into a gallop.

Belle leaned into the Friesian, giving him the rein he needed to run. The hellhounds were gaining ground fast, their snarls and snaps growing louder as they closed in. Trusting in her Friesian to stay the course, Belle let go of her reins and aimed behind her. Unfortunately, the hounds weren't keeping a steady pace. They zig-zagged around each other, dropping back and then drawing closer. It was like they were using the fog, letting it hide them just long enough that she couldn't fire.

A howl called Belle's attention back to the road ahead. A new hellhound was on the approach. Charming couldn't slow though. If he did, they'd be overtaken by the pack. Belle swore and aimed, ready to stop the charging hound.

A branch blocked her gun's sight—en route to knock her out of the saddle. Belle gasped, flinging her left leg over the saddle's front swell and dropped to the side of the horse. With one foot in the stirrup and one hand grasping the saddle horn, she aimed for the lead hellhound. The low branch swept over Charming, touching his ears, and Belle fired.

The hound yipped once, then plunged into the snow. Charming drifted too close to the road's edge, avoiding the dead hound. Belle thrust herself back against his body, her right arm extending out behind her. A passing tree grazed her cheek with its rough bark. Belle breathed out and fired at one of the hounds behind her. He dropped, making the one behind him stumble. *Four bullets left.*

With a bit of muscle and some fancy footwork, Belle swung herself back up into the saddle. The fog was less dense now. Even her ear chip's singing was quieter. They were almost out of the ice fog. Belle breathed a bit easier, confidence filling her.

Up ahead, A fallen tree cut off the path. It was big and old, taken down by the heaps of snow piled on from some past storm. Quickly Belle fired behind her, but the hellhounds swerved. The bullet tunneled into the snow instead. *Three left.*

Gritting her teeth, Belle faced forward and leaned into Charming. She grabbed hold of his mane, kneading her knuckles into his neck, and asked for more speed. He responded and charged the tree. She positioned her body correctly, feeling the stallion's muscles beginning to gather. At just the right second, Charming leapt. For a moment, horse and rider sailed through the air together. Then Charming's hooves connected with the ground, bringing them smoothly back into the gallop.

Staying low to Charming's neck, Belle watched behind them. The hellhounds bounded over the fallen tree with considerably less grace. One tripped, tumbling into the ground, but it recovered fast.

Belle was thrown into Charming's neck as he unexpectedly

came to a sliding halt. Hurriedly, she pushed herself up and raised her gun to defend them, expecting the hounds to be nearly on top of them. Except, they'd stopped at the edge of the road; snarling and growling—but not attacking!

Cold wind whipped Belle's body, sending a chill up her spine. The hellhounds backed away as it slammed into their faces, rustling their heavy fur. Not taking her eyes or revolver off the enemy, Belle swung her leg over the saddle horn and hopped to the ground. She trained her gun onto one hound and drew her second revolver. Closer she stepped, half taunting them.

Shockingly, they continued to disengage. Their teeth snapped angrily at the air. Then they turned and she watched them fading, then disappearing into the waning ice fog. Belle stood there, mouth agape, unable to believe that they had gone—that the moment she turned her back, they wouldn't come charging out at her.

Charming pawed impatiently, his hoof striking smooth cobblestone. Belle looked in surprise at the masonry they stood on, then followed it to the gate which had stopped Charming's mad run. Tall, iron bars stood three times as high as Belle. At its center was the shield for the Vakrein royal family. Wild, thorny rose vines wrapped the bars and traversed the entire length of the connecting stone wall.

Belle stepped closer to the gate, reaching out to touch one of the blooming roses. As she did, the heavy fog cloaking what lay beyond seemed to move away. Gasping at the massive castle, Belle stopped in her tracks.

She whispered in awe, "Castle Vakre Fjell."

It was colossal in size, rivaling the surrounding mountains. The many pointed rooftops reached to high peaks, with a single tower surpassing them all in height. Flags attached to these high piers fluttered in the wind. A hundred windows, taller in length than her own house, decorated the castle's stone walls. Every corner of the building was sharp and severe, radiating its strength to those outside. But the roofs were curved just enough to lend a bit of dainty elegance to the overall appeal.

Had Henri sought shelter here? Her eyes skimmed the bridge, but the wind kept it clear of snow. Belle grabbed the gate, intending to test its lock, but it clicked open at the slightest pressure. Pushing the gate the rest of the way, she stepped through and Charming followed.

"Halt!" A man emerged, aiming a rifle in her direction.

Swiftly, Belle trained her revolvers on the stranger. She eyed his military clothing suspiciously. "How did you get here?"

A weapon cocked over her shoulder. "Drop your weapons."

Whoever they were, they had her. With slow, exaggerated movements, Belle turned her revolvers upward in surrender. The man she couldn't see yanked the guns from her hands, then took her sabre.

"Now walk." The first soldier jerked his gun, pointing to the castle.

They spoke Vakrein, which Belle fortunately knew. That at least told her they were from here, but it also raised many more questions.

Belle didn't move, speaking in his native tongue. "Please, I mean no—"

"Walk, witch, or we'll shoot you where you stand," he threatened.

The pure hatred on his face told Belle not to disregard it. She turned onto the bridge, forcing her sigh inward. Her feet stilled. The walkway was wide, flat, and without railings. Below was a long drop into a rocky canyon.

Belle had the sensation that she was standing on the thinnest of ice. One wrong move and it would shatter, sending her a thousand feet to her death. Fear tensed up her muscles, making her breathing shallow.

A gun barrel shoved into Belle's back, forcing her forward. The bridge didn't immediately crumble. Squaring her shoulders, Belle hid away her insecurities and walked on.

*Men.* The thought hit Belle like a blast of cold air. There were humans in Vakre Fjell! All this time the world thought Vakre Fjell had been lost. Here was proof that not all Vakreins had fallen into sin. How many more were there? Why didn't they come for help? Was her father here, and if so what did they do with him?

# Chapter Nine

*I hid behind the tree line, my remaining wolves growling at my side. They're hungry and frustrated that I held them back. Watching the soldiers march Belle toward the home of her new prey, I smiled.*

As they approached the castle steps, the immensity of the building was daunting. It made Belle feel so small—so squash-able. There were more soldiers guarding the entrance and a stable hand came to lead Charming away. Belle wanted to protest but instead kept silent as they escorted her inside.

The ceilings were high, higher than even her cathedral's. Her head tilted back in awe of the arched peaks. Her boots stepped from elaborate marble floors to lush red carpets. The walls in the entry hall were of the finest masonry with simple flourishes de-signed to turn the eyes upward.

"Go tell General Kogsworthe another has arrived," one of her escorts said to a waiting servant boy.

Belle's heartbeat quickened. *Another has arrived.* Someone else had come before Belle! It had to be Henri.

With a nod, the boy turned and rushed down a long hall.

Silence fell, but Belle's mind screamed with relief. She glanced at her captors. They remained turned away from her. Almost as though they mistrusted the sight of her.

While the chance was available, Belle swept her hand across the button at her hip. It unlatched and her skirts dropped, hanging to her ankles. One soldier looked back at her. She pretended not to notice his attention and smoothed her dress. She leaned forward, catching her reflection in a mirror. Her hair had fallen down in several places. She tucked back a strand or two, but there wasn't much she could do to save it.

Abruptly, the soldier behind her approached. Belle saw him coming in the mirror and made to move away. He grabbed her arm, preventing her retreat. Then, with his free hand, he worked at undoing the clasps at her shoulder. He watched her closely, his eyes glowering at every inch of her face. The buckle came loose and the knife harness slid from her chest. The soldier took the knives and harness and rolled them up, then haughtily tucked them beneath his shoulder. Only then did he move back to his previous position.

An unbearable amount of time continued to pass in silence. Belle shifted uncomfortably from foot to foot. It disturbed her that they did not take her cloak or offer her something to drink, some place to sit, while she waited. She had broken no law, but their treatment thus far made Belle feel less than welcome.

A stout man eventually walked into the hall accompanied by the servant boy and two other soldiers. He had a full, brunette beard and hair cut short. His uniform was pristine, as were his many medals and symbols of rank. At his side was an officer's sword that was not just for decoration. On his back was a white fur cloak edged in brown with no hood. The medallion holding the cape in place was a gold rose.

General Kogsworthe, Belle presumed, had a stern demeanor.

His movements were simple, precise. She straightened as he neared and didn't blink or blush as he scrutinized her.

"These were found on her person." The soldier handed over her knives, guns, and sabre. "She carried a shotgun on her saddle, as well."

"Thank you. Dismissed." General Kogsworthe's voice was gravelly and harsh. He gave no other reaction.

The soldiers left. A gust of cold wind raced in at their departure, tousling her loose locks and cloak. General Kogsworthe signaled for the soldiers he brought to flank Belle. With nothing more than a reproachful look, he began walking away.

Guessing that he meant for her to follow, Belle started after him. The soldiers stayed close but did not stop her. The General said nothing as they walked. He stayed two paces ahead and never once looked back. Lifting her skirts, Belle ascended a great staircase in pursuit.

It was wide and curved. The ceiling here was domed in the arches with gold crown molding. She wanted to stay in the stairwell and marvel at its craftsmanship, but when they moved on to a new floor, Belle found herself in awe once more. It was similar to the entry hall in many ways. It had the same high ceiling and simple, but elegantly shaped walls.

Suits of armor stood along one wall, looking like eyeless guards. The opposite wall was lined with mammoth-sized windows. They reached to the ceiling, curving softly at the top, and their width was the length of several paces. The rich-colored draperies were a marvel of amplitude and fine quality. Satin ropes pulled them back, opening the room to the mountains beyond—Snowcapped, rugged, and impassable.

They walked by many closed rooms and portraits of former kings and queens. At the far end of the long hall, just before the end, they turned down yet another hall. From these windows,

Belle could glimpse the courtyard below and the windows in the opposite wing. The marching seemed endless. Despite Belle's highly active life, she wasn't used to this sort of exercise; nor was her corset made for it.

"Pardon me, sir." Belle finally said, keeping with the Vakrein tongue. "I'm only looking for my father. I believe he might have come to this castle."

General Kogsworthe didn't respond and neither did his men. They continued on as though she hadn't said anything at all. Belle decided not to ask any more questions. Clearly, they didn't have any intention of helping her. In fact, she didn't really know what their intentions were.

At the end of this hall were two more armed guards. They stood at attention until one opened the door for them. Belle's stomach clenched at the sight of where she was headed.

A narrow, stone staircase spiraled upward. The steps were thin and steep, only providing enough room to walk single file. Kogsworthe went first. One of Belle's guards stepped in between her and the General. The other remained at the back, staying close as they stepped into the small space. The stone walls were moist and mold grew in the cracks.

The only light came from the occasional inset niche where a candlestick was placed. They ascended for some time, all the while the staircase wrapping up and up. Belle was in no hurry to reach the top though. She knew where they were going now. A staircase like this only led to one place . . . A tower dungeon.

They reached the top landing and, after the confines of the staircase, it felt like freedom—briefly. It was dark and dank. The room opened into two spaces; one was a cell with the only window, too high to be reached, to provide natural light for the entire dungeon. The other space was mostly hidden by darkness, but Belle could make out chains and cuffs hanging from the walls.

The idea of being locked up here terrified her. She wanted out as fast as possible. She wanted back down to the main floors where lush carpets and handcrafted sculptures hid the horror above.

Kogsworthe and the Vakrein soldier positioned themselves around the room, facing the cell and blocking the staircase. A groan came from the cell, making Belle notice the bundled up man huddled against the bars. Without seeing his face, she knew who it was. Henri was hunched into himself, struggling to keep his cloak pulled tightly around him. He visibly shivered, his breath forming in the air.

"Père?" Her voice faint, she stepped closer.

Henri tilted his head. Surprise lit his eyes. "Belle?"

"Oh Père, you're alive." Forgetting about the armed men at her back, she dropped to her knees next to Henri. She grasped his hands around the bars. Through both his gloves and hers, she felt the chill in his hands.

"What are you doing here?" he rasped. "You can't be here."

"I came to find you, Père, and take you home." Feeling her anger rise up at this clear mistreatment, Belle turned to the General, "Why is he imprisoned? What crime has been committed?"

Kogsworthe did not answer, making her blood boil. A glint of light caught Belle's attention. She squinted her eyes, trying to make out what was in the dark, empty space behind the General. There was something there, something with texture, but she just couldn't see it.

Henri pulled at Belle's arm and she turned back to him. He gripped her sleeve, fear emanating through his features. "This place is wrong Belle. They aren't like us. They're hiding something. Something evil."

"What do you mean, Père?"

He inhaled deeply to answer and his breath rushed out in a cry, his hand jerking to his side. Reaching through the bars, Belle moved about his clothing till her fingers came back red. She looked beneath his cloak and found he was covered in his own blood. He was badly wounded on both his arm and his chest.

"He's injured. Why hasn't he been treated? I ask again that you justify this imprisonment!" Belle glared at each man, daring them to continue ignoring her.

"What is your name?" General Kogsworthe said in English, his true British accent coming out.

Belle answered through clenched teeth. "Belle LeClair of Glace and this is my father Henri LeClair."

His thick eyebrow tipped upward. "Why are you here?"

"My father was missing. I came looking for him," Belle said quickly, relieved that they were finally talking. "He's in bad condition. He needs—"

"How are you still human?" Kogsworthe asked.

The question surprised her, cutting off any quick answer. How was *she* still human? Belle might have asked him the same thing. But it was clear he wasn't going to answer her questions, let alone help Henri. He expected explanations from her though and that gave her an idea.

"Let my father leave with everything he arrived with and I will willingly tell you anything you want know." The General raised his chin, showing just a hint of surprise. She continued, "But if you don't, than I won't say a word."

Kogsworthe scratched his beard, weighing her claim. "We could torture it out of the two of you."

Something in the other corner growled. Fear ran up her spine. She squeezed Henri's hands. The sound stopped so abruptly, Belle questioned if she'd heard it at all. Or if the darkness of this tower was already getting to her. There *was* something wrong with this place. That much was certain.

"You could torture me, but know that I have a surprising

tolerance for pain. So does my father." She turned back to Henri; afraid that if she stared at the General too long her true fear would show. Henri's face was pale with a green tint. He wasn't well and in his weakened state, sickness was inevitable. He needed to be home. Licking her lips and stoking her courage, Belle said to the Vakrein General, "Besides, why go through all that trouble. Just let my father go. Without treatment, he'll be dead in a few days anyway."

General Kogsworthe considered this, then turned to his soldiers. "Take the man, put him on his horse and send him through the gate." Look at Belle he said, "The woman goes in the cell."

Relief washed over Belle, but a rattling fear followed. She stood as the soldiers came over. At the clanking of keys sliding through the cell lock, Henri became alert. He glanced around in confusion. "What's happening?"

"They're letting you go, Père. You can go home and get better." She tried to smile.

"And you?" He grabbed the bars, attempting to pull himself up as the guards walked in. They gripped his arms, half carrying, half dragging him out.

She secretly clenched her skirts, trying to control her fear. "I'm staying."

"No. No, Belle. You must leave!" Henri's distress shone in his eyes and the lines of his face. He seized the bars, stopping the progression away from the cell. Then, with unexpected strength, Henri jerked from the guards and lunged for Belle. His arms wrapped tightly around her. She hugged back, memorizing his scent of machine oil and metal. He whispered pleas in her ears, bringing tears to her eyes. "Belle. No. Don't do this!"

Her father was ripped away from her. The soldiers lugged him toward the staircase.

"Wait," she said, sadness and fear bubbled up inside her. "Please. Just a moment."

Moving to embrace her father in one last au revoir, Belle held up her hand. Kogsworthe blocked her path. She pulled up short, refusing to touch him. The soldiers pulled Henri out of sight, their boots thudding violently. His shouts echoed against the stone walls.

General Kogsworthe swept his hand toward the cell. Belle hung her head in defeat, averting her eyes. Below, the door slammed. The silence was jarring. Henri was gone. Without protest, Belle walked into the cell.

The General pulled the door shut and locked it. Listening to him leave, waiting till he was gone, she grabbed the cell bars. Tears streamed down her cheeks and her head rested against the rusted steel.

*Lord, guide my father home.*

# Chapter Ten

Hours and hours past; day turned to night. The only light came from a single candle placed within an iron lantern. It dangled on a chain from the room's center. Belle watched the flickering flame.

She was perched on moldy, soiled hay, leaning against the moist wall. This portion of the castle was not heated and the wind seeped through the stone. Belle clutched her cloak about her in the same manner that Henri had.

Sleep evaded her. Worry and random thoughts filled Belle's mind. Will her father make it home? Will he survive if he does? How were these Vakreins still human? Why hadn't they made themselves known before and why was she being held captive? What exactly was the evil Henri had spoken of?

And occasionally, she wondered what was hidden in the corner.

From time to time, Belle thought she heard movement, scraping against the stone floor or a sigh-like huff of air. No matter how hard she stared, she saw nothing. If she had her revolvers, the dungeon wouldn't be getting to her already.

Belle sniffled. The continuous cold was making her nose run. Her back ached from the improper position and her eyes were raw from tears. Resting her head against the wall, she tried to sleep.

The dungeon door creaked open and shut with a shocking bang. Belle quickly stood. She attempted to smooth her clothing and hair. She didn't want them to see her looking weak. Finally, they were going to question her. She was surprised it took this long.

Candlelight bounced with each clop of the person's heels. At first Belle expected General Kogsworthe to return, but the steps were too light. They lacked the heavy thud she would associate with the military man's boots. Belle clasped her hands before her as the stranger appeared.

The man was tall and slim. The candlestick he carried cast a yellow glow over his long chin and nose. His hair was pale blond and wavy, despite being pulled back. His clothes had been hastily put together; the corner of his white undershirt stuck out of his pants. The heaviness of his eyes suggested that he'd only just awoke, but it wasn't yet late enough for anyone to be rising.

He stopped before her cell and finally looked up at her. His eyes widen for a brief moment and he looked behind him into the shadows of the other cell. Turning back to Belle, he introduced himself. "Mademoiselle, greetings. My name is Laramie Petit." He bowed. "I am his Royal Highness's Offisielle Rådgiver and Keeper of the Royal Seal."

"And what is an Offisielle Rådgiver?" she asked, forgoing the correct response to his introduction. Belle always followed the rules of society, but so far her treatment had not been warranted and she no longer felt the need to be polite.

Laramie thought for a moment, possibly searching for the correct French words to describe his title. "I am the Official Adviser. It is my job to take an interest in all things that concern his Royal Highness."

"I suppose a *person in need* doesn't warrant his concern then." Belle pursed her lips, letting the ice flow in her tone.

"Not so." The thin man touched his pointed chin, considering his response. "But it is whether you are, in fact, a 'person' or even 'in need' that we were unsure of."

Belle had no idea what he meant by that. Of course, she was a person, what else would she be? She said nothing though, taking a lesson from General Kogsworthe, and allowed no confusion to show on her face.

Looking away from her, Laramie pulled a long key from his pocket. It slid against the cold metal. The lock screeched as he turned it. *Clunk*, the bolt unhitched.

"However, the matter has been put to rest," Laramie said and opened the cell door. "I have come to see you settled into a proper room."

Belle hesitated briefly. It was all so odd to her. Afraid this was a jest—that he'd suddenly change his mind—she stepped out of the cell. Monsieur Petit closed the door behind her; the bang echoed off the walls. Belle watched him from the corner of her eye and he gestured for her to take the stairs first.

Gathering her skirts, Belle made her way down the stairs. The descent was slow. She kept one hand up, ready to brace herself against the walls should she fall. Laramie followed quietly behind, holding the light up to help her see.

The silence was becoming agonizing, and she blurted the first question that came to mind. "Why would you need to settle the matter of whether I am human or not, Monsieur Petit?" She tried not to let her voice echo. "What else could I possibly be? Certainly not a hellhound."

"Hellhound . . . Is that what you call them?" His soft tone was curious.

"Of course." Belle reached the bottom of the steps and moved aside in the tiny area to let Laramie reach the door. "You call them something different?"

He knocked twice on the hard wood, then said to Belle with complete seriousness, "We call them *cursed*."

A soldier guarding from outside opened the door. Laramie nodded to him as they passed and led Belle down the hall. The lighting within the castle had been dimmed considerably since she last walked through. It cast everything in a foreboding shadow. Monsieur Petit still carried the candlestick and Belle's pace kept her just within the flame's glow. "You never answered my question before."

Laramie didn't respond right away. He was the sort of man who considered everything he said before he said it. "It is not a question for me to answer, but you will get your answer in time. In fact, I would say that many of your questions will be answered quite soon."

They didn't speak as he led her back to the grand staircase and ascended to the third floor. Belle relished the lush, red rug and wide steps as they went. Her hand rested upon the thick banister. Already the dark tower dungeon felt like only a brief nightmare.

The idea to turn and dash to the front door crossed her mind, but she shoved it away. That would have been the most foolish action for her to take. If somehow Belle made it past the front guards, she'd then have to get Charming without the soldiers catching up to her. Not to mention that they still had her weapons, and she was *not* leaving without her revolvers. Gosh, Belle missed their weight at her side.

On the third floor, the layout was identical to the one below. It was quickly becoming clear how easily one could get lost in such a large castle. Laramie stopped at the intersecting hallway. There were guards stationed down one hall. Before Belle could ask what the guards were protecting, Laramie gave her the answer.

"This is the West Wing," he said. "The Royal Apartments are down there. They are off limits." He looked at Belle, forcing her to meet his eyes. The candlelight exaggerated the length of his nose. "I know that royalty holds a certain fascination to people, especially young women. Do not fall prey to such a thing. Stay out of the West Wing. Do you understand?"

Belle nodded with a gulp. It sounded to her like a death threat, which made sense. The Vakrein royal family wouldn't want strangers wandering around in their rooms. The idea of risking the penalty of death just for a glimpse of them seemed absurd. But, no doubt, others hadn't seen it her way.

Monsieur Petit then took her down an adjacent hall. They stopped at a large door, high and arched like the windows. It was identical to all of the others she'd seen that night.

Already unlocked, Laramie pushed the door open. "Your room."

It was about the same size as Belle's bedroom at home, save for the incredible ceilings. Ivory walls were accented with intricate gold molding. The furnishings were extravagant. There was a large canopy bed, draped in the finest silk materials. A vanity desk was topped with an extensive mirror; various beauty items sat upon it. Two tall glass doors, draped with sheer white curtains, opened onto a small stone balcony. Golden tassels pulled aside the soft fabric, centering twin peaks as her room's main décor.

Directly across from the luxurious bed was a likewise massive hearth. It was elegantly designed to match the room perfectly. Somehow, despite the high ceilings and almost imposing view, it managed to make her feel safer. A fire roared in its mouth, exuding a warmth meant to chase away the chill of a previously unused room.

An older woman was bent over the fire, sending up sparks with a poker. She glanced up as they entered. A smile spread across her face. "Oh hello, my dear! I'm so happy to have someone new to look after."

"This is Edvina Gulbrandsen." Laramie cleared his throat. "She is the Majordome for this floor. It is her job to tend to our guests."

Belle curtsied. "It's a pleasure to meet you."

"No, no. The pleasure is all mine!" she beamed. Her light, graying hair was pulled back in a soft bun. It was perfectly suited to her rounded shape. She reached over and grabbed Belle's hand, leading her over to the vanity and pushing her onto the seat. Belle was already warming to her. "I've been looking after the same people for the last five years, with no one new to shake things up. Trust me, I'm just happy to see a fresh face. Specially one as pretty as yours." She started pulling the pins carefully from Belle's hair, letting it fall down her back. "I hope you don't mind, I figured you might be hungry and ordered the kitchen to bring you up something. My husband is one of the chefs, you know. He'll make sure you're fed well."

"I am quite hungry, thank you." Belle smiled.

As the woman worked her fingers through Belle's hair, then grabbed a brush and gently started combing, the tension in her body melted away. The mechanical fingers of the Governess back home simply did not have these talents. This might not be so bad after all. A good night's sleep, some answers, and Belle would be on her way by tomorrow night.

"Mademoiselle?" Laramie's voice made her open her eyes. He'd come farther into the room and stood so that she saw him in the ornate mirror. "I'll be leaving you now. Madame Gulbrandsen will get you anything you need. Otherwise, there will be guards posted outside your door. Goodnight."

"Thank you and goodnight." Just like that, dread seeped back in.

For just a moment, Belle had started to think she was a guest. First enthralled by the warm fire and lavish room, then lulled by the enchanting Edvina. But the guards outside were statement enough. Her surroundings may have changed, but this was still a prison.

Edvina chatted on, unaware of the worry spiraling inside Belle. She braided Belle's hair for the night, had her soak in a hot bath, then let her eat until she was full—and truly the food was delicious. By the time Belle crawled into bed, with Edvina unrolling the thick canopy around her, it was much harder to stress over this new prison. The soft mattress relaxed her muscles even further and sleep swept in like a horse with wings to take her away.

Belle's eyes shot open. In an instant, she was awake. Was it morning? There was no fogginess or sleep trying to pull her back in. When she stirred, there were no aches in her body. It all felt odd.

That's when Belle noticed that two things weren't right. First, she was back in her clothes from the day before. Like someone had removed her nightgown and put her in the dress while she slept. Second, this wasn't the same bed or room she'd fallen asleep in . . .

. . . and she wasn't alone.

# Chapter Eleven

This room was most decidedly not Belle's. The balcony and fireplace were in the wrong places, and the room felt lived in. Belle didn't care about all that. Her full focus was on the man sitting at a desk in the adjoining office. He moved his quill pen over some papers, not having noticed she was awake.

She pushed herself up with the intent to sneak out, to perhaps get help. He glanced up at her, freezing her movements. They stared at each other. Belle hardly breathed for fear of his intentions.

"Please, do come in," he said and turned back to his writing.

Confused, Belle climbed from the obscenely large bed, where she'd been lying atop the covers. She glanced, out of habit, at the fireplace. It was larger than the one in her room and carved to look like it was being overtaken by rose vines.

She stopped just outside the office. "Pardonne-Moi, but where am I and how did I get here?"

The man put down his pen and stood. Belle inhaled. His shoulder length, light brown hair was left loose and combed back behind his shoulders in thick, luxurious waves. Baby blue eyes sat beneath strong, authoritative eyebrows. Likewise a similar strength set in the straight lines of his jaw and perfect nose.

A deep blue coat draped his athletic frame. It was accented by a high collar, gold embroidery, and tasseled shoulders. An assortment of silver and gold, star-shaped medals were pinned to the front. A blue sash crossed from his shoulder to his hip, where a gleaming sabre rested.

*Royalty.* She hastily curtsied and apologized for intruding.

"No need to apologize. I was the one who brought you here." The man's voice was smooth, reminding Belle of poured honey. She would bet a week's wages that he had a beautiful singing voice.

"You brought me here, monsieur?" The idea of being carried in this man's arms thrilled her.

"I did. Please, come in." He gestured to the open floor before him.

To her left was another fireplace, but this one was smaller than the other in order to adapt to the smaller space. Across from it, the desk was piled with papers, books, and ink bottles. On the wall, between full bookcases, was a map of God's Cup and the surrounding countries.

"I am Prince Aleksander the First, of House Haraldsson, Crowned Prince Regent of Vakre Fjell," he said, snapping her attention from the interesting décor. Belle stared at him in shock, words lost entirely. He wasn't just some far-removed cousin or uncle as Belle had assumed—he was *the prince!*

"I'm . . . sorry . . . I didn't know," she stammered and quickly dropped into a curtsy even lower than her first.

"Please, do not worry. Our situation is very unique. Traditional expectations must be alleviated for the circumstances," was his diplomatic response. "Now, what is your name?"

Drawing herself up straight, she answered, "I am Belle LeClair of Glace."

"It is a pleasure to meet you, Belle LeClair of Glace." He was the epitome of regal, but his eyes were so open. They welcomed her in. "Where in Glace are you from?"

"Contefées, your Royal Highness."

"Oh?" he said excitedly and came around his desk to stand closer to her. "My father loved Contefées. He said it was a charming town. I had always hoped to visit."

"Did he visit often?" Belle shifted on her feet, feeling a little uncomfortable in his presence.

"Only a few times, long ago." The corner of the Prince's full lips turned up just slightly. The effect pulled her in. Belle couldn't imagine how dazzling it would be to see his full smile.

"I love Contefées," she added hastily, realizing that she'd been staring. "The world doesn't know a stronger town."

"I do not doubt that. After all, you and your father were able to brave your way here. That is no small feat." He crossed his arms, the fabric pulling tight around his muscles. She gulped as he asked, "What does your father do?"

"He is an inventor by trade, but leader of the Hunters by profession." Belle absently fingered the rosary at her hip.

"Hunters? What do you hunt?" He seemed genuinely interested.

"Hellhounds, of course. We protect Contefées from them."

Aleksander's face fell. The openness that had been in his eyes dulled. "You call them hellhounds?"

Belle frowned at being asked this a second time. The repetitive question had the effect of sobering her. "Yes, and I'm told that you don't."

He paused before responding softly, "No, we call them something else."

With her nerves finally adapting to the presence of royalty—attractive royalty—she searched his face. "'Cursed' is the term Monsieur Petit used."

"Yes, we call them cursed, along with other things." Aleksander moved away from her and stood before the window. His eyes were full of faraway thoughts.

"What other things do you call them?" she pressed, hoping to get more solid answers from him.

He breathed deeply and quickly turned back to her with renewed interest. "I'm more keen on knowing why you call them hellhounds."

Sighing, she answered flippantly, "We call them hellhounds because they are demons of Hell."

"Demons?" he asked with surprise. "And what makes you think this?"

Belle shrugged. "The Bishop recognized them. He said that it could happen to the truly sinful."

"Bishop. The Catholic Church?"

"Of course." Her eyes moved over the contents of the Prince's desk, looking for a clue or something that might glean her some real answers. "They employ us to hunt the hellhounds, in order to save their souls."

"How many have you killed?" he asked quickly, with the tilt of his head.

She turned her attention back to him, having found nothing obvious. "I am unsure of the exact number, your Royal Highness. But whole villages, at least."

Sadness crossed Aleksander's face. He tried to shield it from her, but his eyes betrayed him. He walked over to the hearth and stared into the fire. Immediately, Belle realized her mistake and regretted her honesty. Of course, this news would hurt him. To him they are not hellhounds, they are his people—his *cursed* people.

"Aside from Vakrc Fjell, have any other countries suffered this same fate?" Unlike his eyes, his voice did not give away his emotions. By all means, he sounded fortified.

"No." Ashamed and mentally berating herself, Belle kept her answer simple.

"No one in Contefées became one as well?" He still didn't look at her.

"Not to the best of my knowledge, your Royal Highness."

He placed a hand on the mantle, resting his weight. "So it is only Vakre Fjell then. That is good."

A long silence followed where the Prince was so lost in his sad thoughts, he seemed to forget she was still there. Belle took half a step forward, wanting to remedy the pain she'd caused. "I'm so sorry for my candor, your Royal Highness. I should have been more delicate."

He barely turned toward her, giving her only a glimpse of his blue irises. "No, I wanted honesty."

"And honesty you deserve, but I was insensitive." Belle looked down at her hands, rubbing them together. "I sometimes fear that I've grown too cold to what I do." A plethora of corpses flew through her mind, each one accompanied by its own memory. "But when my bullet resides in the body of a child, indifference is my only defense. Otherwise, I think I would be undone."

Aleksander looked at her fully now. "You've killed children before?"

The words stung, but there was no accusation or judgment in them.

"Yes, I have killed children . . . women, men, and elderly." She inhaled a slow, shuttered breath. "All hellhounds are the same in size and desire to kill. If we didn't stop them, they would come for us."

"That's a very difficult responsibility to bear." By the look in his eyes, she knew he understood. He had to shoulder the suffering of his people and she had to carry the weight of protecting hers.

Belle never thought she would find sympathy and understanding from the ruler of Vakre Fjell. He asked, "Your title is Huntress?"

"No, my gender does not change my title. I am still a Hunter. The church did not want the distinction to be made. They feared that it would encourage other women to follow." The unfolding honesty left Belle feeling light and bold. "May I ask a question, your Royal Highness?"

"Of course."

"Why did you carry me here and . . . how did I get back into my own clothes?" Belle reached up to move a strand of hair and realized that her hair was fully done up. Now that was impossible.

"Carry you? No, mademoiselle, I didn't carry you." The Prince shifted uncomfortably.

"Then how did I get here?"

"You're not really here." He paused, a strange look on his face. "This isn't real. It's a dream."

Belle's hand dropped. "Excusez-moi?"

"It's complicated. So please bear with me." His chest extended with a deep breath. "We call it moon dreaming. You are in a dream setting of my creation." At the sight of her disbelief, Aleksander pushed on. "Touch the fire, feel the flames. You cannot be burned here."

She couldn't believe what she was hearing. Had this Prince Regent lost his mind? The openness had returned to Aleksander's face. In fact, his eyes appeared to be daring her. Glancing between him and the fire, she decided to give it a try. He'd be easy enough to prove wrong.

Belle stepped over to the fire and knelt before it. Heat seeped through her skirts, warm and tingly. She removed her glove, then hovered her bare hand inches from the flame. The heat pressed against her skin but didn't burn. She reached further and the flames licked around her fingers . . . but there was no pain. Warmth, but nothing more.

"It's not real," she said with astonishment and stood. "It is a dream. Forgive my repetition, but how?"

"I cannot meet you in person. When my kingdom was cursed, I was . . ." Aleksander searched for the right word. "Imprisoned. But since then, I discovered the ability to moon dream and pull others into them. It is the only way I'm able to have contact with others and it's how I rule my kingdom."

"You're imprisoned?" This alarmed Belle. She immediately felt the instinct to help him. "Who imprisoned you? Someone in this castle? Tell me, I can help."

He put up a hand, silencing her. "No, I cannot be helped. What has taken me is a terrible, truly evil thing."

*Evil thing.* "My father said there was something evil here."

Aleksander nodded. "He's right. There is nothing that can be done for me now, but I at least have freedom here."

Though he gestured to his room, Belle recognized the falsehood in his words. This wasn't freedom, and he knew it. He may be refusing her help, but that didn't stop her from investigating.

So she played her question to be mere curiosity. "Where are you now?"

"In the waking world, you and I are sleeping," he answered, misconstruing her question.

"Your Royal Highness, I must ask." Belle stepped closer to him. If he wouldn't tell her where he was imprisoned, he could give her other answers. "How was your castle not affected by the . . . curse? What happened to your kingdom and why has nothing been done about it?"

"I am sorry, mademoiselle." Aleksander touched his chest. "I brought you here to find out who *you* were. We had every reason to distrust you, but in this evening I've realized that you are not what we had thought."

"What did you think I was?" Belle tilted her head, thoroughly surprised by the odd response.

"I would like to tell you, but you're waking up," The Prince said with chagrin. "I'm trying to keep you here, but your body is pulling you back."

"But . . ." Belle looked down at herself. She looked the same. She felt the same. "What about my questions?"

"Do not worry, mademoiselle, I vow to bring you back here tomorrow night and I will answer all of your questions." With this, he bowed.

# Chapter Twelve

here was the sound of moving fabric and light streamed onto Belle's face. She groaned, covering her eyes.

"Time to rise, mademoiselle," lilted Edvina's voice. "It is late into the morning and I cannot allow you to sleep any longer. Young ladies should not spend the day in bed. People will talk."

Belle forced open one eye to see the curvaceous woman tying back the canopy drapes. She quickly shut her eye again and pressed her face into her pillow. Her dream came back to her then in vivid detail. It felt so real. She could even recall the sound of Prince Aleksander's voice and the light blues in his eyes. Had her mind invented the whole thing? Perhaps that's what happened when one spent the night in a cursed castle.

There was a soft knock at the door and Edvina called for the person to enter. Belle heard the careful, but fast footsteps that followed. She once more popped open an eye as the smell of cooked meats and coffee reached her. A young lady in plain clothes quickly set a small table near the fireplace. When she finished the task, she spared a glance at Belle. Red colored her cheeks when she realized she'd been caught. Averting her eyes, she bowed and left the room.

"Come now, Dear." Edvina patted Belle's leg through the

covers. "That food had to be walked all the way up from the kitchens. Wait too long and it'll be cold."

With an accepting sigh, Belle pushed herself up from the bed. Edvina was there right away with a thick robe to wrap around her. Belle pulled it tight, rubbing her cheeks against the fabric, and sat at the table. As Edvina poured her a cup of the steaming coffee, Belle grabbed a croissant from a mounded pastry dish. She dipped it into her coffee and took a bite, enjoying the robust flavors.

"Have you had breakfast yet today, madame?" Belle asked while Edvina, set to making the bed.

"Please, Dear, call me Edvina. I can't stand to be called madame." She smacked a pillow several times with surprising force. "I'll have my breakfast when my duties are done."

Belle sipped her coffee, burning her mouth a bit. "Please, sit and eat with me then. There's more food here than I can eat and *I* can't stand to eat while someone else works."

Edvina stood, placing a hand on her round hip and cocked an eyebrow. "You insist?"

"Absolutely. I'll just die if I don't get my way," Belle lied with a half-grin.

"Well, we can't have that." She came over, taking the chair from the vanity to sit across from her. "Mm, everything smells wonderful. A terrible taunt for one's stomach."

"Too true." Belle plopped the last of her pastry into her mouth. She rolled it around on her tongue, savoring the fluffy bread.

Conversation flowed easily between Belle and Edvina like they were old friends. Edvina did most of the talking but asked many questions about Belle's life back home. The topics stayed light, never once drifting to grimmer things.

About halfway through their meal a troupe of maids came with hot water to fill Belle's bathtub. It actually confused Belle at first, given that she was so used to a tub that filled itself. When she mentioned this to Edvina, the woman was fascinated and wanted to know all about Belle's modern conveniences.

"Bonjour, mademoiselle." Laramie followed one of the maids, carrying a tray of bathing items, and stopped in the doorway. This time he appeared fully rested and his clothes were in impeccable order. "Pardonnez-moi. Edvina, a moment?"

Setting her coffee down, Edvina joined Laramie in the doorway. The two proceeded to talk in hushed whispers. Belle wiped her mouth on a napkin and watched the maid unload her tray onto a side table. It was an assortment of soaps for Belle to choose from.

"Excusez-moi, what is that?" Belle asked the maid, pointing to one tiny unmarked bottle.

"Rose oil, mademoiselle," she said timidly, then finished emptying her tray and left as a different maid came in with yet another bucket of water.

"Rose oil?" Belle interrupted Laramie and Edvina. They both looked at her in confusion. "Why is there rose oil for my bathwater?"

Edvina smiled gleefully. "His Royal Highness said you smelled like roses and—" Laramie grabbed her arm, cutting off her words. She gave him the nastiest of glares as he spoke for her. "She means that *I* said you smelled like roses and the prince made the suggestion to send rose oil for your bath."

Edvina's eyes quickly widened, then she admitted sheepishly, "Yes, of course, that's what I meant."

"I see." Ignoring the look passing between the two, Belle thought again of her dream. "I had a dream about his Royal Highness last night."

"Hmph, no surprise there. A pretty thing like you, the Prince *would* visit you straightaway," Edvina grumbled, walking over to the bed to finish the job she'd started earlier. "Just once I'd like to moon dream with him."

*Moon dream.* Belle gasped. That's what the Prince had called his visit in her dream. "You mean the dream actually was real?"

"Yes, mademoiselle, it was real." There was no jest in Laramie's eyes. As this new reality sunk in, he bowed. "If you'll excuse me, I'll be going."

"Oh wait!" Belle stopped him. "I'd like to check on my horse if I could, and maybe take him for a walk."

He frowned. "I'm afraid you're restricted to your room for now, but I'll see if I can get permission. I see no real harm in that."

Belle was dismayed. She'd really thought that after her meeting with the Prince, she was no longer a prisoner. Then again, he'd have to be careful, wouldn't he? First impressions can always be deceiving.

She smiled halfheartedly at Laramie. "Thank you, I'd much appreciate that."

Even though Belle never left her room, the morning went by in a flurry. After her bath, Edvina brought a stylist for her hair and a seamstress to get her measurements. All the while, Edvina was her hostess and activity coordinator. She spoke freely about nearly anything that popped in her head, except when Belle pried about the curse or the Prince's imprisonment. Then she was suddenly too busy commanding servants to answer.

The staff all had interesting reactions to Belle's presence. Some were nervous, others were afraid, but many were eager to just be near her. No one spoke out of turn though and when any of them got to gawking, Edvina was quick to snap them back to work.

"Apologies, mademoiselle. It has been a long time since we've had anyone new in the castle. People are simply excited," the Majordome whispered to Belle as the seamstress laid blue fabric over her shoulder and examined the effect in the mirror, then changed it for something gold.

Belle smiled softly in reply. It was all a bit overwhelming. Her normal morning routine was quiet; just Belle and Pixie as she readied. Her mechanical Governess did all that the castle needed a dozen royal servants to do. But then, Belle enjoyed the company and having someone to talk hair and clothes with. Her life had become so dominated by male presences that Belle had forgotten how wonderful female companionship could be.

Charming tugged against the rope, guiding them toward the outer wall. Stepping off the shoveled path and into the thick snow, Belle followed lazily. The cold air felt nice on her skin and the quiet was refreshing.

A figure followed in the distance. Belle ignored him. It was only a guard; one of two that accompanied her. The courtyard was entirely empty otherwise, which Belle figured might have been by design. Still, she was grateful they'd given her permission to walk Charming.

She was so relieved to find him well. Belle had examined him thoroughly, searching for some sign of mistreatment. Instead, she found that her stallion was in good temper and his coat shined, as though they'd brushed him all through the night. He'd nuzzled her affectionately when they reunited, nickering like a worried mare. Now he was more interested in the rose vines that clung to the outer wall.

Belle rapped his nose lightly with her knuckles, discouraging him from eating one of the blossoming flowers. They were everywhere, completely surrounding the castle grounds. The outer wall was too high for a person to climb, but not too high for these roses. The red and green was lovely against the gray stone and snowy terrain.

The roses didn't just stake claim to the outer wall though. They worked their way up the castle walls too. Her eyes followed the vines up and up, till they wrapped around the archway and railings of a balcony many floors up.

Belle's dream from the night before flashed in her mind and she remembered the stone balcony in Prince Aleksander's room. Was this the same one? Belle squinted, trying to see inside the room for a clue.

The large, glass balcony doors were open. The deep colored curtains fluttered in the light breeze. Beyond was only darkness. Then it shifted, or rather something in the archway moved, allowing her eyes to focus on the smallest of details. Steady, bright eyes stared back at her. The beholder was tall—nearly as tall as the archway itself.

*"What has taken me is a terrible, truly evil thing"*, Aleksander had said. Belle stepped back, bumping into the wall. This was it. Those were the eyes of the thing that was holding the Prince captive. Staring into those eyes, there was no doubt that they belonged to something of true evil.

That must be why the West Wing was off limits. Not just because it was the royal family's apartments, but because it's where Prince Aleksander was being held. Imprisoned in his own room. Belle imagined him chained to the wall of some makeshift cell; starving, cold, and dying. If the last five years had been long for her, how much worse had they been for him? Was the rest of the royal family imprisoned too?

Belle jerked her eyes away, angrily gripping the lead rope in her hands. Here were innocents in need of protection—at its core, wasn't that the very reason the Hunters existed? Belle had to do something. She had to kill whatever held the Prince captive and somehow free this kingdom.

But how? Here was an entire castle of soldiers and guards. If they weren't able to kill the evil thing—then how could she? They had guns, swords, and training. They even had numbers. If it was possible to stop Prince Aleksander's captor, then they would have done so already. It would be arrogant of Belle to assume that she could do it, when they had not.

And why hadn't they? She saw no reason for their lack of action. No matter how hard she searched her thoughts, Belle could find no good cause for them not to take a stand. There had to be something she was missing; something she wasn't thinking of.

The Prince had promised her answers when they last met. She'd just have to be patient until that night for them. If only her father was here to advise her—to tell her what to do or be wary of.

Worry shot through her chest at the thought of him. She wasn't too concerned whether he had made it home or not. Henri was tough—the first to kill a hellhound when no one knew they existed. There was little doubt in her that he had survived. But she wanted to be sure, and she wanted him to know she was well. At the very least give him peace of mind that she wasn't still locked in that awful dungeon tower.

Perhaps when she met Prince Aleksander in his moon dream, she'd ask him to send word to her father. After that, she would find out all she could about the Prince's captor. Then there was simply the guards at her bedroom door and her lack of weaponry to contend with. One obstacle at a time, though.

"Mademoiselle?" Belle looked over. One of her guards stood a few feet away. He was big with a nose that had been punched a few too many. "I'm to escort you back to your rooms now."

Belle nodded. A stable hand was already traipsing through the snow to return Charming to the barn. She absently rubbed the horse's muzzle and looked back up at the open balcony. The eyes were gone. Whatever had been watching her had moved away.

Hopefully, the evil thing knew that it would look upon her again. Next time, she might just be there to kill it—kill it and save the Prince.

# Chapter Thirteen

he hearth's mouth was awash with fire. Heat mixed with the cold air that rushed against Belle's back. She blinked several times, surprised at how awake she felt and she'd only just gone to sleep. Belle was back in the Prince's room and this time she was standing, facing the door.

Belle glanced toward the office, but it was empty. She turned toward the cold, flowing air. Aleksander was out on his balcony, looking at the distant mountains. Deciding not to say anything, Belle just watched him.

He wore a loose, white shirt. It was tight over his broad back, accenting strong, defined shoulders. Black pants hugged his hips and Belle struggled not to gawk at the perfectly sculpted body beneath his casual clothing.

Aleksander was relaxed; just a man in his room and not a ruling prince. He rested his hands on the stone railing. His head tilted to the sun, lighting the straight lines of his jaw. Nothing held his hair back. Instead, light brown locks fell freely over his shoulders. Aleksander's eyes were closed and he sighed. Even in his informal state, he exuded power and what Belle could only describe as pure masculinity.

With slow steps, Belle moved to stand next to him on the balcony. She was careful not to invade his space or disrupt his peace. It was an honor that he allowed her to see him this way.

Looking below, she confirmed that this was, in fact, the balcony from yesterday's walk. Roses were everywhere. They wrapped around the thick railings and climbed up the archway. Some were buds, but most were full, red and in beautiful bloom. Their fragrance wafted in the air, causing Belle to breathe deeply.

Seeing the view beyond his room, Belle understood why Aleksander was so relaxed. Soft, blue skies stretched above the great mountain range beyond the castle walls. Gray clouds were approaching in the distance. A few snowflakes drifted past Belle's cheek. A storm was coming.

"It's beautiful." She was nearly breathless.

Aleksander sighed again. He'd been looking in the distance with Belle, but now he turned to go back inside without a word. She was about to ask him if something was wrong, then a boom came from the mountains. It was loud and heavy. Like something smacked hard enough against the air, that it cracked. The Prince turned with her and they looked in the direction of the noise.

The snow beneath the tallest peak broke away like splitting ice. It fell in an avalanche for hundreds of feet. The rumble of it reached even them. By then a ripple had started. An invisible force spread and grew, as though the air itself was warping. It swept down the mountain and over the smaller peaks. It rushed through the forest, bending trees beneath its force. It rumbled over the ground and crashed into the outer wall—just as the Norwegian Sea crashed into the cliffs. Residual force barreled over the wall and smashed into the balcony.

Aleksander was thrown off his feet, into his room. He slammed against the floor. Belle was launched into the stone archway. Pain jarred through her shoulders and down her back. She crumbled to the balcony floor, gasping for air. As she fought to breathe, Belle looked back at the Prince, but her vision blurred. All she saw was his crumpled, unmoving form.

Belle closed her eyes, focusing on staying calm until her lungs were finally able to pull air back into them. What in Hell was that?

A hand carefully touched Belle's shoulder. She glanced up and saw the Prince leaning down to help her stand. He had changed. His hair was neatly pulled back and he wore a suit more suitable for public. Aleksander seemed completely unharmed or shocked by the unexpected attack.

"My apologies." He grasped her arm and brought Belle to her feet. His hands kept hold of each shoulder in gentle assurance. "I should have given you a warning of what this would be like."

Already Belle was starting to feel steady as if she pulled from his strength. His eyes focused so fully on her and sent her nerves aflutter. But his close proximity made her only want to lean into him completely and be engulfed by his strong embrace.

"I'm all right. Thank you for your assistance." Belle patted one of his arms, encouraging him to let go of her. He did and moved to give her some space. Part of her was disappointed by the separation, but another part of her was relieved by it. Normally she was not so affected by a man's presence. "What exactly was that?"

"That was a memory. My memory, actually, of the day my kingdom was cursed." He looked down and then out at the mountains like he was remembering it all over. "I wanted to give you the full effect of what it felt like and to do that I had to be completely focused, so I couldn't be here with you at the same time."

"The air rippled," was all Belle could seem to say.

"That was the curse as it was cast." He placed a hand on Belle's lower back, guiding her off the cold balcony, through his room, and into his office. Aleksander stepped over to the map on his wall and ran his finger along Vakre Fjell. "The spell originated here, on Mount Gunnhild, and after speaking with you, we believe it expanded to the coasts and nearly to the Glace border. Anyone within the spell's radius was cursed with a type of lycanthropy."

Belle stared at him. There was so much in that statement that confused her. "Lycanthropy? Spell?"

Aleksander walked past, brushing her at the same time. The action sucked the air from her lungs. He pulled a red book from his shelf, flipped through the pages, and handed it to her. The language was English and the text was broken up by crude depictions of half-men, half-wolves.

"Lycanthropy is a curse that allows a man to become beast. My subjects can't change back from their wolfish forms unless they die, and that makes them different from lycanthropes." He tapped the old pages where her eyes skimmed. "But I think some form of that curse is what has befallen them."

Not looking up from the text, Belle said, "According to this, to become a lycanthrope, you have to be bitten by one, be born to one, do one of these more absurd actions, or it can be a divine punishment. Only the last one seems possible for an entire kingdom, and it is consistent with what the priests have said."

Aleksander shook his head. "What happened to my people was a divine act, yes, but not meant as a punishment. And it was not Satan who did it—at least not the Satan you know."

He pulled another book from beneath a pile on his desk. It was already open to the place. It was not written in English, French, or Norwegian; the language was unfamiliar to her. It looked old, the pages already showing the signs of age. What caught her attention was the full-page drawing. It was a hellhound; wild and ferocious. The creature, mouth open, was about to rip a knight from his horse. A chill went through her.

"This is written in Old Norse. It tells of a god named Fenrir. It calls him a monstrous wolf." Prince Aleksander pointed to the picture. "That's a picture of him there. Look familiar?"

Belle nodded. "You can't possibly believe that all of your subjects were turned into Norse wolf gods?"

"No, I do not." Aleksander smirked delightfully down at her, his face so close that Belle could see the trace of his eyes and the way they seemed to ponder her. Blushing, she averted her gaze. He moved away to look over his books, pretending not to notice her bashful reaction. "Though, I do believe that Fenrir is the cause of what happened to them."

Belle ignored the foolish insecurity and crossed her arms. "Let's just say I believe it's possible for there to be more than one god and I'm not saying that I do. But aside from this picture, tell me why this theory has any more credence than what my bishop has said."

"Because I met the woman who created the curse." He raised his chin. "And she mentioned Fenrir's name."

"What? A woman?" This was not the reply Belle had expected. "I think you need to start from the beginning."

"Yes, mademoiselle." Aleksander smiled and it reached up to his beautiful, blue eyes. "The moment that curse swept through my kingdom, my people became great wolves, and my castle became a prison to everyone within."

"The whole castle? I thought only you were imprisoned?" Belle relaxed her arms, moving them to rest in front of her.

"My prison is different." He paused, thinking, then tried to explain further. "If anyone from within the castle grounds tries to leave, they are immediately cursed like the others. We lost several good men in learning this."

Finally, a piece of the puzzle fell into place. Now Belle knew why there was a castle full of able people, but why none ever came for help. She also realized then that there would be no way to send word to her father. The only person that could leave this castle was, in fact, her. "Why was I not changed by the curse when I broached your lands?"

"Perhaps because you were not touched by it originally?" He

held up defeated hands. "To be frank, mademoiselle, I do not have an answer for that."

"What about why the castle was unaffected?"

He smiled at Belle again, causing her body to feel strangely light.

"That I do know. For two days we didn't have answers. With telescopes we could see that the closest village and shipyard had been lost, but there was no reason for any of it. No sign of any human that had walked away untouched." His gaze drifted off and Belle knew he was remembering. "Then *she* came. She was not human—she looked human, but there was no question that she was something else. This woman called herself a norn."

"Norn?" The foreign word felt odd on her tongue.

"They are otherworldly beings sent by some universal power to change fate." Aleksander turned toward her. "I can show her to you, if you would like to see her."

"Would it be like before?" Belle wasn't sure she wanted to experience anything that intense again.

"Yes, but I won't give you the full experience." He stepped closer, gently taking her hand. "I'll just let you see her in my memory and I'll be with you this time."

The warmth of his hand seeped through her gloves and sent tingles through her arm. "Okay, I'd like that. Thank you."

"You should close your eyes. It'll make it easier for you to adjust to the change."

Belle obeyed, feeling the tingles reach her stomach. Aleksander was so close to her . . . asking her to close her eyes. Briefly she imagined what it would be like to have him kiss her. Her lips began to part at the very idea.

"You may open them now," Prince Aleksander said, sounding farther away.

Belle hadn't felt her surroundings change or Aleksander let

go of her hand. Her eyes opened. Belle instinctively stepped away when she saw the woman. She was tall, thin, and draped in a luxurious, blue cloak. It was trimmed in silver with matching archaic symbols decorating the cloth. Shining metal armor wrapped her chest, arms, and shoulders. A large, evil-looking dagger was strapped to her front waist. Everything she wore had strange symbols carved into it. Visible just beneath the cloak were small, cat-like black eyes and white skin.

"Terrifying, isn't she?" Aleksander stood a few feet away, watching the woman. "Be grateful you can't hear her voice too."

"Why can't I?" The norn talked to someone that Belle couldn't see; she assumed that it was Aleksander. Belle looked around, but the room was hidden in blackness. The only thing in full detail was the woman.

"Some of it is personal," The Prince replied vaguely. "She did tell me that *she* created the curse and that my kingdom was chosen by the wolf god, Fenrir, to receive this great honor, but that something had gone wrong. She said the roses that grew around the castle protected the people within from the curse."

"How did the roses protect you?" Belle watched the norn, who stood with an air of invincibility.

"She said another norn had interfered long ago and planted seeds, embedded with the power of fatum, to protect this castle. But the roses only held the curse at bay. If we step beyond them, we succumb to the curse."

"That's why the roses grow and bloom here all year long." Belle was beginning to understand, but at the same time it was all still strange to grasp. "You said that norns are sent by some universal power. Is that what this wolf god is?"

Belle had a horrible thought then . . . Could Aleksander's captor be this wolf god? She recalled the image of him ripping a soldier from the saddle, and a chill ran through her. With all of his evidence, and the norn before her, Belle was becoming inclined to believe Aleksander's version of events over that of the church's. So if what he said was true, how was she to kill a *god*?

"No. The information I've found on norns has been scattered and brief, but the texts have been very clear. Norns are the most powerful beings and as such obey only the universe, not even the gods." As Aleksander walked toward Belle, the strange woman faded and the blackness formed into the shape of his study. Oddly, she felt safer here, away from the norn. Aleksander went to his desk and picked up the book written in Old Norse. He tapped the pages thoughtfully. "I'm not sure how or why, but somehow Fenrir has convinced a norn to change fate for him."

"Thank God the universe sent a norn to plant those enchanted roses." Belle walked over to the window to look at the creeping rose vines below. So much information rattled through her brain. "The norn that placed the curse, why did she tell you all of that? Why did she talk to you at all?"

"She wanted me to join Fenrir willingly." He started flipping through the book. "Of course, I would not follow a god who would do this to my kingdom."

Belle turned to look at him. "Why *did* Fenrir curse your kingdom?"

"I believe this is why." Aleksander gestured to the book. "After the norn came here, I started searching for all I could find on the wolf god and I came across a poem titled, *Völuspá*, and it reads that a woman came to the forest Járnviðr, 'and bred there the broods of Fenrir.' I believe that this Járnviðr, which the poem also calls Iron-wood, is Vakre Fjell Forest. 'In the east sat an old woman in Iron-wood and nurtured there offspring of Fenrir'. The poem is mostly about killing the god, Odin, but I think Fenrir sent this norn here to create his broods, as it says."

Belle was completely enraptured. She loved the way Aleksander read so easily from a book written in an all but forgotten language. Suddenly, she wanted badly to meet this man in person. "Is it this wolf god that has you imprisoned?"

"In a manner of speaking," he answered, not looking up from the book.

"So he is not the thing I saw in your quarters yesterday?" Belle tilted her head, trying better to see the Prince's face. "He's not what's holding you prisoner?"

"What holds me is not your concern, mademoiselle. Put it from your mind." Aleksander looked at her through the veil of his lashes, the lines of his mouth flattening with sternness. "If you wish to help my kingdom—and therefore me—find a way to defeat the norn and to lift this curse. Only then, I feel, will we stop Fenrir's plans."

Belle straightened in subtle defiance, but she was not foolish enough to think she could go against a Prince Regent. Nor was she about to press her luck with one. "What is Fenrir's plans? Why do all of this?"

"Why would any god want to make an army of blood-thirsty wolf spawn? To wage war and conquer." He said it casually as he closed the old book, but Belle's throat had gone dry.

It didn't matter if they were great wolves or hellhounds, created by Fenrir or Satan, the end result was the same.

## Chapter Fourteen

Aleksander closed the heavy book with a sigh and reached up to press his fingers against his eyelids, weary from the past week of endless research. He glanced at her, tilting his head curiously. "Have you been to see our gardens yet?"

Belle peered up from her own set of dusty pages and raised an eyebrow at him. "No, your Royal Highness. I'm restricted to my rooms if you recall."

"Ah." He scratched his chin, looking a little sheepish. Then he leaned back in his chair and folded his hands in his lap. "Well, that just proves the point I was about to make."

"Which is?" Her interest piqued at his unusually playful manner.

"We've been cooped up in this study for too long. For five nights we've had our noses stuck in these dusty old books." He reached across the table and took the book from Belle's hand. He snapped it shut. "My brain is turning to mush. If I'm forgetting something as simple as your castle restrictions, then I must need a break."

"Your evidence is certainly sound." Belle grinned. "But I thought you wanted me to go over all of your research; see if I can find anything you may have overlooked?"

After the Prince's order to not concern herself with his captor,

Belle had decided to follow his lead and search for a way to break the curse, or defeat the norn. She didn't dare ask Prince Aleksander about his captor again, not after his reaction from before, and no one else was willing to divulge in the topic—not even Edvina.

"For nearly a week's time, you've been reading these old books, and you've seen little else." He stood and tugged down the sleeves of his black brocade coat. Belle noticed the cuff links were custom embossed with the family seal. The Prince then offered his hand. "You cannot convince me that a visit to the royal gardens is not warranted."

Belle couldn't deny that she'd been dying to see more of the castle. Technically she was a prisoner and this place was cursed, perhaps even evil, but it was the only castle she was likely to ever be in. She wanted to see all of it, enjoy the grandeur that was so different from anything in Contefées.

Taking his hand, Belle let him guide her out of her chair. She closed her eyes as he instructed. A gust of cold wind snaked up her skirts, causing her to clutch his hand in surprise. But only when he said so, did she open her eyes.

They were in the courtyard; a section Belle had not yet wandered too. Before them was a glass building lined with stone and steel supports. A hard-edged roof led up to a domed glass top, like a church made of glass. Glass that was frosted on the outside and coated with steam on the inside.

Keeping hold of her hand, Aleksander escorted her up the few steps and under the steel awning where he held the door open for her. Heat wafted out the door, wrapping around her like water as she entered. Moisture was thick in the air. She breathed deeply, enjoying the heavy feel of it inside her lungs.

"Do you like it?" Aleksander closed the door behind him, shutting off the stream of cold air.

"Oh, I do." Belle smiled as she gazed around the room.

Never had she seen so much green—so much color! Flowery vines climbed walls, tendriled arrangements hung from the ceiling, and small aisles separated the many rows of exotic flora. "I love the cold beauty of God's Cup, but I have never seen anything like this."

"My mother loved flowers and insisted that our castle's arrangements rival that of the warmer kingdoms." The Prince kept off to the side, watching her smell the largest yellow flower she'd ever seen. "I think the enchanted roses did more to this castle than just protect it. We've been able to grow any foreign or strange flower my mother wished."

"It must have been very hard for your mother, losing her husband and then seeing her lands cursed." Belle marveled at a ladybug crawling along a thick, green leaf. Did they have the bugs imported too? The Prince didn't say anything and she turned to look at him.

He was staring down at a flower, but not really seeing it. "After my father's passing, my mother wanted to go out and see the people. She knew they were mourning and she wanted to mourn with them . . ."

Aleksander didn't finish his story, and Belle didn't need him to. The muscles in her chest tightened. She swallowed hard to relax them. "The Queen was outside the castle grounds when the curse hit."

"She was." He turned away from her, hiding his face and the tears she saw him fighting back.

His body had become tense, stretching the fabric of his clothes. Belle wanted to reach out, smooth her hands over his back and comfort him with her touch. Instead, she fiddled with the trim of her dress and searched for something to say. "Your sister was in France though when it happened. Thank God for that."

She waited for his reply, but Prince Aleksander gave none. Allowing him space, Belle walked over to the archway opening into the other half of the greenhouse. Over here there were rows and rows of food. There were enough fruits and vegetables to feed the entire castle.

"What about your family?" Aleksander finally said. Belle glanced over at him, askance. He had turned back to her and the lines in his face had relaxed. "Have they been affected by this curse?"

"Yes, my mother was killed by a hellhou—wolf—about three years ago," she began, grasping hold of her own emotions. It was difficult to talk about the hardships her family had endured. But with Prince Aleksander, she felt the desire to be forthright. "My father had thrown himself into the cause, giving up his inventions for the last five years. My sisters were sent away after my mother's death."

"So your family has been torn apart by this." He paused, waiting until she met his eyes. "We have that in common then."

"Many families have that in common, your Royal Highness."

"Not like us, I'd imagine." He formed a connection to Belle with his eyes, conveying the certainty he put behind his words.

Belle couldn't look away and she couldn't argue. Her breathing became shallow. "No, I suppose you're correct."

The moment stretched on with neither one speaking and she was perfectly content to bask in the stillness of his stare. Aleksander stepped towards her, then broke eye contact by casting his gaze over a row of tomatoes. "It's a shame your father no longer invents."

Finally, she inhaled. "Oh no, he's built things over the years."

Aleksander's eyebrows rose, showing his baby blues even more. "Truly? What has he invented?"

"Many things." Belle shrugged. "Currency counters, self-filling bathtubs, heated carriages . . . He even built an automaton pixie for me as a child. It still works to this day."

"Amazing." He smiled at Belle. Like his eyes, it was so open—so welcoming. Her heart felt like it was expanding in her chest. "I would like to see these inventions someday."

She returned his smile, unable to prevent it. "He'd like that."

Aleksander's eyes danced over her curved lips. Then he blinked and gazed back into her eyes. "So tell me, how did the world react to the news of actual demons on Earth?"

"The same way it reacts to most things. A large uproar in the beginning, but soon they all lose interest." Belle stepped back into the flower garden, slowly walking down one of the rows.

"What about the King of Norway and Sweden? Did old Charles have anything to say about it?" Aleksander said, his footsteps following closely behind.

"He sent ships to investigate, but the ports were overrun with hellhoun—wolves—then." Belle glanced behind her, admiring the Prince's long frame and perfect posture. "When these reports reached King Charles, all he said was that he knew he was destined to rule over two countries, but he never expected three."

"Charles never was afraid to speak plainly. So if he intended to retake Vakre Fjell, why hasn't he arrived at my gates yet?"

"The cursed. Some say he's biding his time, letting the wolves eat themselves into starvation. Others say he's just afraid of them." Belle found a green, metal bench along a frosted window. She pulled out the pearl and gold skirts of her dress to sit. Each day a new gown was brought for her and they were all finer than anything she'd ever worn. "The only thing they seem to agree on is that King Charles would see any country coming to your aid as a threat to what he believes is his by rites. And no one wishes to go to war with Norway and Sweden."

"Other countries aren't worried about the potential Hell on Earth threat?" Aleksander fiddled absently with a wall-climbing vine. They were all over this area. Belle felt nearly surrounded by the leafy plants.

"They are. So they make sure the Catholic Church has all the resources it needs to keep the hounds contained."

"Oh, of course. As long as it doesn't become a direct threat, there are other things to worry about." Aleksander nodded, accepting this terrible statement so easily. "What of the public? Do they have an opinion on the matter?"

"A very mixed opinion, actually." Belle frowned. She didn't like the path their conversation had taken. Every word she spoke made the world seem so cruel and uncaring. That wasn't true for everyone—it wasn't true for her. "Most believe the church, that the Vakreins were sinful and turned by the Devil. Some won't even admit that they had family or friends living here because they're afraid that they'll be marked by it. Many in the scientific communities, however, believe there may be more to it."

"Really?" Aleksander's face lit up again, much the way it did when he asked about Henri's inventions. He sat on the bench opposite her, tugging his vest and straightening his shoulders. "And what have they said about it?"

"Oh, many things . . . Many theories." She wanted to keep the conversation here, in a place that lightened the Prince's mood. "They petitioned the church incessantly in the beginning, but even now they still try to get consent. The church won't agree though and in this situation, the church has all the power."

"Consent? For what?"

"Oh, I'm sorry." Belle fumbled, realizing she'd left out the most important part. "The church has received requests to autopsy some of the bodies and to capture a live hound for experiments."

Aleksander sat back abruptly, his brows scrunched with a look of horror on his face. "Please, tell me, the church has denied every single request of that nature."

Belle gulped down the sinking feeling in her stomach. "Every one."

"Good." He pushed off from his seat and walked over to the glass wall to stare out. It was an act Belle was beginning to recognize as something Aleksander did when his mind was troubled. Without turning, he said, "For once, I actually agree with the Catholic Church."

Chewing her lip, Belle fought the urge to ask, knowing it might upset the Prince, but in the end it just wasn't in her nature to keep quiet. "Giving consent could mean that the scientists learned something valuable. A cure perhaps."

"A cure? You saw the norn, albeit through my memory, but tell me that does not convince you that this is beyond the control of man?" Glancing abruptly over his shoulder, his stern glare pinned her, preventing her from doing anything other than blink. "My people have suffered enough." Sorrow swept into his eyes and he looked away. "I wish for them to rest in peace and I certainly don't wish for those still living to be experimented on—even as evil as they may be now."

Belle fidgeted quietly behind Aleksander's turned back. How could she say those things to him? Twice now, she failed to see the hellhounds the way he did, as his cursed people. She chose instead to see them as everyone else did, as the wild man-killing devils that were presented on the surface. She hurt Aleksander every time she did this and showed herself to be as cruel as Bishop Sauvage. Unable to bear it, Belle pushed herself up and started to walk away.

She stopped unexpectedly and peered back to the Prince. "You must forgive me, your Royal Highness. For years, I've lived on the other side of this. We call ourselves Hunters, but we were the hunted ones. It's hard, even with all I've learned, to see them through your eyes."

"I suppose that's true for both of us." He looked at her and she watched as his deep inhale raised his chest. "Is that all of it then? Nothing more I should know about the outside world?"

"There are the raiders." Belle bit her lip, not wanting to burden him further. Aleksander raised an eyebrow and waited for her to go on. "Every year a group comes along, usually some out-of-work mercenaries. They think your kingdom is ripe for the picking. They're always arrogant, always certain that they'll be the ones coming back with the crown jewels. And they always die." Belle crossed her arms, half grinning as she remembered the last group. "Some raiders came through town recently and caused a bit of a dust up with my Hunters. I convinced them to at least wait until after my father left for Skjebne Port, so as not to endanger his journey any further. Since we haven't seen them, I can only assume they went the way of all the others."

Aleksander leaned into his hip, a mischievous smile curving his lips. "Imagine their surprise if they had reached the castle and found it full of armed soldiers."

Picturing it, Belle giggled along with the Prince. She partially wished they really had been the first mercenaries to reach the castle.

# Chapter Fifteen

There was a knock on the bedroom door as Belle sat by the fire. She was reading yet another history book Aleksander had sent to her. So far, she'd found nothing that he hadn't.

"Oh look," said Edvina as Laramie stepped through the door. "The Keeper of The Seals has decided to grace us with his presence."

"How very droll of you, madame." He frowned at her.

Belle chuckled. Laramie pretended that Edvina's casual approach to decorum vexed him, but Belle suspected that it didn't bother him as much as he put on. "We haven't seen you for a couple days, monsieur. What brings you?"

His attention turned to Belle and his demeanor actually seemed to brighten. The lines of his face tilted upward and his shoulders drew back ever so slightly. The small light in his eyes even danced. "His Royal Highness has extended your castle privileges."

Now it was Belle's turn to brighten. She snapped her book shut and stuffed it behind her. "Really? To where?"

He smiled, his lips pressing into a thin line, and eyed her coyly. "The library, mademoiselle."

Belle gasped and was out of her chair immediately. "The library? Truly?"

Edvina leaned over her chair's arm, the curve of her bosom squeezing dangerously at the rim of her dress. "Child, all you do is read. Are you really that excited to see *more* books?"

"Oh, Edvina." She was almost breathless with excitement. "You have no idea."

"No, I really don't." Edvina turned back to her needlework, mumbling something about how that much reading couldn't possibly be good for the mind.

"I'll escort you." Laramie held out his arm, encouraging Belle to come and she didn't hesitate.

The two guards that continually manned Belle's room followed a few feet behind as they traversed the very long hall. This time they're pace was more leisurely and Belle took her time admiring the fine details of the castle. The immense windows allowed plenty of daylight to illuminate everything perfectly, leaving little in shadow.

"Laramie," Belle said, pulling her eyes from a painting of warring angels. It reminded her of her Hunters. "When will I be permitted to go home?"

"Do you wish to leave?" He glanced curiously at her.

"Admittedly, not as much as one might think," she said with a shrug. "I'd like to see my father, but I'm also learning a great deal here about the cursed. Some more research and we might find something to help us, maybe even reverse the curse."

"I'd imagine spending so much time with the Crowned Prince is quite enjoyable as well." Laramie looked at her through the corner of his eyes, not hiding his smirk.

Heat colored Belle's cheeks and she smiled with embarrassment. "I do enjoy his company very much. I enjoy all of your company, of course."

"Of course." He said nothing more, but irritatingly continued to smile.

Though, if Belle were honest, she more than enjoyed spending time with Aleksander. As the week had gone by, she'd found a great deal of comfort in his presence and took pleasure in discussing their research together. However, after yesterday's moon dream of the garden, Belle's thoughts now strayed toward the unseemly. When she was supposed to be researching by the fire, she'd caught herself thinking about his soft smile and open blue eyes. A page later, it was his strong back and the next second had her imagining him with his hair loose and free around his shoulders.

What was coming over her? She'd never thought of Gastone this way. Sure, she'd imagined being married to him; tried to envision what it would be like. But this was more like she'd lost control of her mind—she wanted to focus on reading, but it wanted to think of Aleksander.

"So, you're the one the castle has been buzzing about," said a light, feminine voice.

A beautiful, young woman stood just ten paces away. She was tall and thin, dressed in pink satin with white lace trim. Her soft, blond hair was swept up in a complex design that allowed for only a few free tendrils. She was flanked by two guards of her own; they watched Belle with wariness.

Laramie stepped between the two women. "Your ladyship, allow me to introduce you to Mademoiselle Belle LeClair of Glace." Belle gave her best curtsy, knowing this woman would see every mistake. When she finished, Laramie gestured to her ladyship. "Mademoiselle, this is Lady Liv Calland. Her father is one of the Five Lords of Vakre Fjell."

"I do say, you're as pretty as the men have been saying," Lady Liv said, allowing for no more formality.

"Thank you," Belle added quickly, not wanting to appear thrown. "You're a vision as well."

The Lady waved the compliment away.

"Yes, but you're new." She moved closer, ignoring the anxious guards. "Is it true that you kill the cursed?"

Belle pursed her lips at that wording, but judging by the easy expression on Liv's face she hadn't meant anything by it. "We call them hellhounds, but yes, I kill them to protect our town."

"Fascinating." She lifted and dropped a shoulder. "My father won't let me near weapons. Since my older brother will inherit the estate, my only concern is to be pretty enough to marry well."

Belle opened her mouth to reply, but a series of barks drew it shut. Her muscles tightened, her hand instinctively reaching for the revolvers that were not at her side, even as her mind recognized the barks as being that of average dogs. Still her heart quickened its pace and her gaze looked toward the sound.

Down the hall, near the royal apartments, came a troupe of five energetic dogs. They bounded around a young servant boy, who was attempting to guide them down the hall. One of the black and white beauties saw Belle and Liv, barked happily, and raced toward them. His pack mates excitedly chased after.

Belle crouched down as they approached. The lead dog shoved his face happily into her hands, panting as she scratched behind his ears. Two of the following dogs leapt up onto Laramie, nearly knocking him over. The servant boy rushed to pull the dogs off of him, apologizing profusely.

"And who are these gentlemen?" Belle laughed, standing up after giving the dog one last scratch.

"They are Prince Aleksander's dogs." Liv kept back, not interacting with the dogs jumping around her. "He raised them from infancy."

The servant boy shooed the dogs away, encouraging them to follow him down the stairs.

"What breed are they?"

"Siberian Huskies." Laramie brushed white fur from his coat.

"They were a gift from the Russian Emperor on the Prince's eighteenth birthday. His Royal Highness used to love riding through the woods with them."

"Your Ladyship     " said one of Liv's guards. He looked uneasy, his eyes glancing between her and Belle.

Liv sighed.

"Ever since you and the other outsider stumbled into our castle, my father has had guards posted at my side." She raised a keen eyebrow at Belle. "As rumor has it, his Royal Highness enjoys your company very much; my father really should be quite comfortable with your presence by now." Liv waited a breath for Belle to comment and shrugged her shoulder when she didn't. "Alas, fathers will be fathers and I prefer to keep my disobedience to a minimum. Good day, mademoiselle."

Belle gave a quick, slightly wobbly curtsy. "Your Ladyship."

Liv walked past but stopped abruptly. "I do hope his Royal Highness loosens his chains on you soon. I think we would be fast friends."

With that, she winked and continued her stroll down the hall.

"I can see you don't really know what to make of that," Laramie said, noticing the way Belle stared bewilderedly after the noblewoman.

"I'm afraid I don't. As a Hunter, I don't have much female companionship." She turned and they started once again toward the library. "The only nobles I know are the Count and Countess of Contefées, and their son."

"A bit out of your element with her then." Laramie chuckled. "Lady Liv Calland is bored. At her age, she should be using her good looks and noble-born education to snag herself a good marriage. Instead she's cooped up in this castle and the only decent match available to her is ruling over a cursed kingdom—and himself imprisoned. Like most occupants in this castle, I think she's just eager for distraction."

"Prince Aleksander is her only decent match?" Belle didn't like the icky feeling that idea placed in her stomach.

"Actually, the Prince and Lady Liv would be a very good match." Monsieur Petit nodded to himself at the idea. "It's why her family came to court in the first place."

"They didn't come because of the King's death?" Belle raised her eyebrows, the unpleasantness in her stomach expanding. "Edvina said that's why so many of the noble families escaped the curse."

"That is true. Only Lord Ostrem was not so fortunate, as he'd accompanied the queen into the villages the day it all happened." Laramie tipped up a finger like he was discussing some bit of history. "House Calland, however, had arrived days prior so that Lady Liv and his Royal Highness could become better acquainted."

Swallowing hard, Belle's eyes drifted to the floor.

Noticing her silence, Laramie looked down her at from the corner of his eyes and added, "Prince Aleksander is the only one here *not* looking for distraction, unfortunately for House Calland."

After ascending many more stairs, passing several shut doors and bowing servants, they reached the entrance to the library. Two looming white doors with gold handles barred her entrance.

"This is where I leave you," Laramie said as her guards moved past to open the doors. "Stay as long you like. When you're finished, your guards will walk you back to your room."

The doors swung open with immense gravity and Belle heard nothing more that Laramie said. Eyes wide, her hand went to her chest to see if her heart still beat. "Oh, my."

Books, two floors worth, spanned walls that reach endlessly away from Belle. She stepped onto the marble floors, past massive, pink-marbled columns with solid gold tops and bases.

Laramie instructed the guards to silently close the doors behind her, but she paid no notice of them.

The ceiling was comprised of a series of separately painted domes. Belle stared up into the one above her. Baby blue skies were the backdrop of purple-hued clouds. Beautiful angels, dressed for pleasure in a vibrant array of colors, lazed upon them. Their white and gold-tipped wings reflected back the library's natural light. They laughed and mingled—many of them were reading. A white Pegasus was bursting through the clouds, to the delight of those around it.

Tears danced on Belle's eyelids. The painting was so beautiful, she could hardly look away. But she did, forcing her gaze onto everything else. A lightness of spirit she hadn't known for some time settled into her.

She walked over to a hand painted globe, so immense that it would take at least two men to spin it. Her fingers grazed over the edges, alighting on the most amazing details of each region. Then her eyes turned to the walls and Belle moved farther into the library.

Each wall was a sectioned bookcase. Their awnings looked like crowns made of gold waves. The books were kept neatly on each shelf, not too tight and not a one laying lopsided; they covered every topic, in every language. At the end of each bookcase, a new case angled into a high arching window. Of which, each had its own gold crown. Glorious natural light spilled in to illuminate the entire library. It was the only source of light. There was no place for lamps and candles here.

"Might I help you find something?" The female voice came from behind, rattling off the stark silence and nearly startling Belle half out of her wits.

Belle spun around to face the speaker, fighting the quickening of her heart. Seeing the petite woman, Belle was surprised yet again. She was thin and a few inches taller. Her hair was drawn up into a severe bun and tiny bifocals rested on a mouse-like nose. Shockingly though, she wore men's clothes. Her vest was green and black over a white shirt. Her only other accessory was the tight, ebony gloves that she wore.

"Madame?" The woman asked and Belle realized that she'd been gawking.

Collecting herself, Belle extended a hand. "Mademoiselle, actually. Mademoiselle Belle LeClair of Glace."

"Ms. Tops of the Library," she said with a smirk and politely shook Belle's hand. At Belle's raised eyebrow she explained. "I am the Librarian of this castle and my father was before me. He raised me here. My life is this library."

"Oh, and your father, has he retired or does he work alongside you?" Belle noted the streak of gray in the woman's hair.

"No, he passed away five years ago." Ms. Tops' Vakrein accent was thick and un-lightened by the years of practice many of the castle servants had.

"I'm so sorry." Belle frowned. "The curse?"

"Nah, heart attack," Ms. Tops said matter-of-factly and waved a hand. "Now, tell me, what are you here to read?"

"Anything on Norse Mythology, specifically the norns."

The Librarian pressed her lips together and turned to walk away. "You're just like Aleksander then, only interested in one thing—the curse. Gods help me, I hope I get some interesting readers someday."

Shocked by the woman's formal use of the Prince's first name, Belle followed dubiously after. Gold reliefs edged the white walls, the top corners of which were inlaid with the golden heads of kings, queens, angels, and gods. They guided her eyes back up into another section of domed ceiling. Similar to the other mural, angels lounged happily among the clouds. It was like each domed ceiling was actually a window to heaven and she was simply getting a glimpse of one small part.

A pink, white, and gold archway was the entrance into the center of the library. On each side was a slow spiraling staircase. Belle stopped as they reached the closest.

The library's circular center was lined with books, but here were also many bronze and gold statues. There was a woman with large wings, clothed in battle armor, and carrying a spear. An older man sat upon a throne with one raven perched on his shoulder and the other on his forearm. Another woman beyond him rode in a chariot, her eyes looking far beyond the library. Yet another statue was a hulk of a man. He carried a mace and a battle ax, as well as a massive broadsword at his side. Like the other statues, he wore a helmet in the shape of wings. His back was draped in bear fur, the head of the animal biting his shoulder. From its ear hung a large gold ring. Next to that statue—

"They're Norse gods and Viking royalty," Ms. Tops interrupted Belle's revere. "Come along now. I'm curious to see if you can find something the Crowned Prince hasn't."

# Chapter Sixteen

Belle opened her eyes once again to find herself in someplace other than her bedroom. The library sprawled before her, taking away her breath as it had the first time. She glanced around to find Aleksander standing near the massive world globe. He spun it easily with one finger—a feat he would not be able to do if this were not a moon dream.

He looked up, meeting her eyes. A smile quirked his lips and Belle couldn't prevent herself from smiling in return. "I would be lying if I didn't say that I was eager to hear what you thought of our great library. I would have given anything to have been with you when you first saw it."

"I wish you had been there." Belle walked over, laying her hands gently on the globe's wooden frame. "Glorious, your Royal Highness. There is no other word for it." She looked into his eyes, trying to convey the full wonder of what she felt. "I've never seen anything like it."

"My Offentlig Rådgiver had said you were awestruck, that you had no words." Aleksander said, using Laramie's official title.

"Oh, I was." Turning away, Belle cast her gaze back around the library taking in every bit of its majesty. "But this entire castle makes me feel that way. Everything in Contefées is much smaller in comparison. Only the mountains and the cathedral even come close to the grandeur that is everywhere here."

"And what word would you use to describe Ms. Tops?" He came around the globe, keeping just feet away from her.

"Shocking," was her gut reaction.

"That she is," He still smiled as he gazed intently upon her.

Thinking of the woman's confidence and pert manner, Belle added, "And wonderful."

Aleksander laughed, its sound was hearty, from deep in his chest. "I knew you'd like her."

"Oh I did. Very much." Belle turned around to face him, her skirts ruffling around her movement. Pressing her chest out slightly, she added playfully. "Perhaps I shall start adorning men's fashions."

He looked down at her, his voice came out like warm honey. "And what a sight you would be."

Belle looked away as a heavy blush filled her cheeks. She put a hand on her chest, attempting the calm the sudden excitement there. "Your Royal Highness—"

"Mademoiselle," he cut off whatever nervous reply she was about to mutter. He stepped even closer, reaching out like he almost meant to reach for her, and said softly, "I'd like very much for you to call me by my name from now on."

Feeling a warmth mingle with the strange nervousness that Aleksander brought out of her, she dropped her hand and clasped them at her front. "Then you shall call me, Belle, from now on."

He nodded and looked at her with unguarded eyes. Their openness tugged at her, wanting to pull her in. Not for the first time since the garden, Belle wondered at the unfamiliar way he made her feel. But this time, she also wondered at how he felt about her.

Fingers taking hold of the polished banister, Belle started down the long staircase leading to the library's bottom floor. Ms. Tops hadn't made an appearance the entire afternoon that Belle had been there. It made no difference though. She'd found the shelves on Norse Mythology that Ms. Tops had taken her to yesterday. In her arms, Belle now carried a small stack of volumes she had yet to read through.

The sound of footsteps drew Belle's eyes up as she neared the bottom. A young man approached with purpose. He watched Belle with confident and curious eyes. At the base of the staircase, he met her.

"My sister did not exaggerate when she spoke of your beauty." He reached out, taking Belle's books. "And she would know, being the pinnacle of beauty herself."

"Is it Lady Liv Calland that you speak of?" Belle asked, taking his cue to be forward. The man was of noble birth, or at least wealthy, judging solely upon his fine clothing.

"It is." Supporting the books in one arm, he snatched up Belle's hand and pressed his lips to her glove. "Lord Audun Calland, at your service."

Calculating eyes stared through dark lashes at her. The man was handsome, there was no doubt. He had a slimmer frame than Aleksander or Gastone. His hair was also kept short, every strand in its proper place. He straightened, smiling at her with dashing white teeth. But his eyes held Belle's attention. His body language, his voice, was kind, but the coldness in his eyes ruined the facade.

"What brings you to the library, your Lordship?" Belle asked, trying to ignore the uneasy feeling he cast upon her.

"You." He started toward the hearth, carrying the books with ease. "The servants said you were using the library and I thought I'd come meet you."

"And you are not required to have guards at all times." Belle inquired as she followed him. "Especially when around me?"

The moment they came within the fireplace's radius, the heat from it was tangible. As expected, the hearth was larger than normal. One could stand on the opposite side of the library and see the enormous blaze from across the room. The fireplace was elegant in its design with a gold and white frame. At the crown of the frame was the torso of an armored angel. She was fierce and beautiful. Her large white wings were spread out, fading into the woodwork.

Audun set her books upon a small table next to a high-backed, velvet red chair. It was precisely where Belle had intended to do her reading.

"I am not as delicate as my dear sister." He faced her again, patting a jewel encrusted dagger at his hip. "I see you are in fact researching the curse as the servants have been saying. Any luck?"

"None so far. The Crowned Prince has been very thorough in his own research and I've uncovered nothing that he hasn't already." She frowned, unable to deny her own disappointment in this.

"Well, I'm not surprised. What could a commoner uncover that our king-to-be cannot?" Audun leaned against one of the chairs, not batting an eye at his statement.

"I am not *just* a commoner, your Lordship." Belle bristled, fighting to answer respectfully. "I stand on the opposite side of this curse and, therefore, see it in a different light. I believe that is why your king-to-be has given me this task."

"Ah, that's right. You're a—what did they call you—a Hunter." Audun stood back up, taking a new interest in her. "You're a killer." He chuckled, sliding his eyes up and down her body. "Nothing common about that."

"Protector is more accurate," she responded, her body tensing to his leer.

He waved a dismissive hand. "Clearly you aren't like other women, so I won't waste your time with idle flirting. Shall we?"

Belle crinkled her eyebrows at him. "Excusez-moi?"

"A dalliance, my dear." He reached out, running his fingers along her arm. "Some maids actually think that by striking up a romance with me, they'll have a chance at bettering their situation. But I am a noble, deserving of a noble wife and barrens. You're clearly intelligent for someone of your station, so you likely already know this. It could be a very freeing experience for the both of us."

"It's time for you to leave, your Lordship." Belle stepped away from him, bumping into the chair behind her. Not once had his gaze left her chest and only now did he meet her eyes. Determinedly, she added, "Insult me no further and I will choose to forget this ever happened."

"You're actually refusing me?"

Belle raised her chin in answer.

Audun's chest filled with air, the muscles in his jaw flexed from the gritting of his teeth. This was not the reaction he had expected from her. His eyes racked up her frame again. This time it was a criticizing gesture. "You know the soldiers talk about your legs? They said when you arrived that you had your dress hiked up like some French prostitute."

"If you will not leave, than I will." She made to do just that, but Audun stepped in her path.

"Show me what the soldiers saw?" He motioned with a thrust of his head, staring down at her billowing skirts.

Belle gasped. "I will certainly not!"

Now, more than ever, she wanted her revolvers. She wouldn't

even need to draw them. The very sight of them at her side would be enough to dissuade him.

"Never has a woman refused me." He glared at her in pure shock.

"Apparently, it is time that one did."

His nostrils flared, his fists clenched, and his eyes went back to her skirts. Belle knew what he was going to do the second he decided to do it. Her body tensed in anticipation.

"I will not let some filthy commoner belittle me." Audun lunged for her skirts.

As his hands went for her dress, Belle grabbed his dagger. He clawed at her legs, attempting to drag up the layers of fabric. Swiftly, she drew the knife and brought the blade to his throat. She applied pressure, making sure he felt it. His hands stilled as a hiss slipped through his teeth.

"I have killed more men, women, and children with this one hand over the span of one night than you will in your entire, privileged life. Do not mistake me for some common trollop. Now back up," she ordered.

"You whore," he spat and carefully stepped back.

Belle was really getting tired of men calling her that. A droplet of blood ran down the dagger's blade. "Well, this is one whore who won't be giving you a complimentary peep show."

"When I'm done with you, you'll wish you had." He sneered, eyes bulging with anger. How could she have thought he was handsome before? "What do you think will happen when I say that you pulled a knife on me? The word of Lord Calland's heir or that of the French intruder; who will they believe?"

Belle glared, but before she could reply, a massive tome appeared over Audun. It came down suddenly, slamming heavily into his head. He wobbled, his eyes rolled, and down he went.

From Audun's unconscious form on the floor, Belle looked at her rescuer.

Ms. Tops nodded to Belle, still grasping the large book in her hands. A thin strand of silver hair had come loose from her bun. "I've had quite enough of his noise in my library."

Belle laughed, relieved to see the woman. "What book is that?"

"The Complete Collection Of Greek Gods And Their Myths." Ms. Tops heaved the book up and carried it over to one of the side tables. It thudded when she released it. "Lord Gaubert thought he could romance the widowed Lady Ostrem with a few select readings of Aphrodite's exploits. I don't know if he was successful, but he did manage to spill wine on it. Thankfully, I was able to save it."

"Yes, thankfully, indeed." An idea then fell into Belle's mind, like it had been dropped from the heavens. "Ms. Tops, has Aleksander ever read any books about Greek Mythology?"

The Librarian adjusted her glasses thoughtfully. "Not since his youth, when it was part of his studies. Why?"

"It was a norn that created the curse. According to Norse Mythology, a norn is a controller of fate." Stepping over Audun, Belle went excitedly to Ms. Tops. "In *Greek* Mythology there are beings that control fate as well, but they're not called norns. They're actually called fates. Still, what if these beings are the same? And what if the Greeks wrote something about them that the Norse did not?"

Ms. Tops looked at her approvingly. "We have exactly three books dedicated to fate lore and four-hundred and eighty-one which mention them."

Belle teasingly pretended to think on it, then nodded. "Let's start with the three first, I think."

"Of course, mademoiselle." Ms. Tops pointed to Audun. "Help me get his Lordship into the chair first?"

"Oh yes." Belle had already forgotten about the awful man in her excitement. She walked over to grab his hands while the Librarian took his legs. "What will you do about him?"

"Let him sleep his anger off here." Ms. Tops grunted as they lifted him up and dropped him ungracefully into one of the armchairs. "You need not worry about him accusing you. He'd never admit that two women got the best of him."

"What about you though?" Belle stuffed his dagger back into his belt loop. "I'd hate to leave you here with the brute."

"Belle, Dear, worry not," she began with a smile. Belle raised an eyebrow at the use of her first name. Ms. Tops used it as formally as she did Aleksander's. "I'll simply step out when he awakens and he'll leave with no further harm done." Ms. Tops moved around Belle and headed toward the other side of the library. "Now let's get you those books, so you can impress Aleksander."

Belle followed and was about to deny wanting to impress the Prince, but then decided, since the Librarian used her formal name that she would ask something else. "Ms. Tops, what should I call you from now on?"

She glanced back only briefly. "Call me Ms. Tops, Dear."

Belle frowned.

# Chapter Seventeen

fter receiving the three books on Greek fates, Belle was escorted back to her room. As she swept through the thick white doors, she was greeted by the aroma of roasted goose. Edvina was assisting another servant in setting a small dinner table.

Immediately she came over to take the books from Belle's arms. "You're just in time, Dear. Any luck today?"

"Perhaps." Belle took a seat at the table and the other servant laid an ivory napkin over her lap. "I don't wish to get any hopes up, but I may have at least found an area that the Crowned Prince hasn't covered yet."

"Wonderful!" Though her voice was bright, the excitement didn't really reach Edvina's face. Being stuck in this castle for so long likely made it difficult to get excited too soon.

The woman came over, taking her seat opposite Belle. As she did, Belle asked about Edvina's day. Here the woman truly brightened. She talked about the latest castle gossip, her day-to-day overseeing the rooms in her charge, her husband needing an inch added to his waistband, and the latest public fight between Lord and Lady Dahling in one of the drawing rooms.

They waded through the meal and indulged in the wine. Edvina's enthusiastic storytelling had Belle forgetting her own dramatic event in the library. After dinner, Belle curled up in front of the fire to begin reading one of the books she'd brought from the library. Edvina had the dishes cleared and the table removed, then she went off to check on her rooms.

When she returned it was time to ready Belle for bed, and by then the Hunter had already read several chapters. Standing in front of the mirror, Edvina helped remove the fancy purple and white gown Belle had been given today.

"Oh, my dear, what happened?" Edvina's fingers, leathery from hard work, glanced across the red marks on Belle's thigh. Belle was surprised to see them, she hadn't thought Audun had been able to grab her so roughly. "Please tell me you haven't taken up with one of the guards? I had high hopes for you and Prince Aleksander."

Shocked, Belle waved away the woman's hand. "Of course not! My God, Edvina, really."

The older woman shrugged.

"Even us career women need love." Then she turned an accusatory eye on Belle, reminding her of her own mother when she'd caught Belle trouble making. "If it wasn't from a love affair, then how did you get it?"

Belle crossed her arms, unable to not turn her eyes away. It was bad enough that she'd had to go through it, did she really have to talk about it? Knowing that Edvina would not let up, she said, "It was Lord Audun Calland. He . . . propositioned me and didn't like that I refused him."

Edvina's hand shot to her mouth, stifling a gasp. "He tried to *force* you?"

"No, I don't think he intended to take it that far. I think he just wanted to humiliate me." Belle dropped her hands, raising her chin. "But he underestimated me and I made sure he knew it."

Smiling, Edvina slapped Belle's shoulder. "Good for you,

Child. Some of these soft-handed lords need a lesson in class."

"Well, he got one." Belle blushed some under the woman's praise.

Gentle hands grasped Belle's shoulders, causing her to look up into the mirror; into Edvina's eyes. "But you'll have to tell his Royal Highness."

Belle's stomach dropped, hating the idea of repeating the story to Aleksander. "I knew I'd have to tell someone. If I didn't, Audun might do worse to some girl who couldn't defend herself. But I thought I'd tell Monsieur Petit."

With sympathetic eyes, Edvina shook her head. "No, Dear. You're the Prince's charge. Under his protection. If you go to anyone else with this, it'll show a lack of confidence in him."

"But that's absurd! I have full confidence in him."

"It won't matter. That's how others will see it. That's how the Prince will see it." She squeezed Belle's shoulders. "They put on a lot of airs, but don't be fooled, men are very sensitive creatures. You wouldn't want to stop your romance before it even started, would you?"

Belle spun around, scowling down at the short woman. "What is this you keep going on about? Me and Prince Aleksander?"

"What?" She looked around the room, as if she could find what caused Belle's confusion. "Is the Crowned Prince not handsome enough for you?"

"Well of course he is. The man is beautiful." She stepped around Edvina, moving over by the fire. "But he is a Prince—who is soon-to-be king—and I am a hunter—no, a peasant."

"So?"

Belle wheeled on Edvina. "So! Royalty marries royalty. No matter what old fairytales say, there is no hope of a happily ever after for the Crowned Prince and I."

The idea was absurd. Belle didn't mean to have a temper with Edvina, but the silliness of this whole conversation was vexing. It just wasn't done. It would be so easy for her to fall for the Prince, but it wasn't as though he would reciprocate. Really, what would be the point if he did?

"Oh, my dear." Edvina sighed, her eyes softening in a way that immediately calmed Belle's anger. She gently took Belle by the arms and guided her back toward the mirror to look at herself. She reached up and began pulling the many hairpins from Belle's hair. Softly, the curls started to fall free, to bounce at her shoulders. Edvina spoke as she worked. "Better to have a grand love that is fleeting, than one that is ordinary and lasts till death." Pulling out the last pins, she added. "As a woman bound for an early grave, wouldn't you agree?"

Feeling her heart double its pace, Belle realized that she did.

"There's something that I need to tell you," Belle said as Aleksander flipped through the only book in his study on Greek mythology. When she told him about her idea, he'd stared at her in disbelief. He then confessed to being narrow-minded and unwilling to see the curse through the eyes of anything other than Norse theology. Quite suddenly he was renewed and eager to get back into their research, but this time with a focus on fates. As Belle watched his excitement grow, she found her own nerves quailing. "It's about Lord Audun Calland."

Aleksander's hand abruptly halted in mid-turn. He slowly lowered the book and strangely guarded eyes looked back at her. His face was a straight mask, only his fingers rubbing the old pages between them hinted at his emotions. "You've met Audun, have you?"

"Yes." Belle shifted her weight between her feet, trying to keep herself from looking away in embarrassment. "We met yesterday in the library."

Jerking slightly, Aleksander's eyebrows came together in confusion. His fingers stopped their fidgeting. "And?"

"He ... um ..." Try as she might, Belle couldn't look at Aleksander directly. The words she had to say were just too much.

There was a thud as Aleksander dropped the book roughly and came around the desk quickly. He stopped a few feet from her, his fingers clenching in and out of fists. "What did he do, Belle?"

Taking a deep breath, she decided just to be done with it. Belle looked at Aleksander and forced the awful words out. "He attacked me. Tried to force himself ..."And that's where her throat betrayed her, cutting off the rest.

Judging by Aleksander, she'd said enough. His body was tense. The muscles in his jaw flexed. He took slow, deep breaths. "Tried?"

"Yes, I used his own dagger against him, but it was Ms. Tops' interference that really ended it."

"I'll give her a raise," Aleksander said matter-of-factly. "But not until after I've dealt with Audun."

Chagrin bled into Belle's stomach. The Prince had so much to handle already and she felt terrible for adding to it, even though the logical part of her knew that none of this was her fault. "Perhaps nothing more is needed. Surely being subdued by two women is enough."

The muscles in Aleksander's cheeks softened and the shield that had appeared over his eyes vanished. He looked at her in the same open way he always had. Stepping the last few feet toward her, he took her hands in his and cradled them gently. Only then did she realize they were trembling.

"My father was a very proud and fierce man, who instilled every value and lesson he had into me." Aleksander's thumb softly ran along her wrist, sending waves of calm through her. "Audun learned his way of thinking from another man, or possibly men. For him to learn the proper way of treating women, he must also learn it from a man. Do you understand?"

"Yes." She nodded. "I believe I do."

He stared down at her, still holding her hands, as he pursed his lips in thought. "How do you feel about a distraction?"

"I'd love one." She sighed with relief, so glad that it was over. "What did you have in mind?"

"I think I'd like to tell you about my family." He blinked slowly.

Just like that, the room changed. Belle gasped. Gone was the study and in its place was an immense hall. The floor was a map—an incredibly detailed map with mountains, waves, and the painted names of each country. Natural light flooded the room from one wall of tall arching windows with frames of gold and heavy draperies. The only furniture was a large desk, covered in various bits of parchment and one feathered quill, on one end of the room. And many knee-high statues. They were various ships, cavalrymen, cannons, and men-at-arms. Looking more closely at them, Belle noticed that they each carried different flags. There was a set for every army in the world.

"This is my war room. I learned battle strategy here as a boy." He let go of her hands and motioned to the floor. "On this floor map, my ancestor kings planned wars." He brought his hand up and pointed to the desk. "On that desk, a thousand treaties and laws were signed into being."

Belle looked from the floor to the desk, trying to imagine all those that had come before. She felt the weight of the history in this room. Then she looked at Aleksander with awe, seeing that he proudly carried that weight. Knowing that he so excitedly shared it with her, made her own chest feel too heavy.

"My family can trace its lineage clear back to the first Viking kings, through the line of Eirik Haraldsson the First." Aleksander swung his hand up, pointing to the ceiling. There was a master-piece that, like the library, some talented artisan had no doubt toiled under for years. Here the ceiling was all one piece. Two battles, seemingly of different eras, were being waged. Between them, on a clouded dusk sky, an army of angels watched. Aleksander pointed to one army along the painting's edge. This was an army of both men and women. They wore heavy Viking armor; carried swords, axes, and bows. "He was nicknamed Eirik Bloodaxe after his war with the frost giants."

Belle examined the Viking king wielding a two-headed ax against a creature made of ice. The invading army of otherworldly giants had jagged skin, their eyes were an icy blue, and they carried frosted swords. Where the frost giants walked, ice spread from their feet. Eirik showed no fear as he led the front siege.

"The Haraldsson line would eventually be unseated from the thrown and lost in time for many centuries. Destined to rule as we were, our lineage gave us favor with King Fredrick the Third who granted us lordship over Vakre Fjell. A century later when a different ruler of Norway tried to remove us from power because of our faith, we fought back. And became kings once more." His hands swiveled to the other side of the ceiling. Men fought from mountains. Ships battled at sea. "Two battles, from two distinct times in our history and Valkyries in the center looking for warriors to carry to Valhalla."

"You know your history well."

"It's important to know our history if I am to rule. I must understand my ancestors and make sure my rule continues to honor the kings who came before me." Aleksander shrugged in an un-princely way.

"Do you believe the story of frost giants?" Belle crossed the room to stand before a mural that nearly consumed the entirety of a wall. Here was a picturesque painting of Vakre Fjell, before the castle had been built. The land was majestic, fertile, and entirely untouched by man. A blond haired god, Belle recognized as Thor from her reading, with a red cloak and shining armor stood before the mountains. With a massive hammer, too big for a normal man, Thor was pushing back one of the mountains and creating the deep chasm that now surrounded the front of Castle Vakre Fjell. "Or this?"

"Well, that is most certainly a myth. A story told around the fire." Aleksander laughed and a delightful smile curved his lips. "But then, not long ago I would have said the same about the tale of Eirik and the frost giants. After what happened here, even that seems possible to me."

Belle turned her attention back to the frost giants above. She examined their details, trying to imagine if they were real. The very idea of them walking the ground, spreading their cold with each step, sent a chill through her. Aleksander was right though, given everything she'd seen, why could that story not be true?

"Since we're here, how do you feel about war games?" Aleksander walked purposefully to the room's center.

"Is it similar to chess?" Belle enjoyed playing chess with Henri and the other Hunters.

"Similar yes, but based in reality." He stepped around the pieces to stop by a handful of galleons and fire ships, bearing the French flag. "You shall be France, I will be Vakre Fjell, and the goal is a classic scenario—world domination."

She returned his wicked smile and moved over to her pieces. Her gaze swept to the details below; from the rocky oceans to the icy ends of the Earth. Taking a half step back, she looked at the depiction of God's Cup. Strangely, a section of Glace was mis-colored, defining it from the rest. Contefées fell within this stretch of land. "Why is this section off-colored?"

"Because five years ago it was meant to be mine."

# Chapter Eighteen

Staring at Aleksander, Belle couldn't quite fathom what he just said. "I'm sorry, did I hear you right? That section of land is supposed to belong to Vakre Fjell?"

"Begin setting up your defenses and I will explain everything." Aleksander casually indicated the grouping of war vessels around France. "Anything with a French flag is yours to maneuver." He took hold of a large galleon ship and lightly pushed it across the floor. "Let me ask you a question first. Has the French Emperor married?"

"Yes, he—" Belle looked up from her own game pawns. "Well, he married your sister, Princess Adelis."

Aleksander nodded, not turning from his strategic planning. "That is good. It was part of the trade."

"What trade?" She moved a large cavalry statue to France's border.

"How well do you know *your* history, Belle?"

"Not as well as you." She smiled playfully.

"Charming." Aleksander chuckled. "In the 1650s, Norway traded a section of Vakre Fjell to Glace, do you recall that?"

Belle thought and a brief recollection of her history lessons returned. "A portion of Vakre Fjell went to Glace in exchange for the hand of a French princess. Contefées was part of that trade—Oh, is this the same land?"

"It is." Aleksander nodded enthusiastically. "The current French Emperor made a request for Adelis' hand and my father proposed that we recreated the trade from the 1650s. My sister marries the French Emperor and he grants our land back to us."

"If this deal took place five years ago, why hasn't it happened?" Belle could hardly believe the idea that by now she should be a Vakrein citizen and not of France. It seemed too strange an idea to her.

"Now that is the question to be asked." Aleksander moved two more of his pieces into motion. It appeared that he intended to take the rest of God's Cup first. "Once he'd met with my sister and a marriage was inevitable, he was to sign the treaty and then marry her. I now know he married her, but it seems that the curse may have halted his signature. I intend to find out why."

"And then what will you do?" Belle asked, intrigued by this bit of royal drama.

"I will make sure our agreement is fulfilled."

The following day came and went in a flurry of research. Every second was spent reading the books on Greek mythology. Unfortunately, Belle's endless reading had yielded nothing new. When Aleksander pulled her into a moon dream, as per their routine, she was eager for a break.

This time they walked the courtyard, enjoying an unnaturally warm day. A slight breeze fluttered a curl across Belle's cheek. She tucked it back with a gloved hand. Closing her eyes, Belle let the soft wind caress her face. It felt so real to her, even then.

"And what did you name this clockwork pixie?" Aleksander asked.

Belle smiled and opened her eyes. He stood just past her,

looking out over the clouded mountain range. In some ways, the mountains reminded her of the Prince. They were strong and proud, claiming their piece of the earth. They were also beautiful; a majesty unmatched.

"I named her Pixie," she answered.

Now he looked at her, returning the smile she gave him. "Pixie. Truly? That's the best you could do?"

"Yes, I know, it was a bit on the nose, but it fit her."

Aleksander laughed. "Of course it did. I'm surprised you didn't name your horse, Horse, instead."

"Oh my, your Highness, I'm sure you don't mean to imply that I do not have an imagination," she teased.

"I'm afraid, dear Belle, that is just what I'm implying." He turned to her completely, hands clasped behind his back and a grin brightening his face. In these moments, he seemed the freest.

Belle palmed her heart. "Well, I believe I am offended."

"I am sorry." He tilted his head. "Truly a shame that no one has brought this to your attention before and perhaps prepared you for this embarrassment."

Belle's mouth shot open in surprise. She rebutted, "Well then, you've left me with no choice, I must throw down the gauntlet."

"Indeed? A challenge? On what grounds?" Aleksander asked, as amused as she was.

"I claim that you have no more imagination than I." She plucked off her glove, one finger at a time. Feigning disgust, Belle tossed it to the ground. "Do you accept?"

Prince Aleksander struggled to push away his smile. "This is a most serious charge, so I must. It is my family's honor at stake."

A giggle slipped out of Belle as Aleksander bent over to pick up her glove. "Truly, it is."

"So how do you suggest we settle this?" He held the glove in his hand, moving the fabric between his fingers.

"I couldn't help noticing that," Belle began, getting her emotions back in check. "Even though this scenery is all in your head, you haven't done anything interesting with it. I mean, you create whatever you want, correct?"

"Yes, I can." A knowing washed over his face. "What is it that you would like me to change for you? I'm sure the creativeness of it will astound you."

"No doubt." She inclined her head and then thought for a moment. Quickly the idea came to her and she was too eager to hold it back. "A dragon."

Aleksander blinked twice at her. "A dragon."

"If you cannot do it, my prince, I understand, but then I must insist on an apology." She fluttered her eyelashes and smiled at him innocently. "For I will have won the challenge."

"You are a dangerous woman, mademoiselle." He stared at her lips, his whimsy suddenly gone. A flurry of butterflies swept up in her stomach, stealing her own lighthearted merriment away. Aleksander's eyes met hers and he held them, then with an abrupt turn, his focus shifted back to the mountains. "At any rate, you mustn't worry. I will give you a dragon."

Belle swallowed hard, still unbalanced by his actions. Her hand went to her corseted stomach, trying to settle the lightness that had overtaken her. For the first time in her life, Belle understood why some women insisted on sitting a spell because they unexpectedly felt faint. No doubt it was always on the account of a man. Did all men know the effect they could have on women? Did Aleksander? If they did, they should certainly refrain from looking and speaking to a woman in such a way. Belle, for one, did not care for the way she suddenly felt so delicate.

"How should he look?" The Prince kept his back to her. Belle took his cue and turned her attention to the mountain range.

She cleared her throat. "He should be large and his scales should shimmer in the light."

Aleksander didn't respond. Belle stepped up beside him and saw that he had closed his eyes, mentally creating the fantasy creature. Her own eyes studied the steadfast arches of his eyebrows and the cheeks that looked soft to the touch.

A roar bellowed from beyond the mountains. It reverberated through the air and smacked against the stone walls behind them. Surprised, Belle looked to the sound. The Prince opened his eyes.

From behind the snow-covered peaks, an actual dragon appeared. Great wings carried him into the sky, higher and higher into the blue. He roared again like it was a call to war.

"My God," Belle said breathlessly.

She took a step forward, lips parted in awe. Belle could hardly believe it. The dragon turned in the sky, each beat of his wings thudding against the air and keeping him aloft. He came up on them quickly and swooped down, as though he did intend to eat them.

Belle unconsciously tensed. At the last second, he stretched out his wings and soared up to the castle turrets. His claws dropped down onto one spiraled tower, knocking snow and shingles loose. The dragon opened its mouth. Fire erupted forth, rippling out into many scolding swells. It spread into the sky before gradually extinguishing.

"Oh, that's wonderful!" Belle said with a breathless laugh.

Then quite suddenly the sky dimmed as if dusk were setting. Belle looked to the Prince in confusion. His eyes were closed, allowing him total focus. Then all at once, the courtyard was illuminated. Every rose brightened like a flame. Every tree and bush shined with a celestial light. The vines that crawled the walls were like glowing, green snakes.

Belle gasped, spinning to take it all in. Then one by one, new plants began to grow. They were large, exaggerated versions of the exotic lovelies that grew in the greenhouse. These too glowed in an array of reds, purples, blues, whites, and more colors than the rainbow. Belle reached out to touch a flower that was as large as she. It was velvety soft.

"Oh my, Aleksander . . ." She looked up at him.

The Prince plucked a luminescent rose from the surrounding stone wall. He twirled it in fingers and walked toward her. The rose's light touched his skin with soft shadings of red.

Aleksander watched her. The look in his eyes, of utter intensity. "Do you like it?"

Gulping, Belle choked on nerves to answer. "It's truly beautiful."

"No, you're mistaken," he said plainly, coming within arm's reach of her. "My father taught me what true beauty is, and this is not it."

"Oh?" was her doltish reply.

Closer still, Aleksander came. His arms went around Belle, causing her to stop breathing. She thought he was going to hug her, but then she found him fiddling with the up-pulled ringlets of her hair. Belle raised her face just slightly, bringing her lips only inches from his neck. The desire to touch him was almost unbearable.

When Aleksander withdrew, the glowing rose was gone. Belle instinctively reached back to feel the flower nestled in her hair. He took her hand from the petals, guiding it before him and splayed out her fingers. Slowly, with an impressive delicacy, he slid Belle's glove over her skin. Aleksander took care, nudging the fabric on one finger at a time. "You are as beautiful on the inside as you are on the outside. It is a quality that is lost on most women. Belle, you are a *true* beauty."

Belle stared at their touching hands, then turned her gaze up to his eyes. His own lovely blues ran over her eyelashes and down her cheekbone, taking in every detail of her face. She struggled to breathe, her heartbeat was little more than a speeding flutter within her chest. Leaning in just slightly, she hoped for a kiss—a physical expression of those lovely words. She found that she didn't want to just hear his feelings; she wanted to touch them—experience them upon her.

"Belle! Mademoiselle!" Someone shook Belle's shoulders roughly. "You must wake up."

A horrible sensation swept through Belle's body. It was somewhere between disorientation and nausea. Pushing herself up, Belle blinked and grabbed her head. The glowing courtyard was gone . . . Aleksander was gone. Disappointment shattered within her.

"You're in the library, my dear," said Ms. Tops, who leaned over her. "You fell asleep here. Laramie has come to fetch you."

Body aching, Belle stretched. Her mouth was dry. The memory of Aleksander's closeness, of her desire to kiss him, came back to her and she knew exactly why she was so parched. Belle was filled with a sudden awareness of the Prince now. Her skin buzzed from the strange, new emotions he'd put upon her. He was in her thoughts, his name was on her tongue, his touch on her hand, and it was hard to deny that he might have a hold on her heart as well.

Taking a second to adjust herself, Belle stared at the roaring fire before her. The hearth was so inviting it was no wonder she had fallen asleep while reading. No more than a few hours could have passed, but her dream felt much longer—as though she'd spent a full evening with the Prince.

Not wanting to keep Laramie or Ms. Tops waiting, she stood and quickly pushed the wrinkles out of her dress. Even Ms. Tops helped to fluff and fix Belle's crushed hair. The library was dark. Aside from the fire, there were no other sources of light. All around her was a vast blackness. Belle found that she didn't care for libraries at night. It was a bit too spooky for her taste, and it ruined the newfound tingles on her skin.

"Come, Dear," Ms. Tops encouraged, taking the lead.

She held a candlestick aloft, its wax melting and dripping down the long taper. Belle stayed close, listening to their echoing footstep and seeing the glint of gold from the wall inlays and the finely painted book spines. The library's center, the circle of statues, was the worst. The subtle illumination along their faces and sharp weapons made the figures appear far more menacing than during the day. Clutching her Greek books to her chest, Belle couldn't wait to get out of there.

Ms. Tops pushed open the library door when they reached the entrance. Though the hallways were only lit by candelabras every few yards, it was still brighter than the library. Laramie, holding a candlestick of his own, turned at the sound of the door opening. The usual two guards waited at his side.

"Here she is, monsieur," Ms. Tops said, holding the door as Belle past through. "Don't reprimand her too harshly, I believe his Royal Highness had her in one of his dreams. You know how hard those are to wake from."

Laramie nodded to Ms. Tops. "Thank you, madame."

"But, of course. Good night, Belle." Giving Belle a wink, she turned back into the library and the door pulled closed on its own.

"So *were* you in a dream?" Laramie gestured for her to walk alongside him.

"I was, yes. I'm surprised Ms. Tops guessed." Belle kept pace with Laramie, relieved that he didn't seem angry with her. The clopping of heavy soldier boots followed behind and, after the unsettlingly dark library, she was grateful for it.

"She has an eerie intelligence." Laramie looked over at Belle as they rounded the stairs. "I'm sorry she had to wake you. I've been awoken abruptly from a moon dream before and I know how unpleasant it can be."

Putting a hand on her unsettled stomach, she said, "Not quite the same as waking from a normal dream is it?"

"No, not at all." They fell silent as they traversed the rest of the way until they reached the guest rooms. Then Laramie turned a half-smile toward her. "To forewarn you, Madame Gulbrandsen was worked into quite a tizzy when she summoned me to fetch you. Worried like a mother hen."

"Oh, dear." Belle laughed.

One of the apartment doors swung open and someone stumbled into their path. Laramie drew up short and Belle halted only a pace behind him. At first Belle didn't recognize the person, but then her eyes focused as the candlelight fell on the man. Belle bit back her surprise.

Lord Audun Calland grasped an open wine bottle. He wavered in place as his glossed eyes moved from Laramie to Belle. Even in the dim light, she could see that there was more wrong with him than drunkenness. One eye was swollen, his skin blackened. His lip had been busted and Belle would have guessed there were more injuries she couldn't see. When her gaze shifted to his disheveled clothes, she found a fair bit of dried blood.

"My Lordship," Laramie said, bowing.

Audun stared at Belle, seeing and not seeing her. He raised the mouth of the wine bottle to his forehead in a sort of mock salute. Then his gaze shifted wildly around the hall. Lips pursed, he gave them a wide berth and continued without looking back. Laramie signaled for one of the guards to follow the Calland heir.

When Laramie saw the look on Belle's face, he added, "Best not worry about that."

# Chapter Nineteen

elle sighed and sunk lower into her morning bath, listening to the servant girl read from one of the Greek books. It was the usual stuff, a story of a hero who came in search of changing fate. Every chance Belle had she was reading the new material. She even requested that a servant read aloud while Belle bathed. There was no time to be wasted.

The door burst open with a clatter. Belle reflexively covered herself and the servant girl jumped in surprise. When she recovered, clutched her chest, the girl mumbled in Vakrein about losing her place. The intruder was Edvina, who came and went as she pleased and didn't notice the shock she'd created.

"Oh dear! Oh dear!" she worried audibly as she shuffled through the tray of bathing amenities. "So much to do!"

"Edvina, what is it?" Belle asked, watching the woman frown.

"Well, he's given us no time!" The woman picked up a bottle, read it, and then chose another. She glanced at Belle quickly with wide eyes. "It is exciting though, isn't it?"

"What is?" Both Belle and servant girl said in unison.

"The ball, of course!" She opened up one of the bottles, sniffed it, and poured the oil into Belle's bathwater. Realizing that they were staring at her, she added, "Don't tell me you don't know? The Crowned Prince is throwing a ball. Tonight!"

The servant girl jumped up, letting the poor book tumble to the floor. She squealed something incomprehensible with her Vakrein accent. Edvina turned and hopped with the girl, including her own excited giggles.

Then she paused and said to Belle, "In your honor!"

"Me?" Belle sat up, pulling her legs into her chest. The bath was starting to get cold. It was still so strange to Belle that she couldn't just flip a lever to add more hot water. "But why?"

"Don't be daft, Child." Edvina waved her off. To the servant girl, she said. "Come, there's a lot of preparation to be done."

With no other word to Belle, they left. The room went silent; no sound other than the wind outside, the sloshing of the bathwater, and the crackling fire. It was odd to be alone, since that hardly happened in this castle. Normally there was even someone there to wrap her in a towel as she climbed from the tub.

Belle stood, shivering as the water ran off her body. She stepped out of the tub and grabbed the towel laid nearby. Quickly, she started to dry herself. Leaning down to dry her legs, Belle noticed that she'd gotten water on the book. She swore and snatched it up, dabbing at the pages. Ms. Tops was going to chastise her for sure.

Her eyes glanced over the pages she dried, realizing that she hadn't read them before. Her hands stilled, noticing one emphasized section.

I.   *The Laws of Fatum as spoken by the Oracle of Delphi:*
II.  *Once the path is set, a Fate cannot leave it.*
III. *A Fate wields a universal power unto her path and unto all else, she wields none.*
IV.  *Only by her own power can a Fate be destroyed.*

"Oh my God." The words came out as a whisper. She clutched the pages with barely contained excitement. Something new! Something that could lead to lifting the curse.

Belle rushed to the door with book in hand. She stopped short of the handle, realizing that she had to dress. But there were more obstacles than just proper clothing standing in her way. Aside from the library, the guards would permit her to go nowhere else. She had to get the book to the Prince, but until Edvina returned there was nothing Belle could do. Not even a moon dream would work, since it was daytime and the act required them both to be asleep.

Instead, Belle dried and threw on one of the many silk nightgowns kept in her wardrobe. Sitting by the fire, she reread the page several times and the surrounding chapters. By the time Edvina reappeared, Belle had taken to pacing as she attempted to fully comprehend the Laws of Fatum.

"My goodness, Child," Edvina said as she came through the door and took one look at Belle's fretting. "You'll worry yourself into your death bed. What is it?"

"Edvina!" Belle marked the page and rushed over to the woman. "This needs to be taken to the Crowned Prince. He must read the page that I've marked."

Edvina took it from her, glancing over the book. "Oh, did you find something?"

"It could possibly be . . . the hope that Aleksander was looking for."

"*Aleksander*, is it?" Edvina looked at her with a sly smirk.

Belle frowned. "Really, Edvina. Now is not the time."

Edvina chuckled, her whole body shaking. "All right, Dear, I'll make sure it gets to him right away."

The woman disappeared outside the door, leaving Belle ringing her hands. After several minutes, Edvina came back. This time without the book.

"Don't fuss, he'll be reading it soon," Edvina said. "Now, we have to talk about your hair."

Belle looked at her strangely, her hand going to the nighttime braid. "My hair?"

"Oh yes. What you wear to the ball is out of our hands, but your hair will keep us plenty busy." She started ushering Belle over to the vanity. "That stylist had better get here soon."

And he did, along with a small team. They combed and oiled each lock, layer by layer, prepping it for the complicated design he had planned. Hours drew by with Belle seated patiently. Only once, at Edvina's insistence, had she been allowed to stand and stretch her limbs.

Edvina was busier than the stylist, overseeing the entire affair. Servants came and went frequently, each with some new problem that needed to be solved. As the Majordome for the guests, it was Edvina's job to make sure they all had everything they needed for the event. A few times she was even pulled away to see to a problem in person. The stylist was just finishing up when Edvina returned from her last excursion.

"It's lovely, Dear," she said as one of the assistants handed Belle a mirror.

Holding the small mirror up, Belle turned her head from side to side. Her curls were piled high onto the crown of her head. Each ringlet was tightly set in place. Only a handful of hair hung without restraint. It laid down her back's center like a waterfall of curls. The expensive oils had done their jobs, giving Belle's hair a brilliant, controlled sheen. Belle found that she could hardly stop staring. Her Governess machine back home had given her many lovely and complex hairdos, but this was something that only talented, human hands could do.

The bedroom door burst open and a whole troupe of people traipsed through. It startled Belle, causing her to almost drop the mirror. The assistant took it back with a smile.

"I have done it." The head seamstress parted the crowd with

her proclamation. She wore a simple but ornate black and white dress. Glasses hung on a chain at her chest, measuring tape on a loop at her hip, and a marking pen and several pins were stuffed in her bun. "I'd been designing it for days now, per his specifications. Then just like that he wants it done all in a day. Never mind that every lord and lady in this castle suddenly wants work done."

"Is it the dress?" Edvina clutched her chest with overwhelming excitement.

"Of course." She gave Edvina a very dry look. "His Royal Highness commissioned this dress nearly a week ago, for Mademoiselle LeClair. And despite the little time he gave me to do it, I have created a masterpiece."

Belle looked over the crowd, trying to find any sign of a dress, but there were too many people. They had piled in, filling up half the room. Judging by their attire, many worked for the head seamstress and others were servants that had clearly come along just for the reveal.

"Enough." The seamstress waved an arrogant hand at the twittering servants. "Let them see it then."

The crowd started to shift, all vying for a glimpse and making room. Through the doorway and up the center of the crowd came two younger seamstresses. They gently carried a mannequin. Upon it hung the dress. They set it down and stepped back.

Belle was speechless. She pushed off from her chair to come closer to the gown. Her hand tentatively reached out to touch it but stopped short for fear of hurting it somehow. Edvina and the dozen other people in the room all gasped and commented on the dress's beauty, but Belle heard none of it.

"Green. He chose it for your eyes," The seamstress said quietly, leaning toward Belle. "The skirts are solid silk so that the green can shine from the light. As you see here in the bodice." She softly grazed a hand over the piece. "The gold embroidered reliefs are the only other color I allowed." Moving closer to the dress, the seamstress spoke louder, walking them all through the design. "The chest line is low, but not so low as to be scandalous. The sleeves are not connected to the dress." She stepped behind the ensemble and untied it. "This part wraps your bicep." It was green with the same gold embroidery to match the bodice. From the wrap hung similarly-colored sheer fabric, long enough to reach past her hands. "This part hangs loose and will look lovely twirling around you on the dance floor, much like your skirts."

"It's beautiful," was all Belle could manage, but her pleasure was clear and the seamstress smirked.

Edvina clapped her hands. "Well, we're running short on time. There comes a point when fashionably late is simply late."

Very quickly, the room cleared of everyone, but the head seamstress, the stylist, Edvina, and two assistants. Belle was little more than an object at that point. She was to stand still as they dressed her behind the dressing screen. Eventually, with the corset tight and the detachable sleeves wrapping her arms, Belle stepped out into the open. The stylist rushed over, quickly correcting any loose strand of hair and affixing it over the dress and down her back.

There was a knock at the door. Edvina called for them to enter. In walked a young woman who's simple clothing and hair told Belle that it was another servant, but her clothing was unique to indicate that she had a specific job in the castle that wasn't of the norm. In her hands, she grasped a large, thin box.

"His Royal Highness sends a gift," she said waiting for everyone to fall quiet and look her way. She opened the box and each person gasped. "A selection of the crown jewels to be worn for tonight's event. They were last worn by Queen Catherine. God rest her soul."

"Oh." Edvina clutched her chest, tears starting to form in her eyes. "His mother's."

Belle stepped closer in wonderment of the jewels. One necklace, a bracelet, earrings, and a broach; a matching set. The jewels were green emeralds surrounded by diamonds and gold. The necklace's focal point was three large emeralds grouped together by ribbons of diamonds and four hanging sets of jewels. It reminded her of an upside down crown. The broach was a similar design, except with one teardrop green emerald hanging from it. The earrings were the same tear-shaped emeralds hung by more diamonds.

The keeper of the crown jewels handed the box to Edvina and with gloved hands she removed the necklace. Belle found herself growing straighter as the fine jewelry was placed upon her skin. It was surprising how heavy it was. The same was done with the earrings and bracelet. Only the broach was handed to the stylist, who clipped it into Belle's curls at the crown of her head.

After finishing touches and some last minute primping, they guided her over to the mirror. Belle stared at herself in awe. The bodice of her dress gripped low onto her torso, giving her a slim frame. The low cut corset hugged her chest, both emphasizing it and displaying it without being distasteful. The deep green skirt swept out around her, giving Belle a delicate look that she was not used to. The design of her styled hair was regal, but still very womanly. All of this combined with the sheer, sweeping sleeves, and the set of emerald crown jewels turned Belle into someone of elegance and grace.

She found it was difficult to breath and swallowed hard to keep from crying.

"Tonight." Edvina touched Belle's cheek with the back of her hand. "You—*are*—royalty."

# Chapter Twenty

Warmth shown in Laramie's eyes when he came to escort Belle. He complimented her beauty, saying that the Prince had done well in his choices for her attire. Being reminded that Aleksander was behind all of this sent her heart into a tizzy of flutters and her mouth into a grin that she couldn't force away.

All the while they walked, Laramie instructed her on what to expect from the night and slipped in a few tips. Belle could hear the crowd of guests on the floor below as they neared the final staircase. Only then did Belle begin to grasp the large number of people in the castle who weren't servants. Over the past weeks, she'd only seen a few in passing and met even fewer.

They came to the top of the stairs. Men, women, young, and old, all mulled on the floor below, waiting for the call to dinner. Like Belle, they were dressed in their finest clothes and jewelry. The atmosphere was charged, the very air vibrated with their excitement.

Keeping Belle's hand rested upon his own, Laramie guided her down the stairs. Belle's heart beat painfully within her chest. Most everyone was too preoccupied with their conversations to notice her, but some did and they gestured for others to look as well. Soon half the guests were gawking at her with interest.

Reaching the last few steps, Laramie subtly indicated for Belle to wait. He stepped over to a servant dressed in a fine royal uniform, holding a large golden staff. Laramie whisper to the man who then banged the staff on the ground. The racket it caused echoed off the marble and stone walls, silencing everyone.

Then he shouted, "Mademoiselle Belle LeClair of Glace!"

Time seemed to stop as all eyes turned to her. Belle clenched her teeth, unsure of what to do. Laramie stood off to the side, watching her. Belle took hold of her skirt and carefully walked down to the crowd. Whispers reached her ears and redness crept up into her cheeks.

"Excuse me, your Lordship," said a familiar feminine voice. Belle searched for the owner of the voice and Liv appeared, as she ushered a man out of the way. Beaming from ear to ear she came over to Belle, as though it were perfectly normal, and grabbed both her hands. She then spoke so that only Belle could hear. "Let us look like we're the best of friends. Then they'll stop gawking like fools and I get to look like I'm in on something that they are not. Does this agree with you?"

Belle squeezed the woman's hands back, beyond grateful for her aid. The guests indeed went back to their conversations and only those closest kept turning an eye her way. "I am much accepting of this arrangement."

"Wonderful." Liv stepped back, not letting go of Belle's hands. "Now as proper friends, we must compliment each other's attire. Yours I see comes with a rather *royal* set. Am I correct?"

Belle glanced away, feeling slightly sheepish. Was it bad for her to be wearing crown jewels? Certainly Aleksander wouldn't have dressed her inappropriately, and then sent her to the wolves . . . so to speak. "Yes, they are."

"Every girl here will be jealous." Liv gave her a wink. "The dress, the jewelry, the hair . . . it's all divine. Really brings out your eyes."

"Thank you," Belle said, finding her nerves starting to settle. She gave Liv a quick look over. The young woman was equally lovely, draped in a blue and white satin with long white gloves that reached past her elbows. All of her hair, save for a few blond ringlets was piled up upon her head. "You are a vision."

"Then you and I shall make quite the attractive duo tonight." She moved to Belle's side, hooking her arm with Belle's and started to steer her into the crowd.

Another series of bangs called everyone to silence, but this time the sound came from the other side of the room. From a source that Belle could not see. "Dinner is served!"

"You will sit next to me, won't you, Darling?" Liv asked as they walked with the steady flow of the crowd, heading toward the dining hall.

"Of course, you won't be able to get rid of me."

Liv laughed. The sound was delicate and soft. The epitome of the saying music to one's ears. Liv was everything a lady should be and for the first real time in Belle's life, she envied another woman.

"Now you must do away with the sheepish behavior I saw just a moment ago. Everyone here is your better, but such behavior is for the servants," she whispered seriously into Belle's ear as they walked. "Are you a servant?" Belle barely shook her head. "No, you're not. You're a guest of his Royal Highness, Crowned Prince Regent, Aleksander the First. Show them the confidence that comes along with such an honor and you'll fit right in. I've been told by many sources that you have confidence in bounds, so let's see it."

One long table filled the regal hall. It was set with the finest of dishware, but no food or wine had yet been brought out. Belle followed Liv, who seemed to know exactly her place at the table. Servants weaved themselves throughout the crowd, helping those who needed it. In moments, everyone was seated and through the doors came a long stream of platter-laden servants.

They walked in a perfect line around the table. There was one tray carrying servant for each guest. Their hands swooped down, like a perfectly choreographed dance, to place the first course.

Smiling, Belle glanced over at Liv, who wiggled her eyebrows. That's when Belle noticed that the head of the table was empty, yet a servant was still there to place a setting. Liv saw where she looked. "That is where our host would sit. Since he cannot be here, against his will, a place is set in his honor."

"That's a nice sentiment." Belle watched the servants making the rounds, filling glasses with red wines. "It shows a great deal of respect."

"His Royal Highness has our respect and admiration, there is no doubt about that." Liv sipped her just poured wine.

Soon she introduced Belle to those seated closest. Two of them were the infamous Lord and Lady Dahling that Belle had heard so much about. They seemed to treat each other with as much disdain as one would treat an enemy. They were all polite to Belle, asking her many questions about the world outside. Every now and then the Lord and Lady Dahling would make a quip at the other's expense, which everyone else would pretend not to hear.

Course after course came and Belle learned not to eat so much of any single one or she would fill up far too soon. The food was divine and her wine glass was kept full. The conversation was also free flowing. If anyone was uncomfortable at Belle's presence, they were too well mannered to show it.

Belle learned a fair bit about Liv as the meal drew to an end. She was as intelligent as Laramie had said, as she was highly educated. She was also nothing like her brother, whom Belle hadn't seen all night. Liv admitted that she had little in common with Audun and they rarely spent time together. He had his duties and lessons growing up and she had hers, they were as good as strangers. Liv also admitted that she envied her brother's position and his future running their family's estate. Being a Lord's wife didn't seem to be as stimulating, she said.

When dinner ended, they relocated to the ballroom. Aside from the library, it might have been Belle's favorite room. White walls with heavy and elaborate gold moldings to match. From the ceiling hung immense chandeliers with dangling crystals and burning candles. Great windowed doors surrounded the whole ballroom. They could be opened during the few warm summer months to let guests mingle in the courtyard, but now they were shut tight allowing only a marvelous view of the surrounding mountains. An orchestra played upon a stage at the far end of the room. The ballroom was perfect for the music, it held onto the notes and let them swirl their round sounds among the guests.

Liv introduced Belle to many more people and some came over with the pretense of greeting Liv, but with the intention of meeting the strange outsider. Belle curtsied more times than she could count and she was grateful that Edvina had been helping her practice over the last week. Reading all day made her muscles ache and aside from her walks with Charming in the evening, it was the only exercise she got. It had certainly paid off. Belle was able to greet each new person comfortably without fear of embarrassing herself. Liv stayed by her side, discreetly giving advice and encouragement.

Eventually, Belle was asked to dance and she was much grateful for it. Though she could hold a good conversation, she quickly grew weary. Dancing? That she could do all night. And she did. As soon as one song ended and she curtsied a farewell to her dance partner, another came to take his place. They were young men, old men, handsome, and not so. Liv was kept just as busy and occasionally they smiled at each other in passing.

These dances were not like the heart-pounding routine that Jack had performed with Belle back at their Noël party. They were more reserved and contained like Gastone's dance had been. She was twirled in a waltz and smoothly guided into a two step. A few times, the dancers formed long lines that meant for them to weave throughout one another. With their partner, but often separate.

Belle was just about to accept a dance from a rather portly man when Liv intervened. "I'm afraid, Lord Gaubert, that the mademoiselle and I have reached our feminine limits. You gentlemen have provided us with far too much entertainment tonight."

She gave him such a sweet smile that he accepted the refusal with a gracious bow.

"Have you truly reached your limits, Liv?" she asked as the young lady took Belle's arm and started escorting her out of the ballroom. "Because I could certainly dance for many more hours."

"Oh certainly could I, Belle, but we've already consumed several hours of the night." Liv patted her hand, as they casually walked. At some point, they'd started using each other's first name and Belle hadn't even notice it happen. "We don't want to give the wrong impression by being the last young ladies to leave, do you take my meaning?"

Belle nodded and Liv said a quick goodnight to some guests but didn't stop their pace. They left the ballroom and two sets of guards took up positions around them. Liv ignored them like a woman who'd dealt with it her whole life.

"Have you heard, Belle," Liv said after awhile of quiet walking. Aside from the guards and a passing maid, there was no one around to hear them. "My brother received quite the thrashing?"

Belle tensed, afraid of how much Audun might have admitted to her. "I did see him last night. It was apparent that he'd been through an ordeal."

"Indeed, he told only my father what happened and that only

seemed to make my father mad at *him*." She raised her eyebrows at Belle to emphasize the point. "I've tried to coax the servants into talking because they know everything that goes on in this castle, but all they would say was that he got what he deserved."

"Oh dear," was all Belle could think to say. She really didn't want to lie or hide things from Liv, but she also had no desire to reveal the events of that day.

Liv shrugged. "He likely did. The man is a pompous, self-entitled git."

Belle laughed in surprise. Most likely that was a proclamation that Liv wouldn't have made in front of others, but Belle was glad she felt comfortable enough to say it around her. "You know, Liv, I think I like you very much."

Liv pulled Belle closer until they walked shoulder to shoulder, and squeezed her hand. "I am so glad to hear that because you are the most interesting person in my life."

Not wanting Belle to be caught without a chaperon in the hall, Liv followed Belle back to her bed chambers and then bid her a goodnight. Belle stepped into her room to find it dimly light by only a few candles and the fire. Edvina was asleep in an armchair, her mouth hanging open.

Belle noticed something on the bed. It was a box; a box wrapped and tied with a satin red ribbon. Belle picked up the package, being careful not to wake Edvina. She turned over the small note card. In cursive writing it read: *Joyeux Noël, Aleksander*.

The gift was early, as Noël wasn't for another five days. But Belle's heart warmed at the gift all the same. She sat down on the bed's edge and placed the gift upon her lap. Sliding the ribbon free, she dropped it next to her. The box's top was removed next. A fist-sized, silver heart sat beneath, within the center of a red cushion.

Pulling the heart from the box, she realized that it was heavy and thicker than it first looked. Upon closer inspection, she saw that the heart's surface was carved into roses, vines, and various elegant designs. On the bottom were three small pegs for the heart to rest upon. Between them was a small hole for a key. Belle ran her fingers along the seams and crevasses of the satin box, till she found the brass piece. It fit perfectly and turned several times with ease.

At first Belle was confused when nothing happened, then she realized that the top of the heart was actually a lid. Slowly, she lifted it and music began to twinkle out. Within the heart, beneath a glass face, were hundreds of tiny gears. They clicked, turned, and spun together.

The song it played was a waltz, but not one she was familiar with. Most popular waltz songs reminded Belle of young, flippant love with their upbeat and short notes. But this song was slower—heavier somehow—with long notes.

It made Belle think of warm nights and starry skies.

# Chapter Twenty-One

Belle stood in the Dining Hall. The table was filled with every tasty dish it could hold. She smiled, knowing what this was. Aleksander was recreating the ball, down to the last detail. Without looking down, Belle knew she wore the same green and gold gown. Her hair was swept up in the same cascade of dark curls and the weight of diamonds and emeralds completed the ensemble. There was a nervous twitch in her stomach; Aleksander was going to get to see her like this.

He was nowhere in the dining hall, but that wasn't a surprise. The food in a moon dream would be a disappointment compared to the real thing. Passing it by, Belle walked to the grand ballroom. At the room's center, there he was.

He looked much like the first moment she saw him. His soft hair was loose but combed back, falling behind his shoulders. Only one medal draped from around his neck; a combined cross and star. A white-gloved hand sat formally before him.

Somehow, standing there in the middle of the ballroom, he reminded her of a lion. So regal. So awe-inspiring.

Walking toward him, Belle couldn't hold back her smile. She truly looked and felt like a princess, and was about to dance with the most interesting and beautiful man she'd ever known. Her heels clicked against the marble. Thousands of candles illuminated the room with light that chased shadows and flickered off gold inlays. Blackness filled the windows, but brilliant stars rested among them. It was just like the night before but, with only Aleksander before her, the beauty of it all was enhanced.

"Mademoiselle," Prince Aleksander said with a formal bow.

"Your Royal Highness." She curtsied, long and graceful.

"You are every bit as beautiful as I had imagined." His eyes rested on her with a loving softness, making her heart skip.

"Thank you for the gift." Belle looked him in the eyes, unable to look anywhere else. "The music box is lovely and the song is enchanting. What is it?"

"It is titled *A Starry Waltz,* composed by a budding talent. He was lost to the curse, but he at least had the chance to present the composition to my parents on their anniversary."

"I am honored that you would give the song to me then. I'll treasure it always." Thinking over the last week, she added, "Thank you for so much more than that. This dress, the jewels, the library, the garden—you've given me so much that I will hold dear forever."

"Then your presence here was a gift to both of us." He extended his hand, smiling down at her. "May I have this dance?"

"You may." Belle took his hand and he led her into position.

They separated and bowed. There was a moment, when they stood, where they just looked at one another. Then he stepped up to Belle and took her hand in his, with one strong hand at her waist. Aleksander closed his eyes, took a deep breath. The moment he moved to begin the dance, glorious orchestral music lilted into the air. *A Starry Waltz* and it was even grander in its true form. If this song was love—it was forbidden, but it was forever.

He maneuvered her effortlessly, like gliding on air. Any inexperience she had in dancing was lost in his elegant movements. Belle twirled, her satin skirts floating around her. Aleksander brought them close together, their chests just barely touching. She could hardly breathe as she looking into his eyes. Her whole body felt light and tingly.

Their eyes never separated throughout the dance. It was graceful. It was heavenly. She was lost in him. How long they danced, Belle didn't know. Only when she was standing next to Aleksander, her arm wrapped within his as he steered her toward the open doors, did her scope widen.

Cold air swooped around them and they stepped outside onto a stone veranda. Belle's eyes were drawn right to the sky. It was so beautiful, each star dazzling. The full moon shone in silver perfection among them. "Breathtaking."

"There are no skies in the world as beautiful as the ones you'll find in God's Cup." Aleksander led her over to the railing.

It was warmer tonight than usual and the scents of the surrounding garden wafted around them, as though it were summer. Belle wondered how much effort it took for him, to give her so much detail. Even the quieted music drifted from inside.

"Have you seen many other skies in the world?" Belle asked, pleased that he still held her arm.

He looked up with remembrance in his eyes. "I have seen a few, yes. You?"

Belle laughed lightly, shaking her head. "Oh no, this is the only sky that I know."

"You are wonderful," he said abruptly, gazing down at her.

Belle smiled and looked away, certain she was blushing under his attention. Prince Aleksander's fingers slid along her jaw and turned her face up to his. He was so close to her, closer than when they danced. His other hand came up to caress her cheek and his full lips moved just inches above hers. Lips parting in anticipation, Belle's heart beat wildly.

Aleksander leaned. Belle's eyes started to close as she watched him. She wanted his kiss. She *yearned* for his kiss.

But he stopped. He closed his eyes, inhaling deeply.

"Someday I *will* kiss you." Aleksander opened his eyes and stared deep into the depths of hers. "But when I do, it will be real . . . Not a dream."

The Prince stepped away from her, and Belle felt the cold more profoundly without him near.

"For now though, there is no place I would rather be." Tingles swept through her, as he brushed a curl back from her face. "If I never lived another free day in my life, this night would last me till my dying day."

Belle lost her smile. Everything in this dream had been more than perfect, but it was only a dream. She'd spent weeks in Vakre Fjell getting to know the people and gradually falling for their prince. Even with recent discoveries, their efforts had produced little to go on. But then, there was still one portion of this curse that he hadn't opened up to her about . . .

"What is holding you captive, Aleksander. Is it Fenrir himself? Is it something else?" Belle forced out, daring to broach the forbidden topic. "If you would just tell me, I might be able to do something." Aleksander's arm dropped and he turned away. Grasping the banister, he stared at the mountains' reflection in the moonlight. She went on. "My father has a friend in America who specializes in unusual creatures. He might know a way to kill whatever it is that has you, or he might even know of a cure for your people. I can go to him—"

"And what if this man cannot help?" The Prince asked softly.

"Then I'll keep looking," Belle answered without hesitation. "I'll go anywhere, do whatever I have to, to help you. However long it takes."

"You'd give your life to lift this curse then?" He still didn't look at her, his voice calm, but guarded.

"Of course." She reached out, gently touching his arm.

"No." Aleksander's voice tensed. His muscles clenched beneath her finger. "Too many have lost their lives to this curse. I won't allow you to do the same."

Belle withdrew her hand, uncertain of the ire she felt building in him.

"I've been such a fool." Aleksander sighed, covering his face with his hand. "I've sought out your affections and allowed myself to believe there was hope . . ."

She waited for him to finish, but whatever thought had been on his tongue had faded back into him. Belle searched for something to say, something to bring him back out of this spiral—a spiral she feared was pulling him away from her. "But what about the laws of fatum? It tells us—"

"It tells us nothing," he cut in angrily. Aleksander inhaled, calming himself. "*Only by her own power can a fate be destroyed.* There's nothing there, Belle."

"But there might be. That's why I want to seek help." It felt like she was pleading for her life. Any wrong word could end it all. "Someone might see something in it that we don't. I'm willing to find them."

"The problem is"—he looked at her, sadness pouring from his blue eyes—"I'm not willing to let you."

"What are you saying?" It was too late. Dread seeped through her skin, icing her blood. "I can help you. I can free you, I know it."

Aleksander shook his hanging head. "No, Belle. I cannot be saved. Not—" He looked over and faltered at the sight of her. "Oh my Belle, my beauty. Do not cry."

He gently pulled her into his arms and wiped away the tears

with his gloved fingers. Belle hadn't even known she was crying. His arms remained comfortingly around her, but the gentle words that followed were not what she wanted. "You can't help me, Belle. I know that you've killed hundreds of terrifying monsters, but even your skills won't help me."

"Please, Aleksander. Just let me try." She touched his cheek.

He pursed his lips and ran his hand up to the nape of her neck. "No. I need you to let this go." He sighed. "And *I* need to let *you* go."

The words hit Belle like a dagger through the heart. Coldness bled from her veins and into her skin as he stepped away from her. A wall was building up between them. She could see it in the growing hardness of Aleksander's face.

"You will leave tomorrow." He turned away. "You are no longer my prisoner, mademoiselle."

Belle sucked in air as more tears streamed down her cheeks, and this time she felt them; hot and painful. Blackness fell around her and the Prince faded away.

"Wake up, mademoiselle." Belle felt a thumping on her shoulder. "You're having a nightmare."

Belle opened her eyes, but she didn't move. All over she felt numb. As though her entire body refused to accept the Prince's refusal. How had that happened? The night had been going so well, then suddenly it changed. A few more tears tumbled down her cheeks onto the already wet pillow.

"What is it, Child?" Edvina asked as she tied back the bed's draperies. When Belle didn't acknowledge her, she paused in her duties and frowned. "Come now, have some breakfast. That'll help you feel better."

Forcing Belle out of bed, she guided her over to the table of steaming food. But Belle had no appetite. She felt sick and it was more than an aching heart. Her body felt weak. Nausea rolled through her stomach. No, she didn't want food. Not even the coffee tempted her.

Edvina tried to coax Belle into admitting what bothered her, but Belle wouldn't budge. It wasn't that she didn't want to tell Edvina. It was more as though she didn't have any words. They weren't buried or hiding, they were just gone.

Then Edvina theorized that maybe Belle just needed a good bath to warm her bones. As Belle stared into the hearth's fire, not really seeing the flames, Edvina hurried the servants. Soon she had enlisted twice as many as usual and the tub was filled and steaming, in record time. Belle sank into the hot water, not hearing Edvina's reassurances that this would sooth what ailed her, and laid her head upon the rim.

"Oh, dear." Edvina's voice barely broke through Belle's haze. "Are you sure this is the right dress?"

Blinking, Belle realized that time had been lost to her and her bathwater had gone cold. She looked over to see Edvina standing in the doorway, gazing down at the garment brought up by one of the assistant seamstresses.

"Yes, madame," came the reply. "The request was clear."

Even from across the room, Belle recognized her gown. The same blue dress she'd arrived in. Spasms rocked her chest. She covered her face with watery hands as the sobs took her. Edvina was at her side in the breath of a second, pushing back her hair and cooing softly.

The words came back to Belle then. Like a tidal wave, they purged from her. Edvina was quiet as she listened.

"I'm so sorry, my dear," she said sadly when Belle finished. "It appears that the Crowned Prince is even more stubborn than I knew. I wouldn't have encouraged you toward him if I had thought it would end this way."

Belle knew this was true and held no ill will toward the woman. In fact, she was grateful for Edvina's care toward her. Soon she was out of the tub, dried, in her own dress, and standing before the mirror with her hair styled. All the while, Edvina acted as her crutch, encouraging strength and wiping away the occasional tear.

It was strange looking at herself this way. After so many days of expensive gowns and jewelry, her own clothing never looked so plain. Red eyes, with large circles beneath them, only added to the dreary image.

"Beautiful." Edvina patted Belle's arm softly, giving her a smile in the mirror.

There was a knock at the door and Edvina left Belle looking at her reflection to go answer it. There was some whispering, then Edvina stepped aside to let Laramie in. He met Belle's eyes through the mirror. The gloominess in the downturn of his mouth and eyes told her that he already knew everything.

"Bonjour, mademoiselle." He shifted the items in his hands. "I have some things for you."

Intrigued, she came over. But her stomach clenched at the sight of her weapons.

"I've been instructed to return your weapons to you." He handed over her revolvers and throwing knives. She looked down at them, running her fingers over the star shooting across the barrel. Monsieur Petit smiled softly. "I'm sure that comforts you some. I know how anxious you were without them." Belle gave him a halfhearted smile and Laramie went on. "His Royal Highness also requests that you mail these letters upon returning to Contefées." She accepted the small bundle as he spoke. "They are letters to various heads of state, updating them on our situation. As well as one of a more personal nature to his sister, the Empress of France."

"Mademoiselle," Laramie said, causing Belle to look up from the sealed letters. "I'd just like to say—"

"Pardonnez-moi." A young servant popped his head in. "Monsieur Petit, you're needed. Lord and Lady Dahling are causing quite the ruckus."

"Not now," he grumbled.

"But monsieur, Lord Dahling has fashioned her Ladyship's undergarments into flags, which now hang from their windows."

Laramie rolled his eyes, then gave Belle an apologetic look. "Your horse is being readied. Servants will be up for your things. Remain here and I will return to escort you."

Belle nodded, following him to the door. Laramie pounded down the hall, bickering to the servant. She glanced over, expecting there to be a guard about to shoo her back into the room. But there wasn't. The two soldiers who'd been by her door every second of every day, since she'd arrived, were now gone. Apparently, Belle was no longer a threat.

Of course, she wasn't the threat. Not in this castle. No, in this castle the only threat was a monster—a *thing* that held the Prince captive and was so terrifying that an entire castle of soldiers were too afraid to confront it, or even talk about it. Belle wasn't afraid though; she'd faced her own fair share of monsters. In fact, if this kingdom was too afraid to save itself, then she was just what they needed.

"What are you doing, Dear?" Edvina asked, holding the letters that Belle had shoved in her hands. "Belle?"

But Belle didn't answer. She walked down the hall, strapping on her weapons and feeling more like the Hunter she was with each step. Her stride was determined. Nothing would stop her from entering the Royal Apartments. One way or another, before leaving this castle, Belle was going to face Aleksander's captor.

# Chapter Twenty-Two

A t the end of the hallway were two large doors, designed in such an immense way that they stood as the focal point of the hall. Belle crept across the royal carpet, passing by lesser doors. Her eyes were fixated on the closed entrance.

*Stay out of the West Wing,* Laramie had said, and now the very air seemed to whisper it.

She passed no servants and, surprisingly, there were no guards in this portion of the castle. The only sounds came from Belle's soft footsteps and the wind as it rushed past the great windows.

Sweeping beneath the gazes of stone Valkyries, Belle reached the ominous doors at the end of the hall. Hand held just inches above the gold handles, she looked back. No one came. Not even the statues watched her.

Resolute, Belle pushed. The door swung open with a groan. She stepped in quickly and shut it behind her. It closed so loudly, despite her efforts, Belle was certain that it echoed all through the West Wing. She cringed and then looked at the room beyond, and gasped.

It was a bedchamber, as she expected, an all too familiar bedchamber. Prince Aleksander's quarters. Except unlike when he met Belle in her dreams, this room was not in perfect condition. Something terrible had happened here.

There were no candles and the hearth was without a warming fire. The only light came from the balcony where the doors were left partially open. Swirls of snowflakes fluttered in. Belle's visible breath added emphasis to the room's cold temperature.

Her gaze roamed over the bedchamber, shocked further at its state. Tables and chairs were overturned. Glass glittered on the floor. Books and all sorts of smallish bits had been strewn about. Whoever destroyed this room left nothing untouched.

Then Belle saw the claw marks. They were large, bigger than she'd seen before. They tore through carpet, draperies, and wood. She walked about the room, looking for any hints of where Aleksander had been taken. The room, aside from the destruction, appeared to be mostly untouched. There were no signs that anyone came through here on a regular basis. Belle went to the fireplace.

The mammoth structure was made of stone with carvings of the rose vines that Vakre Fjell was famous for. She crouched into its mouth and raked her hands through the ash. Her fingers came out black, but with no hint of recent warmth. Belle would wager that this room hadn't been heated in a long time. It was very strange.

The wind picked up and swept into the room. It sent chills over her skin and rustled the pages of the books lying discarded on the floor. Out of habit, Belle went to the balcony to close the doors. First checking the weather, she leaned just outside. The sky had been swallowed up by gray. Snow came down with the wind, soaring at unimaginable speeds. It was going to be quite the storm.

Belle looked down at the stone balcony outside. Flourishing roses spread over the entrance and encircled the small wrapping balcony. They bloomed with glorious red heads, so soft that she wanted to rub them against her cheeks. Their vines were thick and flexible, and dotted with menacing looking thorns. She touched one gently with her fingers, marveling at its beauty. So lovely; thriving in a place as cold and forgotten as this room. It amazed her.

Something scraped on the floor behind her. Belle turned, expecting to find Edvina or Laramie come to retrieve her, but that wasn't who was there. Belle lunged back in fear, slamming into the balcony archway.

A beast towered over her, only feet away. He was twice the size of any hellhound and he *stood*; not on four legs, like the others, but on two. His physique was more masculine and human in shape than it was wolf. There was no mistaking the claws at the end of each finger, the fangs barely contained in his muzzle, and the predatory eyes that glared at her now.

This was no ordinary hellhound; this was something else entirely. Something new; something worse. As fear grappled her heart, he studied her—instead of attacking, as he should have, with primal instinct.

Belle's mind raced, grasping at the truth that had come rushing to her. Aleksander had lied. It *was* Fenrir holding him prisoner—no *manner of speaking* about it. The creature before her was exactly what she'd seen in that old book not long ago. Now she knew, and now she understood that she couldn't fight it—not a god.

Belle had to warn the Hunters. She had to tell them what was hiding in Castle Vakre Fjell. They had to prepare. With well-trained reflexes, Belle drew a revolver. Being only feet away, there was little need to aim. She pulled the trigger.

The beast was fast, leaping to the side, and the bullet struck the wall. He faced her in a crouch and roared. Her instincts erupted, screaming for her to run. Belle rushed for the door, firing with each step. The beast disengaged and took cover.

Grabbing the door handle, Belle ripped it open and dashed

out. She held up her skirts and sprinted down the corridor. Only once did she spare a glance behind her. Fenrir wasn't following. She turned down the hall, unable to get enough distance between her and that *thing* fast enough. Belle whisked past servants, not bothering to apologize for her rudeness.

"There you are, mademoiselle!" Laramie called as he ascended up from one staircase below. "I was just looking for you. Madame Gulbrandsen said you had rushed off." Belle reached the second-floor landing and turned onto the grand staircase, not missing a step. Laramie looked at her curiously as she neared. "What's wrong, Belle?"

"You know exactly what's wrong, I'd imagine," she said in a rush of breath.

The color drained from his face, making him look pastier than usual. "What do you mean? What happened?"

"All this time you could have said something. You could have warned me," Belle spat as she stopped two steps up from him. "But you were too afraid and now the world might pay for it."

Belle shook her head in disgust. She knew her anger was misplaced. They had their reasons for keeping silent, even if it was just fear. But she couldn't help thinking about what that might have cost everyone else.

Laramie raised his eyebrows, parted his lips just a little, then saw her drawn revolver. His eyes widened and he stepped toward her. "What did you—"

Belle lifted her gun, aiming between his eyes. "I cannot stay here a moment longer."

There was a heartbeat's hesitation where neither was sure what the other was planning to do. Then they separated. Laramie hurriedly climbed the steps, rushing the way she'd come. Wasting no time, Belle ran for the castle's entrance.

No guards tried to stop her. But Liv was there, waiting outside.

Charming was saddled, with the few of Belle's things strapped to the back. A stable hand held him, talking casually with the Lady. Both had their backs to the wind and looked up at the sound of her appearance.

"So it's true. You're really leaving?" Liv asked, her arms crossed tightly against her chest, more for warmth than anger.

"Yes." Belle stepped around the woman and shoved her boot into the saddle stirrup.

"You can't mean to leave so quickly." Liv watched her closely, displaying confusion across her face. "You haven't said au revoir and there's a storm coming."

"I'm sorry, Liv, but I cannot stay." Belle launched herself into the saddle and took up the reins.

She cued Charming into a gallop.

"But you'll die out there!" Liv shouted. "Wait, Belle!"

Belle dropped her head as tears started to fall. She hated leaving Liv, knowing they'd become friends. She wasn't the only one; Laramie, Edvina, Ms. Tops, and others. But how could they not have told her what—who—was in that castle? Henri had tried to warn her, tried to tell her that there was something truly evil there. Belle hadn't listened. She let herself be swept up in the kindness, the grandeur, and the curiosity. It had distracted her.

A loud roar echoed into the air. It was otherworldly. The sound curled with anger but drew out with a keening that seemed somehow sorrowful. It matched Belle's pain in a rather profound way.

Two guards yanked open the gate, as she raced toward them across the perilous bridge. Charming flew by them and into Vakre Fjell Forest. The road was gone, hidden by snow, and this time there were no hoof prints to lead her. Belle gave Charming his head, allowing him to take her home. Horses always knew the way home. It was instinct.

The storm whistled through the trees and groaned overhead.

Already the snow was coming down steadily. Belle leaned into Charming, trying to block some of the wind. Her ears and cheeks starting to burn from the cold, her fingers becoming numb. It wasn't long before Castle Vakre Fjell was well out of sight and they were in the thick of the forest.

Charming pushed onward, finding a steady pace to carry her home as quickly as possible. The storm was determined though. Soon the falling snow was thick, like a continuous surge of endless white. It became difficult to see. Trees appeared out of nowhere. Branches jumped out, trying to rip her from the saddle.

Belle had to trust in Charming. Only he could keep his senses in the blizzard. But his pace began to slow. His head came up, his ears searching. When Charming stopped completely, Belle knew it was not because of the storm.

She tried to slow her breathing, listening for the coming hellhounds. Her whole body trembled; the cold crawled over her skin and slipped into her lungs. Belle held up her gun, watching the barrel shake within her unsteady grip.

The cold was sobering, freezing the wild emotions from before. Quickly, Belle removed the cap from the bullet chamber of her gun. *Empty.* She'd used all of her bullets shooting at Fenrir. When she'd aimed it at Laramie, the threat had been empty. It was unlike her to be so reckless, and that fact was starting to become apparent.

Not able to think on it further, Belle reached for her bullet pouch. Her fingers touched only the fabric of her dress. Her pouch, of course, wasn't there. It'd been packed away by some servant. She was entirely unprepared for this journey.

Charming nickered and danced in place. She felt his uneasiness. Quickly, she stashed the empty revolver and retrieved the other. A quick check told her it had been loaded.

There was a blur to her right, the sound of a snarl. *One*, she counted. A branch snapped on her left. *Two*. Then there were multiple growls over her shoulder. *Oh God.*

Belle pointed her gun and they came into view. *Bang. Bang. Bang.* She fired in rapid succession. Smoke twirled up from the barrel as the bodies dropped. There was no time to breathe. Another hellhound came from the left. Belle swiped two knives from her chest harness and flung them. They buried into the hound's fur and he went down with a clipped yipe.

Two more hellhounds attacked from different directions, giving Belle little time to react. She put the first down immediately, but her defense was too slow for the second hound. Her bullet lodged in its heart, as the creature barreled into Belle and knocked her from the saddle.

The impact was jarring, but not as bad as it had been the last time a hellhound got the better of her. Belle scrambled to her feet. Another two hounds approached, as though they had decided to attack in teams. She straightened her shoulders and shot the first easily. The second hound ran across its friend without missing a step, gaining speed with its anger. Belle fired. *Click.*

Her eyes widened. The gun was empty. Belle stepped back, reaching for the last of her knives—knowing that she wouldn't be able to draw them in time. The hellhound came within feet, his fangs bared and eyes gleaming.

Charming lunged in front of her, blocking the hellhound. The stallion reared up and slammed his hooves down at it. He stomped, huffed, and grunted. The hound snarled. Charming reared and thrust his hooves down again, pushing the creature away. It growled but cowered from the large horse.

Charming kept on him, forcing him farther away from Belle. The blizzard swallowed them up when they were only meters away. Belle pressing her back against a tree. She listened for the horse and hound, catching their sounds on the wind, then those were gone too.

Pulling the last of her throwing knives from their harness, she gripped them in each hand. Wind howled through the forest, carrying thick snowflakes upon every available inch. There was white everywhere, it filled the air and gathered upon her handmade dress and fallen hair. She was starting to feel damp, and that was dangerous in this cold.

"Charming!" she called. All she heard was wind and snow. Her breath puffed on the air.

Belle was alone.

# Chapter
# Twenty-Three

elle's clothing and cloak were now worthless. The cold seeped through them and it felt like her skin was slowly freezing. She leaned into the tree, trying to use it to shield her front. Her hair whipped in the wind.

Charming still hadn't returned and Belle was left to worry about him. She couldn't walk home, being as she had no bearing on where she was. Belle would give anything to see those gas-lit lamps right then.

Growls snatched her out of the daze the cold had lulled her into. Belle squinted, attempting to see anything other than white. Then she did. Bits of black. Flashes of yellow. There were many of them and, judging by their growing snarls, they were circling her.

The smell of warm blood had drawn the hellhounds in, but the scent of their dead brethren was making them wary. They knew she was a threat and they were gauging just how much of one. Soon the hounds would decide that the risk was worth it and they would come at her.

Belle's mind raced through her options. If she threw her knives from a distance, she could kill two. Then all that remained were the spring-loaded bayonets attached to the base of both her revolvers. They were Belle's last line of defense, but each hellhound had to be deadly close. Even if she managed to kill one, perhaps two, they'd soon overwhelm her. Or she could kill herself. The small thought whispered from the back of her mind. It would be better than being torn up while she was still alive.

Tears returned. Belle knew she couldn't take her own life, even as the idea came to her. But she would still die today. Part of her knew this would always be her likely demise—she wasn't ready for it, all the same. God willing, they'd go for her throat. End her quickly.

With shaking hands, Belle held up her throwing knives and blinked away the tears. She planted her feet and let the tree guard her back. To be sure, it was no substitute for her Friesian. The first hellhound to charge could be her last and final kill. Belle would certainly be taking at least one with her.

An immense howl broke through the rage of the storm, making her jump. It sounded in the distance. It was hearty and fierce, like a call to battle. The voice was familiar, like the mournful keen she'd heard at the castle. The idea that Fenrir might have followed her chilled her to the core.

Just beyond her line of sight, there was a growl. Belle jerked at the sound. A fight ensued with snarls and snaps. Then a whimper. Seconds of silence, then it started again. There was a blur as a hellhound tried to run, but something bigger took it down. For a moment, the snow seemed to open up, giving her a glimpse of multiple hounds running toward it. They jumped on the hulking figure and disappeared into the blizzard.

Growls, snarls, barks, whimpers, and a deafening roar. It sounded like it was all around her. Belle searched through the trees and sheets of snow, but couldn't see them.

Quite suddenly, there was silence. She didn't move, hardly breathed. Belle only listened.

The blizzard moaned on, but within its cries she heard the subtle sounds of a lone whimper. Then it stopped. A moment past and she wondered if maybe they were all dead, even whatever had saved her.

Crunching snow dashed away that spark of hope. Belle clenched her knives once more. Through the white cascade of snowflakes, a large dark figure began to emerge. She knew who it was right away. Fenrir.

He moved through the snow with great sweeping steps. Graceful and controlled. His fur became defined along with his massive claws and pointed ears. Belle couldn't just throw her knife. He was too fast for that. She had to wait until he was close—too close—before she struck.

Just when Fenrir was about to step into full view, a sterling light burst before him. Belle blinked in surprise. When a hellhound corpse became human, the light was gold. This wasn't like that at all; this was flawlessly silver. When the light disappeared, the wolf god was gone. In his place was a man.

Belle's breath caught in her disbelief. His steps seemed to falter, but he didn't stop. He stepped just inches from her knife. Her jaw dropped.

*Aleksander.*

It couldn't be. He was trapped in a cell, only to appear in her dreams. There was no way he was standing before her now. It was impossible.

With a casual hand, the man pushed away Belle's knife and she didn't stop him. He wore slacks and a loose, partially open white shirt. His untied hair whipped freely in the wind. It was the same look he'd adorned the day the curse hit. There were several large and bleeding gashes over his body, but he didn't seem to notice them. The man who looked like Aleksander stepped up to her, stopping only inches away.

"Belle . . ." The way he uttered her name was so breathless, it was as though saying it too loudly would shatter its existence. His hand went to her cheek, cupping part of her jaw and neck gently. Their eyes met. His were familiar soft blues. Soft blues, that seemed to reveal all of his emotions.

The words that tumbled out of her were of complete, joyful surprise. "It *is* you."

Aleksander answered by leaning in and capturing her lips with his. The kiss was soft, careful, but there was a surety to it. She tasted his need. He didn't want to devour her though; he just wanted to kiss her. His lips slowed, lingering against hers. The warmth of his mouth and body caused Belle to tingle in response.

Gradually, Aleksander drew away from her. His eyelids fluttered, then his eyes rolled back in his head. Belle anticipated his fall, throwing her arms around him. His weight was too much and she was pulled down with him. Into a heap, the Prince crumpled into the snow. She pushed the locks of hair from his face. He was unconscious.

Belle called for Charming again and again as she tried to wake Aleksander. He didn't respond. She checked his wounds frantically. They were deep and in need of stitches, but they hadn't bled enough for him to faint. Something else was wrong.

"Stay with me, Aleksander," Belle shouted over the wind. Tearing a strip from the hem of her dress, she attempted to staunch the bleeding as best she could. Belle then removed her cloak and placed it over the Prince. She watched for hellhounds and leaned in the snow to caress Aleksander's hair soothingly. "Don't leave me now."

He gave no reaction, no indication that he heard her. Dread filled her stomach, bringing with it a fear for the worst. She called for Charming again, and that worry only increased when the stallion still didn't return.

Minutes drawled by. Belle anxiously searched for alternatives should Charming not return. If he . . . She couldn't even think it.

Not then. Not when both she and Aleksander stood on the preci-
pice of death as well. She needed her Friesian; she needed him to
live.

Belle pulled her eyes away from Aleksander's face at the sound
of crunching snow. Out of habit, her hand went to her weapon.
She squinted her eyes in the sound's direction, seeing just a shad-
ing of some tall form in the heavy, falling snow. Belle exhaled in
relief—a smile broke over her face. It was Charming. He passed
among the trees, his long legs lifting high over the snow. Soft nick-
ers rumbled in his throat, and she stood to greet him. Thankfully,
he was unharmed, but Belle doubted that the hellhound was.

Leading Charming to stand beside Aleksander, she coaxed
him into laying down. Once again, grateful they'd practiced such
a large repertoire of tricks. First Belle put her cloak on, then she
lifted the Prince by the arms. It wasn't easy; he was no small
man. With a great deal of determination, she dragged Aleksander across the saddle and onto the back of her stallion. Belle then
urged Charming to stand. The horse came up fast, but steady with
the Prince in tow.

Moving quickly, Belle unclipped the rolled blanket at the back
of her saddle. Aleksander was hardly dressed for being out in the
woods. She tossed it over him and rifled through her saddlebags
to find the small pouch of bullets and Electro-Phonic Chip. She
hooked it around her ear and tested the signal. Not surprising,
Belle was out of range. Reloading her guns, she tied her bullet
satchel to her waist and then retrieved her knives from the human
corpse. Ready for any attacks that were to come, it was time for
Belle to get the Prince to safety.

"All right, boy. You need to lead us home." She came over to
Charming and lovingly caressed his velvety muzzle. He puffed hot
breath against her fingers. "Walk on."

Charming started in some direction that looked to Belle like any other. She walked alongside, keeping vigilance of their sur-roundings since there was no room in the saddle for her. Alek-sander hung over the horse, his head and arms bouncing with the stallion's movements. Belle tucked the blankets tighter around him. *Please be okay.*

The surging snow made the journey extremely slow. The wind pushed against them like it wanted to stop them from leaving. Af-ter an hour, possibly longer, Belle's body involuntary shook. Her toes and fingers felt like they were being repeatedly stabbed with small needles. The pain was incredible.

But she kept on. One foot forward and then the next, Belle pushed through the pain and weariness. She had too. Aleksander needed her. He'd risked his life, risked his kingdom—all to save her.

There was a crackling in Belle's right ear. At first she was con-fused, the cold making her brain sluggish. Slowly, she realized her communication chip was grabbing a signal. Hope flaring in her chest, she tapped the device and croaked, "Hello? Hello?"

Belle pressed the button again and waited. Her attention fad-ed in and out as they walked. They had to keep walking—they couldn't stop. Maybe they weren't going to make it? Belle couldn't fight the cold much longer. Aleksander still hadn't stirred. The storm was winning.

"Belle? Are . . . there?"Andre's voice reached her. It was faint and Belle's daze made her response slow.

"I'm here," she rasped. "I'm here."

"We're coming, Belle."

"I don't know where I am." She had stopped walking without realizing it. Charming stood at her side. Belle's ears caught a faint hissing sound, followed by a series of muffled pops. An orb of light appeared above her. Belle gasped at the sight of the lamppost; her first sign of something familiar. She'd been standing almost directly beneath it and still hadn't been able to see it through the storm. "I'm by a lamppost, but I can't see any others."

"Just stay where you are. We're coming to you," Andre reassured.

Belle wasn't going to argue. Her strength was gone and what little she had was trying to keep her warm. Brushing away the layer of snow that coated Charming's head and neck, she cooed to him, telling him what a good horse he was and thanking him for getting them this far.

Then Belle stepped over to check Aleksander. His skin was cold though it was hard for her to tell, and his breathing was shallow. There was little she could do for him now. She adjusted his blanket and then laid her face next to his, resting her arms over him. At least she could block the wind. She could still do that.

Belle didn't realize that she'd fallen asleep until Charming's body shook with his loud whinnies. She remained slouched over the Prince, unable to straighten or twist to see who approached. Belle heard shouts. Someone brushed her hair away to touch her face, but she couldn't seem to open her eyes. Belle recognized her Hunters' voices and inwardly smiled.

There was a great deal of commotion and Belle found herself suddenly being lifted. She whimpered from the pain, feeling like each movement shattered her frozen veins. Someone cradled her gently against their chest. Belle felt a saddle beneath her and the motion of a horse. Gentle hands rubbed her arms and back, bringing some warmth back to the surface. Gastone's voice reassured her that she would be all right. Belle rested against him, letting him bear all of her in that moment.

Gastone smelled like wood upon the hearth and the dust that settled on a good workhorse. In an instant, Belle could see her home; see her father within her mind. And just like that, she felt safe.

Letting herself doze, Belle knew she couldn't fight the sleep. Though the thumping of boots on metal soon roused her.

"Jack, ride into town and get the doc. Take a carriage. Be careful, the storm will slow you down, but we can't wait for it to pass," commanded Henri. Her heart soared to hear him sounding so strong. "Andre, take the gentleman into the guest room and, Gastone, take Belle to her room. Nicolas and Delano—"

"I stay with him," Belle croaked with sudden desperation. It took all of her energy, but she lifted her head from Gastone's chest to look at her father.

There was a long pause where Henri contemplated her, and she stared determinedly back. Then with the perfect poker face, he amended, "All right, put the gentleman in the bed and Belle in an armchair nearby. Get every available blanket. It will probably make it easier on the doc to have his patients in one room anyway."

His commands went on, but Belle stopped listening and relaxed back into Gastone's warm embrace as he headed for the stairs. In front of them walked the mute Jean. He carried the Prince slumped over one massive shoulder with no trouble at all. Her eyes again grew heavier with each ascending step.

Belle awoke only when she felt the fire engulfing her fingers.

# Chapter Twenty-Four

Belle's eyes shot open from the pain and she tried to jerk away her hands, but Andre held them firmly. "Easy now. It's all right. You have frostnip."

Everything suddenly came into quick focus. Her hands were not being held in fire, but in a bowl of warm water. Patches of solid white marked her fingers and was warning enough to sit still.

"Had you been out there much longer, we'd be dealing with full frostbite," Gastone said, tugging at the ties of her boots. Sliding a pail of water between them, Andre got started on her other boot. Belle's feet were in for the same treatment as her throbbing fingers. Gastone gave her a reassuring smile. "You'll be fine though, once we warm you back up."

In the bed beside her lay Aleksander. He was sound asleep, looking more soft and vulnerable than she'd ever witnessed. Just like Belle, he was mounded with blankets. Delano came in just then, carrying bricks warmed on the fire to wrap within Aleksander's blankets.

"There is something extremely familiar about him that I cannot place," Henri was saying to Jean.

His brow was creased and he scratched his jaw in thought. Jean nodded his agreement. The scarf he wore today was blue and gold.

Belle cleared her throat to quote the Prince verbatim, "He is Prince Aleksander the First, of House Haraldsson, Crowned Prince Regent of Vakre Fjell."

Everyone stopped their work and stared at her. Henri, however, never looked from Aleksander and his eyes lit with recognition. "My God, it is him. How?"

Belle winced as Gastone placed her bare foot into the bowl of water. Andre followed with the other. Exhausted, she rested her head against the side of her chair. "He rescued me in the woods. Without him, I'd have been eaten by the cursed—hellhounds."

Gastone released her ankle and looked up at her. "Why was the heir to the Vakrein throne alone in the woods with you?"

Taking a breath, Belle started from the beginning. She told them of the moon dreams and the memories that Aleksander shared with her. She explained about the curse, the norn, and Fenrir. She told them all they needed to know, leading up to the beast. Then she described *him*—how his body was different, how he stood on two legs, and how he acted on more than animal instincts. She admitted her rash assumption that the beast was Fenrir himself and how she'd raced into the forest when she was least prepared. Finally, she told them about how the beast came after her, and saved her. And how he'd turned into Aleksander.

"You're saying he became human . . . while he was still alive?" asked Andre.

Belle nodded.

"Remarkable," said Henri, sitting in the only other chair and staring off into the distance.

Andre frowned, as he dried his hands with a small towel. "The Prince never told you that he was . . . one of them?"

"No, I had come to believe he was a prisoner and that the beast was his captor." Belle shook her head, looking back on her last moments in Castle Vakre Fjell. "I thought they were all cowards. But I was wrong. I think *I* might have been the coward."

Chagrin crept into her chest at the way she'd run out of there; at the way she'd treated Laramie and Liv.

"Why was Prince Aleksander able to become human again, when the other . . . cursed . . . can't?" Henri asked, either ignoring her self-chastising or oblivious to it.

Shrugging, Belle gave the only reply she could, "I don't know."

The doctor arrived a little later. He shooed everyone from the room, except for Belle, and set to work. He was unusually sober, but it was early yet. The dark circles under his eyes were the only giveaway that he wasn't in the best shape. Doc didn't ask her questions, unless they were medically related. He treated Aleksander first, sewing and patching up his many wounds. Then he took a look at Belle's hands.

"As natives, you two should know better than to go out into a snowstorm," he scolded.

"Is he going to be okay, Doc?" Belle looked past him to watch Aleksander sleep.

The doctor nodded. "Yes, he should be fine."

"When will he wake?"

"I suppose when he wants to," Doc said, standing and removing his glasses to clean them. Noticing Belle's odd expression, he explained, "There's no reason for him to be unconscious now."

"But I thought with the cold and the blood loss . . ." She trailed as Doc shrugged.

"It's possible those things are the cause, but he's young and healthy. He should bounce back as quickly as you do." Walking over to the door, the Doc picked up his medical bag and turned to her. "Let him rest. I'm sure he'll wake up soon. I'll be around here for when he does."

Belle remained wrapped in her blankets, watching Aleksander sleep for several hours. Her father checked on her often. She asked about his health and was relieved to hear that, after being cared for by the doc and a bit of bed rest, he was just fine. Belle's Hunters peeked in on her too. They didn't bother her with many questions, but did welcome her back. Friar Clemens came with hot soup and drink. As she ate, he filled her in on all the comings and goings of LeClair House while she was gone.

Business as usual was most of it. Though there had been a few debates-turned-arguments on how much longer they had to wait before coming for her. When Henri was forced from Castle Vakre Fjell, it'd been made clear that should he or anyone come for her, Belle would be killed—If he was patient, he might see her again. So Henri had forbidden any sort of a rescue.

The advocates for her rescue hadn't gotten any support from the church or local law officials either. No one knew what to make of the discovered Vakrein survivors. There was even some concern that hunting hellhounds on Vakrein land could lead to political turmoil between Vakre Fjell and France.

From the sounds of it, tensions had been high. Even the mercenaries had given up their treasure hunt, leaving town as the village grieved for its lost Hunters. If Belle had been gone for much longer, it all might have come to a disastrous breaking point.

Clemens was gathering up her empty dishes when the doc returned. Henri was just behind him and asked for a word with the Friar. They both stepped out of the room to speak. Belle's attention was drawn to the doc, who came over to check her fingers.

"Good. Good. Your color has mostly returned." He reached into the medical bag at his side. "I'm going to wrap the tips of your fingers, as well as your feet, to keep the cold air off of them. You can remove the bandages in the morning."

Henri came back into the room, his boots heavy on the

wooden floor. "Would it be safe for her to take the carriage into town, Doc?"

"As long as she stays warm and takes it easy, I think that would be fine." Doc glanced at the smoking pipe in Henri's hand and frowned.

"Town, Père?" Belle looked over at Henri, surprised by his request. "Is that necessary? I really think I should stay with his Highness."

"I believe the Crowned Prince will mend just fine whether you are here or not." He leveled her with a stern look. "But word will spread quickly of your return. It will be good for the townspeople to see you well. They could use a boost in morale, given what they've recently lost."

"Of course, Père. I should pay my respects," she said, feeling the guilt that her father was impressing upon her. Belle wanted nothing more than to stay and wait for Aleksander to wake, but Henri wasn't asking much. These were his men he referred to. She owed them a great deal. "I'll . . . a . . . just go make myself presentable first."

"That's my fille." Henri came over and kissed her on the forehead.

As he straightened, her father placed his brown pipe between his lips and inhaled. She smiled and, with that, he gave her a wink. But as soon as Henri was gone, her smiled faded. She looked back at the slumbering prince. Belle had this sinking feeling in her stomach. It nagged at her to stay if only she could.

When Belle entered her own room, she was attacked. Pixie came at her like a flying bullet. She fluttered around Belle, touching her hair and face to confirm it really was her. Belle giggled as Pixie placed a cold kiss upon her nose.

It was strange being back in her own room. The large view of the ocean rivaled the beauty of Vakre Fjell's mountains, and Belle couldn't decide which was better. From her self-filling, heated tub to the Governess machine helping her dress and styling her hair, the process was efficient—but a little lonely. Already, Belle missed Edvina's continual gossip. It would be just what she needed to keep her mind off of worrying for Aleksander. Though she'd never say so to Pixie who did her own fair bit of chattering, like she hadn't "spoken" to a soul in ages.

Pinning on a burgundy hat, accented with white ribbons, and pulling on gloves to match, she was ready for town. Belle stared at herself in her tall, oval mirror. She looked every bit the proper young lady.

If Belle didn't, the townsfolk would judge her more harshly than they would others. Should she lack in any way as a female, they'd blame it on her hunting—claim that it was just unnatural for a woman to kill. So Belle learned early on the importance of appearance and that if she carried herself as the best sort of lady would, people found it easier to accept her as both Hunter and woman. *The opinions of others are not the most important things in this world*, her mother used to say, *but one is still subjected to the reality of them.*

Tying up the laces of her boots, Belle looked over at Pixie. She sat on the bed moping, her metal arms folded angrily around herself. It took some time to convince her that Belle intended on returning in a few hours. Pixie finally nodded and said farewell by hugging Belle's hand, and squeezing with all she had.

From there, Belle was soon seated in the carriage with Friar Clemens in the driver's box. Iron coils, mounted on the wall, pumped a steady flow of heat into the compartment. A wonderful modification—like the driver's enclosed box—that worked with only a bit of vigorous cranks of a handle.

Worn from her journey, Belle leaned back in her seat to look out the window. Snow was falling, but the storm had let up. It was no longer hard to see and the wind had stopped. They shortly rolled into the town square, which was deserted due to the weather. *So much being seen by the townspeople.*

Helping her out of the carriage, Friar Clemens followed her into the cathedral. He placed a gentle hand on her arm. "I wish to pray and will be here when you're ready."

He stepped into a pew near the back and knelt. There was only one other person in the great cathedral. They too were praying and didn't even look up as she past. Belle paused as she neared the clergy's office, hearing voices inside. The last thing she wanted was to talk with the Father, or the Bishop, about all that had happened—especially the Prince. She knew what their stance would be on it and it wasn't something she had the energy to deal with right then.

Silently she slipped by and into the cold stairwell that lead to the catacombs below. Belle went straight to the Hall of The Hunters and pushed her rosary key into the keyhole. She stepped back, watching the gears and bars spin and slide about the surface. The noise ricocheted of the stone walls with soft clicks and heavy booms.

The door swept open and Belle stepped in. Faced with the long row of wall graves before her, she wished the town greenhouse had been open. Without her usual offering of roses, her visit seemed lacking.

First Belle went to the far end, finding the newly made nameplates. There she said her final adieus to Franck and the other Hunters who'd perished. Belle's heart ached for their families and even for her father. She hated to imagine the pain of losing one's own hunting party.

Belle was just saying a prayer for her mother when the door's locks were activated. She waited, curious as to who was also coming to visit. The door opened and Belle was surprised to see Gastone come through it.

He stopped just inside and waited for her to look over at him. "I was speaking to the Father and Bishop Sauvage. I saw you walk by."

"Might I ask what prompted your visit to them?" Though she already suspected the answer.

"They needed to know you had returned." He watched her with his dark eyes. It felt like a challenge. "And about the wolf prince."

Belle sighed. "Don't call him that."

"And what should I call him then?" He moved several steps closer, the muscles in his arms and shoulders tense. "Would demon-prince be more accurate?"

"No, it wouldn't," she scoffed, turning away from him and choosing to look down the long hall of tombs. "And calling him Prince Aleksander would be just fine."

"Why do you care what I call him?" Gastone came the rest of the way, grabbing Belle by the arm and turning her to look at him. "What is he to you?"

"He is a good man." Belle put her hands up on Gastone's chest, preventing him from pulling her any closer. "He doesn't deserve to be disrespected because of what's been done to him."

"Done to him?" Gastone scowled, not loosening his grip on her. "How do you know anything was done to him? How can you believe anything he said when he already lied to you about what he is?"

"You're right. I don't know if I can believe him or if anything he said was true." Belle looked up into Gastone's eyes, which were hooded by heavy black eyebrows. "But he will explain himself when he's better, and I won't condemn him before that."

Gastone squeezed her arms, almost too tightly. "You care about him, don't you?"

"Of course I—"

"And by that," he interrupted when she'd been about to feign innocents to his implication. "I mean, that you care about him in a way you have no right to care about a prince."

Anger bubbled up inside Belle, rearing its head like Aleksander's fire-breathing dragon. She shoved Gastone away.

"And you have no right to speak to me of this?" She stepped around him, heading for the door.

"He won't marry you, Belle," Gastone said, stopping her. "He'll discard you when he's done and, long before that, you'll be excommunicated from the church."

Pain sliced at her heart. Not just at Gastone's words, but at the very idea of it. Advice from a recently good friend came to the forefront of Belle's mind then. She pushed back her shoulders and stuck out her chin. "Better to have a grand love that is fleeting, than one that is ordinary and lasts till death."

With Gastone's jaw clenched in fury, Belle pulled open the hall's door and left with not another word.

# Chapter Twenty-Five

pon returning home, Belle's first task was to check on Aleksander. The doctor was there, leaning over the Prince as she entered the room. Unpinning her small top hat, she paused at the man's focus.

"Is everything all right?" She brought the hat in front of her, lightly cradling it with gloved hands.

Doc quickly looked over, apparently unaware of her presence. "I'm afraid not, Belle. His Highness has a fever."

"What does that mean?" Worriedly, Belle fiddled with her hat and noted Aleksander's flushed cheeks.

"I do not yet know." Doc ran his hand down to Aleksander's wrist and gripped it. With his free hand, he withdrew a tin pocket watch and flipped it open.

Belle watched him; not speaking, not wanting to interrupt. Anxiety danced through her veins. There was so much she didn't understand—so many questions she wanted to ask the Prince. Even now, in his slumber, he was a mystery to her. More than anything, she feared for his well-being. After all his deceptions, she still wanted him to be well.

"Belle," came Henri's voice from the doorway. She turned and he beaconed her into the hall. In a hushed voice, he asked, "How is he?"

"He has a fever." She tried to keep her tone even; not show any of the fear she felt. "Doc is trying to figure out why."

Henri nodded, glancing only briefly into the room. "I've been thinking, with all that's happened, it's time Jack swear his oath." He looked Belle in the eyes, forcing her to stare back into his deep browns. "Tonight, if possible."

"We can't." Belle turned away from Henri, unable to keep herself from watching Aleksander. "Not with his Highness taking ill. I shouldn't have left him before."

"You being here wouldn't have prevented his fever." When she only crossed her arms, Henri stepped closer to ask in hushed tones, "Do you have feelings for the Prince?"

Belle's jaw dropped a little. Her heart palpitated. First Gastone's reaction and now her father was asking her outright. Did they see something there when she didn't fully know her own feelings?

With bated breath, she whispered, "I believe so."

There was a moment of long, drawn out silence. Henri contemplated the side of her face, then looked at the Prince. He chewed his tongue. "The Prince's actions would certainly indicate he has feelings for you."

Belle's racing heart seemed to agree.

"Your love will not be an easy one," Henri said, though more to himself.

A smile danced on her lips as she imagined it. "But it would be grand."

He nodded, almost like he conceded the point. "Grand loves aside"—Henri touched Belle's shoulder—"there needs to be an Oathing Ceremony tonight."

She turned to him finally. "Père, I cannot leave—"

Henri grasped both her shoulders.

"The future is uncertain, Belle. You are a Hunter *now*. We

need you *now*. We do not have the men to spare. Not now, not after—" His voice caught on the loss he felt. Belle caressed his arms, feeling his pain as her own. Pursing his lips, Henri pushed down his sadness. "You're their leader, Belle."

Glancing uncertainly to watch Aleksander's chest rise and fall with labored breath, Belle sighed. "Okay, tonight."

The cathedral doors creaked open. Friar Clemens peered out. "They're ready for you."

The Hunters had been waiting outside for only a few minutes as the church was readied. This was something Belle had done for many Hunters; many Hunters who were no longer alive today.

The cathedral had been emptied and closed since only fellow Hunters and church clergy were allowed to witness the Oathing Ceremony. Outside, the fountain's lantern was lit, glowing beneath a darkening sky. Word of the event spread quickly and many townsfolk had come to leave burning candles on the waterless fountain, offered with prayers for the new Hunter. Here they would wait for the final part of the ceremony to bring Jack outside.

Several villagers shouted to Belle, welcoming her back, and others wished Jack good luck. Belle stepped before the opened doors and waited for it to begin. Henri and the remaining semi-retired Hunters stood before the dais at the other end of the building. Wearing their finest clothes, their shoulders were back with top-hats under arms and sabres at their sides. Henri was at the forefront, standing next to Father Sinclair and other clergymen. Candles flickered all around them.

There was a noticeable absence with the loss of Franck and the others. A pang hit Belle in the chest when she again thought of missing their funerals. It would always be something she regretted.

Together, the waiting Hunters and clergymen began to sing. Baritone and tenor voices rang out, echoing off the marble in perfect accord. The Gregorian chant surrounded her as Belle walked past Friar Clemens and into the immense cathedral.

Gastone and Andre fell into step just behind her, walking side by side. Jack followed them, alone at the procession's center. Then came Delano and Nicolas, with Jean at the back. The group's matched strides were slow, gathered. They moved as one through the hallowed hall, letting the harmonious voices guide them.

Pride and honor swelled inside of Belle. She held her head high, leading her Hunters. With rosary in hand, the beauty of the cathedral, and the masculine voices humming through her, Belle never felt more connected to the divine. Whatever god or gods there were, she was certain they watched.

Drawing up before the other men, Belle locked eyes with her father. His lips quirked a slight smile and she was able to single out his voice from the others. The familiar sound wrapped her in warmth.

Her final position was just in front of Henri. Gastone took his place on her left, on the other side of the aisle. The song drew to an end, the men singing out a long and lovely *amen*. It was silent as the other Hunters filed in. And finally, Jack moved to stand before the dais between Belle and Gastone.

Father Sinclair led the ceremony. Speaking in Latin, he formed the cross over his chest and everyone else did the same. From there he went into an opening prayer similar to the way he began Mass.

When he finished, Father turned to Belle and asked, "Why do Hunters gather here today?"

She replied the same as she had several times before. "We bring you a faithful soul in hopes that he may be returned a Hunter."

The Father nodded and turned his gaze to Jack. "Does he know the words to be spoken?"

"He does," Belle replied.

"These words should not be said lightly. They are an oath to God, a creed to man." Father said solely to Jack. His voice was loud, filling the church. His tone most serious. "They cannot be broken. As you stand before me, do you take heed of this?"

Jack breathed deeply. "Yes."

The Father nodded and gestured to the floor. "Then kneel and speak."

As though the very weight of impending responsibility rested on his shoulders, Jack lowered himself down to one knee. He bowed his head, gathering his breath, and began. "O Holy Angel, attendant of our wretched souls . . ."

They watched silently as Jack recited the holy words. Belle glanced at her Hunters and her eyes met Gastone's. He didn't react, but she knew his thoughts as surely as she knew her own. He was remembering the day they had taken the oath together. Gastone, Andre, and herself had all knelt as one and said these very same words. They would then stand by later as Delano, Nicolas, Jean, and others took their vows.

Each of them had been so proud and so ready to offer up their swords for the cause. They all had their own reasons for making the sacrifice, but each also understood the severity of the commitment. Belle remembered how the cold marble felt against her knees. How heavy the creed was as it fell from her tongue. More than anything she remembered how the experience had solidified a bond between her and the other Hunters. She was one of them; would always have their back and they would always have hers.

Light filtered through the massive stained glass windows,

casting the room in vibrant colors that mingled with the warm candlelight. The light touched Jack's face and fell over his golden locks. Watching, as he recited the creed, Belle knew Jack was experiencing the same thoughts and feelings that she had on her initiation.

Formed the holy trinity over his chest, Jack finished the oath, "In nomine Patris, et Filii, et Spiritus Sancti, Amen."

Jack raised his head but did not stand. From a velvet pillow held by a friar, Father Sinclair took an object. He stepped before the American and presented what would be Jack's rosary.

"The church offers you this sacred item to honor you in this sacrifice." Father Sinclair indicated the rosary. "Will you protect it, as it will protect your soul?"

Jack replied, "I will."

"Then rise, Hunter. Take this gift and may your first act be one of remembrance."

As commanded, Jack came to his feet and the rosary was placed in his hands. His gloved fingers ran over the gilded metal and Belle unknowingly did the same with hers. With no glance to them, the Father turned, leading Jack to the catacombs. There he will enter the Hall of the Hunters for the first time, and alone. In there he will read the nameplates, feel the silence, and pay his respects to those who came before.

This part of the ceremony is often the hardest for many. It's a glimpse into their life as a Hunter. In their beginning, they see their end. Those laid to rest in the Hall of Hunters had performed the same ceremony, spoken the same creed, given the ultimate sacrifice, and someday the new Hunter will be put to rest alongside them.

At the thought of death, Belle's mind flickered back to Aleksander—though he'd been there at the edge, keeping her anxious the moment she left his side. She looked at the windows as if she could determine by them how much time had past. Steeling her fears, Belle used the silence to pray for Aleksander; pray that he would live.

Jack soon returned, his expression solemn, and took up his previous position. Clasping his hands before him, rosary dangling from his fingers, Jack nodded his readiness to the priest. Father Sinclair then gestured to Henri, who came forward holding a velvet pillow of his own. Upon it were two custom revolvers. Belle was pleased to see that they were not made in the same style as her own, with long, curved handles. These were westernized to fit Jack's particular tastes, with hard edges, short handles, and silver-plated.

"The Hunters offer you these weapons to protect you in this sacrifice," Henri recited, holding the pillow out. "Will you use them always with honor?"

"I will." Jack met his eyes, throwing meaning behind his words.

"Then, Hunter, take this gift and may your second act be one of preparedness."

Removing the old revolvers he'd brought with him from the New World, Jack handed them to Gastone. He then picked up the first pistol offered by Henri. For just a second he admired them, then popped open the bullet chamber. Belle held opened her pouch of custom-made bullets and poured a handful into his palm. He then preceded to load his guns. As he finished, he snapped the chamber back into place, gave the revolvers a twirl around his fingers, and slide them into his holsters. Liking the feel of it, he flashed her a smile and a wink.

"Now, for the final offering." Friar Sinclair held out a hand, directing them to leave the church.

Jack turned and led the procession back down the aisle. Friar Clemens was there with another, and together they opened the doors. Cold air tumbled in, causing gooseflesh to rise on her arm. The crowd outside had tripled in size. Every man, woman, and child huddled together with excited anticipation. They broke into cheers as Jack appeared. He tipped his hat to a few ladies, making them flutter and bat their eyes.

Standing in front, apart from the crowd was Marshall Baine. He was the official holster to the Hunters. He bred the Friesians, trained them, and chose each horse for each Hunter. He was in no way formal, wearing clothes for warmth and work. Monsieur Baine smiled with big lips that parted a thick beard. In one hand was the lead rope to a young, dark stallion. In the other was a crier's bell. He rang it several times, calling the crowd to silence.

"The townspeople offer you this steed to guide you in this sacrifice." Marshall presented the beautiful horse with pride. "Will you trust him, as he trusts you?"

"I will." Jack rushed down the steps to meet the horse. He ran a hand over his forelock and stared in awe.

"Then mount, Hunter," Marshall said more quietly and with a devilish glint in his eyes. "Take this gift and may your third act be one of camaraderie."

Grinning, Jack took the reins. He shoved his foot in the stirrup and pulled himself into the saddle. Immediately, he sat with more pride and confidence than Belle had ever seen from him on one of the spare horses.

"Good townspeople of Contefées!" Father Sinclair called from the top of the cathedral steps and all eyes turned to him. He raised a hand toward Jack. "I give you, your new Hunter."

Boisterous cheers filled the air. Belle clapped obligingly, but already her thoughts were back with Aleksander.

# Chapter Twenty-Six

The ride was slow and quiet. Belle watched the shadowed trees pass, but mostly she stared at the stars shining above. On winter nights, they were always the brightest.

Reaching LeClair House, Friar Clemens dropped her off at the lighthouse, then drove the carriage into the stable. He would care for the tack and see to all of the horses. His own small room was there—an alteration to the original plans since he refused to take up space in the house. He was safe even in the stable though, which was fortified with as much steel protection as the house. It gave the Hunters peace of mind to sleep beneath the sea, but Clemens insisted that if the stable were ever attacked, it would hold long enough for them to rescue him.

Belle opened the lighthouse door, wondering what Hunter was keeping a lookout from above, and stepped into the drafty building. Momentarily she flashed back to the dark tower of Castle Vakre Fjell. Uncomfortable shivers skimmed down her spine. Quickly, Belle used her rosary key to unlock the elevator and entered the steel chamber.

Normally, after exiting the lift, Belle went to the armory to remove her cloak and weapons. But her impatience was too much. She first wanted to check on the Prince. Down the grated hall and up the wooden stairs she went to the spare room he'd been given.

The blankets were thrown off Aleksander. His shirt was open and pushed aside. The doctor had a wet sponge, which he was pressing to the Prince's torso. Another damp cloth rested on Aleksander's forehead. Belle rushed over and put her hand to his cheek. It was hot to the touch though the wet cloth was cold.

Aleksander murmured unintelligibly, his eyes creasing with distress. Then he suddenly relaxed and rested soundly. Belle looked in horror at the doc.

"That's new," Doc said, bringing himself upright and dropping his sponge into the bucket at his feet. "He's been doing it every few minutes for the last half hour."

"What is it?" Belle gestured for the bucket, intent on taking over so that Doc could rest.

He passed it willingly and slumped into his chair. At only a glance, the doctor looked rough. His shirt was damp. His sleeves rolled haphazardly up to the elbow. Belle went to work as he pulled a silver flask from inside his unbuttoned vest.

"Hallucinations . . . Fever dreams." There was a pause as he gulped whatever was in the container. "The fever is overheating his brain, making it overactive. It can cause a person to imagine all manner of strangeness."

"Could it kill him?" Belle rung out the sponge, then gently ran it over the Prince's stomach and chest.

Aleksander's muscles were tone, defined by the many forms of combat training he was required to learn growing up. His broad chest expanded with his breathing. His stomach muscles tensed with whatever wildness tormented his mind. It was impossible not to notice how beautiful he was, as she attempted to cool his hot skin.

"I imagine that it will actually." Doc was staring at her when her gaze shot to him. He was not jesting. His abrupt answer was meant to be like the quick setting of a bone; painful, but fast.

With a sigh, he removed his glasses—wiping his forehead with his sleeve in the same motion—and began to clean them. "I've been monitoring him closely, Belle. At the rate this fever is progressing . . . he won't make it to daybreak."

"What's wrong with him?" Belle stared at the doc. Suddenly the whole world muted and grayed. "Is there nothing you can do?"

"I'm trying to keep his fever down, but I don't know what's causing it or the coma." Doc leaned forward, bracing his elbows on his knees. "As a normal patient, he's perfectly healthy. But he's not normal, is he?"

Belle dropped the cloth back into the bucket and went to the head of the bed. She cupped Aleksander's cheek, enjoying the feel of his smooth skin against her palm. This was the Aleksander she knew. Not that beast in the castle. That was something she didn't know at all.

"Aleksander has two halves. There's this half—his human half." She grazed her knuckles over his cheekbone, wishing she could see his eyes. Finally, she looked at the doctor, who watched her thoughtfully. "But his other half is cursed. Maybe this fever isn't coming from his healthy human form, but from the beast he was before?"

Doc opened one of his hands, then dropped it. "I'm a man of science, Belle. What you suggest isn't something I know anything about."

"Perhaps not, but if anyone knows anything about this curse, they'll be living at Castle Vakre Fjell." Belle turned toward the door. "And I know just who to ask."

"What do you mean?" Doc questioned, but she was already out of the room and headed toward the armory. He jumped up and followed after. "You can't mean to ride for the castle tonight?"

"You said it yourself, Doc. He'll be dead by sunrise." The doc was close on her heels, as she went down the stairs. "If I wish to save him, I see no other option."

"But, Belle, you just got back and it's too dangerous." They turned into the armory.

"What's too dangerous?" Gastone stood within, one leg propped on a bench where he was just sticking a blade into the sleeve of his boot.

He slid his foot back to the floor, drawing himself to his full height and not looking in any mood for games. He wasn't alone either, the rest of Belle's hunting party was there. They'd returned early from the celebration to perform the nightly hunt; she knew this without having to ask. They each stopped their preparations to look at her and the harried doctor.

"She's riding back to the castle," Doc blurted, his eyes bulging. "Tonight!"

"What?" Gastone scowled, a vein appearing in his forehead.

"The Prince is dying," Belle said calmly. She addressed the entire group, refusing to give Gastone her sole attention. After all, he answered to her and not the other way around. "Doc says he won't make it to morning. I'm going to ride swiftly, straight on to Castle Vakre Fjell. If anyone knows how to help him, they will."

Belle expected Gastone to fight her immediately, but he shook his head and turned away. Roughly, he shoved a hand through his black hair.

"We'll go with you then," Jack said, patting the new pistols at his side.

"No, this is about speed. There and back, as quickly as possible." She grabbed her cloak, throwing it over her shoulders. "Also, our border still needs to be protected. The hunt can't be delayed."

"It would still be wise to take a few of us with you." Andre had been tinkering with the inner workings of his mechanical arm. He snapped the metal door shut, tugged up his glove, and returned the tiny screwdriver to his jacket pocket. "We won't slow you down."

Belle considered this. "Fine. You, Jack, and—"

"Me," Gastone volunteered.

She'd been about to pick Jean, wanting her second-in-command to stay with the other group. But seeing the determination in Gastone's eyes made her concede. He was picking his battles. He knew he couldn't convince Belle to stay, but he wouldn't let her go there alone again.

"Fine. Jean, Delano, and Nicolas will stay and hunt our borders." She looked them each in the eyes, making them all nod their understanding. "Let's get to it then."

Silently, they went through their weapons, checking for problems and ammunition. The doctor wished them luck and returned to his patient. Belle asked after her father, as they walked to the elevator. Nicolas said he was still at the tavern, having some drinks in honor of his fallen Hunters. Belle was disappointed she couldn't say au revoir, but it was probably for the best—no doubt, Henri would have refused to let her go.

Charming was well rested when she found him in his stall. Belle hated to ask more of him, but he was still eager for duty. With steady but swift hands, she ran a heavy brush across Charming's black coat. Each stroke brought the many strands into perfect alignment. Next came the blanket and then the saddle. The smell of dust and oils wafted around Belle as she carried it to her stall. The leather creaked with each movement. Aside from their working, the stable was quiet. Each rider was lost in their own thoughts and tasks.

Finally, Belle slid the metal bit into Charming's mouth and drew the crown of the bridle over his long ears. Taking the reins, she steered her Friesian out of his stall. Gastone was exiting at the same time; the others were about to do the same. Belle met his gaze. After all these years, their movements had been synchronized. But only their movements, their thoughts—and emotions—certainly weren't the same. She looked away.

As she'd always done, Belle led them out of the barn. With one discreet motion, she buttoned her skirt over her right hip, then placed the toe of her boot into the stirrup. In the cold night air, beneath the light of a single lantern, they mounted together.

Riding to the border, Belle waited for her Hunters to settle. She then lowered her head, "Oh Holy Angel. Attendant of our wretched souls and afflicted life."

The others then joined and her heart beamed at being beside them once more. *Poof. Poof. Poof.* The gas lamps began to illuminate, turned on by Friar Clemens in the stable.

Signing the cross over their chests, they finished. "In nomine Patris, et Filii, et Spiritus Sancti, Amen."

There was a moment of thoughtful silence, then Belle said to the three who would remain behind, "Good hunting."

They each nodded and Delano replied, "Same to you."

Without another word, Belle cued Charming. Gastone, Andre, Jack, and herself galloped into the dangerous forest of Vakre Fjell. This time it was not with the intent to kill, but to save—if they were fast enough.

# Chapter Twenty-Seven

I ran. Smoothly over the fresh and old snow, I swept. I was fast as the Hunters I chased. Faster even, if I wanted to be. I ran alongside the four of them.

They're focused, watching for my wolves, but not intent on engaging them. No, their goal was speed. I can only guess as to the reason, which is why I followed.

The rage inside me wanted to kill them though—To step before them and slaughter each one with my bare hands. I could. It would be easy. Like crushing a snowflake.

I stared at the head rider, watching her search for the blur of me she'd just seen. I wanted to kill Belle the most. She was supposed to kill the Prince—not fall in love with him. The fool of a girl. I needed Prince Aleksander out of the way and both her and Henri failed to do what they were trained to do. Worse yet, the Prince had been able to do something impossible. He fought the curse and became human again. All because of the beauty I watched now.

Oh how I wanted to kill her; punish her for messing with my fate. But then, the Prince wasn't with them and he was the real threat. Fenrir was still intent on bringing Aleksander to his side though. I could disobey Fenrir; I answered to the Universe—not some god. But such bad blood that would cause. No, if I wanted *to rid myself of Prince Aleksander I'd have to, once again, rely on someone besides myself.*

*My wolves could do it. Fenrir could not fault them for their wild hunger, nor could he blame me. Yes, they will kill the Prince for me. And I will kill the beauty.*

*I breathed deep, savoring the idea of a good slaughter here in the woods. I reached over and petted the wolf who'd come to my side. He growled at the passing riders, his hackles rising down the spine of his back.*

*"Let's wait for your siblings," I said to my spawn. "I'll call some from the mountains. When the Hunters attempt to return the wretched prince to his castle, you'll have a feast. And I'll have my way."*

Icy air whipped across Belle's face, fluttering her loose curls and lifting the fur cloak off her back. She clutched the reins, leaning into Charming's mane for speed. *Thud. Thud. Thud.* The sound of his heavy hoof beats were muffled by the powdered snow beneath. Belle glanced over her shoulder.

Gastone was just off to her right and Andre on her left. Jack followed close behind from the rear. They too gave their horses rein, letting them run without hindrance. Thick puffs of breath rolled from the nostrils of each stallion, only to be swept up by the passing wind.

Turning her eyes to the trees, Belle searched for hellhounds. They hadn't seen any. Except once, they'd seen something. Something that looked human. Then there was the growl. It was low and rippling, flowing over them with all its yearning hatred.

It unnerved Belle, causing her to hurry Charming even more. Whatever was out there, human or not, Belle wanted to avoid it.

Relief was like warm butter in her chest, when she saw Castle Vakre Fjell looming over the trees.

Two soldiers watched them approach. One recognized Belle and signaled for the gates to be opened. The Hunters swooped past, nodding their thanks as they went. Every few paces along the bridge were great stone torches. They blazed, illuminating the night and lighting their path to the castle.

They didn't halt but continued their run across the bridge. Only when they reached the great front doors did the Hunters slow. A hostler rushed over to take their horses. Belle shooed him away.

"Monsieur Laramie Petit. Get him—" she started to command, then the doors burst open.

A troupe of worried people rushed out. Laramie led them. They hurried down the steps, and he held up a hand to hold them back. Particularly General Kogsworthe who looked ready to have her arrested . . . again.

"Thank the heavens you're alive, mademoiselle." Laramie came right up to Belle, taking her hand softly in his. "The beast, tell me, what fate befell him?"

Her heart clenched at the heartache she saw in his eyes. Even now, he wouldn't betray his Prince's secret though he feared that Belle had killed him. She leaned over, bringing her head close to his.

"He lives," she said, watching the relief wash over his face. He turned to tell the others, but Belle held tight to his hand and pulled his attention back up to her. "He's human, Laramie. I watched the beast become Aleksander right before me."

His eyes widened and his blond eyebrows rose. "That's not possible."

"Isn't it?" she asked, fishing for any shard information.

"No!" Laramie violently shook his head. "The curse trapped

Aleksander in that wolfish body. His mind and soul were still the same, but he couldn't . . . get out. "

*Trapped.* That's what Aleksander meant when he said he was a prisoner back when they first met. That seemed like so long ago now. It hadn't been entirely honest, but to imply that the beast was his captor wasn't completely untrue either. That's if any of this was true. Why would Aleksander lie about it if it were? Belle shook her head from all the confusion.

"I *swear* it," Laramie added, reading her reaction as mistrust—which in some way it was.

"There's more." Belle relaxed some, wanting to believe Laramie. "After he became human, he went into a coma. Now he has a rising fever. Our doctor says he won't make it to the morning if we don't do something."

"My God." Laramie's face turned a ghostly white, the wrinkles around his mouth and eyes looking even more pronounced. "What did the doctor say caused it?"

"He says that Aleksander is healthy and that the there's no reason for the coma or fever." Nervous energy zapped through Belle's heart. The fact that Laramie didn't produce an answer straight away terrified her. "But what if the fever wasn't coming from Aleksander as a human, but as the beast?"

"He was healthy as a beast too, I'm afraid." Laramie looked at the ground, his thoughts taking him to other places. Then his brow quirked up with whatever thought just past into his mind. He looked back at Belle. "Did you say he became human in front of you?"

"Yes."

"Aleksander hated what the curse turned him into. He searched tirelessly for a way to reverse it. But he never could. No matter what he tried, he could never change back." Laramie's face softened suddenly like something had fallen into place and he was comfortable in his certainty of it. "Until you. You saw him and ran from the castle. And he chased after. I'd wager that Aleksander had never been more desperate to be human, then right then—with you . . ." His eyes drifted and his voice grew faint. "And now that he's free, he wouldn't be willing to give it up. Even if the curse kills him instead."

"You think he's still fighting the curse to stay human?" Belle ran through Laramie's words, trying to keep pace with his stream of thought.

"That's precisely what I think, mademoiselle." Laramie stared her in the eyes, forcing all of his intensity into his gaze. "He fought the curse back—for you—and he's still fighting it."

Heart clenching within her chest, Belle swallowed. "So how do I help him fight it?"

Laramie shook his head. "You don't."

"What?" Belle raised her voice slightly at the unthinkable.

"There is no stopping the curse." His lips pursed and his head tilted sympathetically. "You know this. Think back to your research and what you found there."

Belle didn't have to. She remembered all too well what little they'd managed to find. "So there's nothing we can do? He's going to die?"

"No." Monsieur Petit patted her hand. "Tell him to give in to the curse."

"You want me to tell him to become that . . . beast again?" Belle asked, incredulous. Tears formed at the rim of her eyes. She blinked and swallowed them down, causing a painful lump in her throat.

"It's the only way he'll get to live." Laramie lifted Belle's chin, forcing her eyes back on him. "And you're the only one who can get him to do it. *You* have to save his life."

"Okay." Belle sat back in her saddle, taking up her reins. "No matter what happens, I'll return him to you."

Laramie bowed and stepped back. "Godspeed."

Belle's eyes fell to the slumbering Prince and then to the doctor sitting next to him. Doc's back was to the door. He held Aleksander's wrist and his head rested in the palm of his other hand. His posture was slouched, entirely defeated.

"How is he?" Belle grabbed a rag from the wash bin and rung it out. Gently, she sat on the bed and replaced the cloth over Aleksander's forehead. She noticed the beads of sweat on his skin as she did so.

"His fever hallucinations are more frequent." Doc sat straighter and grabbed his glasses from the nightstand. "But his temperature has leveled out, at least for now. What about you? Did you learn anything?"

"Maybe." Belle didn't spare him a glance.

She had eyes only for Aleksander. He shivered despite how warm he was to the touch. Occasionally his breathing would accelerate or his muscles would clench, disrupting the calm sleep.

When there seemed to be nothing more to say, Belle removed the cloth and dropped it back in the bucket. Her heart pounded in her chest. She had no idea if this would work. In fact, she doubted that it would. But she couldn't let that show in her voice. Belle had to be the woman that Aleksander needed her to be. Confident and in control.

Belle took a deep breath and when she was finally at ease, she leaned in to place her lips next to his ear. Her hand almost instinctively went to his hair. She made small graceful strokes, letting the locks slide through her fingers.

"Aleksander, listen to me," she said quietly. There was a subtle shift in the Prince's muscles and she wondered if he really could understand. Elation and hope shot like a bullet through her. Doc's chair creaked as he shifted to listen. Belle ignored him. "I need you to let the curse take you. I know you're fighting it, but it's going to kill you if you don't give in." She paused, searching for the right words. "Your people need you, Aleksander. You're all they have. Giving in, isn't giving up." The words came out of her easily then. Belle forgot about the doc and the surrounding room. There was only her and Aleksander. "We'll find a way. I'm not ready to let you go."

Belle stayed close to him, continuing to caress his hair, even when there was nothing more for her to say. What felt like an eternity passed and nothing changed. Belle dropped her head, tears forcing their way to the surface. What more could she do? What other options did they have? A droplet of salty sadness landed onto his cheek.

Belle whispered, "*Please.*"

Just like that, as though her pleading was more than he could bear, Aleksander's muscles began to spasm. Belle moved back and watched in amazement. Angelic ringing hummed in the air. A giddy smile broke over her lips and she looked at the doctor. He was pressed against the wall, terror written on his face. But Belle was elated. It was working! Aleksander had heard her and was shifting back.

Thin rays of silver light jutted out from the Prince's skin, illuminating the room like a beacon. Belle watched them dance over his body until they were too bright and her eyes burned to look away. Whiteness exploded over her eyelids, then suddenly vanished along with the noise. The room went terribly silent.

When her eyes finally adjusted, the Prince was gone and the beast was in his place. Even at rest, he was massive. The room felt suddenly smaller. He dwarfed the bed that his feet now hung off of.

Doc gasped something about the holy mother, Mary and formed the cross over his chest.

Belle smiled at him. "It's all right, Doc. He's still just the Prince. He still needs us."

The doctor couldn't seem to look away, which was understandable. She wasn't sure he'd ever seen a hellhound up close, let alone whatever the Prince was. Belle angled her head to draw the doc's attention. "Okay?"

Finally, he looked at her and recognition flashed in his eyes. Doc nodded, swallowing hard. As long as he didn't forget that it was Aleksander he was looking at, that was all she needed from him.

Turning back to the Prince, Belle leaned back over him just as she had before. This time she spoke into large, pointed ears and her fingers combed through thick fur. "Good Aleksander. You're going to be fine. I'm right here with you."

A moan rumbled from his chest, reminding her so much of a sighing dog.

# Chapter Twenty-Eight

With Aleksander finally resting soundly and Doc keeping watch over him, Belle found her father in his workroom. Henri leaned over his desk, tinkering with some new device. He looked up when Belle walked in and she had to stifle a laugh. Resting on his nose was the most absurd looking glasses she'd ever seen. They featured many lenses of varying size and color. There was even a suspended candle with a mirror to reflect the light.

Henri took off the glasses and to hug Belle, telling her how glad he was that she was okay. Feeling ashamed, Belle was quick to apologize for leaving without word. He understood her reasons, saying that the doctor had filled him in completely when he returned from the tavern. Now all he wanted to know was if she learned anything from her trip back to Vakre Fjell.

So Belle explained everything from her conversation with Laramie to Aleksander turning back into a beast. When she was done, Henri was at a loss for words. Then he pulled his glasses back on and said, "Machines are much less complicated than the divine."

Belle agreed and confessed to exhaustion. Henri kissed her on the forehead and wished her goodnight. As Belle climbed into her bed, with Pixie snuggled in her own tiny nest, Belle was aware that she wasn't as tired as she'd led Henri to believe. But she was more than eager to sleep—and perhaps to moon dream.

Hours later Belle threw her off her blankets. She sat on the edge of the bed and brushed her hands through her hair, letting out a frustrated sigh. Pawing the wall, she found the tiny brass turnkey. Small flames appeared around the room with only a twist. They grew as she turned the key further, casting the room with dim lighting before she let go.

Belle glanced over, watching Pixie's chest rise and fall with simulated breathing. She'll stay there, in her decorated egg, for many more hours still. Perhaps the Prince was moon dreaming with her because he certainly hadn't been with Belle. Her sleep had been dreamless until stress finally woke her.

Knowing her thoughts would keep her awake, Belle climbed from her bed. She went to her wardrobe and withdrew a simple blue dress. She slipped it on and grabbed her brush. Standing in front of the mirror, she dragged her long waves of curls in front of her shoulders. Belle stared at her green eyes, the softness of her hair—just stared, not really admiring. Then she noticed the saddlebags sitting by the door, hidden by the many shadows in her room.

Belle walked over to pick them up. The smell of worn leather swept into her lungs. In one pouch, she found her father's pocket watch. In the other bag was Aleksander's letters to various recipients. She ran her thumb over the top address, thinking of Aleksander's fingers moving his pen across that very parchment. Her imagination pictured him leaning casually over his desk, as rays of sunlight crossed the room. But that was impossible, wasn't it? The Prince would have been the beast when these letters were written. This couldn't be his handwriting; it had to belong to Laramie then.

Feeling somehow slighted by this realization, Belle pushed the letters aside. Beneath was the music box Aleksander had gifted to her. Removing it, she set the saddlebags back down. Adoringly, she touched the rose engravings, then lifted the metal cover. *A Starry Waltz* twinkled out. In an instant, Belle's memory took her back to that dance in the ballroom. The feel of her hand in Aleksander's, the soft look in his eyes—it all came back to her.

Hurt permeated into her thoughts and the memory vanished. Belle hated feeling this way. She worried for the Prince but felt scorned by his secrets. When she expected him to call her into a moon dream and explain everything, he didn't. The snub of it was a painful offense. Oh, how she wanted to throttle him.

Frustrated at Aleksander, and her conflicted self, Belle tossed the music box onto her bed. She needed some space. Out of her room, then through the parlor and toward the elevator she slipped. Halfway there, she turned into the Observation Room.

Passing beneath the large, metal archway, Belle stepped onto stone floors. The walls of this room reached up and kept reaching until they angled into a wide arch. But the walls were not walls; they were immense glass windows held together by strong metal beams and large bolts.

Her boots clicked against the hard stone as she walked across the room and over to a lone pedestal. Belle grabbed a lever and flipped it into the up position. *Ke-chug.* Great gas-lamps illuminated the green and blue hues of the watery depths outside her sunken house. They shone out like sun rays, reflecting through the seawater.

Belle then turned the knob of a smaller gas-lamp. It cast yellow light over the room's three desks and various gadgets. This was her father's second study; a place he came to do research instead of building inventions. During the day, he could study the ocean or the sky. At night, before lowering LeClair House deep into the sea, Henri could even study the stars.

However, Belle liked this room for quiet thinking. She walked over to the windows. A single fish wiggled closer to the warm gaslights, eying her suspiciously. Ignoring him, Belle stared into the outreaching beams of light and watched the changing colors of the water.

Dread appeared as she opened herself to the flood of worries. What if Gastone was right? What if Aleksander had lied to her about everything? He had kept it from her that he was that beast. What else had he kept from her and why did he not pull her into a moon dream? The Prince had to know that she had questions, that she needed to talk to him. Avoiding her now could only mean bad things. Belle's chest constricted. She could be wrong and leading them all to their deaths. Her foolishness could be the Hunters' downfall. Belle felt like she was going to be sick.

She grabbed her stomach, clutching the dress fabric, and took long deep breaths through her nose. Over and over again she mentally told herself to calm down, everything was going to be fine. But the awful feeling didn't leave.

"Belle?" Turning around, she saw Henri. The lamplight fell over his face, creating shadows and exaggerating the textures of his facial hair. "What are you doing here at this hour?"

"I'm afraid that my mind is too unsettled for sleep at the moment." Belle gave her father a halfhearted smile.

"What troubles you?" Henri walked over to the Constellation Apparatus at the room's center.

It was a scaled down replica of the orbiting planets and stars. Much like a globe, it rested upon a tall, wooden pedestal and took the shape of a sphere. Though, instead of being a map that sits upon the surface, the celestial bodies were suspended by thin wires to make them appear weightless at the device's center. Circling it all were two intersecting gold-plated rings. The carvings upon the rings, and where the rings came together, were measurements of time. It was one of several devices Henri used for his research.

"I had expected the Prince to pull me into a moon dream and explain everything to me, alleviate my concerns." Belle followed her father, watching him examine the position of the simulated stars. "He did not, and now I'm questioning myself as well as him."

Henri scratched his beard and tilted his head to get a different angle on the constellations. "I suppose I can understand your concern, but beyond that, what would cause you to doubt the Prince?"

"I . . ." Belle searched for an answer. "I do not know."

"Did you not trust him before? Did your instincts ever warn you away from him?" Henri straightened and looked at her as he asked his questions, then crossed the floor to one of his desks. He opened a leather book and scribbled notes within. "When you went back to Vakre Fjell seeking help, did Monsieur Petit say anything that would give you pause? Or ring untrue?"

"No! No, nothing like that," Belle rushed out to stop his flow of questioning. "I've never felt cause to mistrust them."

"Then you must have faith in them." He snapped the book shut and looked at her. "And faith in yourself. You're a LeClair, your instincts are impeccable."

"But what about what you said in the dungeon?" she added, not completely able to shake her discontent. "About there being true evil in that castle?"

Henri looked off into the dense ocean water, his eyes shifting just out of focus. His voice was soft, sad, as he remembered. "I'd watched many of my old friends die violently that day—all for the sake of my invention, no less. Sitting in that dank dungeon on *that* day . . . everything looked evil to me. I'm an old man, Belle. Too old, I think, for all this."

His thoughts still looked so far away.

Belle stepped across the cold floor to grasp his big, callused hands in hers. "You're not so old as you think. Tired perhaps, but so am I."

He smiled warmly, chasing away their dark thoughts, and squeezed her hands.

"What *are you* doing awake so late?" She curled an eyebrow as the sudden thought came to her.

Henri chuckled. "As tired as I may be, work still invigorates me the same as it did when I was a fanatical, young lad."

"What are you working on?" Instantly Belle was taken back to her childhood when she would spend hours watching Henri work and sharing his inventions with her. She was so grateful for the distraction now.

"I'm experimenting with a substance called aether." He grabbed something from his desk and placed it in Belle's hand.

It was a small glass sphere that was encircled by two brass rings, much like the Constellation Apparatus. Holding it up in the light, Belle marveled at the substance within the globe. It was a swirl of purple and yellow electricity. The snapping lightning curled in on itself and traced the shield of glass; always in motion.

"It is the quintessence of air," Henri said, causing Belle to look at him sideways and he rushed on to explain. "It is the unseen force between you and me—even the blackness between the stars." He sighed, his eyes drifting into the depths of the orb. "Its uses are endless. Without it birds could not fly, light could not travel, and gravity would not exist."

"How did you come by it?" She turned the object over in her hands, trying to imagine the aether surrounding everything.

"Monsieur Genov," Henri answered, giving the name of his American colleague—the one that specialized in unusual creatures, and was also an inventor. Belle's father picked up a redwood box from his desk. "He managed to harness the mysterious element and is using it to give ships flight."

"Flight?!" Handing the orb back to Henri, he tucked it safely into the dark, velvety folds of the box.

"Yes, indeed, flight." Henri grinned, excitement dancing in his eyes. "He says they'll be called airships and, with the help of this fantastic substance, the first commercial flight is underway."

"Remarkable," Belle whispered.

"Imagine, great, white sails could be soaring the American skies as we speak." They were both silent as they did just that. Henri then chuckled and came back to himself. "Marvelous. Anyway, he sent me this sample to experiment with."

"That was kind of him."

"Genov has both an engineering and entrepreneurial mind. He thinks big." Henri waved his arms, emphasizing his words with his hands. "Great locomotives and now airships. Whereas my mind tends to veer toward more practical applications. We think differently, you see, and as inventors we have an obligation to explore all avenues." He placed the box within a drawer in his desk and used a key from his breast pocket to lock it.

"Perhaps you could do something with heating?" Belle touched Henri's shoulder and leaned to kiss his whiskered cheek. "A portable heating source, for those without a carriage. Could do well in areas such as ours."

"Indeed, one must have cold blood to live in God's Cup, or perhaps very hot blood. I'm not really sure which makes more sense," Henri said with a chuckle that shook his shoulders. "Are you going to bed?"

"Yes, I may not have all of the answers yet, but you've eased my mind considerably." She gave her father a hug and he squeezed her back.

"I am glad. Give it time, my little Bellerina." He smiled, using his childhood nickname for her. "Sleep well."

# Chapter
# Twenty-Nine

A fist slammed several times against her bedroom door. The bangs ricocheted off the metal walls. Belle was jerked from her sleep.

Jack called for her, shouting, "The Prince is rampaging. We need you now! Belle!"

Just like that, with a toss of her covers, Belle was up and out of bed. Pixie flew past her, chittering excitedly. There was no time to dress, so Belle grabbed the sheer robe from next to her bed and draped it over her. Pixie landed on her shoulder, clutching the white fabric.

As Jack started banging again, Belle went to the door and opened it.

"Enjoy your beauty sleep, Princess?" he said quickly, before turning to jog down the hall.

"I'm no Princess!" She followed after, her robe and hair fluttering about her. Belle shouted over the bangs, "What's going on?"

"His *Highness* woke up and went feral," the cowboy said over his shoulder with more irritation than worry in his voice. "Doc got out and shut him in the room. Not a scratch on the ol' boy somehow."

The fact that Belle hadn't heard the ruckus was a testament both to her deep sleep and the thick metal walls. Belle didn't ask any more questions as they approached the group gathered outside Aleksander's door. Everyone was there, including Bishop Sauvage and Father Sinclair. Belle was dismayed to see that they had come now, of all times. Doc stood at the back, looking like he needed a drink, and the Hunters all had weapons at the ready.

Belle halted just as something slammed into the wooden door. Bits of wood splintered around thick black claws. Everyone froze as the fingers gripped and ungripped the wood. Then with an angry roar, the Prince jerked his hand free.

"This is preposterous. He needs to be put down," the Bishop argued to Henri.

Belle's eyebrows shot up. "You want to kill the Vakrein Prince? Are you *mad*?"

Bishop Sauvage's nostrils flared and he glared contemptuously. "That ceased to matter when he became the devil incarnate."

"My God." Belle shook her head, then pushed past Jean and Gastone who stood in front of the door, waiting for it to give way—or a decision to be made. Someone called for her to stop, but she didn't.

With no weapons on her body, Belle grasped the brass doorknob and turned it. She pulled the door open and made to step forward. At the sound of the intrusion, the beast was across the room too fast for her mind to keep up. His roar blasted her ears, sending an instinctual fear into her bones. A massively clawed paw came down toward her.

It froze. The creature that was Aleksander towered over her, nearly a foot taller than the man she knew. He stared down at her. Anger curled his lips, but his eyes flashed recognition. Aleksander was so close to her, his breath wafted against her hair. Gradually, his paw dropped to his side. He never looked away.

Pixie's metal joints literally shook at the nape of Belle's neck where she'd taken refuge. Belle didn't move; didn't speak. She allowed the rage and tension to seep from the room. He was a beast of monstrous proportions, but Belle knew him. She knew that beneath the rage and terrifying exterior was her prince. The evidence was in his blue eyes—eyes that were now wolf-like—and the way they looked at her.

Belle dared to speak. "It's all right. I'm right here."

Aleksander's breathing slowed. His head dropped just an inch closer to hers. Belle placed her hand carefully on his chest. The fur was soft to the touch and the heart beneath pounded strong and steady. His muzzle grazed her hair and she felt the intake of breath as he scented her. With her free hand, Belle gestured to the Hunters behind her. Several clicks indicated the lowering of guns, but she didn't fool herself that there still weren't a few pointed his way.

Belle pulled back just slightly to look into the Prince's eyes again. "Will you wait in here for just a moment while I settle this? I won't be long and I'll be right outside this door."

Prince Aleksander stared at her, making her wonder if he could even understand her in this form. Then he stepped back, drawing himself to full height. He really was unlike anything they'd ever seen before. A hellhound with a body that was truly a blend of man and beast, that somehow walked on two legs . . . She would have thought it was impossible.

Aleksander glared at the other Hunters, his eyes sending unspoken warnings. As Belle reached for the door, he looked back to her and held her eyes until the second the door closed. She took a deep breath, settling and preparing herself, then turned around.

Gastone spoke first. Anger radiated from him. "What the hell was that?"

"Golly," said Jack, looking at her with wide eyes. "I never thought I'd say this to a lady, but you've got some serious balls—"

Jean smacked the back of his head.

"You could've been killed," Gastone went on like he hadn't spoken.

"She could've gotten us all killed," Nicolas added, but it was more of a matter-of-fact statement than one of accusation.

"No, I know him," Belle piped in before anyone else could. "I knew he wouldn't have hurt me."

"Bull—" Gastone's finger went up like he was about to truly give her a verbal thrashing, but he stopped himself. He closed his eyes, balling his hand into a fist.

Henri picked up where he left off. "He does not seem like the civilized prince you described to us."

Gastone pointed at her father, indicating that he'd taken the words from his mouth.

"It is him. He's just confused," Belle said to her father. He was the only one she had to convince. "A lot has happened to him in such a short amount of time, but I know the man *inside* of the beast. He is a good man."

A snort of derision turned everyone's attention to Bishop Sauvage. "A flight of fancy from a female reaching her childbearing years, nothing more." The comment was such a slap in the face, Belle found herself almost dumbfounded. She risked her life for the church and this was how they saw her? The Bishop preached further, "His very existence is a blight against God. You must do your duty!"

"No!" Belle shouted, starting to lose her temper. "You are wrong about him and killing him, at the very least, would be an act against the Vakrein crown. Would you risk open war?"

"If it must be done, then so be it!" Bishop Sauvage's face was beat red at this point, spit flying with his words. Father Sinclair stood back, unease rolling off of him.

"That's enough," Henri interrupted, stopping the escalating argument. "I do not know what the correct course of action is, but it does not need to be decided right now. We will revisit this after we've all had time to think it through." Henri's eyes darted to each person, waiting for objections that would never come. "Bishop, Father, I'll ride with you into town. I have some business there."

"Merci. I believe that is best," Father Sinclair said, speaking for the first time.

Henri let the clergymen leave first. Bishop Sauvage looked down his nose at Belle as he went. Henri, however, paused just long enough to grab her hand and stare meaningfully into her eyes. Belle didn't know if he was trying to tell her something, but either way she knew what she had to do.

"Doc," Belle said quietly so that her voice wouldn't carry down the hall. The Hunters tilted their heads to listen. "For general anesthesia, do you use Chloroform or Diethyl Ether?"

"Chloroform, of course," he said like the question was an affront, which Belle assumed was a doctor thing. "How do you know about general anesthesia?"

"She reads a lot," Nicolas said, his eyes widening for emphasis. The others chuckled and nodded.

Belle frowned, but otherwise ignored them. "The *British Medical Journal* had an article on the use of it. I'd like to test one of those uses presently."

The doctor curled an eyebrow, then looked sidelong at her. He unscrewed the silver flask in his hand and tipped it to his lips. After a gulp, he asked, "You wish to go into a chemically induced sleep?"

"What?!" exclaimed Gastone with all the appall of a spinster listening to scandalous gossip.

"Not just me, the Prince as well." She glared at Gastone, imploring him to keep his voice down, in case the churchmen hadn't left yet. "In order for us to communicate, we must moon dream. For that to happen, we must both be asleep."

"Then wait till tonight and go to sleep naturally." Gastone looked as though he wanted to shake her. Every muscle in his body was tightened to the hilt.

"I fear we may not have time. The Bishop is out for blood." Belle looked to her Hunters, making her case. "He does not care if I get the answers I need from Prince Aleksander first."

"What sort of questions?" Calming significantly, Gastone leaned against the wall and closer to her. His tone was soft, vulnerable even.

"What is he? How was he able to turn human?" Belle said quietly with a shrug of her shoulders. She didn't want Aleksander to hear her through the door, but she was also feeling a bit vulnerable herself. "Why did he keep it from me?"

Andre reached out and gently squeezed her arm. "All very valid questions."

"It's dangerous, Belle," Doc said, pressing his lips into a thin line but still looking like he was prepared to cave. "If the Chloroform is not administered correctly, there is a chance you may not wake up."

"I have full faith in you, Doc." Belle turned and grabbed the doorknob. "But let me speak to his Royal Highness first, make sure he's willing."

"One of us should come in there with you." Gastone pushed off the wall, ready to be that one.

"No, it'll be easier if we're alone." She waved him off and twisted the knob.

Gastone grabbed her hand, preventing her from opening the door. He held out his personal revolver. "At least take this. For my peace of mind."

Belle frowned, most certainly not wanting to. She took it with a sigh and stuffed it into her robe's pocket. It was too heavy for the garment, causing the fabric to hang oddly. Suddenly remembering the other object she had stashed, Belle reached up into her hair and extracted the mechanical pixie hiding there.

"Take her to my room, will you?" Belle said, releasing the fairy into Gastone's calloused hands.

Gastone nodded. Pixie grasped his curled fingers, staring at Belle with wide, black eyes. A string of notes sang from her throat. Belle touched her gently on the nose, then opened the door to Aleksander's room. He was standing in the corner as she stepped through and closed the door behind her.

The room felt too small. She remained by the door and he in his corner—a corner that barely fit him. His chest shook with his labored breathing, his shoulders slouched, and some of his wounds had reopened. Despite his display of beastliness before, Aleksander was not fully healed from his transformation. It was abundantly clear now that his excursion was catching up to him.

"Aleksander, it's time you gave me the truth," she said plainly.

The Prince met her stare unblinkingly. With a deep breath, Belle made her proposal.

# Chapter Thirty

Belle remained near while the doctor worked. She didn't touch Aleksander or speak openly to him. Instead she sat in a corner chair, watching quietly with her hands folded in her lap.

In the time it took for the Doc to retrieve his necessary equipment from town, Belle had donned the blue dress from her visit to the Observation Room and pinned her hair up in a simple bun. It wasn't her best look, but at least now she was somewhat decently dressed for the company of men—and beast.

Also, somewhere in that time, a tension had formed between Belle and Aleksander. It was mostly coming from her, she was certain, but there was nothing for it. The moment she'd stepped into Aleksander's room to explain the Chloroform idea, she'd started to feel it. Belle didn't want to be near the Prince. She didn't want to look at him, talk to him, or have anything to do with him. The feeling was uncomfortable like it was a substance inside her that just didn't belong and forced everything out of place.

She couldn't wait for this to be over and she prayed their relationship would return to normal. Belle wanted it to feel comfortable again, safe. She wanted the fear of what he might soon tell her to finally go away.

In Aleksander's room, all of the furniture had been overturned.

A chair was in pieces and there were jagged scratches marking the metal walls. Had he tried to claw through it? Even the bed had been flipped and landed several paces from its place. They'd had to right it, just so the doc could work.

Aleksander sat quietly on the bed. From time to time, his eyes turned to her and they connected with just a look. Like they did now. Belle marveled at the way his eyes had changed. The soft, light blues were gone and these wolf eyes were intense, focused. Like iridescent half-moons resting within each eye. They pulled her in, the ferocity of his gaze was like a magnet holding her in place. She couldn't move; could barely breathe when he had her. They terrified and fascinated her all at once.

With a snarl, Prince Aleksander broke their connection and glared at the doc. Blinking, Belle took deep breaths.

"Sorry. So sorry." Doc squirmed but continued fixing one of the stitches at Aleksander's side.

Belle understood Doc's flustered reaction to the Prince. She was feeling the same. He went against everything she was taught and she at times struggled to reconcile that it was Aleksander behind those wolf eyes.

"How much longer will you be, Doc?" Belle opened her watch necklace to check the time.

"I'm done," he said, carefully taping a bandage in place. "Now we just have to administer the Chloroform."

"I should ready myself then. You'll be all right without me?"

The doc nodded and waved her away as he removed some apparatus from his medical bag. But, to Belle's surprise, she hadn't been talking to the doctor. The query had come out abruptly, with no thought behind it, and had been meant for Aleksander. The Prince understood this and nodded in a way that was too human for a wolf.

With no more words necessary and fully aware that Aleksander watched her closely, Belle opened the door and left. Outside of the room, she suddenly felt like she could breathe again. Like somehow Beast-Aleksander sucked all of the air straight out of the room. Her heart and instincts were completely at war with one another. Her heart recognized Aleksander. It saw past the terrifying exterior and even the brilliant eyes, and found the man within. The man who had her questioning all she knew. Her instincts, however, couldn't seem to tell the difference between Aleksander and the hellhounds she hunted.

Heading into her room, Belle changed back into her nightclothes and robe. She then slid into bed and waited for the doctor. Pixie fluttered about her, singing a strange melody that Belle suspected was being made up on the spot. Weariness was just starting to weigh heavily on her when there came a knock at the door.

"My apologies for making you wait." Doc slipped into her room and shut the door behind him. "It took a bit more Chloroform to put him down than I expected."

Belle raised an eyebrow and frowned.

Pausing in his step, the doc had the good grace to look sheepish. "Apologies again, poor choice of words."

"So he's asleep then?" Belle tucked the blankets nervously around her waist.

Now that she was moments away from talking to Aleksander properly, butterflies were moving into her stomach. It was silly for her to be nervous at the idea of talking to him. She'd spent more than enough time with him over the weeks and was quite comfortable in his presence. Or, at least, she had been before. Now, dare say, things were different. The course of events that were to come depended entirely on their impending conversation. Moreover, Belle's heart sat in the balance.

"Just nearly." Doc was saying, but Belle hadn't really been

listening. "I have Andre watching over his treatment. Now please, lie down."

Belle scooched herself into position and Pixie watched from her perch upon the headrest. The doc held up the device he'd been readying. The bulk of it was a glass cylinder attached to a foot long hose. It was a duplicate to the one she'd seen in Aleksander's room.

"Here's how this works. This part here goes over your nose and mouth." Doc held up a hand-sized, concaved object that was connected to the other end of the hose. "You'll breathe deeply. Air will be pulled into the inhaler, through the Chloroform, up the hose, and into the mask. This will give you a blend of both oxygen and Chloroform, which should regulate your dosage safely."

"How long before it begins to take effect?" Belle asked, starting to feel nervously sick.

"Not long," was the doc's deadpan answer.

"How long will I be asleep?" Perhaps she was stalling now.

"Depends. Most likely about forty-five minutes to an hour." Not waiting for her to ask another question, Doc reached forward and placed the mask over her nose and mouth. "Take hold. Now long and slow breaths, if you will."

Grabbing onto the mask, so that the doctor could let go, she held it against her face. It was cold, and she hated the harsh feeling of it against her skin. Stealing herself, she inhaled. A sickeningly sweet smell filled her nostrils. Belle scrunched up her eyebrows, immediately not wanting to breathe anymore in.

Doc's stern gaze held her firm. "Slow and deep. Just relax."

Belle chose to focus on his stare, ignoring the wretched scent and her nervous energy. In and out, she let her chest inflate with his. In and out. Slow and . . . deep . . .

Fire filled Belle's vision. She looked around, feeling strangely disoriented. It took her a moment to realize it, but she was in Aleksander's private office at Vakre Fjell. The windows were frosted over, the fire was in full burn, but somehow it all looked dull to her. Belle reached out to caress the cold windowpane. Yet, more oddness struck her. There was no doubt that none of this was real.

"It's that . . . Chloroform. It has put a fog in my mind," came Prince Aleksander's voice. He stood behind his desk, his hands typically clasped behind his back. He shook his head in irritation. "Nothing feels right to me. I find it disorienting."

"I feel it too." Despite herself, Belle's heart leapt at the sight of Aleksander. She realized suddenly that she'd missed him. Turning toward the Prince, she put her hands together at her front. Only then did Belle notice she wore one of the dresses from her stay at Castle Vakre Fjell. The regal outfit and the elegant design that Belle knew her hair was swept into, gave her confidence. With that came the needed fortitude to get down to the brass tacks. "You're a hellhound."

"No," Aleksander said forcefully, with barely a breath between their words. He stared at her defiantly. "I *am* cursed, but I am not *like them*."

"Then what are you?"

"*Mánagarmr,* that's what the norn had called me the day she came to my castle. I don't think she even meant to say it." He brought his arms in front of him, crossing them over his chest.

"And what is that?"

"It means Moon-Hound; also One Who Hates and The Enemy." Aleksander chose a book from on top of his desk, opened it to just the right page, and held it out to her. "Do you recall the poem Völuspá?"

"Yes, I remember." Belle looked over the book he gave her,

seeing the same pages he'd shown her the day he first told her about the curse.

Aleksander's eyes drifted as he recited from memory the words that were written before her. "'*In the east sat an old woman in Iron-wood and nurtured there offspring of Fenrir*' but the line went on further. It read, '*a certain one of them in monstrous form will be the snatcher of the moon.*'"

As the Prince spoke, the words began to change before her eyes. Where once had been blank space, the old paper became stained with aged ink. Belle looked up at Aleksander in surprise.

"You hid this from me." Suddenly she realized the extent Aleksander had gone to in order to keep his secret. Belle had read many books during her time in Vakre Fjell, but most of those had been in one of Aleksander's moon dreams. "How many books did you alter just so I could read them without discovering what you are?"

"Only this one. The other books I gave you never mentioned me." He glanced away, looking uncharacteristically guilty. "All the books that did . . . those were kept with me."

"What did the other books say?" Belle set down the book she'd been holding, ready to hear it all.

From within his desk, the Prince pulled out two more immense volumes. He opened the first and slid it to her. "The poem, Gylfaginning. '*from this race shall come one that shall be mightiest of all, he that is named Mánagarmr; he shall be filled with the flesh of all those men that die, and he shall swallow the moon.*'" Over top of it, Aleksander placed the next book. "'*Unfettered will fare the Fenris Wolf and ravaged the realm of men, ere that cometh a kingly prince as good, to stand in his stead.*' The poem Hákonarmál."

Aleksander remained silent as Belle attempted pathetically to process it all. She stared at the words, hardly believing any of it. That he had kept it from her, yet by these words she could not see why. This was all a moon dream still, could she even trust what she was seeing?

"I don't understand, Aleksander." Belle looked up at the Prince, unable to help the tears in her eyes. "Why would you keep this from me? Why would you lie to me?"

"At first it was simply a matter of trust. When that past . . ." He swallowed, his face looking pained at the sight of her distress. Aleksander placed his hands on his desk, dropping his head like the weight was too much. "I was afraid you would hate me. You were a Hunter and I was a beast. For you . . . I wanted to be just a man."

Belle couldn't speak. She felt entirely overwrought with raw emotions and circling thoughts.

Aleksander sighed, continuing in her silence, "In time several things were becoming clear to me. First, that I loved you. Second that you appeared inclined toward me as well. And third, that there was no breaking the curse upon me. I was never going to be the man you deserved." The Prince pushed off his desk and walked to the window. He said quietly, "So I sent you home."

"And that made me angry," blurted Belle, overtaken by her own memory. Aleksander turned to her in surprise, his lips upturning at the sight of her own smirk. He'd said he loved her! Despite all of Belle's still valid fears, the Prince's admission made her feel incredibly light. "I wasn't going to let the beast keep us apart. I intended to confront it. To save you."

"You shot at me," Aleksander teased, making Belle blush at her actions. Then his smile faded as he remembered. "The look on your face, when you saw me . . . it was everything that I had feared."

Belle's heart ached at seeing the event through his eyes. Her actions had been unknowingly cruel. "Why then did you chase after me?"

"What must've you thought upon seeing such a monstrous beast? What of me? My people? I couldn't bear to think of it. Then I realized that I would never see you again. Our time together would end with fear and gun smoke." Aleksander came away from the window, grasping Belle's small hands within his. His blues eyes gazed intently into her own. "I had to make you see. Not just so you wouldn't bring an army back to my doorstep, but because I needed you to know that I was there. That the man you were growing to care for was still reaching for you. That he wasn't lost."

Tears streamed down her cheeks from the waves of relief that flooded her. Belle freed her hands, expecting her hopes to still yet be dashed. "I wish you had called to me sooner. It was torment," she whispered breathlessly. "Not understanding what you were and fearing that you were avoiding me."

"I'm sorry. I tried," he answered. "Fighting the curse weakened me. I can't remember anything after becoming human again in the woods."

"That's why you destroyed our guest room?" The emotional pain was fading fast from Belle. His words were like an herbal salve on an open wound. "You were confused?"

"I was angry that you weren't there." Aleksander raised his hands and grasped her cheeks. Belle looked up into his fierce blue eyes. He pushed back her hair, his eyes tracing the lines of her face. "I'd feared the worst. I was so relieved when I saw you were safe."

"I understand completely. I thought I was going to lose you when you wouldn't wake before." Belle thought back to his fevered sleep. Then she grabbed onto his hands, holding them firmly against her cheeks. "But you're still not safe. We need to get you back to Vakre Fjell."

"What do you mean?" The Prince pulled away slightly, but didn't let go, and looked at her with creased eyebrows.

"I think the church means to have you executed."

"What?" He dropped his hands incredulously. "The murder of a foreign monarch . . . They wouldn't dare."

"It's the Catholic Church, Aleksander. They *would* dare. They would act now and convince the world governments of their righteousness after." Belle grabbed up one of his hands, holding it tightly between two of hers and looked at him beseechingly. "Your kingdom would either be abandoned then or it would be taken up as a cause of evil that needs to be rid from the world. Your people need you to protect them. Without someone on the throne, they'll be tossed to the wolves—excuse the turn of phrase." He frowned at that, but she peddled on. "It's time for us to wake up, your Royal Highness. We need to get you back to your castle."

Prince Aleksander looked at her, considering something. "You're with me?"

"Irrevocably so."

# Chapter Thirty-One

et the horses ready, we're taking the Prince back now," Belle ordered the gathered Hunters.

She'd called them together as soon as she'd woken. Doc had informed her that she and Aleksander had been asleep for forty-eight minutes. Which was too much time, as far as Belle was concerned.

"But the church hasn't approved his return yet," Delano stated, standing with the others outside her bedroom door.

"We can't allow the church to execute him. He may look like a beast, but there's still a man under there." Belle had to convince them. Asking them to go against the church was asking a lot, but she had to make them see it her way. "He's clearly not the Devil and he's not a hellhound. If he were Satan, why would he bother with any of us? Have you ever seen a hellhound save a Hunter, as he did me?"

"I certainly haven't," answered Nicolas.

Jack leaned against the wall, crossing his arms and propping up a cowboy boot. "Wouldn't be much fun hunting them if they did."

"The church isn't out there hunting like we are." They seemed to be listening and hope unfurled inside her chest. "Think of all you've seen—not just recently, but in these long years. We cling to what the church tells us, but we all know that this curse isn't as simple as Heaven and Hell. You know they'll refuse to see him in any other light."

Silence followed. The Hunters looked to one another and wrestled with their own uncertainties. Gastone, who was normally the first to speak up, remained stoically quiet. It was Andre this time who scratched his arm, like the metal beneath had an itch, and said, "I have no qualms about killing a Vakrein prince, but if I'm going to, I want to be honorable about it." He gestured to Aleksander's door. "Killing him here, like he's a wounded dog, it isn't honorable."

Jean banged on the wall twice with a grunt. He finished with a nod of agreement, then crossed his arms. Jean couldn't speak, but his body language spoke volumes. This caused a ripple through the group as they each started to concede this point.

"So you're with me?" Belle asked, echoing Aleksander, and looked to each man. "The Prince goes back to Vakre Fjell and then we see how the church wishes to proceed?"

"I'll agree to that," Andre said first and the others followed suit.

Except for Gastone. He watched them all with his stony expression and said nothing when they all looked to him for his answer.

"Gastone?" Belle prompted.

He took a deep breath. "I'm in."

Belle clapped her hands together once but reined in her relief. She had no intention of listening to the church on this matter. The beast was Aleksander—and he . . . she'd give her life for. For now though, Belle just had to get him back to Castle Vakre Fjell. There he would be protected by his soldiers. If the church chose to strike against him, she'd just have to deal with that when the time came. God willing, it wouldn't.

"Okay, Hunters. Ready yourselves and the horses. We leave in an hour. Tell no one." They all nodded and dispersed to do as she ordered. Belle returned to her room to ready herself properly for the journey ahead.

With hair styled and fully dressed, Belle took a right into the armory. Jack was there loading a rifle. The boy was magnificent with a pair of revolvers, but nothing packed a punch like a rifle. Andre was there as well, making adjustments on his mechanical leg.

Jack snapped the gun's lever into place. It was now loaded and ready to fire. He rested the barrel against his shoulder and tipped his hat at Belle.

"I see you look lovely no matter what you wear, ma'am." His American accent fell off his tongue like a built-in charm device.

"Why thank you, Mr. Jack Lloyd." She couldn't help being playful. Her mood had improved dramatically after her moon dream with Aleksander. Having the air clear, despite their impending danger, made everything seem better. Imitating an American accent better than she'd expected, Belle teased further, "You're not too bad yourself."

He stumbled back, clutching his heart. "Oh lord, it's like I'm back home again."

Andre snorted and glanced up at Belle. "How's the Prince?"

Starting with her throwing knives, Belle began strapping herself with weapons. "I checked on him before I came down. He's weak, but he can travel."

"Do you really think you can trust him?" Jack asked. Fully plated with weapons, he stayed for the conversation.

Andre pulled down his pant leg, waiting for her answer.

"With all my heart." Belle grabbed one of her revolvers and began loading it.

Andre stood, taking his own rifle from the wall. He gave Belle a knowing look. "I suppose there's no hope for it then?"

"None at all." Belle smiled, which Andre returned before leaving with Jack.

Belle quickly readied. She ran through the checklist, knowing that time was of the essence. Revolvers, knives, spare bullets, sabre, and she cocked a bullet into her shotgun. With all she could carry, she left the armory.

As she stepping into the hall, Gastone and Jean were walking toward her. They were both wearing their dark cloaks and their weapons glinted from the indoor lights. Gastone carried his rifle strapped to his back, a personal preference that Belle didn't share. Rifles were heavy and Belle already had enough material weighing her down.

"The horses are ready," Gastone said, stopping several feet away at the sight of her. His manner was stern and closed off. He may have agreed to this, but it didn't make him happy.

"The Prince is still very weak. I'm not sure he can make the journey on foot." Belle looked between the two men, focusing on the task ahead rather than addressing Gastone's emotional state. "Harness two horses to the flatbed for him to ride on. Friar Clemens will have to drive it. I'll head up to get the Prince."

Jean nodded authoritatively and turned to leave. He walked several paces before realizing that Gastone hadn't followed. The large Hunter stilled, watching them both warily. His inability to communicate efficiently perhaps giving him an aptitude for observing the subtleties that others lacked.

Gastone said nothing, instead stared at her as though he wished to. He clutched his jaw, thinking something over. Ultimately, he thought better of whatever he'd wanted to say and simply nodded. Then he turned and pounded past the watchful Jean, who seemed relieved and followed after.

Rifle in one hand, Belle went up the stairs to Aleksander's room. Taking a collective breath, she opened the door  Aleksander lay curled up on the bed. It looked incredibly uncomfortable, being as the bed was clearly too small for him. He raised his head and looked at her with his wolfish eyes.

"It's time to go," she said simply.

With a casual exhale, the Prince pushed himself up and stepped off the bed. Belle had only ever seen the beast standing on two legs but was not surprised that even on all four he was impossibly large. Hellhounds were two, even three, times larger than a normal wolf. Aleksander made them look like pups.

Belle walked alongside him as they made their way down the hall. His claws clicked against the wood floor and his paws padded heavily with each step. Knowing that small talk was impossible, Belle decided to feign comfort in their involuntary silence.

As it was still daytime, LeClair House was above sea level. Which was fortunate, because Belle had no idea how Aleksander would have fit in the lift. As it were, his wide shoulders barely squeezed through the front door. Grabbing her fur cloak before leaving, Belle draped it over her shoulders. The white fur grazed softly against her skin as she pulled out her gloves and tugged them on.

With a little extra luck, the sun was shining when Belle stepped outside where Aleksander was waiting. His dark fur rippled from the breeze and his nose was tipped up, scenting the air off the Norwegian Sea. Distant gray clouds warned them of coming snow. Gauging its distance, Belle was certain they could reach Castle Vakre Fjell before the clouds made landfall.

"Your transport is ready, your Royal Highness," said Friar Clemens from beside the aforementioned flatbed.

It was harnessed to two strong horses, but even Belle worried that it wouldn't be enough to pull Aleksander. Nicolas, Delano, and Andre were already mounted up and waiting. Jack was just approaching their assembly upon his new steed, with her Charming in tow. Leaving Aleksander's side, Belle placed her hands on her Friesian's muzzle and greeted him. He puffed delightedly into her palms.

"Your Highness, if you please," Friar Clemens prompted, pulling the Prince's eyes from Belle.

With a subtle groan, Aleksander approached the flatbed's rear. The horses shied at the sight and smell of Beast-Aleksander. Comforting pats and words from their riders settled them, but their flicking ears and wide eyes showed their unease. Only Charming seemed unbothered by his presence. Belle supposed that carrying Aleksander on his back would have such an effect.

The Prince ignored the animals' hubbub. With an easy leap, he alighted onto the flatbed. It pitched side to side with his weight. The wheel axles moaned and the boards creaked in distress. Aleksander quickly laid down to steady the wagon.

As they waited for Jean and Gastone, Belle gave Charming a quick look over. She checked his hooves for problems, made sure he was groomed properly, and then went over his tack. Everything was as it should be, girth tight and all. Belle stuffed her rifle down into the saddle's scabbard.

"Jack," Belle said, reaching down to tie up her skirts. He looked at her, showing no ungentlemanly interested in her flash of skin. "I never got to ask you, what name did your horse get?"

Monsieur Bane, the Hostler, named the stallions he gave to the Hunters. All the names were regal in theme, chosen with the intention of honoring the impressive breed. Their names were also indications of their heritage. Magnificent and Magnanimous, for example, were given similar names due to their sharing of the same bloodline.

"Knightly," Jack answered with a proud grin.

Giving them both a quick appraising eye, Belle then mounted "It suits him, and you."

Jack welcomed this complement by tipping his cowboy hat. As he did, Gastone and Jean approached a trot. The unofficial royal guard was now complete. Friar Clemens climbed into the driver's seat of the flatbed and took up the reins. Everyone looked to Belle.

Pressing back her shoulders, Belle gave out her travel instructions. On a hunt, everyone entered the forest in a certain order with Belle going first. This wasn't a hunt however and Belle wasn't leaving Aleksander's side; though she didn't plan on admitting that last part outright. This time Gastone would take the lead, Andre and Jack behind him, Jean would guard Aleksander along with Belle, and Nicolas and Delano would take up the rear.

"Any questions?" No one spoke up. "Then let's get this prince back to his castle."

"Here, here!" Several Hunters heartily agreed.

Belle signaled and, moving as a single unit, they made their way to the forest edge. The Hunters took up their positions seamlessly. She guided Charming over to walk alongside the wagon, glancing at Aleksander the same moment he glanced at her. They couldn't speak to one another, but each look held a thousand words.

The group stopped a second later. The forest didn't appear as ominous during the day as it did at night and without falling snow the visibility went much farther than normal. Belle wasn't fooled though. Death could be awaiting them just beyond those trees.

Belle pulled her hood up and bowed her head. The other Hunters did the same. She was quiet for a moment and then she began, "O Holy Angel."

The others took up the creed. Their voices fell into a rhythm, chanting together. Aleksander shifted next to her and Belle knew without opening her eyes that he was watching her, listening intently to the oath so few had heard before. The words memorized long ago, fell from her lips and soon the prayer drew to its end. Each Hunter raised their heads, opened their eyes, and formed the cross over their chests. "In nomine Patris, et Filii, et Spiritus Sancti, Amen."

Without a word, Gastone signaled his horse forward. Andre and Jack followed. Belle glanced down at Aleksander. Their eyes locked for a long moment. Then Belle broke the contact, turning her attention to the forest, and cued Charming. Into its depths they went.

*I waited with my hounds . . . We smelled Hunters on the wind.*

# Chapter Thirty-Two

To call them a pack would be an understatement. It was an army of hellhounds and they came from all sides. Belle's ears were filled with a cacophony of gunfire and growls. It was simply one shot after another with no time to think.

Her guns emptied and Belle was forced to hastily draw her sabre, hacking down at the surrounding hellhounds. With Charming about to be overrun, she dismounted to push them back. The stallion covered her side, defending with his hooves.

Shouts and grunts came as comforting sounds to Belle, telling her that her Hunters were still alive. Only at Aleksander did she spare a glance. He maintained the high ground of his flatbed, guarding a terrified Friar against the hellhounds. Fortunately for them both, the hounds seemed wary of Aleksander's large fangs and claws.

A hellhound leapt at Belle. She sidestepped, swiping as she moved. Her blade ran down his body, cutting him open. Sweeping the saber upward, she ran another hound through. Before she could even pull her sword free, Belle grabbed two knives from her chest and launched them at descending attackers. They dropped as Belle removed her weapon from the corpse.

Flipping her sabre backwards in hand, Belle thrust it behind her and speared the mouth of a hound. Bodies piled at her feet as she killed, making it difficult to move. She made to step out of the mess, while slicing at several hellhounds, when a corpse burst into light. Blind, she flinched away. Something solid struck her back, sending her forward. Belle tried to keep her balance, but tripped over the array of bodies and stumbled several feet until she fell face first into the snow.

Dazed and blinking, Belle scrambled for her sabre. Before she could regain it, claws hooked into the flesh of her lower torso. The sudden pain caused her to cry out.

Then she was being dragged. By flesh and muscle, the claws pulled her through deep snow. Alerted by her scream, Aleksander turned from his attackers to see her about to disappear into the tree line.

Puffing out his chest, he issued a roar that shook the very forest. Nearly every hellhound ducked in fear. Aleksander leapt off the flatbed, leaving the cowering Friar behind.

His heavy paws were nimble over the snow, but the hellhound army was quick to recover. Several at once jumped upon him. The Prince twisted under their weight, grabbing one with his paw and flinging it away. Then he engaged the others in a fight of fury. The snarls and whimpers were jarring in Belle's ears.

She had to give Aleksander time to get to her, to get at the hound that dragged, as well as disabled, her so successfully. Belle dug her hands through the snow trying to grab at anything. Her mind raced for alternatives. Her sabre was now well out of reach, her guns were empty, and her last throwing knife was trapped firmly beneath her. The heavy paws on her back prevented her from turning to grab it.

Panic seized her as she was pulled passed a lamppost. The hellhound was dragging her into the woods. There was only one reason for a predator to drag its prey away from the group. Belle lashed out, grasping the metal post. Holding on desperately, she was not willing to be the main course of this wolf's private dinner.

"Aleksander!" Belle cried in agony. The claws pulled on her flesh, threatening to tear her completely to shreds.

He flung a hellhound against a tree with his strong jaws and looked at Belle, roaring at the one who had her. But his attackers were relentless. No matter how many he fought off, they were intent on killing him.

Unfortunately for them both, the hound dragging Belle dug its claws even deeper, introducing her to a whole new kind of pain. Stars danced in her eyes and her grasp failed her. Belle was jerked beyond the trees.

She felt entirely helpless the further and deeper they went. The Hunters and Aleksander disappeared from sight. The sound of battle fell away. Her body swept through the snow, over rocks and fallen branches, leaving an obvious trail in her wake. Belle scrambled about, grabbing for any and everything she could reach. A bush scraped through her grasping fingers and Belle cried out in anguish.

Crunching snow caught Belle's attention. Something was coming, following their trail. It was gaining ground fast. Was it Aleksander? She pictured him bursting on the scene and leaping upon her attacker.

"Belle?!" Gastone's call was shaky, uncertain and racked with worry.

"Gastone!" she shrieked in desperate surprise, her voice strained from the pain.

His noise increased and Gastone rounded a grouping of trees, bringing himself into view. Relief flooded his face at the sight of her, but then he saw the hellhound. His color drained away, a slur of indecent words tumbled from his lips.

The hellhound released its claws from her, tearing flesh as it did. Belle whimpered from both the pain and relief at the loss of pressure. The hound stalked around her and she was finally able to see it. Her eyes went wide with shock.

On two massive, clawed feet it walked—another Moon-Hound. It stopped just to the side of Belle, drawing itself to its full height. With dark fur and solid muscles, it could have been a duplicate for Aleksander. At first her mind thought it was, but then she noticed the eyes. They weren't blue or wolf-like. They were black and unreflecting like deep soulless voids.

The Moon-Hound didn't attack. It remained still, tilting its head in curiosity at Gastone. Belle could have sworn it was smiling as a low growl began to rubble from its chest.

Gastone shifted on his feet, anger starting to ebb from him. He raised his sabre, ready to charge the creature. But he would die; he knew this and so did Belle. The hound's lips curled back, hackles rising, and it widened its stance in anticipation of the strike.

Not ready to let her friend die for her, Belle pushed herself up and grabbed the throwing knife from her chest. Without hesitating, she whipped it at the strange Moon-Hound. The blade stuck in its side, right between the ribs. Jerking in surprise, the hound whirled and looked down at its bleeding side. Then it roared angrily at Belle. The sound was higher than Aleksander's roar but just as terrifying. Perhaps even more so.

Taking his chance, Gastone charged. Before the hound could finish its roar, the Hunter drove his blade through its skull. The creature stilled, its death coming instantly. Gastone released the sword. The body crumpled to the ground.

As the corpse came to a rest, the fur and muscles shimmered. Then, quick as a blink, the Moon-Hound was gone. No lights. No angelic ringing. The wolf was just gone, and in its place was a woman.

They both stared at the dead form, not believing what they

were seeing. She was beautiful, her face exquisitely formed. Her skin was pale, but it was accented perfectly by the blue and silver cloak that surrounded her. A lock of sheer white hair danced in the breeze, like a tendril of smoke. Her eyes were open, those soulless orbs staring at Belle.

"It's her." Uneasy shivers swept down Belle's spine.

Gastone finally looked at Belle. "Who?"

"The norn. She's the one I saw in the Prince's memory." Belle had an undeniable desire to get away from the otherworldly being. It unnerved her that no blood seeped from the sabre in her skull. "She's the one who created the curse."

"She's a norn *and* like the wolf prince?"

"I don't think so. The books said she had a universal power that could be used to complete her fate." Either from laying in the snow or from the fading terror, Belle's muscles began to shake involuntarily. She pushed up from the ground, intending to finally right herself, but pain laced through her body. It spread like searing fire over her torso and into her legs. She dropped back into the snow with a grunt, breathing heavily as she waited for the pain to recede. "My guess would be that she became a lycanthrope in order to kill me. A bit theatrical of her, but she nearly succeeded."

"The books also said that a norn could only be killed by another norn." Belle watched the corpse warily. "Unless you have something you need to tell me about yourself, then we shouldn't linger."

Gastone came over to kneel at her side. He brushed the snow from around her and carefully examined the bleeding wound.

"It's bad, Belle." He removed the scarf from his neck and began to tie it around her waist, covering the injury. The touching was entirely too intimate, but she forgot that when he painful tightened the scarf to slow the bleeding. "I believe I'll need to carry you."

Looking into his brown eyes, and their flecks of green, she saw so much concern there. With a forced smile Belle replied, "If you must."

"I apologize if this causes you pain." He moved to pick her up.

"Wait." She stopped him and pointed to the norn. "Your sabre."

"Leave it." He shook his head and slowly slid his hands beneath her. "Perhaps she'll stay dead if it stays there."

Belle bit back a cry as Gastone easily pulled her up with him. Once he was standing, the pain lessened and his warmth pushed back the growing cold within her body. Belle rested against him unintentionally. The pain was sucking away her energy with each passing second. How much blood had already been absorbed into her corset?

"Don't worry Belle," Gastone said, most likely thinking the same thing. "I'll have you back home soon."

"No. Not home. We push on to Vakre Fjell."

She felt Gastone slow slightly in his steps. "You're badly injured. You need the doc."

"Castle Vakre Fjell has physicians too." Belle kept her tone firm, despite the weakness that wanted to creep in.

"I think the doc should be the one to treat you, not some Vakrein. The other Hunters can continue on without us."

"No, I stay with Aleksander. I will see this through," she said before realizing her mistake. Her address of the Prince by his first name was far too familiar and entirely inappropriate. Pretending that she hadn't said anything incorrect, Belle finished the discussion. "That'll be the end of it, Gastone."

His pacing became more angered and hurried, but Belle said nothing. There was a faint click in her ear and Andre's voice came into her Electro-Phonic Chip. "Belle? Gastone? Are you out there?"

Gastone answered, "We're both alive and we're coming to you."

"Thank God. The area is clear now. You should be safe to come in." With that, there was another click as Andre disconnected his earpiece from theirs.

They remained silent as Gastone retraced his footsteps. Soon she heard her friend's voices and the sounds of the horses. As they stepped back onto the path some of the recently dead hellhounds burst into light.

"At this rate I'm going to go blind," said Nicolas rubbing his eyes.

Jean and Delano were lifting Aleksander from the snowy ground. His head lulled to the side. Blood matted much of his fur. Belle's heart went to her throat, as she feared the worst. Laboriously, they carried him back to the flatbed. Friar Clemens stood on top and lent a helping hand. Gently, he guided the beast to the wagon floor. Jack handed over the blanket from his saddle and Clemens spread it over the Prince. He didn't cover Aleksander's head and Belle suddenly wanted to weep that her prince was still alive.

Jean saw them approach and grunted to alert the others. His body was covered in red, but he didn't appear hurt. Charming nickered and bobbed his head with happiness that she returned. Belle smiled and told him he was a good horse.

"What happened? Is it bad?" Andre asked, limping forward a step. His right pant leg was shredded, revealing thin scrapes where claws raked over metal. Blood was splattered across his face.

"Her back is badly injured. She'll have to ride with me," Gastone answered.

Belle interjected as they reached the flatbed, "Not necessary. I'll ride on the wagon."

This order was met with silence from all around. Belle didn't care. She had eyes only for Aleksander. His, she was happy to see, were also open and staring back. At her request, he issued the most subtle of whimpers.

Clearly angry, Gastone thundered around the side of the wagon. Clemens again helped with the lowering. Belle was placed at Aleksander's back. Heated radiated off of him, as though he were a living furnace.

"Anyone else injured?" Gastone stomped off and mounted.

"Stitches will be needed," Andre answered from atop his Friesian, Valiant. "But only Belle and Prince Aleksander are in immediate danger."

"The Prince should come with us on all of our hunts," Nicolas said, nudging Jean who raised an eyebrow at him. The statement, though Nicolas didn't realize it, was in poor taste. "He was a real rager."

"As weak as he was, yet to dispatch so many—it was quite the remarkable sight." Friar Clemens took up his driver's seat and reins.

"Thank God for that," said Jack, casually twirling his revolvers. "Things weren't looking good there for a bit."

"Let's get a move on," Gastone cut off the talk.

"Onward to Vakre Fjell?" asked Andre.

"So it seems."

There was a snapping sound as Clemens cued his team forward. The wheels began to roll, causing the boards to creak with movement. Charming followed the flatbed of his own accord.

Feeling that no one was paying much attention to them any longer, Belle reached up and placed a hand upon Aleksander's shoulder. The sound he made in response was part sigh and part groan. A few tears tumbled freely as she gently caressed his dark fur; how happy she was that they had both lived, and yet she feared that he wouldn't make it home.

"What about the bodies?" Nicolas asked.

"We leave them," was Gastone's short reply.

There was some hesitation at that, then Andre said, "There's not much we can do about them now, I suppose."

Delano spoke quietly to those around him, though everyone still heard, "They'll eat them ya know? The corpses, I mean. The hellhounds will come back."

# Chapter
# Thirty-Three

*I felt him before I opened my eyes. I can always sense him, feel him watching me.*

*In fluid movement, as I raised my eyelids, I came to my feet. Bits of snow fell from the armor. The wind whipped my white hair about my face. I looked at Fenrir, not yet reaching to pull up my cloak's hood.*

*Standing by a tree, the god twisted a thin silver sabre in the evening sunlight. His youthful face boasted a pointed nose and lean, shapely cheeks. His deep, brown hair was pushed away from his face, feathering down the nape of his neck. It somehow reminded her of a wolf's hackles.*

*Similar to my attire, Fenrir's clothing was at odds with the trends of the human realm. Leather armor, edged in Norse knots, wrapped his shoulders. Otherwise his chest and torso were bare, showing his inhumanly perfect muscles. Fur clothing encircled his waist while a heavy broadsword hung from the side. Beneath one of Fenrir's arms was a silver winged helmet.*

*"They cannot kill you, but they discovered an effective way of disabling you," he said calmly, not looking at me. "Clever of them to leave it in your skull. Would you ever have been free of it?"*

*"It would have been dislodged with time," I responded, unconcerned.*

"The Mánagarmr lives." He discarded the sabre into the snow and finally looked at me. "As does the female Hunter you failed to kill."

I bristled. "My wolves did not slay the Moon-Hound? Even with their vast numbers?"

"Your wolves?" Fenrir's eyes narrowed, looking haughtily down at me. "They are not your wolves, norn. You may be the architect of this fate, but they are my kin."

As though it'd been silently called, a wolf appeared at Fenrir's side. It growled at me as it came to sit by the god. Absentmindedly, Fenrir placed a large hand between the creature's ears.

I watched it, unafraid by its predatory stare. Fenrir could call all of his wolves, have them tear me to pieces, but still I would not die. There is only one thing in existence that could end me, and gods could not wield it.

"I've come around to your way of thinking though," Fenrir said, looking disquieted by my sudden smirk. "The Mánagarmr will not join my cause, not now that he has aligned with the Hunters. You have my consent to end him."

Ravenous excitement filled me. No more sending mortal wolves to kill the Prince. With fate on my side, I will slay him myself. There is nothing to stand in my way . . . except Belle LeClair and her wretched Hunters. "And the female Hunter?"

"Whoever else you wish to kill does not interest me, Skuld." Fenrir's eyes then focused upon my body, staring like he hadn't noticed something before.

He held a hand out and a sudden pain ripped through my side. My hand went to the injury, surprised by the unusual feeling. I looked at the god in shock. How had he done that? Then I saw it; the small knife held between his fingers. He twisted it from side to side, marveling at the glimmering crimson upon the blade.

"This, however, this—is interesting." With uncertain eyes, Fenrir asked, "What is this weapon that has harmed a wielder of fate?"

"You need not fear it, young god. There is only one weapon in all the universe that can kill a god." I reassured him though I am amused by his fear. "For we made it and it is we who keep it, of that you can be certain."

He glared at my thinly veiled threat and pressed the knife into his thumb, testing my theory. No matter how hard he pressed, the skin does not pierce. "It seems this problem is entirely yours then."

Satisfied with himself, he flicked the weapon. It flew through the air and lodged into my chest. I stared down at it, not feeling an ounce of pain. I pulled the weapon free. The wound healed without a drop of blood. I looked from the weapon to the watching god, a foreboding feeling poisoning my earlier enthusiasm. "It is not the blade that harms, but the blade's thrower."

"I see," is all Fenrir said to my realization. He stared off into the distance, his eyes unseeing. I couldn't help wondering what thoughts he was entertaining. Then with a sigh, he straightened his spine. "I have been here long enough; this place wears upon me. I must return to Asgard."

I nodded, knowing full well why the gods do not dwell long in the plain of men. I blinked and before me was a hulking black wolf, bigger even than his wolf spawn. Surrounded by a forest of white, he was hauntingly beautiful. Turning away from me, he jogged deeper in the woods. The other wolf followed, but Fenrir was heading to a place that it could not go.

With Fenrir out of sight, I turned my eyes toward the direction of Castle Vakre Fjell.

The staff of Castle Vakre Fjell was in an uproar upon the Hunters' arrival. Trumpeted fanfare and a chaotic assembly of people ushered them from the bridge and to the front of the castle. Laramie shoved his way through the crowd, chastising some as he went for being in the way and insisting they make themselves useful elsewhere.

"Oh your Royal Highness, what a relief it is to see you returned," Monsieur Petit was saying as he finally reached their cart. He looked to Belle, still laying at the Prince's warm side. "Merci, mademoiselle."

"My pleasure, monsieur." She forced a smile despite her pain.

"But you are both injured." Laramie's relief quickly changed to concern and he looked to some nearby staff. "Have his Highness taken to the royal sickrooms and Mademoiselle LeClair and the Hunters to the public rooms to be tended."

Two unfamiliar men stepped up to the flatbed, intent on lifting Belle to be carried away. As their hands descended, Aleksander twisted in a flash. He snarled and growled at the men, half looming over top of her. The servant men jumped back in alarm and the crowd fell into a stunned silence. Low rumbles still ebbed from the beast.

Belle stared up at him, her breath held tight in her chest. He had moved so fast. From fatal injury to protective wolf in the blink of an eye. It must cost him dearly to be so aggressive in his current state, but as a wolf this was his only means of quick communication. The idea that he must deem her worth such excursion both swelled her heart and humbled her.

"The . . . Mademoiselle LeClair shall accompany his Royal Highness." Monsieur Petit, guessing at the cause of his Prince's agitation, was rewarded with Aleksander quieting his growl and settling back down beside her. Looking satisfied, Laramie clapped his hands to wake everyone from their shock. "Off to it then!"

The crowd immediately began to disperse, not wanting to incur the Offisielle Rådgiver's wrath. The Hunters were encouraged down from their mounts and the horses, including Charming, were taken to the stables. Gastone paused at the castle entrance, staring back at Belle, as the others were led within by overly attentive servants. His gaze gave nothing away, not an ounce of the emotion beneath. He nodded abruptly, a salute to her rank, and walked away.

"Now, your Highness, we are going to have to carry the two of you separately," Laramie said as two white-clothed litters were set alongside them, accompanied by more servants to carry them. Laramie moved aside, mumbling, "Let's not kill the staff for it. We don't have many replacements awaiting."

Belle smirked until she was lifted from the flatbed, sending hot pain ripping freshly through her back. She gritted her teeth to fight the wanting cry within. After all, she shared Laramie's concern for the castle staff. They laid her upon the litter and gripped the ends to hoist her between them. Belle's muscles slowly relaxed into the cot's soft grasp and the pain faded to a steady throbbing. The last thing she saw before resting her head was the sight of four servants struggling to carry the Prince's litter up the castle steps.

The two men carrying Belle followed closely behind. Through the great halls, up the grand staircases, and past many immense windows they were hoisted. Soon Belle realized that she no longer recognized the ceilings in this part of the castle, and still through several more doorways they went.

The last room they entered wasn't as large as the others. The lighting was dim and all was hushed as Belle and Aleksander were transferred into actual beds. Aleksander's bed was large, luxurious, and yet he still barely fit within. Belle's bed had been brought up from the public infirmary and hastily put together, not that she really minded. The entire sick room was more of a royal suit than a place for patient and doctor. It had a calming effect upon her.

When the Head Physician and his many assistants, came in, the room was immediately cleared. Only Monsieur Petit remained, stationed by the door in case he was needed. The doctor, a portly-jowled sort of fellow, glanced over Belle's wounds and instructed a follower on the proper treatment. His attentions then shifted to the Prince and his administrations became more urgent. All but the assistant assigned to Belle were put to work helping.

There was a bit of shouting outside the sickroom door. Laramie's eyes widened at the colorful language emitted from some authoritative female beyond. Then the doors burst open and Madame Edvina Gulbrandsen trounced through. She curtsied briefly to the Prince, who paid her no mind, and went straight to Belle.

"Oh, my dear, I'd heard you'd been injured." She took up Belle's hand, coddling it gently within hers, and leaned toward her. "How very awful. Is it very life threatening?"

The young assistant glanced up from his table of instruments, but it was Belle who answered. "No, no, not at all. Don't worry yourself, Edvina."

"Nothing for it, my dear. I can't help seeing you as a child of my own." Her eyes had turned glassy with tears, as the medical assistant took a pair of shears to cut away the back of Belle's dress. Edvina looked up, mouth open with horror, as her eyes shifted between Belle and the Prince. "Good gracious! Do you mean to humiliate the poor girl?"

The man froze in his cutting, looking at the yelling Majerdome with a touch less color than he had before. Clearly a yelling female was not something he was accustomed to. "M-Madame?"

"The indecency, you fool!" She gestured angrily to Belle's exposed flesh. Then she dashed around to stand between Belle and Aleksander, with arms out as a visual shield. "Do you not have a partition? A sheet? Anything to spare the girl some privacy?"

Belle bit her tongue to keep from giggling. The physician looked at Monsieur Petit for assistance. With rolling eyes, Laramie already had the room door open and was sending someone to fetch just what Edvina needed. He added a posthaste to encourage their speed. In moments, they had returned with a partition, and a wall of white linen was erected between the two beds.

With Edvina finally mollified that Belle's reputation would not be sullied, she took up Belle's hand once more. The assistant set back to work, falling into a rhythm that suggested he'd soon forgotten them both. Belle, however, did not forget him as he pressed a stitching needle in and out of her skin.

When he finished, he needlessly warned Belle of the scars she would have. He went on to say that she should stay the night at the castle, let her wounds settle a bit before riding about. Edvina vehemently approved of this idea and sent for a new dress and to have Belle's room readied.

As the assistant went around the curtain to help with Aleksander, a strange scraping noise drew Edvina and Belle's attention to the corner. Edvina squeaked in alarm when a door, that had once been just a wall, pushed open. Much to their surprise, it was Lady Liv Calland who walked through. She looked around the room like she'd just discovered it until her eyes fell upon Belle.

"There you are. Wonderful!" A delicate smile spread over Liv's sweet face. Her dress was one of soft yellow and black, designed to make her stand out in a crowd. The expensive fabric swished as she moved closer. "You won't believe what I just heard."

"Good to see you again, your Ladyship," Belle said, amused at the woman's unexpected entrance.

"Of course, Darling." She paused to look at Belle affectionately. "Did you know that the castle is filled with secret passageways?"

"I did not, but I see you did." Belle glanced at the square hole in the wall, that Edvina was going to close.

"Only that one passage. Be kind to the staff, Belle, they know things," she said sagely and brushed a bit of hair from Belle's face. "Why, just this day, I was in the library of all places, and this little dove told me all about your harrowing adventure to return our prince to us. When I expressed an urgent need to visit you, she showed me the hidden passage that led me straight to you. Fascinating creatures, aren't they?"

"What are?"

"The staff, Darling, of course." She leaned down and said conspiratorially, "The little dove also said that you'd seen the Crowned Prince as a human again, is this true?"

Belle blushed, but there was no point in hiding it if this *little dove* knew already. "It is."

"Well, you scandalous little minx." Liv swatted Belle playfully and straightened with a mischievous gleam to her eyes. "I haven't seen the real him for years. Quite handsome, isn't he?"

"Very." Belle fought to keep from grinning too widely, suddenly realizing that Liv had no idea the Prince was in the room with them. So caught up in her gossip with Belle, Liv had paid no mind to what lay beyond the partition.

"But you have no shortage of handsome men in your life." Lady Liv wiggled her eyebrows at Edvina, who grinned and shook her head. "I hear those Hunters of yours are quite dashing. Is this true?"

Belle sighed, as though to take stock of her group of men. "Yes, they *are* easy on the eyes."

Aleksander growled from the other side of the cloth wall,

shocking Liv from her playful air. She stormed around the bed, still looking elegant somehow.

"I say, what in the world is that." She jerked the partition aside, intent on chastising whoever made such an undignified sound. She gasped upon seeing the great beast and dropped into a curtsy so low she was nearly on the ground. "Your Royal Highness! I do apologize. I had not realized you were here. Please forgive my intrusion."

She began backing slowly away and Edvina pushed the partition back into place, cutting off view of the Prince. Liv looked over her shoulder, glaring at the giggling Belle. "*Sneaky* little minx."

"I'm sorry, Liv." Belle took a deep breath, trying to force the smile from her face. "I am a terrible friend for not warning you. And worse yet, I must ask a favor."

Liv turned fully toward her, raising a curious eyebrow. "Oh, and what burden do you wish to lay upon me?"

"My Hunters need to be informed that, because of my injuries, I am to stay the night here and that they should return without me." Belle dramatically looked away, then returned her gaze to Liv imploringly. "It must be someone I trust. Can I rely upon you?"

"Little minx, indeed." The corner of the Lady's mouth tilted upward. "This is quite the thing that you ask of me, for that is such a long way for a lady of my station to walk—but you are my friend and you are in need." She nodded with conviction. "I will do this for you."

"Oh, thank you, Liv. You are too good for this world." Belle held out a hand to her friend.

Liv took it, giving Belle a wink. "You and I both, Darling."

# Chapter Thirty-Four

itting together on the loveseat, Edvina ran a brush through Belle's loose hair. With her eyes half-lidded, Belle listened to Edvina's story and watched the fire dance in her room's fireplace. After a meeting with Monsieur Petit and General Kogsworthe, Belle checked in on a sleeping Aleksander, then spent the remainder of the evening resting her injury.

Admittedly, Belle was grateful to be back at Castle Vakre Fjell. It was strange. Home would always be LeClair House and her family would always be the Hunters, Friar Clemens, and the good people of Contefées. But she was also glad to be in the care of Edvina, have the sisterly friendship of Liv, and enjoy the intelligent company of Ms. Tops. The companionship of other women, it was something she never wanted to go without again.

"Anyhow, long story short, the entire castle is abuzz with your epic saga—"

"My epic saga?"

"Well you know, how Prince Aleksander rescued you from the cursed, then turned human to show you who he was. And how you carried him to your home and risked your life in turn to save him, then how you both nearly died upon returning to the castle. It is quite the thing. Anyhow, as I said, long story short, even the strictest of holdouts that you were not to be trusted have come around. You've won over the entire castle, Child!"

"I'm so glad that's all it took."

There was a timid knock at the door.

"Now, who could that be? How very unseemly to come calling so late." Edvina put the hair comb aside and went to the door. She opened it just enough to see who it was and block Belle from view.

"Sorry to disturb, but I've brought something for the mademoiselle," said a male's voice.

"Couldn't this wait until morning when she—"

"It's all right, Edvina. Let him in." Belle stood, pulling her silk robe around her and covering the billowing nightgown beneath.

As commanded, Edvina stepped aside and a middle-aged man, with rosy cheeks, entered. Belle immediately recognized him as a servant who generally worked the stables. He blushed at seeing Belle in her nightclothes. She ignored it, keeping her head high. Whatever it was, it was important enough for him to come here at this hour and she was not about to make it worse by being embarrassed.

"Pardonnez-moi, mademoiselle, I know the hour is late." The saddlebags in his hands suddenly gave a jump, causing Edvina to squeal and grab her excessive bosom. The man held the straps tight, so as not to drop it. "However, something in your bag is upsetting the stable hands. It does not act like an animal and is making very unnatural noises. Now, the boys are not superstitious if you can believe it, but their talk has turned to such nature. I thought it best to bring it to you before they decided to convert."

"A reasonable decision." Belle accepted the bag, which had started to wiggle dramatically.

"Careful, Dear," Edvina whispered, remaining several feet away.

Grabbing the metal clasp, Belle unhooked it. Slowly she began to lift the leather flap, tilting her head to peer inside. Whatever it was flew up in a rush. It burst past the flap and whizzed by her face with only inches to spare.

"What in the world?!" Belle exclaimed, struggling to follow the thing's fast movements.

Edvina screamed, swatting her hair like it had bats in it and ducked behind a chair. The servant stepped close to Belle, removing a small dagger to guard her with. The thing made one fast dash around the room, then dove to the bed and disappeared beneath a pillow.

Belle could hardly believe it. "Pixie?"

There was just a second of nothing, where the pillow shook only a little. Then the thing flew out again and came straight for Belle. It was so fast, she couldn't react. Then little cold hands were touched in her cheek and a small voice twinkled hurriedly in her ear. Belle laughed in her surprise and carefully took the small toy into her hands. She held Pixie before her for the others to see.

"Pixie?" asked the man, looking over her shoulder with his mouth agape. "A real fairy?"

"No, just a mechanical one. My father made it for me one Noël." Belle smiled at Edvina to encourage her out from hiding. She came over hesitantly, a hand still on her beating heart as Belle said, "I had no idea Pixie had come with me. I've only had her out of the house a few times. The snow isn't terribly friendly to metal joints, you see."

"Ja," he agreed with an exaggerated nod. "Well if that's all it was, I'll be going to calm the boys down."

"Goodnight, monsieur. Thank you so much."

"Of course, mademoiselle. Goodnight." He chuckled as Pixie waved enthusiastically to him; a gesture which he reciprocated before leaving.

"As I live and breathe." Edvina now clutched her chest with

two hands and looked as though she were witnessing a miracle. "What marvels!"

"I guess she was tired of being alone in my room and hid in my pack."

Pixie leapt out of Belle's hands and fluttered over to the older woman. She twinkled a song and did several circles around her. Like a gleeful child, Edvina laughed and watched her with gleaming eyes.

Lifting up the saddlebag, Belle looked inside. She shuffled through the various contents and chuckled when she found the decorated egg that Pixie slept in. "Clever little stowaway."

In this moon dream, Belle was alone in the courtyard. She glanced around the snowy grounds, expecting to see the Prince, but he was nowhere to be seen. She frowned, placing her hands on her hips. It just didn't make sense that he wouldn't be here and she would.

"The sun is about to set," came Aleksander's sweet voice, drawing Belle's eyes upward. He stood confidently on the outer wall and stared into the distance, then he turned to smile down at her. "Would you like to join me?"

"I would." She returned his smile, feeling his lightness of spirit in the air. "But I'm not sure how I would get all the way up there."

"Have a little faith." He knelt down, extending his hand toward her. At her skeptical expression, he added, "Come now, give me your hand."

Belle really couldn't see how this was going to work. He was many feet above her! With a shrug, she decided to just go with it. She reached out her hand, taking steps in his direction.

Suddenly the ground pitched forward. It lifted her in the air with a soft acceleration and shifted to help her balance. Belle laughed in astonishment. She took another step. The ground came up to meet her boot. Another step and another, Belle confidently walked the earthen staircase upward to Aleksander.

He grinned charmingly at her, gently taking her hand and guiding her safely onto the outer wall. As both of Belle's feet found firm footing, the ground receded back into its original shape with a groan from the effort.

Aleksander held onto her hand a second longer than necessary, letting his thumb trace her wrist. His blue eyes twinkled. His lips remained upturned. There was a softness about him that had been missing over the last few days. Belle hadn't realized it so much at the time, but now it seemed obvious.

"You seem quite changed, Aleksander." The breath of her voice shook just a little. She was nervous for some reason, but it was more like the excited energy that comes with the first of Spring. "May I ask what has brought it about?"

"Do I?" Aleksander actually looked away, almost sheepishly. He thought for a moment, then gazed out over the mountain range. "I suppose it's due to being home again. Everyone is well. My kingdom has hope. It is a good feeling."

"Wonderful. I am glad for you." Belle withdrew her hand, wondering at what—if anything—came next for them and peered at the mountains. Their steely gray, capped with perfect ivory, had a backdrop of pink and gold. "It really is lovely here."

"However, my change might have more to do with the influence of your company." His words came out in a rush and she looked at him in surprise. "Belle, I've made my affections known. I do not—I will not—hide them, not even now. I love you." Aleksander held out his arms in acceptance, looking to the sky. "I love your fierce spirit. I love that your heart has no limits; you care unconditionally. You didn't need to help me or my kingdom, but you did without want for yourself." The Prince dropped his eyes to the ground with a shake of his head and a chuckle. "I love that your favorite room in my castle is the library. I love that your green eyes remind me of emeralds, that you smell of roses, and that you make me want so badly to be free."

Belle's breath became sparse. Did her heart even beat, for she no longer felt it? "Oh Aleksander, I . . ."

He pressed on at her loss of words, "I only say all of this because I know that I'm about to ask too much of you." With tentative movements, Aleksander took up her hand once more. He caressed her fingers, gazing intently into her eyes. "I am a beast. I am cursed. This hasn't changed." He closed his eyes to take a breath, then forged on. "What *has* changed is that I know now that I do not wish to be without you. You are my hope." Not releasing her hand, Aleksander touched her cheek. "If this curse is ever broken, I'd like to court you—publicly. Would that be agreeable to you?"

Stunned, Belle stared blankly. Then her answer burst out. "Yes! Of course!"

Aleksander's eyebrows raised in shock. His lips began to upturn, but he forced the smile away. "Please understand what you're agreeing to. I may never be free of this curse, or you might have to wait years for me." He squeezed her hand imploringly. "Then when we do go public, there will be opposition. Some noble families will fight us. It will be a strain both socially and privately." He straightened his shoulders, constraining all of his emotions. "I'll understand if you see now that it is too much. I will not force you—"

"Aleksander, I love you," she interrupted him. Belle didn't hide her joy. She splayed it across her face like the sun in the sky. "I'll wait my whole life just to have you, even if I never do."

His hand started to drop hers and he stared at her wearily. "And what of the noble families?"

Looking at the mountain range, seeing the sun dip behind their peaks, she found her answer. "Our love will be like your mountains. Let the winds batter us, we will not give way." Belle turned back at the Prince, who watched her closely. She reached up to touch his face. "I know this because I've never loved anyone the way I love you, Aleksander. Our love may be new, but one day it will be *grand*."

"You don't know what it means to me to hear you say these things." He cupped her hand against his face and tugged her a step closer with his other. "I was stunned the first moment I laid eyes on you. You were afraid but undeniably strong. I didn't know then the effect you would have on me. Then it was my turn to be afraid, to fear that you might not love me in return." Prince Aleksander's blue eyes danced between hers. "You've made my heart sing. I love you, my beauty."

"And I love you, my prince."

# Chapter Thirty-Five

It took several knocks before Belle could pull herself fully out of the wonderful moon dream. She loathed whoever forced her to leave. The knocks came again, rattling her senses further.

"I'm up! I'm up. Just a moment!" Belle threw back the covers with an exaggerated flourish and fumbled her way through the drapes surrounding her bed.

She blinked at the light just starting to illuminate the distant mountains. Was it sunrise already? Belle tied her robe around her. Pixie pushed up from her egg-shaped bed and feigned a yawn. Rubbing her eyes, Belle walked over and opened the bedroom door.

"Apologies. There are two gentlemen to see you, mademoiselle. A Frenchmen and an American." The servant said with only a hint of surprise in her voice. "They say it is urgent."

Belle looked over the woman's shoulder to find Jack and Andre. Though with a description like that, she hadn't expected to see anyone else. They looked windswept, with cheeks and noses red from the cold. Whatever news forced them to brave the forest so late at night must truly be terrible.

"Let them in," Belle said, as unease replaced the moon dream's euphoria. "Have coffee and food sent up, posthaste."

The servant curtsied and turned away. Belle walked over to the mirror. Quickly, she checked her appearance. Really, they couldn't expect much from her this early.

The door opened again and the two Hunters walked in. Pixie released a high jingle at the sight of them and flew excitedly over to Jack. She kissed his cheek while he greeted her in kind.

"Pixie? You brought Pixie with you?" Andre said, eyebrows raised.

"Stowaway." Belle pointed at her accusingly. "Please have a seat, messieurs. I've ordered refreshments, but I assume you wish to tell me why you are here without delay."

"Quite right." Andre walked over, grabbed a log, and tossed it on the fading embers. A few prods from the iron poker revived the sleeping fire. "I'm afraid the church has decided against allowing the Prince to live."

"What?" Sitting down quickly, Belle felt suddenly very awake. "Even after he has returned to his castle?"

"Yes, ma'am." Jack came over to sit, letting Pixie stay on his shoulder. "I believe the words used were 'As long as he is controlled by the beast, he is a threat to us all'."

"Controlled by the beast? So they don't believe that he is cursed then. He's still the devil incarnate to them." Belle shook her head, frustrated after everything they'd been through.

"To be fair, they do not know Prince Aleksander like you do." Andre exchanged a meaningful look with Jack. "And they do not know you like we do."

"Merci." She gave a smile, but it was a struggle with the worry that she now felt. "So what action do they intend to take?"

"They're gathering all the capable men in Contefées—" Andre silenced himself as the door opened.

Servants entered with trays of food and began serving fresh coffee. Belle shooed them away, stating that they were perfectly able to pour their own coffee at this juncture. They curtsied and quickly left.

"You were saying?" Belle took over where the servants left off, first handing a filled cup to Jack.

"They'll be outside these gates by midday." Andre took the cup Belle offered, thanking her gravely. "Their intention is to execute the Prince and I believe they intend to kill everyone here if he is not turned over willingly."

"They said that?" Belle set down the coffee pot.

"Not in so many words."

"But, Belle, there was no mistaking their intent," Jack added.

Sipping from her cup, Belle took in this new information. There was really only one logical step to take first.

"We must wake the General and Monsieur Petit." She set down her drink and went to the door. "There is much to do and the day is already upon us."

The leather slid through the clasp and Belle popped the metal home, tightening the holder across her chest. Then one by one she drove each throwing knife into position. After Belle's sabre was hung at her hip, she removed her revolvers to make sure they were loaded.

The door to Aleksander's room opened. Belle glanced up from looking in the bullet chamber to see Andre entering. He was armed to the teeth, just as she was. With the cover back over the chamber, Belle put her beautiful revolvers in their hostlers.

"'Bout ready?" he asked closing the door behind him. His dreadlocks were pulled neatly out of the way.

"As ready as I'll ever be, I suppose." Belle hated the idea of possibly fighting her family, and her people. Could she really stand against them if this turned to bloodshed? She knew she couldn't, so she'd have to make them see reason.

"How is he?" Andre nodded to the Prince slumbering in his own bed. Since it was easier to defend him here than the royal sick rooms, Aleksander had been moved just hours ago.

"He's holding together. His strength is coming back, but it'll take time for all those wounds to heal." She looked from the Prince to the Hunter. "Andre, I have to ask. How come you're with me and not with the other Hunters?"

Tugging the glove tighter over his mechanical hand, he answered, "The church may pay us, but you lead us. I've sworn my vows alongside you from the beginning and I intend for it to remain that way. For Jack, it's essentially the same." Seeing Belle's thoughtful look, he squared his shoulders and held out his arm. "Till my heart stills."

Warm pride swelled within Belle's chest. Somehow, through all of the bloodshed and loss, she had earned a steadfast loyalty from Andre and Jack. If she never earned a single thing in her life, this would be more than enough.

Belle grasped his forearm. "Till my heart stills."

A horn sounded a long, deep keen from one of the castle battlements. Belle released his arm and placed a hand on her revolver. "They're here. We'd better get out there."

Andre sighed. "Here we go."

Belle looked at Aleksander. He rested peacefully. Her heart surged as she remembered his recent declarations. She wanted to reach out and stroke his cheek but fought the inappropriate desire.

As Andre grabbed for the door handle, the balcony doors flew open with a crash. They flinched in surprise as glass scattered over the floor and frosty wind swirled around them. Belle then looked up and gasped.

Standing confidently on the stone railing of Aleksander's balcony—like an angel of death—was the norn. Her blue and silver cloak whipped about with the wind. Her hood fell back revealing straight, silver hair. Her hand rested comfortably on an evil looking dagger strapped to the front of her lower waist. A smile played on her perfectly red lips.

Belle stepped forward to place herself between the norn and the Prince. She drew her guns. Andre moved beside her.

"Belle LeClair," The norn spoke, unbothered by the Hunters' protective positions. Her voice was lyrical, in a fashion, with a lacing of malice. "If I'd have known you were going to be such a problem, I'd have killed you long ago."

The sound of Belle's name coming from the norn gave her a sickening feeling. Andre glanced at Belle, his brow furrowed in confusion. Likely he was wondering the same thing she was.

"How do you know my name?" Belle asked.

"Oh, I've known you for a long time." The norn floated down to the balcony floor. She carefully placed her hood back on her head, her solid ebony eyes not looking away from them. "I watched you kill my wolves. You were good. A real talent for slaughter. I had hoped you would solve my little Moon-Hound problem, but . . ."

The norn walked casually beneath the archway, cold air pouring into the room from behind her. Belle tightened her grip on her revolvers. Her mind raced. How was she supposed to stop this norn when Gastone had already put a sword through her head?

"Oh Belle, I never thought you'd fall for a—hellhound." She snickered at the term. "But you did something to him, Belle. His resolve was weakening, he was just about to give in to Fenrir." The amusement dashed from her face and she glared at Belle with nothing short of hate. "Then he did something he shouldn't have been able to do. He fought the curse!"

The scream bounced off the walls, sounding like she had the

full force of Hell behind her. Belle's nerves jumped. She didn't know what was more terrifying. The norn calm and collected, or angry

There was a bang on the door. Jack called to them from the other side, but the sound was muffled. He pulled on the door. It didn't budge.

"No one will open that door unless I want them too." The norn smiled again. "You've presented me with the perfect opportunity, Belle. I tried to kill you once, but that handsome Hunter of yours got in my way." She chuckled and positioned herself squarely before them. "Now he's turned against you, distracting everyone else . . . and Fenrir has seen fit to let me kill you and your prince."

As though it were a cue, Andre whipped four knives at her. With unimaginable reflexes, the norn held up her arm and caught one through her palm and two in her forearm. The fourth stuck between her ribs, but these wounds didn't bother her. In fact, it looked as if she'd wanted the knives to injure her.

"Did you forget who I am?" She glared at them both and slowly, painfully, began pulling the knives from her flesh. The skin healed as each blade was removed. "My name is Skuld. I am a norn; the embodiment of fate. You *cannot* hurt me."

Skuld, as she called herself, pulled the last knife from her torso, and Belle felt a sickening terror grow within her stomach. How could they stop her? Nothing would kill her. Briefly Belle considered lunging into the norn, sending them both over the balcony, but she doubted even that would kill her.

Not facing the same dilemma as the Hunters, Skuld gathered the knives in one hand. As though she were an expert, she flung them. All four flew between them, missing them both completely. Belle might have laughed at the poor aim if it weren't for the heartbreaking whine that followed. She turned to find the beast, Aleksander, on his knees just behind them. He'd climbed from his bed, no doubt to fight alongside them. Now he was wounded; stuck with all four blades.

Belle couldn't prevent the small cry that escaped her and she dropped to her knees before him. "Oh, God."

Prince Aleksander's pained eyes watched her meaningfully and she wished desperately that he could speak to her. He still seemed so weak, his breathing labored, and yet he had tried to stand with her. Without warning him of the pain to come, Belle stashed away her revolvers, grabbed the knife in his shoulder, and ripped it free. He half whined, half howled but didn't move. She pulled another from his side and dropped both knives with a clatter to the floor.

Blood made her hands slippery as she grasped a third knife in his stomach. She was vaguely aware of gunshots firing when she removed the blade. Then Andre was thrown, he slammed into the great doors and landed in an unconscious slump. There was no time to react before Belle felt Skuld's cold hand on her shoulder and she was cast away from Aleksander.

For several feet, Belle was airborne, then she slammed into the marble floors and slid many more. Pain sliced through her hip and up her side. On shaking arms, she fought to push herself up. Skuld towered over Aleksander.

"I saved this death just for you," the norn said and from her waist she pulled the long, silver dagger. It glinted in the light, revealing strange and intricate markings.

# Chapter Thirty-Six

Shoving to her feet, Belle pulled her right revolver and triggered the bayonet to snap forward. Skuld raised her own dagger. As Belle ran, she turned the gun in her hand so that the barrel sat in her palm, acting as the hilt to her blade. It was not how the weapon was intended, but it was the only way she could think to possibly inflict serious damage. A wound that might take more than a second to heal and perhaps steal them some more time. Bullets and blood littered the marble floor as Belle crossed the distance. Skuld's dagger began to descend and Belle leapt.

She slammed the bayonet into the norn's shoulder and dragged it down with her. A foot-long wound tore in its wake. The weapon dug into her muscle, causing Skuld to pull back with it. She screamed in outrage and, somehow, pain.

Skuld jerked herself forward, yanking the revolver out of Belle's hand and sending it to the floor. Belle backed away as the norn's angry attention turned to her. Belle's eyes flicked around the room trying to find some way to fight this otherworldly being. Then she saw Aleksander hunched over, still breathing, as he grasped the final throwing knife lodged in his muscle. At least there was this. At least he was still alive. Maybe somehow, he could fight back even if it was too late for her.

Eyes still on her prince, Belle didn't react fast enough when Skuld reached for her neck. Her fingers went around Belle's throat. They squeezed painfully.

"What are you?" she said through clenched teeth and lifted the Hunter from the ground.

Sharp pains stabbed at Belle's lower back. Frantically, she pulled at the norn's fingers. They were cold and immovable. No air could make it to Belle's lungs. She looked into Skuld's eyes in this moment. They ate up her distress as though her pain was nourishment.

"Adieu, little Bellerina," she said with a sickening smile. Holding Belle aloft, like she was nothing more than a feather, Skuld carried her to the balcony. She stopped just below the archway, her expression changing. "No, I don't think I will throw you to your death." She smiled at her delightful idea. "I think I'll let you suffocate instead. That's a more befitting death. *Slow*."

Belle's brow creased in shock of such evil. Her heart raced and she reflexively gulped for air. When none came and her lungs began to burn, she thrashed. She kicked the norn several times, but Skuld paid it no mind. Trying desperately to calm herself, Belle reached for her left revolver. It was gone; likely lost when she was thrown before.

Then Belle went for the throwing knives strapped to her chest. She fingered one of the handles, intent on stabbing the norn in the eye. But her brain was fuzzy and she struggled to pull the knife out. Skuld knocked Belle's hand away and grabbed the sash. Deftly, she ripped it off her and tossed it away. That was it then. Belle had no more weapons. With one last surge of panic and defiance, she swung at Skuld. It was easily blocked.

Pain raced through her body. Belle was acutely aware of every part of her that screamed for air. Tears streamed down her cheeks and she continued to open her mouth, as though somehow air would find its way in. This wasn't how Belle was supposed to die. She was supposed to die with blood—not like this.

Through the fog, movement drew Belle's attention. Aleksander, in his hulking beastly form, rose from his crouch on the ground. Blood leaked down his body as he drew to his full height. In livid silence, like he could feel no pain, Aleksander came over to them with long smooth steps and towered above the unaware norn. He glared down at Skuld, his lip beginning to curl in an unrealized snarl. And just like that, the Prince snapped. Many sharp, deadly teeth bit into Skuld's neck.

A bloodcurdling scream tore through the air and Skuld's hands pulled back in her agony. Belle dropped to the floor, her legs crumpling weakly beneath her. She gasped, desperate for air. Fresh blood trickled down her side from her reopened wounds.

Still latched onto Skuld's neck, the Prince planted a hand on her shoulder. With strong claws, he pulled the armor from her shoulder. He released her just long enough to bite into the now bare skin. The norn seemed helpless to stop the attack. True fear filled those evil eyes of hers.

Suddenly, Aleksander jerked away. His lips twitched. He shook his muzzle, like a dog that didn't like what he tasted. He stopped, ears forward and eyes wide. Belle followed his gaze back to Skuld. Something other than blood spread from the gashes on her shoulder and neck.

It was gray, laced with black veins like some of the marble in the castle. It spread up into her hair and down into her armor. Skuld looked at her trembling hand. The substance swept up from beneath the metal and wrapped around each finger. Then, whatever it was, moved to the armor itself. It sunk into each crevice, leaving nothing uncovered by it.

The fear in Skuld's eyes vanished as she seemed to realize, or accept, what was happening to her. Though neither Belle nor

Aleksander knew what that was. She retrieved the armor the Prince had ripped from her and reattached it. Then with slow, pained movements she pulled her hood back over her head.

"I can feel your glee, *Mánagarmr*. You think that with my death, you and your people will be free." She shot Aleksander a nasty glance. "Your people will never be free."

The Prince stood tall and squared his shoulders at that. He made no angry move for her though. Even if his people were lost forever, it seemed that they'd won. Skuld plucked a fully bloomed rose from the nearby archway. She looked at it fondly, ignoring Belle on the floor completely.

The norn walked toward the Prince, but Aleksander didn't seem concerned. The gray substance had drawn over most of Skuld's body now. Even her cloak was covered. Each step she took was slow and weighted. She stopped before him, twirling the rose between her fingers. "And you will never be rid of the beast."

Her hand lashed out, unhindered by the thing that was consuming her. Skuld shoved the rose into Aleksander's wolf chest. Light burst from where they touched. The Prince's head fell back in a wall-shaking roar. He stumbled away, claws raking at the bloody spot over his heart.

Skuld's face was serene. She exhaled calmly and closed her eyes. The grayness swept down her face, completing its domination. With that, she stilled. If Belle didn't know better, she'd have thought that it was a statue of a sleeping woman that someone forgot to lay down.

Belle clambered to her feet. She felt weak, her throat was sore. Aleksander's bloodied hands were cupped before him and he stared at the rose carved into his chest. He flexed his hands, then let his arms drop with exhaustion.

Cautious, Belle walked over to Skuld and tentatively touched her. Her hand snapped back at the feel of cold stone. Skuld didn't just look like a statue, she *was* a statue. Head to toe. Cloak, skin, and hair—all of it was a solid piece of perfect marble. Belle formed the cross over her chest, speaking the Latin words of the holy trinity.

A burst of silver light flared in her eyes, causing her to flinch away. Only twice had Belle seen that color of light before and, as it faded, she knew it could only mean one thing. Hurriedly, she blinked away tiny stars and saw a human Aleksander standing in the room's center. He looked at his hands again, then touched his silk shirt. Without the fur, his multiple stab wounds were more obvious. The blood was already seeping through his clothes.

He looked at Belle with an awed expression and she knew she returned it. She didn't dare believe what she was witnessing. Her Prince was human! Aleksander started to smile, his chest heaving with excited breaths.

As though he'd been stabbed through the gut, the Prince hunched in on himself. His muscles began to twitch and flex. He grunted in pain, his face contorting from it. Concerned, Belle stepped toward him.

Angelic ringing gave her pause. She looked away just before the light could blind her. When she opened her eyes, her heart fell at the sight of the beast.

Had this been what Skuld meant? Her death freed him but using the rose had somehow forced the Moon-Hound back on him? It was so cruel to give him just a taste of freedom, only to snatch it back.

Not looking down at himself—he knew the wolf form all too well—Aleksander stared at nothing. The sadness in his eyes broke Belle's heart. She stepped into his shadow, forcing his eyes to hers.

There was a part of her that still said this was wrong; a woman should not love a beast. But her heart saw only Prince Aleksander, the man she loved. Belle reached up and touched his soft fur cheek. He closed his eyes, leaning into her hand. A sorrowful moan rumbled in his throat. It made her want to cry.

All at once, Aleksander was engulfed in light. It filled the room and chased all shadows away. It was pure . . . like moonlight. The sweet ringing was as loud as ever. Then it was gone, vanished in an instant.

Belle blinked. Beautiful, blue eyes filled her vision. The Prince was smiling down at her, his face much closer than it had been as a wolf. A ripple shifted over his skin and she thought he was about to become the beast once more. Aleksander closed his eyes. His jaw clenched with strain. After a second, he relaxed and opened his eyes.

His gaze caressed her face, memorizing it at that moment. The tips of his fingers gently touched her forearm. A thrill shot through her. He was touching her. Actually touching her.

"I can control it, Belle. I'm free." His lips spread into the most exuberant of smiles.

She laughed with disbelief as she finally understood. Skuld's death had freed him, but with the rose she made it a part of him—not just something placed on him as it was before. With effort, Aleksander could shift between beast and human.

He didn't seem to realize it now, but he would never be free, not truly. This meant that he was something . . . else. Skuld did not do this to be kind. There were consequences here that, by the joy in his eyes, the Prince didn't see. In *his* mind, he was free.

Unsure of what to say, trapped between fear and happiness, Belle's gaze fell to the rose-shaped wound over Aleksander's heart. She gently moved his shirt. The bloody etching wasn't life threatening, but it would scar.

Prince Aleksander touched her temple. His fingers ran down the side of her face and his palm rested on her cheek. His thumb grazed her jaw, angling her face upward. Meeting his gaze, her breath caught at the smoldering, possessive look in his eyes. "Belle—my beauty—I love you . . . and I'd like very much to kiss you once more."

"My Prince . . ." Her voice trembled with raw emotion as she responded with a breathy, "I love you—"

Aleksander's lips alighted onto hers. They gave soft, gentle caresses. Lip over lip, drawing her in for kiss after longer kiss. His arms encircled her, forcing one of her hands on his chest and the other on his waist. The simple feel of his muscles and warm skin, even through fabric, were enough to melt her. Belle felt the slightest brush of his tongue on hers and he pulled her in for one extended, luxurious kiss.

# Chapter Thirty-Seven

Belle reveled in the feel of Aleksander. His lips, his body, his soft sandalwood scent invaded her senses. It was fully consuming. He was here, touching her. Belle worried not for propriety or unladylike behavior because she had him. At that moment, there was only them.

"Holy Hell!" Andre's voice bounced off the stone walls, jarring the passionate embrace.

Aleksander pulled back from Belle and, in one blinking flash, turned back into a lycanthrope. The hand on Belle's hip became a paw that nearly covered her entire waist. A snarl rumbled past his lips at Andre's unwanted interruption. The Hunter's eyes widened with shock. He stayed on the floor, frozen like a terrified deer.

Belle smiled. "Are you all right, Andre?"

He looked at Belle for a long, thoughtful second. "Uh, yeah, I think I'm fine. What happened?"

A loud crash cutoff Belle's answer. The door's flew open with a bang. Wielding a large battering ram between them, Jack, Laramie, and a group of guards stumbled in. Aleksander pulled Belle back protectively. Edvina followed after, brandishing two deadly candlesticks above her head. They all stopped and looked around menacingly.

"It's all right," Belle said drawing their attention and gestured to the norn. "We're all fine now."

With a collective groan, they noisily set down their makeshift battering ram. Belle raised an eyebrow as she recognized the statue of the god, Odin. Jack quickly went to Andre, leaning over him to check his head. Laramie and Edvina rushed over to Belle and Aleksander while the guards examined the strange stone norn.

"Your Highness, the men from Contefées are here," Laramie said, clearly frazzled. "No attack has been made, but tension is quickly building. General Kogsworthe is trying to delay things, so you can imagine . . ."

Laramie's comment drifted as Aleksander closed his eyes and sighed. Once more his muscles rippled, tensed, and the ringing light sprang forth. She felt his body change, the fur replaced by warm, smooth skin. The claws on her back turned to gentle fingers. When the light receded, everyone opened their eyes. Aleksander's breathing was slow, controlled. He already seemed completely at ease with this new change in his life. There was even a twinkle in his eyes.

"Oh my," whispered Edvina, grabbing her cheeks as everyone else stared, dumbfounded.

"Your Royal Highness, how?" Laramie put a hand to his forehead, looking suddenly flush. "You're human!"

Aleksander placed a comforting hand on his advisor's shoulder. "There is no time now. Later, we'll discuss everything." Lifting his chin, the Prince's tone changed to one of command. "I want two men guarding this statue till I say otherwise. Get the Head Physician and his team here at once." He looked at Belle, a softness flashing in eyes. "Any suggestions on how to deal with your people?"

Belle contemplated this, only distracted slightly by his hand still at her waist. "They came to kill a beast, show them you are still a man. A man controlled by no other."

"I'd do so proudly." He smiled. "Laramie, have our horses readied. We must ride out to meet them."

"Of course." Monsieur Petit turned to act out his orders, but stopped and looked back. "It is good to see you again, your Highness."

Aleksander inclined his head. "It is good to be seen."

Edvina was ready to burst into tears, her smile so big that it crinkled around her eyes. Soon the doctors came. Several tended to the Prince, who insisted they do some quick patchwork—as he had some place to be. Others saw to Andre while Belle had her back stitches quickly fixed. Edvina was put to the task of making them presentable and she did a far better job than was expected. Though she was still smoothing hair and clothing till the moment Belle and Aleksander mounted their horses.

The militia beyond the gate was larger than Belle anticipated. The crowd yelled for blood, shouting over General Kogsworthe as he stalled for time. When Aleksander and Belle started down the long bridge, their horses at a casual pace, the angry militia grew quiet.

They peered over each other and squinted their eyes, trying to see who approached. Belle did some identifying of her own. Immediately she recognized her Hunters. They were stationed around the outskirts of the crowd, watching for hellhound trouble. At the front of the gates were the church clergymen, Henri, and Edgard Chevallier—the Count of Contefées, Gastone's father.

On the bridge were several rows of Vakrein foot soldiers. They were calm and disciplined; just what Belle expected under the watch of Kogsworthe. As the Prince neared, the lines of men separated in perfect unison and the General left the gate to meet his Prince. Belle could see the astonishment in their eyes at the sight of Aleksander, but they did well to mask it.

A hand reached over to tug Belle's wrists, halting her horse. Belle looked at Andre, askance.

"You mustn't ride up there with him," he said quietly.

"It would be bad, you openly siding against your people." Jack rode up alongside her, looking sympathetic. "You do and no matter how this turns out, they'll never forgive you. You don't want that."

An icky feeling sank into her stomach as Belle nodded her agreement. Aleksander reached his general and glanced at her. Surprise swept over his face when he realized that she wasn't still next to him. Then she saw the moment he understood, and the almost concealed hurt that followed.

It made her feel wretched.

Aleksander dismounted, handing his white steed off to another and went to General Kogsworthe. They spoke for several seconds while everyone else looked on. By the end of their conversation, Kogsworthe seemed unhappy. Still, he nodded and stepped aside.

With the body of a man and the bearing of a ruler, Prince Aleksander walked up to meet the Contefées militia—alone. Belle's heart jumped into her throat. She couldn't believe he was approaching the gate without protection. Good diplomacy or not, he was risking too much! Charming danced beneath her, sensing her anxiety. She reached down to calm the horse and inwardly prayed for the Prince's safety.

"I am Prince Aleksander the First, of House Haraldsson, Crowned Prince Regent of Vakre Fjell," Aleksander addressed the militia. His voice carried back to Belle by the cavern walls. He held out his arms, even pushing back his cloak to hide nothing. "I stand before you a man. Not a beast. Human flesh and human bone."

Through the iron gates, he spoke as though they were his own subjects. Each person gave him their rapt attention.

"I stand before you the prince of a cursed kingdom, whose own mother became one of the monsters that stalk this very woods." A murmur rustled through the crowd. Some looked into the trees behind them. No man would say such things about his own mother unless it was true. "Evil came here in the guise of a woman. It thought it could make Vakre Fjell its home. But I and my kingdom *resisted*."

Prince Aleksander pointed to Henri and the Count. "Your Hunters *resisted*. Though evil would not be undone so easily. Threatened by a partnership between my castle and your Hunters, evil came to my quarters this very day. It wanted to kill me and *your* Hunter Captain." He swung his arm around, pointing to Belle. There were gasps and vocalized outrage from the crowd. "But we stood against it. We fought back!" Several people nodded, one shouted a *hear, hear*. "And when evil is met with courage, it cannot stand!"

The militia cheered with approval.

"Do you doubt me?" Aleksander looked to the authority figures in the group. "All the proof you need to the truth of this tale can be found within." He gestured for a soldier to open the gates. "I invite you all to see what evil looks like encased in stone."

The cheering was twice as loud now. The Prince had won them over. It was clear he was no beast as they had been told. Now they wanted to see his proof and someone shouted of celebrating their victory against evil.

Glowering, Bishop Sauvage slunk back into the crowd. Men moved around him, wanting to be closer to the royalty before them. Belle watched the Bishop with unease.

"You mean to say," Count Chevallier spoke up, quieting those nearest. "That you've captured the evil woman that you spoke of—and turned her to stone?"

"What are you doing, Belle?" whispered Andre as she dismounted.

"Stay here." She tossed her reins over the saddle and left Charming with Andre and Jack.

Whatever Aleksander said in response to the Count delighted the crowd. Belle didn't hear. Her attention was focused solely on Bishop Sauvage as she weaved her way in and out of the Vakrein soldiers.

She couldn't say why, but her pace increased. Belle made eye contact with Gastone as the Bishop walked past. Gastone scrunched his eyebrows, noticing her growing distress. Sauvage moved to stand several paces up from him on a small upturn of hill. His face was red, his nostrils flaring. That's when Belle saw the weapon.

She grabbed up her skirts and ran. In response, Gastone drew his sabre. Bishop Sauvage raised his revolver.

"Gastone, the Bishop!" Belle pointed behind him.

Gastone turned. Leaping, Belle splayed out her arms to shield Aleksander. The Bishop pulled back the gun's hammer. Gastone's sword went up.

"Belle, no!" Aleksander's arms wrapped around Belle and he spun her away.

Bishop Sauvage fired. The boom pierced her eardrums, echoing off every hard surface. Aleksander sank to the ground, bringing Belle with him. She clung to him, agony ripping at her heart. Shouts and chaos filled the air.

"Aleksander?!" Belle twisted in his arms. He stared wide-eyed at her. She dragged her hands along his back, searching for blood. "Are you shot?"

"Belle! Belle, I'm fine." He snatched up her hands to hold them firmly. "He missed."

She breathed a sigh of relief, then glared at him. "You fool. You could have been killed!"

"I'm the fool?" He raised an eyebrow with disbelief, a faint smile tipping the corner of his mouth.

Belle looked away sheepishly. "It seems we're both fools, then."

"Your Royal Highness, pardonnez-moi." Laramie appeared beside them, kneeling on the stone bridge. "Might I just point out that lingering down here together might draw inquiries?"

"Right." Aleksander nodded. "Of course."

With the assistance of more than enough people, Belle and Aleksander were brought to their feet and righted. Belle met the gaze of her father. His moving lips wanted to know if she was hurt, and she shook her head. He noticeably sighed.

On the hill, Bishop Sauvage was also being dragged to his feet. They'd tied his hands behind his back. Several guns stayed pointed in his direction.

"Well, it seems we were receiving guidance from someone rather unstable," the Count said. Count Edgard Chevallier carried himself with an intimidating air of privilege and authority. His beard was perfectly trimmed and his attire was impeccable, but his sandy brown hair sported more gray than Belle remembered. He turned to Henri and Father Sinclair. "I say we see what proof the Prince has and should it be satisfactory, as I trust it will, I'd like to begin talks of supplying whatever aid is needed here. What say you?"

"I agree," answered Henri.

Father Sinclair nodded. He looked surprisingly pleased by these turn of events.

"You are all welcome." Aleksander opened his arms and looked at his men. "Someone open this gate already!"

A young soldier rushed over to do just that. The crowd huddled around, eager to get in.

"Your Royal Highness," came the voice of a different soldier. He and another struggled to keep Edvina at bay. "I'm not sure we can hold her much longer."

"It's all right." Aleksander chuckled. "You can let her by."

They happily released her. Edvina ran over as the militia started to stream in. She fussed about Belle and Aleksander, looking for wounds that might have been missed.

"Edvina, please." Belle took the older woman's hand. "We're safe."

"What a fit you two have caused in me!" Edvina inhaled a rather wobbly breath. "Shame on you both."

"So sorry, madame." Aleksander winked at Belle. "We'll be more careful from now on."

"See that you do." She squeezed Belle's hand, then tilted her head with curiosity. "What is Laramie doing?"

They both turned. Laramie stood at the edge of the open gateway to Vakre Fjell Forest. The crowd had already past, leaving him there alone. He was right on the border, one more inch and the curse would take him. He stared intently into the land beyond.

"Laramie, what is it?" Aleksander inquired.

"I am inspired, your Royal Highness." Monsieur Petit faced them. He grasped his hands and squared his shoulders. "Now that the norn is dead and the curse on you lifted, I'd like to see if it's safe to leave as well."

Aleksander didn't respond, his lips drew into a tight line.

"Laramie?" Belle spoke up, worry streaking back through her. "You can't."

"Mademoiselle, it is because of you that I wish to do this. You are a Frenchwoman." The words came out steady with no hint of hesitation. "Yet you risk your life to save our prince. Witnessing this has compelled me to be more than just an adviser."

Belle clenched her teeth, unsure of what to say. Water sat on her eyelids and she tried to blink it away. The crowd had paused, having noticed that something was occurring. They looked to Aleksander. It would have to be his decision. Aleksander gave one nod, the muscles in his cheeks flexing.

Taking a deep breath, Laramie slowly turned. He remained on the edge for several long seconds preparing himself. Belle felt the softest tracing of Aleksander's fingers along her palm and a tear slipped past her defenses. If it wasn't for propriety, she'd be crying in the Prince's arms right then.

Finally, Monsieur Petit gave them one last glance. He took a deep breath and nodded to two soldiers. They raised their rifles, ready to shoot him should he turn.

Gripping his hands into fists, Laramie took a step. Then he took another. His head angled toward the sky. His eyes closed. Everyone waited with baited breath. After a moment, Monsieur Petit lowered his chin and turned back around.

He stared at the crowd of shocked onlookers. The silence was weighty. Then Laramie tossed up his arms and shouted, "We're free!"

As joyous cheers filled their ears, Aleksander smiled down at Belle. A soft breeze lifted the locks of his light-brown hair. His blue eyes twinkled and she knew what he wanted to say, without him even saying it.

# Epilogue

When the French militia returned home, their tales of the
cursed kingdom moved like superheated aether. It was all
anyone could seem to talk about. Suddenly Belle found
herself to be a much sought after commodity. When in town, she
could go nowhere without being asked to recount her time within
the mysterious castle. At home, she was not even safe. Belle received at least a handful of calling cards each day, seeking a private audience. These occurrences only increased as travelers from
outside of Contefées arrived for Aleksander's coronation.

With Vakre Fjell being in need of a king, the event was held
within a fortnight. Nobility and Heads of State from all over God's
Cup were in attendance—In spite of transport to the castle being
limited due to its unsafe nature. Skuld's death may have lifted the
lingering curse from the land, but those previously affected remained as hellhounds.

Despite the threat of otherworldly, ravenous wolves, the great
throne room was filled for the coronation. Belle understood everyone's desire to be there. It was a grand affair, unlike anything
she had hoped to witness in her life. As the crown was placed upon
Aleksander's head, she found herself entirely speechless.

Now, days later, Belle watched as several workers slid a massive stone slab onto the long stone box. Within laid the norn,

Skuld, as though she were a corpse and not a solidified being. They had tried to destroy her, but her marble body proved to be unbreakable. So she was given a grave that was little more than a sepulcher perched among the mountains near Castle Vakre Fjell. Inscribed on the lid was a warning to any who might consider disturbing the crypt.

Father Sinclair spoke over the proceedings, talking of God and the power of his followers. It was agreed between various officials that someone from the Catholic Church should be involved, as a sign of good faith between the two lands. A holy man of the old gods, that were still worshiped by the Vakrein royal family, was also there. He and Sinclair took turns speaking.

Belle let their familiar words wash over her and glanced at Aleksander, or King Aleksander as he was now called. He sat proudly upon his royal horse, in full ceremonial garb. At his side was his father's great sword and on his arm was the shield fashioned for his coronation. A wolf's head, a replica of Aleksander in his lycanthrope form, and a blossomed rose emboldened its face. The gold trim and embellishments glinted in the sunlight.

Aleksander peered down at her, flashing her a wink. She was in love with a king. True to his word, Aleksander was taking steps to make their courtship official. Belle had no idea what that would bring. Would they be able to marry? Or would Aleksander be forced to pursue a proper political match? She had no way of knowing. So at that moment, all that mattered was that Aleksander was free and that he loved her.

A sense of lightness had descended upon the kingdom and much was changing fast. Though travel was now a possibility, not a single Vakrein citizen had agreed to be relocated out of Vakre Fjell. Talks of establishing a trade route between Castle Vakre Fjell and Glace had begun, and there were plans to extend the lamppost paths. Aleksander also sent out a reward for anyone able to release his subjects already befallen of the curse. Until a cure or curse-breaker was found, the Hunters would still be needed.

As the burial ceremony concluded, the norn's crypt was sealed forever. Belle looked to Castle Vakre Fjell resting at the base of the mountains, half encircle by the great gorge. It stood as a beacon of strength and resistance, both impressive and intimidating. Their struggles were far from over, but for the first time—in a long time—Belle saw more than death in her future.

# 𝕿𝖍𝖊 𝕰𝖓𝖉

Belle and Aleksander will return in

# Author's Notes

I love this fairytale. I've seen many movies, TV shows, and read many versions of it. The day I came up with the idea of using hellhounds and steampunk inventions was one of the best days of my life. I tried to pay homage to all the versions I was familiar with; Some easter eggs will be obvious and others won't be. However, this world was still its own. So much hardship and death has a way of changing characters. I've really enjoyed getting to know these altered versions of familiar souls. I can't wait to see who they become . . . now that the fairytale is over.

In order to give this world rules, I drew from various mythologies. Particularly Norse Mythology. It seemed perfectly tailored for what this story needed. All of the poems that Aleksander read from belong to a real collection of Old Norse poems called, Poetic Edda. I know spots were hard to understand, but I refused to alter the original words.

The same can be said for the Hunter's Creed. The creed is a blend of old Catholic prayers and my own wording. If I could help it, I tried to keep the old prayers as close to the original wording as possible.

The thing that made this story particularly difficult, also a thing that I loved, was the cultural diversity. French, Norwegian (The basis for the Vakrein culture), American, British, and even some Irish. I imagined that throughout this story the characters switched almost seamlessly from speaking French, to Vakrein, to English, and back to French. I tried to represent this by slipping in little bits here and there. Such as Père (French for Father), Fille (French for Daughter), and so forth. Vakrein was the hardest to represent. I can type *merci* and most will recognize it. The Norwegian thank you (*takk*) is less recognizable. So instead I tried to represent it in the names, like Vakre Fjell or Mount Gunnhild.

It is my greatest hope that by doing all that I wrote above, God's Cup might perhaps be mistaken for a real place. Or, at the very least, it felt real to you.

Au revoir . . . for now.

# Acknowledgements

First, I'd like to thank my two writing mentors; Tom Nugent and Trisha Wolfe. I've said it many times, Tom taught me how to write and Trisha taught me how to tell a story. Whether they realize it or not, they helped shape me into the writer that I am. I will be forever grateful and indebted for that.

To my family . . . I love you all so very much. Thank you for never telling me that I couldn't do it and for never encouraging me to have a backup plan. Thank you to my mom for always buying me books and never discouraging that desire. Thank you to my dad for always asking where your helicopter is. To Tom, thank you for all the inspiring gun talk. To the three of you, thank you for supporting me completely. To my brother, thank you for asking me how the book was coming along every time you saw me. To my lil sis, thank you for daydreaming with me about what it would be like if my book was ever turned into a movie. I have the best siblings ever—the best family ever.

To Nicholas Smith, my best friend who's not blood related. You were the first to read *The Beast*. I thank you for loving the story as much as I do and for talking about the characters with me for hours.

Big thanks to Stephanie Mooney of Mooney Designs for creating such an incredible book cover, interior images, and a gorgeous map. You've captured it all so wonderfully, I can't wait to see the sequels!

Thank you to Jaye Manus for her patience and mad formatting skills. People can actually read this because of your talents.

I have to give massive props to my betas: Jessica Bolton, Jessyca (Robin) Bull, Cheryl (SheRa) Martin, Taryn Love, Emily Beronja, and Bunny Cates. God, I hope I didn't forget anyone. You didn't have to read the book. You didn't have to send back notes and edits. You certainly didn't get paid for it. Yet, you were all still there for me. I bow down to your incredible awesomeness.

To my amazing—fantastic!—YouTube subscribers. My Tubers and Tubettes are the most beautiful people I know. You helped me stay positive when I had to cut over 10k words from my manuscript or when I was frustrated that it was taking so long. You also understood when my vlogs sucked because I was too busy writing. You dutifully gushed anytime I read bits from *The Beast* aloud and announced how excited you were to read it. You've all been there for me nearly every day for the last year. Thank you. Thank you. Thank you. A thousand times over . . . Thank you.

Thank you to indiegogo.com and all of my campaign funders! Your backing of this book had a foundation that was primarily faith-based. Thank you for lending a hand to an aspiring author. Also, thanks for your patience. We all know this took a lot longer than expected.

To EVERY COWORKER I'VE EVER HAD! You watched me write on my arms, scribble on pieces of paper, and you listened to my excited babble about characters you knew nothing about. Thank you . . . and I'm sorry.

In all honesty, this is only a portion of the people who have had a part in the creation of this novel. I've had many friends and writing partners since I was in my teens. They all influenced me and they all helped push me to this day. I have not forgotten you.

To the Universe and every god that's out there—especially the writing gods—I thank you with every ounce of my being for this gift. Keep the stories coming.

# About the Author

Lindsay Mead lives in Michigan's lower peninsula with her small dog, Suzie Q, and her fish, Oscar. When she isn't writing, Lindsay is replying to comments on YouTube. There she uploads a video every day, documenting her writing, travels, and life adventures.

Get more from Lindsay on:

YouTube: Watch her daily vlog!
www.youtube.com/lindsaylou04

Website: Read her blog and more!
lindsaymead.blogspot

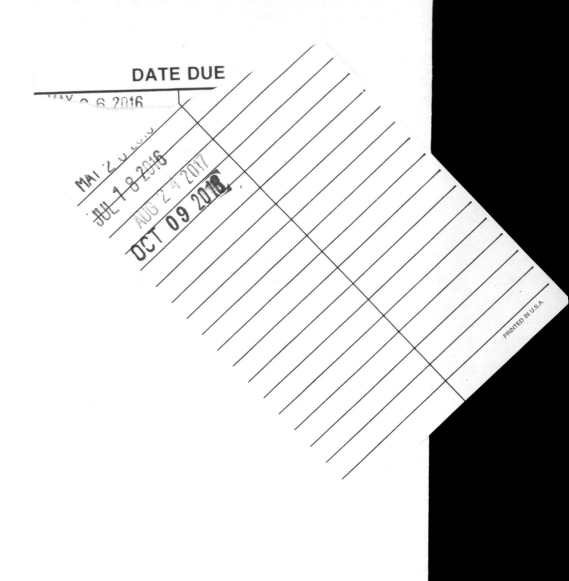

**DATE DUE**

MAY 2 6 2016

MAI 2 0 2016

JUL 1 8 2016

AUG 2 4 2017

OCT 09 2018

Made in the USA
Middletown, DE
30 April 2016